A Private Chiv
A Novel

CW01064493

Francis Lynde

Alpha Editions

This edition published in 2024

ISBN 9789362514011

Design and Setting By
Alpha Editions
www.alphaedis.com
Email - info@alphaedis.com

As per information held with us this book is in Public Domain.
This book is a reproduction of an important historical work.
Alpha Editions uses the best technology to reproduce historical work
in the same manner it was first published to preserve its original nature.
Any marks or number seen are left intentionally to preserve.

Contents

CHAPTER I THE WOMAN ...
WHOSE HANDS ARE AS BANDS   - 1 -

CHAPTER II THE VINTAGE OF ABI-EZER   - 10 -

CHAPTER III "THE WRECK OF THE HESPERUS"   - 17 -

CHAPTER IV THE MIGRANTS   - 24 -

CHAPTER V THE SCALE ASCENDING   - 32 -

CHAPTER VI A MOLEHILL LEVELLED   - 36 -

CHAPTER VII AND A MOUNTAIN UPREARED   - 40 -

CHAPTER VIII A BLOW IN THE DARK   - 46 -

CHAPTER IX THE EYE TO THE STRING   - 52 -

CHAPTER X THE STRING TO THE SHAFT   - 56 -

CHAPTER XI AND THE SHAFT TO THE MARK   - 61 -

CHAPTER XII THE WAY OF A MAID WITH A MAN   - 64 -

CHAPTER XIII "THROUGH A GLASS DARKLY"   - 72 -

CHAPTER XIV THE ANCHOR COMES HOME   - 78 -

CHAPTER XV WHEN HATE AND FEAR STRIKE HANDS   - 85 -

CHAPTER XVI THE GOODLY COMPANY OF MISERY   - 90 -

CHAPTER XVII "AS APPLES OF GOLD IN
PICTURES OF SILVER"   - 95 -

CHAPTER XVIII "LET THE RIGHTEOUS SMITE
ME FRIENDLY"   - 101 -

CHAPTER XIX THE LEADING OF THE BLIND   - 108 -

CHAPTER XX THE DEMONIAC   - 116 -

CHAPTER XXI "A ROD FOR THE FOOL'S BACK"   - 121 -

CHAPTER XXII HOW THE SMOKING FLAX
WAS QUENCHED   - 129 -

CHAPTER XXIII HOW DOROTHY BLEW
THE EMBERS ALIVE   - 138 -

CHAPTER XXIV "WHOSO DIGGETH A PIT
SHALL FALL THEREIN"   - 145 -

CHAPTER XXV "SILENCE IS AN ANSWER TO
A WISE MAN"   - 154 -

CHAPTER XXVI IN THE VALLEY OF THE SHADOW   - 160 -

CHAPTER XXVII SHOWING HOW FAITH MAY
OUT-BUFFET A FACT   - 170 -

CHAPTER XXVIII HOW THE JUDGE GAVE OF HIS BEST - 177 -

CHAPTER XXIX IN WHICH A WILFUL MAN HAS HIS WAY - 186 -

CHAPTER XXXI A FEAST OF MINGLED CUPS   - 194 -

CHAPTER XXXII SUCH FRIENDS ARE EXULTATION'S
AGONY   - 202 -

CHAPTER XXXIII TE MORITURI SALUTAMUS   - 206 -

CHAPTER XXXIV THE WING-BEAT OF AZRAEL   - 212 -

CHAPTER XXXV THE WISDOM OF MANY AND
THE WIT OF ONE   - 217 -

CHAPTER XXXVI IN WHICH A FOX DOUBLES
ONCE TOO OFTEN   - 227 -

CHAPTER XXXVII THE LAW OF THE MEDES
AND PERSIANS   - 235 -

CHAPTER XXXVIII IN WHICH DARTS ARE
COUNTED AS STUBBLE   - 239 -

CHAPTER I
THE WOMAN ... WHOSE HANDS ARE AS BANDS

THE lights of Silverette were beginning to prick the dusk in the valley, and the clanging of a piano, diminished to a harmonious tinkling, floated up the mountain on the still air of the evening. At the Jessica workings, a thousand feet above the valley, even the clangour of a tuneless piano had its compensations; and to one of the two men sitting on the puncheon-floored porch of the assayer's cabin the minimized tinkling was remindful of care-free student ramblings in the land of the zither. But the other had no such pleasant memories, and he rose and relighted his cigar.

"That is my cue, Ned. I must go down and do that whereunto I have set my hand."

"'Must,' you say; that implies necessity. I don't see it."

"I couldn't expect you to see or to understand the necessity; but it is there, all the same."

The objector was silent while one might count ten, but the silence was not of convincement. It was rather a lack of strong words to add to those which had gone before. And when he began again it was only to clinch insistence with iteration.

"I say I don't see it. There is no necessity greater than a man's will; and when you try to make me believe that the honour man of my class is constrained to come down to dealing faro in a mining camp——"

"I know, Ned; but you don't understand. You saw the fair beginning ten years ago, and now you are getting a glimpse of the ending. To you, I suppose, it seems like Lucifer's fall—a drop from heaven to hell; and so it is in effect. But, as a matter of fact, a man doesn't fall; he climbs down into the pit a step at a time—and there are more steps behind me than I can ever retrace."

"But you can't go on indefinitely," insisted the other.

The fallen one shook his head. "That is a true word. But there is only one adequate ending to such a fiasco of a life as mine."

"And that?"

"Is a forty-five calibre bullet, well aimed."

"Bah! That is a coward's alternative, and if you haven't altogether parted company with the George Brant I used to know, we needn't consider it. Why don't you turn over a clean leaf and cut the whole despicable business?"

Brant sat down on the porch step and clasped his hands over his knee. Friendship has its key wherewith to unlock any door of confidence, but from disuse the lock was rusted and it yielded reluctantly.

"I have half a mind to let the game wait while I tell you," he said at length. "It isn't a pleasant tale, and if you are disgusted you can call me down."

"Never mind about that; go on."

"I'll have to go back a bit first—back to the old college days. Do you remember the old woman who lived on the flat below the campus? the one who used to smuggle liquor and other contraband into the dormitories when she came to scrub?"

"Mother Harding? Yes."

"Well, you don't remember any good of her, I fancy—or of her daughter. But let that pass. The year after you went to Heidelberg the girl blossomed out into a woman between two days, and went wrong the day after, as the daughter of such a mother was bound to. I got it into my callow brain that I was responsible. I know better now; I ought to have known better then; but—well, to shorten a long story, she has managed to spoil my life for me, root and branch."

The assayer got upon his feet and swore out of a full heart.

"Good God, Brant! You don't mean to say that you married that brazen——"

But Brant stopped him with a quick gesture. "Don't call her hard names, Ned; I shot a man once for doing that. No, I didn't marry her; I did a worse thing. Now you know why I can't turn the clean leaf. Let the blame lie where it will—and it is pretty evenly divided between us now—I'm not cur enough to turn my back on her at this stage of the game."

Hobart tramped up and down the slab-floored porch, four strides and a turn, for two full minutes before he could frame the final question.

"Where is she now, George?"

Brant's laugh was of hardihood. "Do you hear that piano going down there in Dick Gaynard's dance hall? She is playing it."

"Heavens and earth! Then she is here—in Silverette?"

"Certainly. Where else would she be?"

Hobart stopped short and flung the stump of his cigar far out down the slope.

"Brant," he said solemnly, "I thank God your mother is dead."

"Amen," said Brant softly.

There was another pause, and then Hobart spoke again. "There was a brother, George; what became of him?"

"He went to the bad, too—the worst kind of bad. He laid hold of the situation in the earliest stages, and bled me like a leech year in and year out, until one day I got him at a disadvantage and choked him off."

"How did you manage it?"

"It was easy enough. He is an outlaw of the camps, and he has killed his man now and then when it seemed perfectly safe to do so. But the last time he slipped a cog in the safety wheel, and I took the trouble to get the evidence in shape to hang him. He knows I have it, and he'd sell his soul, if he had one, to get his fingers on the documents. In the meantime he lets me alone."

"He will murder you some day for safety's sake," Hobart suggested.

"No, he won't. I have made him believe that his life hangs on mine; that when I die the dogs of the law will be let loose."

"Oh!" The assayer made another turn or two and then came to sit on the step beside his guest. "One more question, George, and then I'll let up on you," he said. "Do you love the woman?"

Brant shook his head slowly. "No, Ned; I never did; at least, not in the way you mean. And for years now it has been a matter of simple justice. She was bad enough in the beginning, but she is worse now, and that is my doing. I can't leave her to go down into the hotter parts of the pit alone."

For a few other minutes neither of them spoke; then Brant rose and girded himself for the tramp down the mountain.

"I must be going," he said. "I'm glad to have had an hour with you; it has given me a glimpse of the old life that is like the shadow of a great rock in a thirsty land. And I want to see more of you, if you will let me."

"It will be your own fault if you don't. Have you got to go now?"

"Yes. There is a tough crowd up from Carbonado, and Gaynard will have his hands full to-night."

"Wait a minute till I get my overcoat, and I'll go with you."

Brant waited, but when Hobart reappeared he made difficulties.

"You'd better stay where you are, Ned. It's likely there will be trouble and a free fight; and you are new to the place."

"New to Silverette, but not to mining camps and rough crowds," Hobart amended.

Brant still hesitated. "I know, but there is always the risk—the bystander's risk, which is usually bigger than that of the fellow with his gun out. Besides, you have a wife———"

Hobart pushed him into the downward path.

"You don't know Kate," he objected. "She would drive me to it if she were here and knew the circumstances. She knows the camps better than either of us."

Fifteen minutes later they entered Dick Gaynard's dance hall together, and the assayer loitered in the barroom while Brant edged his way back to the alcove in the rear, where stood the faro table. Presently Hobart saw the dealer rise and give his chair to Brant; then the loiterer felt free to look about him.

There was nothing new or redeeming in the scene. There was the typical perspiring crowd of rough men and tawdry women surging to and fro, pounding the dusty floor to the time beaten out of the discordant piano; the same flaring oil lamps and murky atmosphere thick with tobacco smoke and reeking with the fumes of alcohol; the same silent groups ringing the roulette boards and the faro table. Hobart looked on, and was conscious of a little shiver of disgust—a vicarious thrill of shame for all concerned, but chiefly for his friend. And Brant had come to this for his daily bread! Brant, the honour man, the athlete, the well-beloved of all who knew him!

Hobart let himself drift with the ebb and flow of those who, like himself, were as yet only onlookers, coming to anchor when he had found a vantage point from which he could see and study the face of the fallen one. For all the hardening years it was not yet an evil face. The cheeks of the man were thinner and browner than those of the boy, and the heavy mustache hid the mouth, the feature which changes most with the changing years; but the resolute jaw was the same, and the steady gray eyes, though these had caught the gambler's trick of looking out through half-closed lids when they saw most. On the whole the promise of youth had been kept. The handsome boy had come to be a man good to look upon; a man upon whom any woman might look once, and turning, look again. The assayer was not given to profanity, but he swore softly in an upflash of angry grief at the thought that the passing years had marred Brant's soul rather than his body.

None the less, it was shipwreck, hopeless and unrelieved, as Brant had asserted; and from contemplating the effect of it in the man, Hobart was moved to look upon the cause of it in the woman. Perhaps there was that in her which might make the descent into the pit less unaccountable. Hobart would see.

He worked his way slowly around two sides of the crowded room, and so came to the piano. One glance at the performer was enough. It revealed a woman who had once been beautiful, as the sons of God once found the daughters of men; nay, the wreck of her was still beautiful, but it was the soulless beauty whose appeal is to that which is least worthy in any man. Hobart saw and understood. There be drunkards a-many who look not upon the wine when it is red in the cup; and Brant was of these—an inebriate of passion. The assayer turned his back upon the woman that he might the better make excuses for his friend.

Gaynard's bar did a thriving business that night, and the throng in the gambling alcove thinned out early. The dance hall was the greater attraction, and here the din and clamour grew apace until the raucous voice of the caller shouting the figures of the dance could no longer be heard above the clanging of the piano, the yells and catcalls, and the shuffling and pounding of feet on the floor. Hilarity was as yet the keynote of all the uproar, but Hobart knew that the ceaseless activity of the bartenders must shortly change the pitch to the key quarrelsome, and he began to wish himself well out of it.

Brant glanced up from time to time, always without pause in the monotonous running of the cards, and when he finally succeeded in catching Hobart's eye he beckoned with a nod. The assayer made his way around to the dealer's chair, and Brant spoke without looking up:

"Get out of here, Ned, while you can. There will be the devil to pay before midnight, and there is no earthly use in your being mixed up in it."

Hobart leaned over the table and placed a coin on one of the inlaid cards to keep up appearances.

"I'm here with you, and I mean to stay," he insisted. "You may need— By Jove! it's begun."

The dance stopped and the clamour sank into a hush, which was sharply rent by a blast of profanity, a jangling crash of the piano keys, and a woman's scream. Then the two fought their way into the thick of the crowd around the piano. A drunken ruffian was grasping the woman's arm and brandishing a revolver over her head.

"You won't play it, won't ye? And ye'll give Ike Gasset a piece of yer lip? By God, I'll show ye!"

Brant's pistol was out before he spoke. "Drop it right where you are, and get out of here before I kill you," he said quietly.

The man's reply was a snap shot in Brant's face, and, though his aim was bad, both Hobart and Brant felt the wind of the bullet passing between them. The crack of the pistol was the signal for a scene a description of which no man has ever yet been able to set down calmly in black on white. Shouts, oaths, a mad rush for the open air foiled by a fiercer closing in of the crowd around the piano; all this while the ruffian levelled his weapon and fired again. At the death-speeding instant the woman started to her feet, and the bullet intended for Brant struck her fairly in the breast. Hobart heard the sharp snap of the steel corset stay, and saw Brant, catching her as she reeled, fire once, twice, thrice at the desperado. Then the assayer lifted up his voice in a shout that dominated the tumult:

"Silverettes! Out with them—they've killed a woman!"

There was a fierce affray, a surging charge, and when the place was cleared Hobart ran back. Brant was on his knees beside the woman. The smoking oil lamps burned yellow in the powder reek, but there was light enough to show that she was past help. None the less, Hobart offered to go for a doctor.

Brant shook his head and rose stiffly.

"She doesn't need one; she is dead."

Hobart grasped the situation with far-seeing prescience.

"Then you have nothing to stay here for; let us get out while we can." The din of the street battle rang clamorous at the front, and he took Brant's arm to lead him to the door, which opened upon the alley in the rear. "Come on," he urged; "they will be back here presently, and you have nothing to fight for now."

"No." Brant yielded as one in a trance, but at the door he broke away, to dart back with the gray eyes aflame and fierce wrath crying for vengeance. Unnoted of all, the wounded desperado had lain where Brant's fusillade had dropped him. But now he was on hands and knees, trying to drag himself out of the room. Brant was quick, but the assayer pinioned him before the ready weapon could flash from its holster.

"Good God, man, that would be murder!" he panted, wrestling with the avenger of blood, and possessing himself of the pistol. "Come on out of this!"

Again Brant yielded, and they made their way to the open air, and through the alleyway to the mountain path, and so in silence up to the Jessica and to the assayer's cabin. Not until they were safe within the four log walls did Hobart open his mouth. But when he had struck a light and hung a blanket over the window which looked valleyward he spoke tersely and to the point:

"A few hours ago, George, you told me why you couldn't turn your back on your shame, and I had nothing to say. But now the reason is removed, and you have had an object lesson which ought to last you as long as you live. What do you say?"

Brant spread his hands as one helpless. "What else am I good for?" he asked.

"That question is unworthy of you, and you know it. You have your profession; but without that you could still do as well as another."

Brant was still afoot, and he fought his battle to a finish, pacing slowly back and forth with his hands behind him and his head bowed. For all his square jaw and steadfast eyes, rash impulse had been the bane of his life thus far, and the knowledge of it made him slow to decide even when the decision leaned toward the things which make for righteousness. So he fought the battle to its conclusion, and when it was ended was fain to sit down awearied with the stress of it.

"I am not in love with the degradation of it; I think you must know that, Ned. All these years I've had a yearning for decency and clean living and respectability that I could not strangle, do what I would. So you will understand that I am not halting between two opinions. It is simply this: Can a man turn over a new leaf and bury such a past as mine without being beset by a constant fear of its resurrection? Won't it come up and slap him in the face about the time he thinks he has it decently buried and covered up and out of sight?"

Hobart's rejoinder was prompt and definitive. "No. The world is wide, and a few years of one man's life are no more than so many texts written in the sand."

"You're wrong there, Ned. The world is fearfully small, and its memory of evil deeds is as long as its charity is short."

"Let be, then. You are not a woman. You are a man, and you can fight it out and live it down."

Brant acquiesced without more ado. "I was merely stating the case," he said, as if the matter were quite extraneous to him. "You have earned the right to set the pace for me, Ned; and I'll do whatever you say."

"That is more like the George Brant I used to know. And this is what I say: I know a trail across Jack Mountain that will take us to the railroad in three hours. The night trains pass at Carbonado, and you will be in good time to catch whichever one of them you elect to take, east or west. There is no station on the other side of the mountain; but there is a side track for the Hoopoee mine, and you can build a fire to flag the train. Have you money?"

"Yes."

"Enough?"

"Yes; enough to try whatever experiment you suggest."

"I don't know that I have anything to suggest more than your own good judgment would anticipate. Find your allotted corner of the big vineyard and go to work in it; that's about all there is to it."

"How deep shall I dive?"

"You will have to decide that for yourself. You are a Western man now, and I suppose you don't want to go back home. How about Denver?"

Brant shook his head slowly. "Denver is good enough—too good, in fact. I wonder if you will understand it if I say that I'd much rather have my forty days in the wilderness before I have to face my kind, even as a stranger in a strange city?"

"I can understand it perfectly, and the decency of the thing does you credit. And if that is your notion, I can help you. You used to be the best man in the 'Tech.' at map making; have you forgotten how to do it?"

"No; a man doesn't forget his trade."

"Good. I met Davenport at Carbonado yesterday. He was on his way to the Colorow district to do a lot of surveying and plotting, and was sick because he couldn't find an assistant before he left Denver. Shall I give you a note to him?"

"It is exactly what I should crave if I had a shadow of the right to pick and choose."

Hobart found pen and paper and wrote the note.

"There you are," he said. "Davenport is a good fellow, and you needn't tell him more than you want to. The job will last for two or three months, and by that time you will know better what you want to do with yourself. Now, if you are ready, we'll get a move. It's a stiffish climb to the top of the pass."

They forthfared together and presently set their feet in the trail leading over the shoulder of the great mountain buttressing the slope behind the Jessica. The sounds of strife had ceased in the town below, and but for the twinkling lights the deep valley might have been as Nature left it. Since the upward path was rough and difficult there was scant breath for speech in the long climb; and for this Brant was thankful. The scene in Gaynard's was yet fresh in mind and heart, and not even to the friend of his youth could he trust himself to speak freely.

The moon was rising when they reached the summit of the pass, and Hobart pointed down the farther slope to a dark mass hugging the steep mountain side.

"That is the Hoopoee shaft house," he said. "The railroad is just below it. Got matches and cigars?"

"Yes, both."

"Then I'll go back from here. Good-bye, old fellow, and God bless you! Tie your courage in a hard knot, and let me hear from you."

Brant grasped his friend's hand and wrung it in silence. He tried to speak, but the words tripped each other.

"Never mind," Hobart broke in. "I know what you want to say, and can't. It is nothing more than you would have done if the saddle had been on the other horse. And about your—the woman: I'll do whatever you could do, if you stayed. Now, then, down you go, or you'll miss your train. Good-bye."

CHAPTER II
THE VINTAGE OF ABI-EZER

IT is not always given to prescience, friendly or other, to reap where it has sown; or to the worthiest intention to see of the travail of its soul and be satisfied. But if the time, place, and manner of Brant's sequestration had been foreordained from the beginning, the conditions could scarcely have been more favourable for bulwark building between an evil past and some hopeful future of better promise.

The new mining district to which Hobart's suggestion sent him was a sky-land wilderness unpeopled as yet, save by a few pioneer prospectors; his fellow-measurer of mining claims was a zealot of his profession, who was well content to take his friend's friend at his friend's valuation, asking no questions; and the work itself was such a fierce struggle with Nature in her ruggedest aspect as to afford a very opiate of antidotes to reflection, reminiscent or forecasting.

So it came about that the heart-hardening past with its remorseful reminders withdrew more and more into the dimnesses of willing forgetfulness, and the bulwark between that which had been and that which might be grew with the uncalendared days and nights till it bade fair in time to shut out some of the remorseful vistas.

The claim-measuring came to an end one flawless day in August, when the aspens were yellow on the high-pitched slopes and the streams ran low and summer clear in the gulches. Brant helped in the preparations for the retreat from the sky land of forgetfulness with a distinct sense of regret, which grew with every added mile of the day-long tramp toward Aspen, the railway, and civilization, until it became no less than a foreboding. Davenport, well satisfied with an assistant whose capacity for hard work was commensurate with his apparent love for it, had made him a proposal pointing to a partnership survey in a still more remote field, but Brant had refused. He knew well enough that his battle of reinstatement was yet to be fought, and that it must be fought in the field of the wider world. And toward that field he set his face, though not without misgivings—the misgivings of one who, having given no quarter, need expect none.

"So you have made up your mind to go to Denver, have you?" said Davenport, when they were smoking the pipe of leave-taking in the lobby of the Aspen hotel.

"Yes. I have made arrangements to go down on the night train."

Davenport looked at his watch. "It is about time you were moving," he said. "I'll walk over to the station with you if you don't mind."

Brant did not mind. On the contrary, he was rather sorry to part from the man who had been the first to help raise the bulwark of forgetfulness. But their walk to the station was wordless, as much of their companionship had been.

They found the train ready to leave, and at the steps of the Pullman a party of four, an elderly man and three women. One of the women was young and pretty, and she was cloaked and hatted for a journey. So much Brant saw, and then he came alive to the fact that Davenport was introducing him. Of the four names he caught but one—that of the young woman who, it appeared, was to be his travelling companion.

"Well, now, that is lucky all around," the elderly man was saying. "We have been hoping that some one would turn up at the last minute. Dorothy would go, whether or— Hello, there!"

The wheels were beginning to turn, and whatever poor excuse for a launching the acquaintance might have had in a few minutes of general conversation was denied it. Brant had no more than time to hand his charge up the steps of the Pullman, to stand for a moment beside her while she waved a farewell to the group on the platform, and his responsibility, such as it was, was upon him full fledged.

He did not make the most of it, as a better man might. So far from it, he erred painstakingly on the side of formality, leading the way with the young woman's belongings to her section, asking her rather stiffly if he could be of any further service to her, and vanishing promptly to the solitude of the smoking compartment when her negation set him free.

But once alone in the stuffy luxury of the smoking den it was inevitable that the tale of the weeks of voluntary exile should roll itself up like a scroll and vanish, and that the heart-hardening past, and chiefly the tragic valedictory of it, should demand the hearing postponed by the toil-filled interlude in the wilderness. He was well used to scenes of violence, and there was a strain of atavistic savagery in him that came to the surface now and then and bade him look on open-eyed when stronger men blenched and turned away. But now the memory of the tragedy in Gaynard's kennel laid hold of him and shook him in the very stronghold of ruthlessness. He could not pretend to be deeply grieved, for the woman had been little better than an evil genius to him; and yet he would willingly have thrust his own life between her and the destroyer. Instead, she had done that for him, though he did not harrow himself needlessly with the thought that she had intentionally given her life for his. He knew her well enough to be sure that she was only trying to save herself. None the less, when all was said, it was a tragedy of the kind to leave scars deep and abiding, and the remembrance of it might well threaten to be the dregs in any cup of hope.

For his swift retaliation on the slayer he took no remorseful thought, and for this environment was responsible. In the frontier mining camps, where law is not, men defend their lives and redress their wrongs with the strong hand, and one needs not to be an aggressive brawler to learn to strike fierce blows and shrewd. So in the matter of retaliation Brant was sorry only that, for all his good will, he had not slain the ruffian outright.

That the heart-hardening past with its grim pictures should thus obtrude itself upon his return to civilization seemed natural enough, and Brant suffered it as a part of the penalty he must pay. Not in any moment of the long evening did he remotely connect the sorry memories with the young woman in Section Six, who was at most no more than a name to him. Nevertheless, though he knew it not, it was the young woman who was chiefly responsible. If a good man's introduction had not made him accountable for the welfare of a good woman, Brant might have smoked a cigar and gone to bed without this first reckoning with the past.

As it was, he smoked many cigars and was driven forth of the smoking-room only when the porter, avid of sleep himself, had suggested for the third time that the gentleman's berth was ready. Even then sleep was not to be had for the wooing, and the gray dawn light sifting through the chinks around the window shades found him still wakeful.

The sun of a new day was half-meridian high when the porter parted the curtains of the berth and shook his single man passenger.

"Time to get up, sah; twenty minutes to de breakfas' station."

Brant yawned sleepily and looked at his watch.

"Breakfast? Why, it's ten o'clock, and we ought to have been in Denver an hour ago."

"Yes, sah. Been laid out all night, mostly, sah; fust wid a freight wreck, and den wid a hot box."

Brant remembered vaguely that there had been stoppages many and long, but with the memory mill agrind he had not remarked them.

In the lavatory he found the porter ostentatiously putting towels in the racks for his single man passenger.

"Light car this morning, John?" he asked.

The negro grinned. "Yes, sah; you' right about dat, sholy, sah. You-all come mighty close to hab'n a special cyar last night, sah."

"So?"

"Yes, sah. De young lady and you-all had de Hesp'rus all to you' own selves. Po' portah ain't gwine get rich out o' dis trip, sholy."

"No, I should say not." Brant was sluicing his face in the dodging basin at the moment, but a little later, when he had a dry pocket hand, he gave the porter a coin of price.

"Take good care of the lady, John; they don't remember about these little things, you know."

"No, sah—t'ank you kin'ly, sah—dat dey don't. But I's take mighty good keer o' dat young lady now, sah. Is—is you-all 'quaintin' wid her, sah?"

"I haven't so much as seen her face," said Brant, which was near enough the literal truth to stand uncorrected. And a few minutes later he went back into the body of the car to repair the omission.

What he saw stirred that part of him which had long lain dormant. She was sitting in lonely state in the otherwise unoccupied car, and his first impression, at half-car-length range, was that she was a sweet incarnation of goodness of the protectable sort. Whereupon he shut the door upon the past and betook himself to her section with a kindly offer of service.

"Good morning, Miss Langford," he began. "I hope you rested well. We are coming to the breakfast station, and there will doubtless be the usual scramble. May I have the pleasure of looking after your wants?"

Her smile was of answering good will, and he had time to observe that the honest gray eyes were deep wells of innocent frankness; and when she made answer, there was something in her speech to tell him that she was neither of the outspoken West nor of the self-contained East.

"It was kind of you to think of me," she said. "But I think I needn't trouble you."

"Don't call it trouble—it will be a pleasure," he insisted; and when she had made room for him on the opposite seat he sat down.

"We are very late, are we not?" she asked.

"So late that we are not likely to get in before night, I'm afraid. A freight wreck and a hot box, the porter says."

"I thought something was the matter. The train has been stopping all through the night, and I could hear them working at the car every time I awoke."

"I heard them, too," said Brant, though his memory of the stoppages was of the vaguest. "It didn't impress me at the time, but it does now. I'm hungry."

She laughed at this, and confessed a fellow-feeling.

"So am I; and I was just hoping for two things: a good breakfast, and time enough to enjoy it."

"We are pretty sure of the first, because the Van Noy people always set a good table; but as to the time, our being so late will probably cut it short. If you please, we'll go out to the front platform and so be ready to get in ahead of the rush."

She went with him willingly enough, and a little later they were partakers of the swift down-grade rush of the train in the open air. It was before the day of vestibuled platforms on the mountain lines, and when the lurching and swaying of the car made the footing precarious he slipped his arm through hers for safety's sake.

And she permitted it, does some one gasp? Yea, verily; and, since she was much too clean-hearted to be constantly on the watch for unworthy motives in others, thought no harm of it. Moreover, Brant's conclusion that she was neither of the East nor the West was well founded in fact, and this had something to do with her frank trust in him. She was Tennessee born and bred, and to a Southern girl all men are gentlemen until they prove themselves otherwise.

And as for Brant, if she had been an angel of light, preaching repentance and a better mind to the hardened sinner of the mining camps, nothing she could have said or done would have touched him so nearly as this tacit acceptance of his protection. But also it gave him a soul-harrowing glimpse of the bottomless chasm separating the chivalrous gentleman of her maidenly imaginings from one George Brant, late of Silverette and Gaynard's faro bank. How this clean-hearted young woman would shrink from him if she could but dimly imagine the manner of man he was! There was honest shame and humiliation in the thought; and in so far as these may give a moral uplift, Brant was the better man for the experience. None the less, he was glad when the train slowed into the breakfast station and the demands of the present once more shut the door upon the past and its disquieting reminders.

Having a clear field for the run across the station platform, Brant and his charge were the first to reach the dining room, and they had chosen their table and given their order before the other seats were taken. As a matter of course, Brant's order was filled first, and thereat his vis à vis, a hard-featured man in a linen duster and a close-fitting skullcap, broke forth in remonstrance.

"That is the curse of the tip system!" he growled, looking pointedly at Brant and addressing no one in particular. "I object to it on principle, and every self-respecting traveller ought to help put it down."

Brant's eyelids narrowed and the steel-gray eyes behind them shot back a look that aforetime had quelled more than one wild beast of the gaming tables. But he held his peace, and here the matter might have rested if the irascible fault-finder had not seen the look and accepted it as a challenge.

"Yes, sir, I referred to you!" he exploded, hurling the explanation at Brant's head. "I submit it to the entire company if it is fair for you to monopolize the attention of the servants while the rest of us go hungry?"

Now Brant was by nature a very madman of impulse, but the one good thing he had brought out of the hard school of lawlessness was the ability to be fiercely wrathful without showing it. So he said, placably enough: "I am sure you will excuse me if I decline to discuss the question with you. We were the first comers, and my order was given before you sat down."

Here again the matter might have rested, but the hard-featured critic must needs have the last word:

"What I said, sir, had no reference to the matter of precedence. What I particularly object to is the shameless subsidizing of the servants."

Whereupon Brant, who was as yet innocent of the implied charge, took occasion to call the waiter who had served him and to fee him openly in sight of all and sundry. The man in the linen duster scowled his disapproval, but, inasmuch as his own breakfast was served, said nothing. There was a lull in the threatened storm, and Brant was still congratulating himself on his own magnanimity, when hostilities broke out afresh. His charge had finished her breakfast, and he had prevailed upon her to take a second cup of coffee. When it came, the man across the table, who had given a similar order, claimed it for his own. Brant expostulated, still in set terms exuding the very honey of forbearance. The tyrant of breakfast tables fell into the trap, mistook his man completely, and in a sharp volley of incivilities proved that a soft answer may not always deflect the course of righteous indignation. In the midst of the volley Miss Langford rose to leave the table.

That was the final straw, and it broke the back of Brant's self-control. Rising quickly, he leaned across the table and smote the offender out of his chair; one open-handed blow it asked for, and it was given with red wrath to speed it. That done, he took the arm of his companion and stalked out of the dining room before the smitten one could gather breath for an explosion.

Brant marched his charge straight to the Pullman, drawing deep warrior breaths of defiance world-inclusive; but by the time they were halfway across the platform he came to his senses sufficiently to be heartily ashamed of himself; nay, more, to be ready to welcome anything which might come by way of reproach. But whatever Miss Langford thought of it, she was self-contained enough to keep her own counsel, and they boarded the train in silence. In the seclusion of the deserted sleeping car Brant laid fast hold of his courage and said what he might by way of apology.

"I can't ask your forgiveness, Miss Langford," he began; "I know I have put myself beyond that. But I beg you to let me say just one word in my own defence. For years I have been roughing it in these mountains, eating at tables where that man's insolence would cost him his life before he could measure words with the mildest man in the camp. And so I forgot myself for the moment—forgot what was due you. Now I'll make the only reparation I can, and keep out of your sight for the rest of the day."

And straightway he vanished without giving her a chance to reply.

CHAPTER III
"THE WRECK OF THE HESPERUS"

HAVING set himself to expiate his fault, Brant wore out the day in the smoking compartment in comfortless solitude, doing penance by limiting himself to one cigar an hour. It was dull work, but not altogether profitless. For one thing there was plenty of time to think; and for another the expiatory mill had a chance to grind out a goodly grist of conclusions. The first of these was that there were going to be more obstacles in the way to amendment than those interposed by an uncharitable world; that apart from the sharp fight on the firing line, he was likely to have trouble with an insubordinate garrison.

Now a fine scorn of obstacles was another of the lessons learned in the hard school of abandonment, and Brant set his teeth on a doughty resolution to override them in the race for retrieval, as he had overridden them in the mad gallop pitward. Self-respect, or some comforting measure of it, should be regained though the devil himself held the present reversion of it. There should yet come a day, please God, when he would not be constrained in common decency to put the length of a Pullman car between himself and a good woman. Moreover, the past should henceforth be a dead past, and woe betide the enemy, man or devil, who should have the temerity to resurrect it.

The gage of battle thus thrown to the powers of darkness was promptly taken up. After one of the many stops with the troublesome axle the rear brakeman came into the smoking compartment and sat down, as one weary. To begin at once the shedding of the churl shell of the master gambler, Brant nodded pleasantly; whereupon the brakeman passed the time of day and immediately began, railwaywise, to abuse his calling and to ease his mind in respect of the hot box.

"She never has made a run yet without keeping everybody on the keen jump," he declared. "By gum! I've been chasing up and down with the dope kettle ever since one o'clock this morning."

"She?" said Brant, to whom railway speech was an unknown tongue.

"Yes; this here car—the Hesp'rus. Last time we had her it was the back box on this end; now it's the for'ard one under the drawing-room—blazing away like a blooming track torch more'n half the time."

"Keeps you busy, does it?"

"You're mighty right it does. And when I have a job like this, I like to have some blame' fool pilgrim come up and begin to jaw about the soft snap a brakeman has now they have the air brakes."

"Did somebody do that?"

"Sure; first thing this morning. Big chap in a linen duster and smoking cap; same one that—" The brakeman stopped short, as one who suddenly finds himself treading upon what may prove to be dangerous ground.

"Go on," said Brant encouragingly.

"Well, I mean the fellow you had the scrap with. Great Moses! but he was hot!"

"Was he? So was I."

"You'd better believe he was. Came out of that dining room rearin' like a buckin' bronco; said he was going to have the law on you, and wanted the old man to wire ahead for a policeman to meet the train."

"What old man—the conductor?"

"Yes; and Harker told him he couldn't do it, because the row didn't happen on the train; said he didn't know who you was, anyway. Then I chipped in, and told 'em you was Plucky George, the man that cleaned out the six toughs when they tried to run the bank up at Silverette. Holy Smoke! but you ought to've seen old linen duster fall apart when I said that!" The brakeman laughed joyously, but Brant groaned in spirit at this ominous hint that his reputation meant to keep pace with him.

"You'd better believe he was rattled right!" the man went on. "He just went yaller, and the last I saw of him he was up ahead, looking for you so't he could apologize. Ain't that rich?"

"Very rich," said Brant grimly. Then he saw his advantage and made good use of it. "In fact, it is much too rich to spoil. Go find the fellow and tell him I'm in a bad humour, but that he is safe as long as he keeps away from me. Will you do that?"

"Sure," assented the brakeman, getting upon his feet. "I'll do better than that: I'll scare him till he won't get a good breath this side o' the Missouri River."

Brant's eyes narrowed, and in the turning of a leaf the mantle of humility slipped from him and he became Brant the man-queller.

"You will do nothing of the sort. You will tell him just what I say, and no word more or less. Now go."

The man of dope kettles and rear-end signals was no coward, but neither was he minded to pick a quarrel with the hero of a dozen savage battles. Brant let him get to the door and then called him back:

"Where does your run end?"

"Voltamo; next stop but one."

"Then you don't go into Denver?"

"No."

"But some time you may. In that case, it will be as well for you to forget what little you may happen to know about me. Do you understand?"

"You'd better believe I do. I can hold my jaw with anybody when I have to; and I don't have to be hit with a club neither."

"Good. Have a cigar—and don't forget what I say."

The brakeman took the proffered cigar and vanished; and thereupon Brant began to repent once more and to grope for the lost mantle of humility. Here on the very heels of his good resolutions he had balked at one of the smallest of the obstacles, bullying a man in his displeasure and trading upon his reputation as a man-queller like any desperado of the camps. It was humiliating, but it proved the wisdom of the smoking-room exile. Truly, he was far enough from being a fitting companion for the young woman in Section Six.

As he had predicted, the train lost time steadily throughout the day, and an early supper was served at the regular dinner station. Brant went to the dining room with the other passengers, and when Miss Langford did not appear, he sent the porter to her with a luncheon and a cup of tea.

"It is about what I had a right to expect," he told himself when he was once more back in the solitude of the smoke den. "She was afraid to trust herself in the same dining room with me. Why the devil couldn't I have held my cursed temper just ten seconds longer? Here I've had to sit all day and eat my heart out, when I might have been getting miles away from the old life in her company. What a fool a man can make of himself when he tries!"

"That is a fact," said a voice from the opposite seat; and Brant, who had been staring gloomily out of the window at the wall of blackness slipping past the train, and so was unaware that he was not alone, was unreasonable enough to be angry.

"What's that you say?" he began wrathfully, turning upon his commentator; but the pleasant face of the young man in the opposite seat was of the kind which disarms wrath.

"It's on me," he laughed. "I beg your pardon. I spoke without thinking, but what you said about the fool-making faculty calls for general ratification. We all have it."

Brant nodded, and the newcomer relighted his cigar, which had gone out in the explanation. "Going in to Denver?" he asked, willing to let interest atone for impudence.

"Yes."

"Wish I were. I've been out a week now, and I'm beginning to long for the fleshpots."

"You have my sympathy if you have to stop overnight anywhere between this and Denver," said Brant, who knew the country.

"Luckily, I don't have to. I am merely riding down to the meeting point with Number Three to kill time. I have to go back to Voltamo to-night."

Brant laughed. "Do you find it cheaper to ride than to wait?"

"It is quite as cheap in my case; the railway company has to foot the bills, anyway."

"Oh—you are in the service, are you?"

"Yes."

"Engineer corps?"

"No; operating department. I am chief clerk in the superintendent's office."

They smoked companionably for a while, and then Brant said: "Perhaps you can tell me some of the things I want to find out. Who is your chief engineer now?"

"Colonel Bowran."

"Good fellow?"

"Out of sight; gentleman of the old school, you know; West Point, regular army, and all that. They say he won't hire a chainman unless he is a college graduate."

"Is his office in Denver?"

"Yes; right next door to ours."

"All of which is comforting," said Brant. "I hope you will have me for a neighbour. I am going to try for a billet on the C. E. & W."

"Good!" exclaimed the chief clerk, rising at the sound of the locomotive whistle. "My name's Antrim, and you will find me in Superintendent Craig's office. Latchstring hangs on the outer wall."

"And my name is Brant. Do you quit us here?"

"Got to do it—wish I hadn't, now. Glad to have met you, I'm sure. Don't forget to hunt me up. Good night."

They shook hands heartily at parting. It was Colorado, in the day when strangers became friends—or enemies—on the spot; when one unconsciously dropped the "Mr." in an hour, and then slipped easily around the surname to hobnob with Tom, Dick, or Harry in the first interview.

For the exile the little chat with the chief clerk was heartening in its way; and when the train was once more swaying and lurching along its crooked course down the cañon he looked at his watch and figured out the probable arriving time.

"Eleven hours late; that will make it ten o'clock in Denver. I wonder if Miss Langford will find somebody to look after her when she gets in. If she doesn't——"

The interruption was the advent of the porter. The negro had been trying to get speech with his patron for half an hour, but he was much too discreet to deliver his message in Antrim's presence.

"'Bout de supper, sah; de lady in lower Six say, T'ank you kin'ly, sah, and would you-all be so kind and step back in de cyar a minute?"

"Certainly." Brant rose to comply, but he was no sooner on his feet than he was thrown violently all across the compartment.

"Golly Lawd! she's on de ties!" gasped the negro, and the exclamation ended in a yell of terror.

Brant kept his head, and thought only of the young woman alone in the body of the car. With the floor heaving and bounding under him like the deck of a storm-tossed ship, he darted out of the smoking-room and flung himself against the swinging door in the narrow side vestibule. It was jammed, but the glass of the upper panel fell in fragments under his blow, and he was past the obstruction when the end came. The heavy sleeper lurched first to the right, reeled drunkenly for a critical instant on the brink of the embankment facing the river, righted itself with a jerk when draw bars and safety chains gave way, and then settled back to topple over against the cañon wall, stopping with a crash that sent Brant to his knees just as he was starting down the aisle.

The broken glass was still falling from the shattered deck lights when he reached Section Six. The young woman was unhurt, but she was very pale, and the gray eyes were full of terror.

"Don't faint," said Brant very gently, though he was wondering what he should do in case she did. "It is all over now, I think."

"But the others?" she faltered.

"Let us hope that the other cars have kept the track—that it is only the 'wreck of the Hesperus.'"

She smiled at the conceit, and asked what they should do.

"If you will promise not to faint while I am gone, I'll go and find out. There is no danger now."

"I'm not going to faint; but please don't be gone long."

He was back in a moment, gathering up her belongings.

"There is nothing smashed but our car," he explained. "They will leave flagmen with it, and go on to Denver with the remainder of the train. Will you take my arm?"

The wrecked sleeper was already surrounded by a throng of curious passengers and anxious trainmen, and ready hands were extended to help them down from the uptilted platform. But Brant put them all aside, and lifted his companion to the ground as if the right were his alone.

"It is all right, Mr. Harker," he said, singling out the conductor. "I mean, we are all out. There was no one else in the car except the porter, and he isn't hurt."

They made their way through the throng of curious ones, and so on down the track to the train. Brant found a seat in the day coach, disposed his charge comfortably therein, and then, once more laying hold of his courage, sat down beside her.

"I am not going to leave you again until I see you safe in Denver," he asserted; "that is, unless you send me away."

"I didn't send you away this morning," she rejoined, with a smile that went far toward making him forget for the moment who and what he was.

"I know you didn't; but you had a right to. And after what I had done, there was nothing for it but to take myself off."

She did not speak until the train was once more lurching on its way. Then she said: "I thought at the time you were very patient; and—and I think so still."

"Do you, really? That is very good of you; but I think I don't deserve it. My first thought should have been for you, and I might have kept my temper for another half minute."

Now this young woman could rejoice in an excellent upbringing, as will presently appear, and she knew perfectly well that Brant was right. But where is the woman, old or young, who does not secretly glory in a vigorous championship of her rights, even at the expense of the proprieties?

So she spoke him fair, telling him that she was sending for him at the moment of the accident to thank him and to pay him for her supper. Nay, more: she made the next two hours so pleasant for him that they were as but a watch in the night, and their flitting seemed to push his life in the camps into a comfortably remote past.

And so they chatted amicably until the outlying lights of Denver began to flash past the windows; and then Brant bethought him of her further well-being.

"Will there be some one at the train to meet you?" he inquired.

"No; but my street-car line is only a block from the depot, and the car takes me almost to our door."

"I will put you on the car," he said; and this he did some few minutes later, bidding her "Good night," and standing in the street to catch a last glimpse of her as the car droned away to the northward. Then he turned away to seek a hotel, and was well uptown before he remembered that he had not thought to ask her address, or to ask if he might call upon her.

"But that is all right," he mused. "Denver isn't London, and if I can ever pull myself up into the ranks of the well-behaved, I shall find her."

CHAPTER IV
THE MIGRANTS

TIME was, and is no more, when invalids, hopeful and hopeless, thronged the eastern foothills of the Rockies till there was no longer houseroom for them in the cities, and a new word "lunger" was grafted upon the exuberant stock of Western folk speech to distinguish them. Unlike the pioneers of a still earlier day, who crossed the plains with their worldly possessions snugly sheltered beneath the canvas tilt of a single prairie schooner, these migrants for health's sake were chiefly of the class which neither toils nor spins, and to the foothill cities they presently added suburbs architecturally characteristic each after its kind. In these suburbs the trim-built town house of New England is the commonest type, but the more florid style of the middle West is not lacking, and now and then, in the roomier city fringe, there are replicas done in red brick of the low-storied, wide-verandaed country house of the South.

Such was the home of the Langfords in the Highlands of North Denver. Driven from the ancestral acres in the blue-grass region of Tennessee in the late afternoon of his life, the judge had determined to make the new home in the life-giving altitudes as nearly like the old as money and the materials at hand would compass, and he had succeeded passing well. He had bought acres where others bought lots, and the great roomy house, with its low-pitched roof and wide verandas on three sides, stood in the midst of whatsoever Tennessee greenery would stand transplantation from the blue-grass region to the less genial climate of the clear-skied altitudes.

On pleasant Sunday afternoons, when Dorothy was at her mission school and the judge slept peacefully in his own particular chair, when Mrs. Langford followed her husband's example in the privacy of her room, and Will was no one ever knew just where, the hammock slung at the corner of the veranda which commanded a view of the mountains was Isabel's especial convenience. For one reason, there was the view; for another, the hammock swung opposite that portion of the low railing which was Harry Antrim's favourite perch during the hour or two which measured his customary Sunday afternoon visit.

Being very much in love with Isabel, Antrim was quite willing to turn his back upon the scenery for the sake of looking at her. And as between a winsome young woman swinging in a hammock—a young woman with laughing brown eyes and a profusion of glory-tinted hair framing a face to which piquancy and youthful beauty lent equal charms—who but a scenery-mad pilgrim of the excursion trains would think of making a comparison?

In these Sunday afternoon talks Isabel could be abstract or concrete as occasion demanded. What time the young man dwelt overmuch on railway matters, she found it convenient to be able to look over his shoulder at the mighty panorama unrolled and unrolling itself in endless transformation scenes against the western horizon. And when Antrim, finding himself ignored, would come back from things practical to things personal, she had but to close her eyes to the scenic background and to open them again upon the personality of her companion.

Conceding nothing to what he was pleased to call her artistic fad, Antrim was willing to condone Isabel's indifference to railway affairs. His business was a part, the greater part, of his life, but he could understand why Judge Langford's daughter, as such, might easily weary of railway shop talk. True, there had been more or less of it all along in the old days in Tennessee, when the judge was counsel for the railway company of which Antrim's father was the superintendent; but that was because the Langfords and Antrims dwelt side by side and were friends as well as neighbours. Here in Colorado it was different. The judge was an invalid—a migrant for health's sake, with gear sufficient to make him independent of railway counsellorships, and with little left of his former connection save a pocketful of annual passes and a warm affection for the son of his old friend the superintendent.

None the less, Antrim thought that Isabel might bear with him now and then, if only for the reason that she would at some time begin to eat the bread and meat of railway service and so continue to the end of the chapter. This, indeed, he had the temerity to say to her one Sunday afternoon some weeks after his return from the exile of division duty at Voltamo. By which it will be seen that Antrim was a very young man, and as yet no more than a novice in the fine art of love-making.

"I do take an interest in your affairs, Harry; you know I do. I am glad to see you succeeding in something you really like. But I wish"—she stopped, and let her gaze go beyond him—"I wish you wouldn't always talk as if—" She paused again, and Antrim finished the protest for her:

"As if my prospects and your future were one and the same thing, you mean?"

"Yes; it stirs me up and makes me feel resentful. I know I can't paint very much yet, but that is no reason why I shouldn't attain by and by, is it?"

"None in the world. It's only when you side-track me for art that I get restive. No man could be patient under that. Besides, you are never going to be a bachelor of art; you are going to be married to me, and then you can paint for fun as much as you like."

Isabel's retort was emphasized by a piquant little grimace of defiance:

"That is what you have been telling me ever since I can remember. I didn't mind it so much in the boy and girl stage; but when you say such things now, it only makes it more than ever impossible."

"Why does it?"

"Because it shows that you still cling to the idea that my love for art is nothing but a schoolgirl fad. It isn't anything of the kind; and you and father and all the rest of them ought to know it by this time."

"Oh, pshaw!" said Antrim, relapsing into disgusted silence.

Isabel touched the toe of her slipper to the floor and swung the hammock gently. As a comrade, brother—as anything, in fact, but a lover—she fellowshipped Antrim with hearty frankness. They had known each other from early childhood, and the outspoken familiarity of such an acquaintance is not to be set aside by the mere formality of a one-sided love-making.

He was a nice boy, she thought, suffering herself to moralize a little while he was recovering his equanimity. He always looked so well groomed, and his severe taste in the matter of raiment was very creditable. And he was capable, too; every one said that of him. Still he was but a boy; and his smooth-shaven face made him look years younger than he really was; and he wouldn't wear a mustache, as she wanted him to; and—and——

"Why don't you say something?" snapped the subject of her moralizings.

"I was thinking about you, and I supposed you would be glad to have me keep quiet if I would do that."

"I don't know about that. It depends very much upon what you were thinking. I could tell better if I heard the recapitulation."

Isabel tossed her head disdainfully. "Anybody would give me a penny for my thoughts," she said.

"Oh, if it's a pecuniary matter, here"—and he took a coin from his pocket and gave it to her.

"Thanks! I need some new brushes, and father says I am extravagant. Now you shall have what you have paid for. I was thinking that you know how to dress becomingly—and that you are smart—and that your salary is enough to make poor people envious—and that you look absurdly

young—and that a mustache would make you look years older—a-n-d——
"

Antrim sawed the air with his arm as he would have slowed down a reckless engineer.

"That will do; you have earned the dollar. But you won't mind my saying that I can get myself abused for less money. Do you ever have a really serious thought, Isabel? Take time to think about it, and tell me honestly."

Again Isabel's gaze went past him, bridging the bare plain and seeking infinity in the heights rising in mighty grandeur beyond the flat top of Table Mountain. When she spoke, raillery had given place to enthusiasm.

"Could any one live in sight of that"—pointing to the high-piled grandeur—"and not have thoughts too big for any kind of expression?"

"Oh, artistic thoughts, yes; I'll admit that you can outthink most people on that line," he rejoined.

"That is right; gird, if you want to. You are a Philistine, and you can't help it, I suppose. Just the same, art is the real reality, and your petty business affairs are merely the playthings of life. If I could put on canvas the faintest impression, the merest foreshadowing of what you can see over there, every other accomplishment or enjoyment in the world would seem little by comparison."

"There you go again," said Antrim. "Now I like pretty things as well as anybody, but when you try to make me believe that the painting of them is the chief end of man—or of woman, for that matter—why, it's like—" He searched for a sufficiently strong simile, and not finding one, ended rather irrelevantly. "Between you and Brant, I have a hard time of it trying to keep my feet on the everyday earth."

Isabel ignored the tirade and went off at a tangent, as was her custom with Antrim.

"Mr. Brant is a college graduate, isn't he?" she asked.

"Yes, I believe so. What of it?" demanded Antrim, who was so wholly imbued with the afflatus of business as to think small of scholarly attainments.

"Nothing; only I was thinking how much a college man has to be thankful for."

"I don't see your point," Antrim objected. "Take Brant, for instance; how is he any better off than the rest of us?"

"The mere fact that you can ask such a question is its best answer," replied Isabel pertly. "You are a specialist; you have lived in a business rut until you can't see out over the edges. You know that rut well enough, I suppose, but you would be utterly helpless if you should ever happen to be dragged out of it."

"I don't mean to be dragged out of it. A rut is a good thing when you come to know it well. Furthermore, I never saw the time when I was as helpless as the average college graduate."

"That is nonsense," said Isabel sweetly. "And, besides, it isn't original nonsense; you have had it said for you by every self-made man the world ever saw. The college man has this advantage in your own particular field: he can usually take hold of things where other people leave off. That isn't mine; it's father's. But I agree with him."

It was Antrim's turn to scoff. "I don't believe that. I have seen too many of them shoved into railway positions that they couldn't hold down. There was Pollard, on the west end—given a division when he didn't know the difference between a mogul and a switch engine. Nice mess he made of it before he got through."

"That may be; but at the same time Mr. Pollard had probably forgotten more things than most railway men ever know. Now, there is Mr. Brant; he doesn't ever have to talk 'shop.' He knows books, and art, and penology, and a hundred other things."

Whereat Antrim lost patience, as who would not?

"Brant be hanged!" he exclaimed wrathfully. "I am sick and tired of having him held up to me as an example. I wish I had never brought him here!"

"Thank you for nothing," snapped Isabel; and for five full minutes neither of them spoke. As usual, it was the man who finally made the overture toward peace.

"How is the 'Sunset in the Platte Cañon' coming on?" he asked placably.

"It is done—as much as anything of that kind ever is done."

"Shall we go in and look at it?"

Isabel got out of the hammock rather reluctantly, and they tiptoed past the sleeper at the other end of the veranda. In the room which Isabel called her studio she uncovered a canvas on an easel and ran the shades up to get a better light. Antrim made a proper show of examining the picture, and was silent so long that she was moved to say, "Well?" with a sharp little upward inflection.

"It's no use," he admitted good-naturedly. "You say I can't criticise, and when I try, it only makes you angry."

"It is your duty to try, anyway. Besides, I am in a lovely temper to-day."

Antrim had his own opinion as to that, but he stood off and tried to imagine himself at the impossible point of view from which the picture was painted. Failing utterly in this, he drew up a chair and sat down to go over it patiently for small errors in detail. Isabel presently grew restive, knowing well from past experience what was coming.

"It doesn't seem to me that the station at Buck Creek looks just like that," he said at length. "It's a longer building than you have made it, and the platform comes out farther this way."

"Anything else?" asked the artist sweetly.

"Yes; you have put two gondolas and a box car here on the side track. I don't believe there ever were that many cars set out there at one time."

"How dreadfully unfortunate!" said Isabel, with well-simulated concern.

"Yes, it is rather awkward. Can't you paint one or two of them out? Then, you have put this switch stand on the wrong side of the track; the engineer couldn't see that target until he got right up to it, and then he'd be in the ditch."

Isabel said, "Yes—go on"; and Antrim went on, glad enough to have found something which he was competent to criticise.

"Then, these cars again: if you don't paint them out you'd better paint them over. There are no high-sided gondolas on the narrow gauge, and no cars of any kind as big as these you have here."

It was unkind of Isabel to stand at the back of his chair where he could see none of the signs of the gathering storm, and there was no note of warning in her reply.

"Do you really think they are too large?"

"I don't think; I know. And I'll prove it to you," said he, confidently, taking his pencil and a slip of paper, and making sundry measurements on the station building in the picture. "Now, see here: this is what I mean. If you have kept the proportions right on this building, it ought to be about six feet between these two marks. Using that for a scale, you see these cars are about twice as long as they ought to be. And when you come to the height——"

Isabel flung the cloth over the painting and burst out passionately: "That is enough; it's a picture—not a mechanical drawing! I knew there were miles enough between us, but you never miss a chance to count them all over to me. I——"

She choked, and turned quickly to the window, and Antrim, who was slow to anger, tried to make amends.

"I'm sorry," he said. "You know I told you it was no use. I'll admit that I don't know a good picture when I look at it."

"I sha'n't trouble you to look at any more of mine." This to the window.

"I like to look at them; and I'll praise them, too, if that is what you want. But you always say you want criticism."

"And so I do, but I don't care to be made fun of."

"I wasn't making fun of you; I was merely pointing out the things I know are wrong. And what I said may be nothing against the picture as a work of art; it may be a masterpiece, for all I know about such things." This he said, being willing to pour still more oil on the troubled waters.

"You didn't say anything at all about the colouring."

"Because I don't know anything at all about colour—unless it's the colour of your eyes and hair. Let's drop it, Isabel, and talk about something of a great deal more importance—to me. When are you going to put me out of my misery?"

The time was ill chosen, and she answered him accordingly:

"That is dead and buried; there is no use in going back to it."

"Yes, there is," he insisted. "I have waited pretty patiently for a long time, Isabel, and—and—well, I can't wait always."

But Isabel was still tingling with pique, and she replied without so much as turning her head.

"End it, then. I never asked you to wait."

He was on his feet in a moment.

"Don't talk that way," he pleaded; "it hurts. I am not going to urge you any more now, because you are angry about the picture. But I want to say this: I can't take a jesting answer, or an angry one, always. When we speak of it again you must either take me or send me away; and—and you'll listen to reason, won't you, Isabel?"

She continued to look steadfastly out of the window and gave him no word of encouragement.

"Won't you, Isabel?" he repeated.

Still no answer.

"Isabel, I'm going now."

She did not speak or move until she heard the front gate latch behind him. Then she ran to the easel and snatched the cloth from the newly finished picture.

"Oh, I hate you!" she burst out spitefully; and when Dorothy came in, a few minutes later, the offending canvas had disappeared from the post of honour in the studio.

CHAPTER V
THE SCALE ASCENDING

AS for Brant and the successive steps in his reformatory experiment leading up to the good repute hinted at by Isabel's praise, fortune, good and ill, had befallen in this wise.

After the incident on the Denver journey and his instant recognition by a chance brakeman on the train, he had steeled himself, looking for similar embarrassments at every turn. But uphill paths are not always rough or slippery throughout, and in proof of this the beginnings were made easy for him. From the first he met no inopportune acquaintances, and, again, the question of employment answered itself congenially and promptly. Colonel Bowran needed a draughtsman; also, he happened to hold Brant's college in high repute, since its Professor of Mathematics had been an alumnus of his own *alma mater*. This and that, yoked together, ploughed Brant's furrow for him; and two days after his arrival in Denver he was perched upon a high stool in the chief engineer's office, giving himself mind and heart to the practice of a profession which had once been an artistic passion with him.

A fortnight later Antrim came back, the acquaintance was renewed, and Brant exchanged his room at the hotel for lodgings in the quiet private house recommended by the chief clerk. For a few weeks the reincarnated one went about his business circumspectly, spending his days at the office and his evenings with a fresh gathering of books in his room at Mrs. Seeley's, and showing himself in the streets as little as might be. This guarded walk brought its own reward. Not once in his goings and comings did he see a familiar face out of the disregarded underworld; and when the sense of security began to tread upon the heels of continued immunity, he ventured to take another step and went with Antrim to call upon the Langfords.

"They are nice people, and I am sure you'll like them," said the chief clerk. "My father was the judge's oldest friend back in Tennessee, and our houses stood in the same acre. I've known them ever since I can remember."

Antrim signalled a North Denver car, and Brant ventured a single question:

"Large family of them?"

"No; two girls and a boy. Dorothy's good, but not pretty; Isabel is pretty, but not—well, I'll leave her out, and you can judge for yourself. As for Will, he is another sort altogether. I call him an unlicked cub."

Twenty minutes later Antrim was introducing his friend in the double drawing-room of the transplanted Southern mansion in the highlands.

"Mrs. Langford—my friend, Mr. Brant. Judge Langford, this is the hermit I promised to bring you. Isabel, let me present Mr. Brant. Dorothy——"

But the elder daughter was smiling her remembrance of him, and she forestalled the introduction.

"I am so glad to be able to thank you in our own house, Mr. Brant," she said. "Mamma, this is the gentleman who was so kind to me on the night of the wreck."

That was the beginning of it; and Brant's heart warmed within him when he allowed himself to hope that something more beneficent than chance had brought them together again. Later in the evening, however, it cooled, till the former generous glow became a mere memory. The chilling process began in a turn of the conversation which defined Mrs. Langford's attitude toward sin and sinners, and her point of view was that of a mother of marriageable daughters. She had small charity for sowers of wild oats, and was strongly in favour of a social code which should embody a goodly measure of expiation. If every young man were held strictly accountable— were given to understand that every misstep would shut one or more respectable doors to him—the crop of wild oats would grow smaller with every generation.

Brant went dumb before the suggested accusation, was ill at ease during the remainder of the evening, and was much relieved when Antrim finally gave the signal for departure. On the walk cityward (they had missed the car) the chief clerk harked back to this discussion on culpability.

"I could hardly keep a straight face while Mrs. Langford was laying down the law for us," he chuckled. "She has a very dark-brown sheep in her own household—though she would be the last person in the world to admit it."

"So? The son, I suppose."

"Yes, Will. He is only nineteen, but I am afraid he has sounded the pond pretty thoroughly. I haven't kept track of him here in Denver, partly because he has no use for a friend of the family, and partly because I haven't much use for him. But he promised to be a terror when he was only a schoolboy back home, and I have no doubt he is keeping the promise."

"It's a pity," said Brant, thinking of the boy's elder sister.

"It's all of that. There is plenty of good blood in him on the Langford side, but his mother was a Troop, and the Troops have had at least one black sheep in every generation. But the father and mother are to blame, too. They have had one standard for the daughters and another for the son. Will has never known the meaning of obedience, and he has never been required to do anything he didn't want to do. Consequently he is a hardened sinner at nineteen."

"What is his particular weakness?"

"I'm not sure that he has any favourites. To the best of my knowledge he is as impartial as a callow youth can well be. I've heard more about his gambling than anything else, though."

"Quiet games with amateurs? or the other kind?"

Antrim laughed. "The other kind, of course. Penny-ante in a parlour wouldn't be half tough enough to suit him."

"That's bad."

"Yes; especially bad in his case. He is a surly young cub, as vindictive as he is quarrelsome. Somebody will lay him out one of these fine nights, and that will be the end of it."

Brant held his peace for two whole squares; then he spoke his mind freely as to a friend.

"It is none of my business, Antrim," he began, "and I don't know how you stand with the family, but it is a thousand pities to let that boy go to the devil without turning a hand to save him. I don't half like the way you put it."

Antrim laughed again. "You must remember that while you're hearing it for the first time, it is an old story with me. Besides, I shouldn't have a ghost of a chance with him. He doesn't like me, and I don't like him. If I should try to interfere I'd simply get myself into hot water with all concerned."

"Just the same, something ought to be done," Brant insisted.

"I agree with you, but who is to do it? By Jove, I have an idea! Suppose you try your hand. Mrs. Langford wouldn't thank you a little bit, because she would never admit the necessity; so far from it, she'd probably write you down in her black book. But the judge knows, and he'd be your friend for life."

Brant smiled rather grimly at the thought of his becoming a bearwarden for wayward youth, but he answered not a word; and presently their arrival at Mrs. Seeley's put an end to the talk. Contrary to his custom, Brant did not read himself to sleep that night. In room of a book he took a problem to bed with him, lying awake far into the small hours to wrestle therewith. And the name of the problem was William Langford.

CHAPTER VI
A MOLEHILL LEVELLED

FROM Brant's first visit to the transplanted Southern mansion in the Highlands to the second was but a step, which he found easier to take after the talk with Antrim about the black sheep.

After that, finding his welcome all that could be desired, he went often. The judge liked him because he took the trouble to inform himself on the subject of penology, which was the invalid's hobby; Mrs. Langford was disposed to be gracious to him because of his kindness to Dorothy on the train; Isabel openly rejoiced in the acquisition of a critic who knew the difference between a work of art and a photograph; and Dorothy made him welcome for many reasons, most of which she kept under lock and key in the strong room of her heart.

So there were not a few excursions across the river for Brant, and all went well until a certain Tuesday evening in late September—the Tuesday following that Sunday of picture measurings and lovers' partings. Brant had reached the house in the Highlands rather later than usual, and found Dorothy alone with her father and mother. There were unmistakable signs of sorrow in Dorothy's eyes; and when neither the judge nor Mrs. Langford seemed grateful for the company of their guest, Brant cut his visit short.

When he took his leave Dorothy followed him out to the veranda. There had been nothing more than a pleasant friendship between them thus far, but Brant had been watching eagerly for a chance to say or do something which might lessen the distance. Here was the coveted opportunity; and when she gave him her hand at parting, with a halting excuse for the gloom of the household, he made bold to hold it while he said:

"Don't speak of it unless you want to; but—just send me about my business if I am intruding—is there anything I can do to help you?"

"Then you know?" She stopped in tearful embarrassment, and he was too generous to allow her to go on.

"I know nothing, and seek to know nothing—that is, not anything more than you want to tell me. But you seem to be in trouble."

"I am; we all are. And there is no reason why you shouldn't know; it will be in the papers in the morning, and then every one will know. Will didn't come home last night, and—and father found him in jail this morning."

With all his comings and goings, and with all his good will to know him better, Brant yet knew the black sheep as little as might be, and that little by hearsay. The boy was seldom at home in the evening, and on the few occasions when his homestayings had coincided with Brant's visits he had been sullen and reticent, showing forth the fitness of Antrim's epithets. Scanty as were his opportunities for observation, however, Brant had seen that the mother idolized her son and found no fault in him; that Isabel tempered her sisterly affection with a generous measure of contempt; and that Dorothy loved her brother not blindly, but well. And it was with Dorothy's point of view that Brant chiefly concerned himself.

"Where is he now?" he inquired.

"We don't know; that is the sharp edge of it. He was in his room at noon, but when I went to take him his dinner he was gone."

"One more question, and you need not answer it if I ought not to know: What was the trouble last night?"

"I am not sure, but I think that—that—" she stumbled over the wording of it and would have broken down, but Brant ventured a word of comfort and she went on: "They were playing cards, and the police took them all. Will has made mamma believe they were not gambling, but I am afraid that isn't true." She turned away from him to lean against a veranda pillar to cry softly with her face in her hands.

Brant saw the path of duty very clearly; and he saw, too, that it might easily lead him straight to his own undoing. None the less, he set his feet therein like a man and a lover.

"Don't cry," he said. "We must find some way to help him. Does Antrim know anything about this?"

"No; and that is why Isabel went to the theatre with him to-night. They had planned to go, and she knew he would find out if they stayed at home. She would have had to tell him."

"That is all I need to know. Now go in and comfort your father and mother. I can help—perhaps more than you would be willing to believe. Good night."

"One word, Mr. Brant: you will bring him home if you find him, won't you?"

"Certainly. And I'll find him, if he is in Denver. Has he a latchkey?"

"Yes."

"Then don't sit up for him; and don't let your mother, if you can help it. And you mustn't grieve; it will come out all right."

"Oh, if I could only believe that! But I don't know how we can ever repay you, Mr. Brant."

"Wait till I have done something worthy of payment; then perhaps I may tell you—if you will let me. Good-bye."

A car was coming, and he ran to the crossing to intercept it. Half an hour later he was climbing the stairs to the editorial rooms of the Colorado Plainsman, listening to the rumbling of the presses in the basement, and wondering if his slight acquaintance with the man he sought would serve his purpose. The night editor was in, but his desk was yet unlittered.

"Hello, Brant; glad to see you. Sit down. Got a scoop for us?"

"Not exactly," said Brant. Then he took counsel of directness. "It is rather the other way about. I want to cut a slice out of one that you have got."

"Anything in reason. State the case," said the editor briefly.

"It is this: the police raided a dive last night, I believe?"

"Yes, Draco's. It was this morning, though, after the forms were locked."

"So I supposed. Well, there is one name that must come out of the list of arrests—that of William Langford."

Editor Forsyth lighted a cigar and tilted his swing chair to what the night force called the disputatious angle.

"'Must' is a stout word in a newspaper office," he objected. "Who is this William Langford? and why should he play and not pay?"

Brant uncoupled the two queries and spoke only to the latter.

"There are plenty of reasons. For one, he is only a boy; for another, he is a friend of mine."

The editor chuckled. "You have no business to be making maps in the colonel's office," he retorted. "You ought to syndicate yourself to the refrigerator people; they'd save money on their ice bills."

"Never mind about that. Will you do what I want you to?"

"Oh, sure." Forsyth took down the copy hook, found the report of the raid, and blue-pencilled the name of William Langford. "It's rank treason—muzzling the press, you know—but anything to oblige a friend. What else can I do for you?"

"Much; this is only the beginning. Put on your hat and coat and go with me to the other morning papers. I don't know any of the newspaper men; but they will do it for you."

The chair of the night editor righted itself with a crash.

"By Jove! Say, Brant, you've got the cold nerve of your namesake over in the Silverette district; I'll be hanged if you haven't. Oh, I'll go," he went on. "I suppose the other fellows will say there is a woman in the case, and devil me accordingly, but that won't matter. Come on, and let's have it over with."

"There is a woman in the case," said Brant calmly. "Otherwise I shouldn't be here. But she must not be mentioned."

"Of course not. Langford is your cousin, and you are his natural guardian—that's the line. Light a fresh cigar and we'll be about it."

They made the round of the newspaper offices together, and when it was completed Brant thanked Forsyth at the foot of the Plainsman stairway.

"I owe you one, Forsyth, and I'll pay it when I can," he said. "Let me know when the time comes—say some dark night when you need a bodyguard, for instance."

Forsyth laughed. "I believe you would fill the bill about as well as the Silverette man. By the way, is he a relative of yours?"

"No; but I know something of him. Good night." And at the word Brant turned away to begin the search for the lost sheep of the house of Langford.

CHAPTER VII
AND A MOUNTAIN UPREARED

ON the night after the raid Draco's gambling house was running in full panoply as usual; and thither Brant directed his steps upon leaving the Plainsman building. Arguing from experience, he made sure that young Langford would be found in the kennel of the dog that had bitten him; and carrying the deduction a step farther, he was prepared to find the lad playing the part of led captain to some older villain.

It was not likely that the boy had developed a passion for play of his own motion. Brant knew that trade well. It had its master workmen, its slipshod journeymen, its tramps, and its apprentices. He doubted not that young Langford was still of the undergraduate guild; in which case a heroic remedy might yet effect a cure.

This train of reasoning led to certain conclusions. If he should find the boy serving as a stool pigeon for some older man, his task would be comparatively easy. The professional gambler is sufficiently wise in his own generation; and a word to the wise—such a word as Brant knew how to speak—would quickly release the apprentice.

So much for the boy and the first step in his rescue. After that it would be the father's part to keep him from forming a new alliance—if he could.

For himself, however, Brant foresaw price payings of the dearest. The lower world was thickly peopled in the Denver of that day, and he could scarcely hope to win in and out unrecognised. As a citizen of that world his light had not been hidden under a bushel. He was known to the men of his tribe, and the tribe is nomadic, albeit it keeps well within its own marches.

What then? Merely this: It would be passed from lip to ear that Plucky George of the mining camps was in town; that, for reasons best known to himself, he was living for the time in retirement. And thereafter he would better cut off his right hand than be seen in public with any woman whose reputation he valued.

This was the barb of the arrow, and it rankled sorely while he was measuring the distance between the Plainsman building and the kennel of the dog. Nevertheless, he went on steadily enough until he stood before the baize doors screening the interior of the Draconian kennel. But here he hung reluctant for a moment, knowing that he had reached the turning point. Once beyond the swinging doors it would be too late to go back.

So he stopped, and put out his hand and withdrew it, and for the first time in many years the square jaw of him lacked something of its resolute outline. Within he could heard the shuffling of feet, the clinking of glasses, the *b-r-r* of the roulette balls—all the familiar sounds of the life he had put behind him. He was far enough away from it now to begin to loathe it; and yet it drew him irresistibly. What if he should be dragged back into the old paths again? Stranger things had happened; and the fascination of the serpent is not less potent because it is loathsome.

While he hesitated, it came to him like the thrilling of an electric shock that this was one of the penalties he would always have to pay—this calling to him of the underworld to which he had belonged. In a flash of the inner self-sight, one of those glimpses into heart possibilities that not even a good man may prolong to a scrutiny, he saw that he had lied in telling Hobart that his yearnings were altogether for better things. They were not. The woundings of the evil years were not healed, and they might never be. He turned and took a step away from the doors of peril.

There and then he saw a picture of a grief-stricken young woman leaning against a vine-covered veranda pillar and sobbing softly as one who mourns without hope. Then and there the thought of his promise to Dorothy Langford nerved him afresh, and the swing doors fell apart under his hand.

The baize screens were yet winging to rest behind him, and he had no more than taken the measure of the place, when the bartender threw up his hand by way of welcome. Here was recognition on the very threshold of the undertaking; and since it had come, Brant set his teeth and determined to make such use of it as his errand would warrant. So he went around to the end of the bar and waited until the man was at liberty. That was not long.

"Well, say, old pardner—shake! I thought you'd turn up all right. How are they coming, anyhow? Fellow came in here a while back and said you'd killed a man up on the range and lit out. I told him he lied; told him you wasn't the runaway kind; see? What'll you take?"

Notwithstanding Brant was but a short Sabbath-day's journey away from the associations of which the bartender's greeting was a part, he winced at the familiarity of it, at the oaths with which it was plentifully garnished, and even at the underworld *argot* in which it was couched. Then he humbled himself and put his newly found dignity under foot.

"Thank you, I am not drinking anything to-night, Tom. I merely dropped in to ask a question or two."

"Fire away."

"Have you seen a young fellow hanging around here lately—smooth-faced boy, dark eyes and dark hair—dresses pretty well?"

"Why, yes; that's the kid. He's here now."

"Alone?"

"Well, hardly; the Professor has sort of adopted him, I reckon; anyhow, they run together most of the time."

Brant's face flushed as if the man had smitten him, and with the narrowing of his eyes the past laid fast hold upon him and once more the man-quelling demon was in possession.

"There is only one 'Professor,' I take it." He spoke softly, as one speaks to a little child. "You mean Jim Harding?"

"Sure; *her* brother. You ought to know him, if anybody does."

"Yes, I know him." The recusant sinner turned his back to the bar and let his gaze go adrift down the long room. It was comfortably filled. There were pairs and trios and quartettes at the card tables; little groups around the marble games and roulette boards; a front rank of sitters about the faro table, with a standing reserve playing over the shoulders of those in the chairs; and in the midst an uneasy throng revolving about the various centres of attraction, like the slow-moving figures in a timeless minuet.

Somewhere in this devil's dragnet was the boy—the boy who was Dorothy's brother. To keep that in mind asked for an effort, because with the boy he should find his enemy, the man who had traded upon a sister's shame. At the thought the gray eyes grew hard and cruel, and his hand went back toward the bartender.

"Give me your pistol a minute, Tom; I may need it," he said, without looking around.

"It won't do down here, George. They'd hang you too quick for any use."

"Never mind about that; give me the gun."

The weapon was passed across the bar and Brant dropped it into his coat pocket. Then he dipped into the uneasy throng and began a search which ended beside one of the roulette boards. Young Langford was watching the game dry-lipped and hot-eyed, and at his side stood a man who might have passed otherwhere for a schoolmaster. He was tall and slightly stooping, his garments were of the clerical cut, and his lean face was clean shaven. Only in the ferrety eyes was there a hint of the unfathomable wickedness of the man. The nickname of "the Professor" fitted him aptly, and he dressed the part, playing it with all the skill of a trained actor.

To outward appearances no more harmless person than James Harding could have been met in a day's journey; but Brant knew his man. Coming softly up behind, he seized Harding's right wrist and held it helpless while he spoke.

"Excuse yourself to the boy and come out with me," he whispered at Harding's ear; and the vicelike grip turned the soft-spoken words into a command.

Harding's answer was a stealthy movement of his free hand toward his breast pocket, but Brant checked it with a word.

"Don't be a fool, or take me for one, unless you are ready to quit. Do as I tell you, and be quick about it."

There was murder in Harding's eyes what time he was measuring his chance against the weapon in Brant's pocket. Then fear took its place, and he obeyed the command.

"All right," said the boy, without taking his eyes from the spinning roulette ball. "I'll wait here for you."

Brant marched his man to the swing doors and out into the deserted street. Just beyond the circle illuminated by the arc light in front of Draco's he backed Harding to the wall.

"Hands up!" he said briefly.

Harding's thin lip quivered like that of a snarling dog, but again he obeyed.

"Turned hold-up, have you, George?" he sneered.

Brant ignored the taunt and deftly disarmed his captive. Then he spoke tersely and to the point, as one who may enforce his commands.

"You know me, and there is no need to measure words. I brought you out here to tell you what you are to do. You are going to take that boy home and turn him loose; and then you are going to keep out of his way."

"Oh, I am, am I?"

"Yes; and this is the way you are going to do it: You will go back in there and bring him out; then you will walk him up the street and put him into the first carriage you come to. Do I make myself perfectly clear?"

"Sure thing! You've got it all down to a fine point, haven't you?"

"Then you will get in with him and go wherever the driver takes you. By the time the carriage stops you will have explained matters in any way you see fit; only young Langford must be given to understand that it is all off between you."

"And after that?"

"After that I think it will be best for you to leave Denver. It is a fair-sized town, but I am afraid it isn't big enough to hold you and me at the same time."

"And what if I refuse? What if I tell you to go to——"

Brant took out the borrowed pistol and balanced it on the palm of his hand.

"In that case I shall be obliged to make sure of you here and now; and remembering what you are, I'd about as soon do it as not."

The man at bay fought the fear back out of the telltale eyes and tried to laugh hardily.

"You are a pretty smooth talker, George, but you can't bluff me. I don't know just what you are driving at, but I do happen to know that you don't care to get your name in the papers just now. All the same, I'm willing to oblige you—for a consideration."

"How much?" asked Brant, still balancing the weapon.

"A hundred, say, in money, and that little package of papers you took the trouble to have sworn out against me up in Taggett's Gulch."

Brant considered it for a moment, and the man at bay began to have a dim premonition that he had gone too far; that his life hung in the balance while he waited. The terror of it grew with the lagging seconds, and he had opened his mouth to withdraw the condition when Brant spoke again:

"You know very well that I don't have to make terms with you, but you shall have the money. The papers I keep. Now go and get the boy, and don't make any bad breaks. If you do, I shall shoot first and talk afterward."

Harding drew breath of relief and re-entered the kennel with Brant at his heels. Inside the swing doors the latter gave another order.

"Go on and get your man; I'll wait here while you are doing it."

When Harding was about it Brant turned to the bartender. "Here is your gun, Tom; much obliged. And, while I think of it, I'll turn over the Professor's arsenal. You can give it back to him when he calls for it."

A murderous-looking knife, a life preserver, and a set of brass knuckles changed hands, and Deverney swept them into a drawer with an exclamation of surprise.

"Holy Smut! And he let you catch him without his gun!" he said.

"Not much," rejoined Brant pleasantly. "But I shall keep that for a little while. I am not through with him yet. And say, Tom, that reminds me: if that youngster ever comes back here, just pull that 'No Minors Allowed' sign on him and run him out. You won't lose anything, because he will have no money to blow in."

"I'll do it—for you, George. But the Professor will run him in again."

"I shall make it my business to see that he doesn't," Brant asserted; and just then Harding came up with young Langford.

"Hello, Brant," said the cub, with a free-and-easy swagger born of the place rather than of his temperament. "By gad, I didn't know you were a sporting man! Shake hands with my friend Mr. Harding."

Brant scowled, but the boy saw nothing and rattled on: "Going home early to-night. What will you take, gentlemen? It's on me."

"Nothing," said Brant shortly; and Harding drew the boy away.

The pair left the place and went up the street, with Brant a few steps in the rear. At the corner a night-owl carriage was waiting for a chance fare, and Harding opened the door and got in with his companion. At the click of the door latch Brant climbed to a seat beside the driver and gave the order.

"No. 16 Altamont Terrace," he said; and when the horses were fairly headed for North Denver he lighted a cigar and ventured to anticipate success.

But the triumph was short-lived. While the carriage was yet rumbling over the viaduct the little upflash of triumph flickered and went out. For, however worthy the cause in which he had fought and won, it was Brant the man of violence, and no repentant sinner of them all, who had done the fighting. For the time being he had lapsed as thoroughly as if the new leaf had never been turned, and the dregs of that cup were bitter.

CHAPTER VIII
A BLOW IN THE DARK

WHEN a careful man blunders he is apt to make thorough work of it. If Brant had suspected the use Harding would make of an uninterrupted quarter of an hour with William Langford, it is safe to assume that no preventive, however heroic, would have failed to commend itself to the rescuer; and he should have foreseen. Any tenderfoot of them all would have been less blunt-witted, he told himself afterward in much bitterness of spirit. But that was after the fact. While he was smoking his cigar on the box and tasting some of the aloe dregs of the cup of lapsings, Harding was making the most of his opportunity.

"No, Willie, I can't say when I may be back in Denver. A man with a big mine on his hands can't play marbles all the time, you know. Has to look after his ante or they'll steal him blind."

"Of course," agreed Will; and then, "Where is your mine?"

Now one place is as good as another for the location of purely mythical real estate; but, for safety's sake, Harding went far afield.

"It's on the other side of the range; in the Silverette district."

"Is that so? Then you must know all about the Jessica. The governor's got some stock in the Jessica."

"Ye-yes; oh, yes. I know the Jessica, of course. But the Silverette is a big district, you know. My claim isn't anywhere near the camp, and I'm glad of it. Tough town, is Silverette. And that reminds me, how did you happen to catch on to George Brant?"

Truly, Will Langford was a crass young idiot whose ways were very far from being the ways of wisdom, and yet he was not besotted enough to be without an undefined conviction that this smooth-tongued mine owner of pedagogic appearance and profligate habit was not a man to whom family affairs could be properly confided. Wherefore he skirted the question.

"I don't know very much about him. He is a friend of a friend of ours."

"I thought you wasn't fairly on to him, or you wouldn't have introduced me," said Harding, with marked significance. "He is a mighty good man to let alone. You can bet high on that and play to win every time."

The hint accomplished that whereunto it was sent, and Will must needs know more. Harding was crafty enough to make an unspeakable mystery of it until the boy's curiosity was whetted to the keen edge of demanding the particulars for family reasons. Then Harding told Brant's story, carefully suppressing his own connection therewith, and weaving evil deeds and worse motives into the narrative with such a skilful admixture of truth as to make it utterly impossible for the ex-reprobate ever to clear himself without denying much that was manifestly undeniable.

The carriage was turning into Altamont Terrace when he concluded, and the eager listener had time for no more than a word of thanks.

"By Jove, I'm awfully glad you told me about him, Mr. Harding! There are reasons, family reasons, as I said; but I can't tell you about them now. By gad, if he ever shows up here again I'll——"

What the self-constituted guardian of the Langford honour would do is not to be here set down, since the carriage was stopping at the gate. Harding would have given much to know that, and many other things; would have purchased another quarter of an hour with the boy at any reasonable price. But with the carriage drawn up before the judge's gate and Brant sitting on the box, the time was unpropitious. So Harding was fain to bury his desire for further knowledge under a final word of caution.

"I'm glad I happened to mention it. Keep your eye on him and give him the whole sidewalk. I saw him hanging around down yonder, and I was afraid he might get his hands on you; that's why I brought you home. Good night."

Brant heard the last word, and saw the boy go up the walk and let himself into the house. Then he gave the driver the return order.

"Back to town," he said. "You can put us down at Elitch's."

The long drive back to town was full of disquieting reflections for the man who desired nothing so much as to be allowed to atone for past violence by present and future good behaviour, and who was yet constrained to play the ruffler through still another interview with James Harding. Such reflections capped by such consequences are likely to be heart-hardening, and Brant was in no merciful mood when the carriage drew up at the curb in front of the *café* and he climbed down to open the door.

"Come out," he rasped; and when Harding stood beside him, "You will have to go in here with me to get your money."

Harding nodded, and threw in a sneer. "Banking with John nowadays, are you?" But to this Brant made no reply.

As it chanced, the great dining room was nearly empty, and the genial proprietor, known and loved of all men, was at his desk. Brant took him aside.

"John, I want a hundred dollars to use right now. Can you cash a check for me?"

The genial one laughed. It was not his way to cash checks for men whom he knew and trusted.

"Not much," he said. "You can have the century, but I don't want your paper." And he found the money in the little safe behind the desk. "Anything else I can do for you?"

"Yes; I want to use one of the private rooms for a few minutes."

Elitch held up a finger for the head waiter, a stalwart young fellow who looked as if he might be a college athlete working his way through a lean vacation.

"Parker, show these gentlemen to No. 4, and light the gas for them. No orders."

The athletic one led the way to a small private dining room partitioned off in the rear of the public tables. It was a mere box, lighted by a chandelier pendent from the ceiling, and furnished only with table and chairs. When they were alone, Harding dropped into one of the chairs and Brant drew up another on the opposite side of the table.

"Now, then, talk quick and tell the truth—if you can. What did you say to the boy?"

The soul of the real James Harding peered out through his half-closed eyes for a fleeting instant, but the veil was drawn again before one might note the levin-flash of triumph.

"I did what you wanted me to: told him I'd got to go and look after my mine."

"What excuse did you make for taking him home?"

"Told him he shouldn't ought to be out so late. He'll do anything for me, that young fellow will."

"Yes, that is very evident," Brant commented dryly. Then, "What else did you say to him?"

Again the levin-flash of triumph, but Brant did not see it. "Nothing; you didn't tell me to say anything else to him."

"No more I didn't. Well, all you have to do now is to keep out of his way—and mine. Here is your money. Take it and make yourself scarce."

The roll of bills changed hands, and Harding made sure of the price before he spoke again. Then he squared himself against his side of the table and asked if he might have his weapons.

"Deverney has them—all but the gun. I think I shall keep that as a souvenir."

Harding nodded assent, and the shifty eyes were veiled. "That's all right; keep it, and welcome. I'd have made you a present of it if you had asked me for it." He was picking nervously at the tablecloth, and a curious change—a change in which sullen hardihood gave place to something not so easily definable—came over him as he went on: "And about young Langford: I would have turned him loose long ago if I had known you wanted me to; honest to God, I would! You have had it in for me for a good many years, George, but there hasn't been a day in any one of them when I wouldn't do anything you asked—and more."

Brant's acknowledgment of all this was a contemptuous curl of the lip, and Harding tried again.

"It's so, and you know it. We've scrapped a good deal, first and last, but if I've been the jackal, you've been the wolf. I've been thinking a good bit in the last hour or so, and I'm going to say what's in me. Why can't we quit square, for once? I haven't got anything against you; and it seems like after what has happened you ought to be willing to let up on me."

"Oh, it does, does it?" Brant was looking now, and he saw the fear signals flying in the shifty eyes. He was as yet no more than a catechumen in the temple of mercy, as he was learning to his cost, and the man-quelling demon was once more in possession. So he backslid promptly into the prerepentant barbarism and gave another twist to the thumbscrews. "That means that you want something more, I suppose. What is it? Out with it."

"The papers, George—the affidavits you got against me up in Taggett's Gulch. I haven't had a good night's rest since I found out you had 'em, so help me God, I haven't! Wherever I go, and whatever I do, I can feel that cursed hangman's knot pulling up under my ear. For Christ's sake, give 'em to me, George! Don't send me to hell before my time!"

Truly, Brant was yet very far from sainthood, either in act or intention, since he could look unmoved upon the ghastly face of the terror-sick man across the table. Harding leaned forward until his chin was nearly touching the cloth. His shifty eyes were for once fixed and glassy, and the perspiration of fear stood thickly upon his narrow brow. And with the dropping of the mask of self-control, the old age of dissipation wrought its will on the clean-shaven face, furrowing it with wrinkles that seemed to deepen visibly with the dragging seconds.

"Oh, my God! think of it, George," he began again in a husky whisper, "think of what would happen if you were to die! And I'd never get so much as a hint of what was coming till they had snapped the bracelets on me! You couldn't die easy with such a thing as that on your mind; now could you, George?"

Brant looked away and shut his hands until the finger nails bit the flesh. There was a moment of silence surcharged with the electricity of portent— a moment in which the limp figure at the opposite side of the table drew itself up by imperceptible degrees and the glassy eyes of it began to glow with the fires of unrecking ferocity. The athletic young head waiter, drawn to the door of No. 4 by what promptings of curiosity he knew not, had his eye glued to a crack in the panel and his ears strained to catch the reply to Harding's appeal; and knowing nothing of the man, but much of the danger signals readable in the man's face, he wondered at Brant's preoccupation. And when Brant began to speak without looking up, the athlete swore softly to himself, and cautiously tried the handle of the door—tried it and found it locked.

"I have thought about that a good many times, and it has been a comfort to me. You called me a wolf a minute ago, but it is you who have lived the wolf's life, sparing neither man, woman, nor child. Hence it is fitting that you should die as you have lived. Remembering these things, and how you used to wring my soul when you had the power, I think I shall die quite comfortably when my time comes."

"Then die!" yelled the madman, hurling himself in a fierce tiger spring across the table at his tormentor.

Brant was by far the stronger of the twain, but the onset was so sudden and unexpected that he was borne down among the chairs, and Harding's fingers were at his throat before he could gather himself in defense. After that he was helpless, and the dancing gas jets of the chandelier were about to go out in a flare of red lightning when the weight was lifted from his chest and he began to breathe again. Then he saw that the athletic waiter had set his shoulder to the door at the opportune moment; that he had flung Harding into a corner and was standing guard over him with a chair for a weapon.

"Say the word, Mr. Brant, and I'll smash him one for good luck," he said; but Brant sat up and shook his head.

"No; let him go," he said huskily. "I can kill him later on if I need to."

The young man stood aside, and Harding ran out. Then the athletic one helped Brant to his feet.

"He didn't cut you, did he?" he asked.

"No. I believe he was trying to choke me. I don't know how I came to be so careless. How did you happen in?"

The young man laughed, and was not beyond blushing a little. "I guess I might as well make a clean breast of it. Business isn't very brisk at this time of night, and I overheard a little of what was going on—not much, but enough to make me wonder if I could smash the door in if the need arose. I suppose I ought to be ashamed of myself; but it was rather lucky, as it turned out."

"Very lucky, indeed. And there was nothing particularly private about my part of the interview. Has John gone home?"

"Yes. Shall I call a cab for you?"

"Oh, no. Give me your shoulder to the sidewalk and I can make it all right. But I am beginning to think I had a rather close call."

"You did that." The head waiter took Brant's arm, and the course between the tables of the public room was safely steered. At the door the breath of the night air was revivifying, and Brant found speech in which to thank his rescuer.

"Oh, that's all right," laughed the athlete. "It's all in a day's work. Good night."

CHAPTER IX
THE EYE TO THE STRING

IN the Langford household the judge and Dorothy were the only early risers, and on the morning following Will's home-bringing they breakfasted alone together as usual. Dorothy and her mother had sat up for the wayward one the night before; but at the breakfast table the daughter saw that the news of his son's return brought small comfort to her father. The cause of his disquietude was not far to seek. The morning papers lay unopened beside his plate, and he left them there when he retreated to the library.

Being a woman, Dorothy did not thus deny herself the luxury of suffering with full knowledge. She opened the papers and read the reports of the raid on Draco's; and she did not fail to put up a little pæan of thanksgiving when she found that her brother's name was omitted in the list of the arrests. Stopping only long enough to make assurance doubly sure, she hastened to the library.

"Here are the papers, father," she began, and when he looked up from his book and shook his head in refusal, she went on quickly: "You needn't be afraid to read them; Will's name isn't mentioned."

The judge took the papers and scanned them with interest newly aroused. The fine old face of the master of Hollywood, with its heavy white mustache and pointed goatee, was military rather than judicial, and Dorothy was joyed to see the lines of stern sorrow soften a little as he read.

"You are right," he said, after he had scanned the list of the incriminated ones. "Let us thank God that we are spared so much. But I don't understand it."

"Perhaps Will gave an assumed name," Dorothy suggested.

"And so added a lie to his other misdoings?" rejoined the father bitterly. "No, he didn't do that. I saw the record at the police station."

Dorothy was puzzled for a moment, and then a light broke in upon her.

"I think I know how it happened," she said, and then she gave him a brief summary of the talk with Brant on the veranda.

The judge heard her through, and being in nowise less shrewd because he happened to be his daughter's father, he was at no loss to account for

Brant's motive. Nevertheless, he did not forget to be grateful, and he gave the helpful one his just meed of praise.

"It was a thoughtful thing to do, and the man who would think of it at such a time must know how it grinds to have a good old name dragged in the mire," he said warmly. "I shall remember it. Was Mr. Brant with Will when he came home?"

"I couldn't tell. I saw the carriage drive up, and saw Will stop to speak to some one inside after he got out. Then he came up the walk alone, and the carriage went back toward the boulevard."

"Well, it was a kindly deed, well meant and well done, and we are Mr. Brant's poor debtors," said the judge, taking up one of the papers again. "I shall go down by and by and thank him for it."

Dorothy went at that, and when the library door closed behind her the judge put the paper down, ostensibly to polish his eyeglasses, but really because the problem of his old age had grown great enough to banish interest in everything else. He had always prided himself on being a good judge of human nature, and so he was when the point of view was the judge's bench in a courtroom. But it is a wise father who knows his own son; and Judge Langford was just beginning to suspect that his experience with human nature, and his courtroom studies therein, had counted for little in the training of his son. More than this, he was coming to understand that there is a time when a father's lost opportunities may not be regained; that the saving of William Langford, if salvage there were to be, must be at other and alien hands.

That conclusion set him upon the search for his own substitute, and most naturally he thought of Brant. There was that about Colonel Bowran's assistant which made him easily a beau ideal for a younger man whose tastes were not wholly vitiated. He was a man of the world—a much wider world than his present position with the colonel bespoke, the judge decided; and he was of the masterful type out of which boys are most likely to fashion their heroes. If the thing might only come about without suggestion; if— But there were too many "if's" in the way, and the judge fell to polishing his eyeglasses again, letting the summing up of the matter slip into spoken words: "I wish he might be able to tell me what to do with the boy. It is far enough beyond me."

The door had opened noiselessly, and the mother of the problem crossed the threshold in good time to overhear the summing up.

"What is beyond you?" she asked, knowing well enough what the answer would be.

"The one thing that is always beyond me, Martha—what we are to do with William."

The mother had not yet been to breakfast, but she sat down and prepared to argue her son's case.

"Doesn't it sometimes occur to you that possibly you may try to do too much?"

"No," said the judge firmly, knowing by sorrowful experience whereunto the argument would lead. "By some means—I don't pretend to know how—the boy always manages to whitewash himself with you. But I am coming to know him better. We may as well face the fact first as last, Martha. He is thoroughly, utterly, recklessly bad. God forgive me that I should have it to say of the son for whom I am responsible!"

But Mrs. Langford protested indignantly, as was her maternal privilege.

"That is just where you are mistaken—in assuming that he is bad at heart. You don't understand him at all, and sometimes I'm tempted to think you don't want to. Are there no allowances to be made for youthful thoughtlessness?"

"Youthful depravity, you would better say." The judge left his chair and began to walk the floor. "Why don't you call things by their right names? I should think this last affair would open your eyes, if nothing else has."

"Oh, I don't know. Please sit down, Robert; you make me nervous. I had a long talk with him last night, and he told me everything without reserve. I know it was all wrong—his being in such a place—but it was rather foolish than intentionally wicked."

"You make a nice distinction," said the judge, but the sorrow in his voice dulled the edge of the sarcasm. "What is his story?"

"Why, just this. It seems that he has a friend—a Mr. Harding, a wealthy mine owner—and they went around together to see the sights, purely out of curiosity, William says, and I believe him. They just happened to be in this Draco place night before last; and when the police rushed in they took everybody, guilty and innocent. William says his friend tried to explain that they were only onlookers, but it was no use, and—well, we know the rest."

"Yes, rather better than I could wish. As a result of his curiosity, or this Mr. Harding's, I find my son in the police station, charged with gambling."

"Of course, in such a case the charge would be made against everybody."

"As it should be. If William had been at home, instead of prowling about town with a disreputable companion——"

Mrs. Langford raised deprecatory hands.

"Wait and hear the sequel before you do the man an injustice. When Will went downtown last night, feeling desperate and discouraged enough to do anything, this Mr. Harding found him and insisted on his coming straight home—brought him home in a carriage, in fact. A bad man would not have done that."

The judge looked perplexed, as well he might. "Brought him home in a carriage, you say? Why, I thought—" But he did not add what he thought.

"Yes, and that wasn't all. It seems that Mr. Harding knows Mr. Brant, and he told William his whole history. Will wouldn't repeat it—he said it wasn't fit for me to hear—but he told me enough so that I shall know what to say to Mr. Brant if he ever has the effrontery to come here again."

Here was a fresh mystery, but the judge was wise enough not to repeat what Dorothy had told him. Moreover, he knew his son's failings too well to place implicit confidence in any story of his told in a peace-making moment after an escapade. Wherefore he counselled moderation.

"I shouldn't take too much for granted if I were you, Martha," he said. "There are always two sides to an accusation like that, and possibly Mr. Brant may have something to say for himself. Anyway, I should give him a chance."

"That is precisely what I shall do," Mrs. Langford rejoined, with a tightening of the firm lips that boded ill for the man who was to be given the chance; after which she went to breakfast, leaving her husband to the company of his own thoughts—thoughts which were far from comforting.

How much of William's story could be believed? And who was this man Harding who claimed to know Brant? If the latter was the one who had prevailed upon Will to come home, how was it that the boy had come in a carriage with the former? And which of the two had suppressed the mention of William Langford's name in the published lists of the accused? These and many more perplexing questions suggested themselves, and the judge was no nearer the heart of the tangle when he finally went out to seek Brant at the railway offices.

CHAPTER X
THE STRING TO THE SHAFT

AS for Brant, the day following the retrieval of the body of William Langford was a day to be marked in the calendar as the Feast of the Mingled Cups. Having been up rather more than half the night, he was a little late at the office, and he found the chief engineer getting ready to go up the line on the day train.

"Good morning, Brant," said the colonel. "You are just in time. I want Grotter's field notes to take with me. What did you do with the book?"

Brant found the notebook, and began to say something about late hours and their next morning consequences, but the colonel only laughed good-naturedly:

"I know; I was a young man once myself. But if I had it to do over again I'd touch it lightly. Of course, you are new to the West, and naturally you want to see the animals; but even an onlooker has to be careful and not get the smell of the menagerie in his clothes. It's devilish hard to get out."

It was a random thrust, but it went home, and for a few minutes after the colonel's departure Brant saw only the large humour of it. Truly, he had never posed before his chief as a reformed reprobate; but to be mistaken for an innocent youth, fresh from the moral environment of the well-behaved East, was mirth for the gods. Afterward, however, the pendulum swung to the opposite end of its arc. Was it quite honest that he should suffer the colonel—and others—to think better of him than the facts warranted? Obtaining money under false pretences was a crime: was it any less culpable to carry off booty of good repute in like manner?

As far as his chief was concerned, Brant had come to know the colonel well enough to be sure that a most intimate knowledge of the incriminating facts would have little weight with him on the professional side. He was well satisfied with his assistant, and, unlike many employers, he was frank enough to say so. But there was a standing invitation—as yet unused—holding the door of the Bowran home open to the draughtsman. This might not be withdrawn in so many words, but—Brant put himself in the colonel's shoes—it would probably not be renewed.

From the Bowran generalities to the Langford particulars was but a step, and Brant presently began to ask himself curious questions touching the continuance of his welcome at Hollywood if the facts were known. That was a different matter, and he was not long in arriving at conclusions definite and humiliating. The judge would probably set him down as a hypocrite; Mrs. Langford would be horrified; Isabel would want him to pose as the central figure in a certain picture of mining camp life she was painting; Will would fellowship him frankly on the ground of similarity of tastes; and Dorothy—it was not so easy to prefigure her attitude, though pity and sorrow for a smashed ideal might well be the pointing of it.

"That settles it!" said this latter-day flagellant, scourging himself into a fine fury of self-abnegation. "I go there no more. It is only a question of time when they will find me out, and then I should do something desperate."

So he affected to consider the determination taken once for all, and fell to work in a dull rage of resentment. But when that fire burned out for lack of fuel, as all fires will, another and a holier was kindled in its place. At thirty a man does not fall in love at first sight, and in the beginning Dorothy Langford had figured in his thoughts of her only as an incarnation of pure womanhood. But latterly the point of view had been changing. She was no longer a type; she was the eidolon of the type. Brant asked himself a blunt question, and the ink dried between the nibs of his ruling pen while the question waited for its answer. The windows of the map room looked northward, and he got down from the high stool to stand with his hands behind him, gazing abstractedly across the railway yards toward the quarter of the town he had come to know best.

"You have spun the web for me, little girl, and I couldn't break away from you now if the heavens fall," he said, letting his thought slip into speech. "I have just about one chance in a hundred of being able to carry it off without being found out, and I am going to take that chance; I'd take it if it were only one in a thousand."

The outer office door opened and shut, but Brant heard it not. For which cause he started guiltily when some one behind him said:

"You have a fine view from here, Mr. Brant."

Brant spun around as one shot, and found himself confronting the father of the young woman whom he had been apostrophizing. For a moment even the commonplaces deserted him, but presently he recovered himself sufficiently to join rather sheepishly in the laugh at his own expense.

"I was fairly caught," he admitted. "How long have you been here?"

"Not long enough to hear any secrets," replied the judge. "You were saying something about 'one in a thousand' when I came in, and it struck me as being a very natural remark for a young man in a trance."

"It is one of my bad habits," Brant confessed—"talking to myself, I mean. It began when I was a little fellow and lacked playmates."

"It is a very common habit. I once knew an attorney who had it in a most peculiar form. His office was adjoining mine, and he would lock the door and discuss a case with himself. We used to laugh at him a good bit, but he was always the best-prepared man in court."

All of which was quite beside the mark, as Brant well knew; but he made courteous answer, having it in mind to let his visitor pick his own way through the generalities. This the judge seemed to find very difficult, since he made several false starts before coming finally to the object of his visit. Brant set the hesitancy down to pardonable family pride, and stood ready to help when he should be given the chance. At length the judge came to the point and waded reluctantly into the domestic pool.

"I came down to thank you for what you did for us last night, Mr. Brant. My daughter has told me the circumstances, and it was exceedingly good of you to interest yourself in my poor boy."

Brant said "Not at all," meaning thereby that the service had been freely rendered, and the judge went on:

"It was a great relief to us all to find William safe at home this morning. He left us in anger, and I feel quite sure that we have you to thank for his return, though I am wholly in the dark as to how you managed it."

Brant answered the implied question frankly.

"It was a very simple matter. I found your son in company with a man whose influence over him seems to be quite as great as it is sure to be bad. I happened to know this man, and I persuaded him to take the boy home."

The judge leaned back in his chair and matched his finger ends reflectively. "William mentions a Mr. Harding as having accompanied him home in a carriage. Is he the man?"

Brant bowed.

"Then the boy must be very much mistaken in his estimate of Harding. He seems to think he is a gentleman."

"I don't doubt that in the least. Harding has probably been at some pains to make him think so. Just the same, you may believe me when I say that he is the worst possible companion for your son, or for any young man."

"H'm; that is a little odd." The judge was fairly surprised into saying so much, but since he did not go on, how was Brant to know that the odd thing was the exact coincidence of his opinion of Harding and Harding's opinion of him as reported by William Langford? And not knowing this, he went on straightway to his own undoing.

"Odd that he should try to mislead your son? Knowing the man and his kind as well as I do, I should say that any other proceeding on his part would be odd. Harding is a professional gambler."

The judge began to put two and two together.

"You say you know him well?"

"Yes; I have known him a long time, and I owe him an ill turn or so on my own account," said Brant, whose throat still ached from the pressure of Harding's fingers.

"Ah." The judge's mind began to lay hold of something like a sequence of threads in the mystery tangle. "Pardon me, Mr. Brant, if I am dull: but what possible use could a professional gambler make of my son? Surely William's pocket money would be scarcely worth plotting for."

"Certainly not. Harding would be much more likely to give him money than to take it from him. Here is the layout," Brant went on, dropping unconsciously into the jargon of the craft in describing its processes; "Harding poses, let us say, as a gentleman of leisure. He lays siege to some tenderfoot with more money than brains, perhaps, but who isn't altogether blind, and proposes a quiet game for amusement. If he worked it alone the rawest greenhorn of the lot might suspect a trap, but with your son as a third party the thing looks perfectly square. Don't you see?"

The judge rose and walked slowly the length of the room with his hands behind him and his head bowed. When he looked up again the paternal anxiety in his face had given place to judicial severity.

"Yes, I see two things: One is, that you have a much worse opinion of my son than the facts, bad as they are, justify; and the other is, that you seem to have a—an unenviable familiarity with the methods you have been describing."

Brant saw his error when it was too late, and tried to retrieve it.

"Don't mistake me, Judge Langford. In such a case as I have been describing an inexperienced boy might well be an innocent accomplice—indeed, he would have to be to be of any use to his principal. And as to my knowledge, one learns much in the rough school of the frontier."

The judge's hand was on the doorknob.

"I can believe that; pardon me if I spoke hastily," he said. "To be very frank with you, I am in deep trouble about William. If what you tell me about this man Harding be true, the boy is ruined."

"Not necessarily," Brant amended. "Harding has left the city; and if you can keep your son from forming another such intimacy——"

"How do you know Harding is gone?" interrupted the father.

"He went at my suggestion."

"And was it also at your suggestion that the newspapers omitted my son's name in reporting a certain wholesale arrest made by the police night before last?"

"It was."

The judge smiled and shook his head.

"You seem to be all-powerful, Mr. Brant, but I dislike mysteries—even beneficent mysteries. In this matter, however, I am your debtor; let me know when I may square the account." And before Brant could add another word in explanation or extenuation he was gone.

CHAPTER XI
AND THE SHAFT TO THE MARK

NOT until he had passed the judge's questions and his own answers twice or thrice in mental review did Brant realize how completely he had succeeded in raising doubts as to his own obviousness where he fain would have allayed them. Then he grew angry, at his own inaptness in particular, and at an unsympathetic world in general. In its turn the fit of wrath was supplanted by a fever of impatience, and this glowed fitfully through the interminable afternoon which separated him from a possible visit to Hollywood.

Having done a good deed, he had a very human hunger for appreciation—appreciation untinctured by suspicion or innuendo, and Dorothy, at least, would not withhold it. So he believed, and, when evening came, lost no time in presenting himself at the door of the comfortable mansion in Altamont Terrace.

He was shown into the double drawing-room, and it was untenanted—a fact remarkable enough to make him wonder. He had come to know the family habit well, and after dinner, when it was too cool to sit on the veranda, at least four of the five would be found in the living rooms. Was he too early? He looked at his watch. No; it was a full hour a-past the Langford dinner time. In the midst of his wonderings the door opened to admit, not Dorothy or Isabel, but Mrs. Langford.

"You must excuse me if I have kept you waiting," said the lady in the tone which turns the apology into a chilly conventionalism. "I was not expecting any one so early. Is there anything I can do for you, Mr. Brant?"

Brant doubted his ears, and glanced around involuntarily as one who has stumbled into the wrong house.

"I—do for me? Why, nothing in particular," he stammered. "Are—are the young ladies at home?"

"Not to you, Mr. Brant; nor will they be if you should ever happen to call again."

Brant laid fast hold of his sanity and fought for calm speech.

"But, Mrs. Langford," he gasped, "I—I don't understand. What have I done?"

"Rather ask what you have not done," said the lady icily. "But since you put the question, I may answer it. You have come here, not once, but many times, knowing very well that if your history had been known to us or to Mr. Antrim our doors would never have been opened to you. If that is not sufficient, I can be still more explicit, if you wish it."

"By Heaven, madam, I do wish it!" Brant exploded, rushing upon his fate like any fool of them all. But anger was fast supplanting astonishment.

"Very well, sir. Would you mind telling me where you have spent the better part of your life since you left college?"

"In the mining camps." He had a sharp premonition of what was coming.

"And your occupation was——"

"It was not what it should have been, I admit. But is there no room for repentance in your creed, Mrs. Langford?"

"Assuredly; but you have not repented. That is proved by your own act in coming here quite as much as by anything that Mr. Harding says of you."

"Harding!" At the mention of the name Brant saw what his enemy had done and went mad accordingly. "Do you mean to say you would listen for a moment to anything that damnable hound could say of me, or of any one?"

Mrs. Langford retreated to the door.

"Pardon me, Mr. Brant, if I leave you—you are merely making a bad matter worse. A gentleman does not so far forget himself as to swear in the presence of a lady. I think we understand each other, and I will bid you good evening."

When she was gone Brant found his way out of the house, and spent half the night tramping the hills to the westward of the suburb. Under favouring conditions self-respect is a plant of rapid growth, but it is sensitive in inverse proportion to its age. While he was very willing to call himself the chief of sinners, and to deprecate his own temerity in aspiring to a seat at the table of virtue, Brant was no more complaisant under reproach than any Pharisee of us all.

For this cause he filled the hours of the solitary walk afield with bitter revilings heaped upon uncharity in general, and upon social canons as interpreted by the Mrs. Langfords in particular, going finally to his room in a frame of mind in which wrath and desperation far outran grief.

"'Give a dog a bad name,'" he fumed, flinging hat and overcoat into a corner and lighting the gas and a fresh cigar with the same match. "I might have known what it would come to. And all I asked in the wide world was to be let alone!"

CHAPTER XII
THE WAY OF A MAID WITH A MAN

A FORTNIGHT or such a matter after his rebuff in the presence of outraged art—typified by the newly finished "Sunset in Platte Cañon"—and a week after the Draconian episode and Brant's dismissal by Mrs. Langford, Antrim took Isabel to the opera, meaning to have his answer once for all before he slept.

Another man under similar hard conditions might have hesitated to preface his *coup de grace* matrimonial with an evening's amusement; but Antrim was wise in his generation, and he knew Isabel's leanings well enough to be sure that no other preliminary would add more to his chances of success.

Now *Rigoletto*, well sung, is a treat not to be despised even by a jaded theatregoer, and the younger Miss Langford was neither jaded nor lacking the artistic sense which finds its complement in good music. Wherefore she gave a little sigh of regret when the curtain ran down on the last act, and stood up mechanically in her place that Antrim might adjust her wrap.

"Great show, wasn't it?" he said, making a praise-worthy but purely manlike effort to strike the proper note of appreciation.

She did not respond, and when they came out in the lighted foyer he saw the rapt isolation of her mood and resented it.

"Up on top of the mountain as usual, aren't you? Did you happen to come down far enough any time during the evening to think of the thing as a play meant to amuse people?" He tried to say it jestingly, but the whetstone of sarcasm sharpened the words in spite of the placable intention.

"Don't tease me, please, Harry; at least, not now while I'm in the seventh heaven of the aftermath. I'll talk practical things with you by and by, if you like, but just now it would be sacrilege."

Ordinarily Antrim would have laughed, as he was wont to laugh at her extravagances. As it was, he sulked and was silent while they were drifting with the slow-moving human glacier out through the vestibule and during the long street-car ride over to the Highlands.

Since early morning he had been fighting a desperate battle with the Apollyon who disputes the way with that man who is foolish enough to set the day and hour in which a question of moment is to be decided. No sooner had he written it down that Isabel should that evening be brought to hear reason, than an imp of disorder came and sat at his elbow, and after this the business of his office went awry and the day became a lengthened misery.

He had quarrelled with his stenographer, found fault with the operator, and made life burdensome for the office boy. Last, and worst of all, just before the day's end he had fallen into a wrangle over the wires with the division train despatcher at Lone Pine Junction, the upshot of which was to bring the man's resignation, garnished with a few terse "wire" oaths, clicking back through the sounder in the superintendent's office.

So much for the day's tribulations. But since he had not taken the trouble to tell her, Isabel knew naught of these things. Hence it was not until they had left the car and were nearing the Hollywood gate that she began to wonder if his silence were altogether of abstraction.

"You are in a sweet temper to-night, aren't you, Harry?" she said, merely by way of arousing him to a sense of the social part of his duty.

Antrim helped her across the bank-full irrigation ditch at the curb and answered not a word.

"I suppose you are just aching to take it out on somebody," she went on. "If that is the case, you may begin on me. I'm young and strong, and not too thin-skinned."

Still Antrim held his peace, fearing to open his mouth lest a worse thing should come of it.

"Why don't you say something? You needn't go into your shell like a disappointed turtle just because I wouldn't let you spoil my negative of the opera before I could get it developed."

Still no reply.

"What is the matter with you, Harry, dear? Have you lost your tongue?"

"No; I've been waiting till you saw fit to come down out of the clouds; that's all."

"Well, I have arrived. And I am ready to forgive you for being so sulky. My, oh!"

They had reached the gate, and Antrim tried to open it. The latch stuck, and straightway the gate flew across the sidewalk bereft of its hinges. Isabel laughed joyously, and the small explosion served to clear the moral atmosphere, as other wooden profanities are said to.

"Good as a play, isn't it?" growled the young man, and he sought to re-establish the wrecked gate.

"Ever so much better," was the quick retort. "It was positively the most human thing I ever saw you do. You are always so self-contained and precise that you put a quick-tempered mortal like me to shame."

"Did you ever do anything as senseless as this?"

"Haven't I? Come into the house and I'll show you."

He followed her obediently and stood in the dark hall while she lighted the lamp in her studio. When he joined her she was running over a stack of canvases standing in a corner.

"Do you see that?" she asked, slipping out one of the oil studies and giving it to him.

It was a sketchy little painting of Long's Peak, and it was punctured with numberless penknife stabs.

"I did that one day when I was particularly savage," she confessed; "just as you were when you smashed the gate. You don't know how much good it does me to find out now and then that I haven't a monopoly of all the bad temper in the world."

Antrim grinned. "Don't lose any sleep on that score; you have lots of good company. I have been having a tough time of it all day, and the gate business was only the wind-up."

"Poor old martyr! And I have been sticking pins into it all evening! What has been the trouble? Or is it tellable?"

"Everything and nothing. It has just been an off day with me all around. I have quarrelled with everybody I could get at, and with myself more than all. I need a balance-wheel worse than anything, Isabel, and it's for you to say whether I shall have it or not."

He knelt to clear the smouldering fire in the grate, and then got up to walk back and forth in front of it. Isabel sat down and shaded her eyes from the light. Levity was on the tip of her tongue, but she felt that his mood was one in which ridicule would be as the spark to gunpowder. Therefore she met it fairly and tried to reason with him.

"Must we go all over the old ground again, Harry?" she began. "Can't I say something new and fresh—something that will make it clear to you that the worst possible thing that could happen to either of us would be this that you have set your heart upon?"

"I don't think you can," he objected, pausing in front of the mantel to adjust a picture which was three hairs' breadths out of plumb. "But you may try, if you care to."

But having leave to try, Isabel found that new sayings on a well-worn subject do not always suggest themselves on the spur of the moment, and she was obliged to leave the promise unfulfilled.

"It would only be dressing the old things up in new clothes if I did," she confessed, "and that wouldn't bring us to any better understanding."

"It isn't a question of understanding, Isabel; it is your ambition against my love—against reason, I had pretty nearly said. I don't believe you love anybody else; and I—well, I'd be glad enough to take the chances of winning later on what you say you can't give me now. That is the whole thing in a sentence, and it is for you to say whether I shall go away from here to-night the happiest of men or the most miserable."

He said it calmly and with the air of one who has weighed and measured the possibilities of success or failure. Then it was that Isabel first began dimly to understand that Harry Antrim, her schoolfellow and playmate, had somehow come to man's estate what time she had been calling him a boy; and while she replied out of an honest heart, the newborn conviction helped her to choose the words.

"It wouldn't be right, Harry, even if you are willing to risk it and take the consequences, good or bad. I want you to believe me when I say that I don't seem to know anything about the love that reaches out toward marriage; and I am afraid I don't want to. I love my friends, and you more than any of the others; but I would turn my back on all of them if the doing of it would bring the answer to the question which is always and always at the tip end of my paint brushes. It's unwomanly, hard-hearted—anything you like to call it—but it is the simple truth. You don't want to marry a woman who feels that way, Harry, dear."

He ignored the argument, if, indeed, he had tried to follow it, and pressed her to give him his answer.

"Which is it to be, Isabel—Yes, or No?"

She parried the direct demand, not because there was any present uncertainty in her own mind, but because she discerned that in his eyes which warned her to deal gently with him.

"I say you wouldn't want to marry a woman without a heart—a loving, home-making heart, I mean; and that is what you would do if you took me. I have my own little battle to fight, and I must fight it alone, Harry. That is simple justice to you, or to any other good man who might ask me to marry him."

Antrim pounced upon the suggested alternative with unreasoning and vindictive acerbity.

"Any other man, you say. Who is the other man, Isabel?"

The steel of jealousy struck fire at once upon the flint of Isabel's quick temper, and her mood changed in a twinkling.

"You intimated, the other day, that it might be Mr. Brant," she retorted with malice aforethought.

Antrim set his teeth hard to keep back the bitter sayings that came uppermost, and when he could trust himself to speak again tried hard to make her deny his own assertion. "Just tell me there is no one else, Isabel, and I'll be satisfied," he pleaded; but Isabel, caring at that moment very little for Brant and a great deal for Antrim, yet stubbornly refused to give her lover even this small crumb of comfort.

"Then—once more, Isabel—give me my answer. Is it to be Yes, or No?"

"Oh, can't you see? Can't you understand that it must be No?"

"There is no reservation—no little green twig of hope that you can hold out to me?"

"Not as I hope to be sincere, Harry."

"Not if I should wait until you had won or lost the battle?"

The little arrow of self-effacement found its mark, and Isabel hesitated. With the enthusiasm of a young devotee she had striven to unsex herself in the singleness of her purpose, but Antrim's pleading stirred the woman within her, and in that fleeting instant of introspection she saw how frail was the barrier defending her ambition from his love. Honesty, pure and simple—the shame of taking so much where she could give so little— stepped in to save her.

"No, not even then, Harry. You deserve the full cup, and I couldn't be mean enough to offer you the dregs. If I fail, I sha'n't be worth anybody's having; and if I succeed—ah, God knows, but I am afraid I should be still less the woman you ought to marry."

"As you will," he said, and held out his hand. "Let us say 'Good-bye' and have it over with."

She put her hand in his and let him keep it while she said: "It mustn't be 'Good-bye,' Harry. I can't afford to lose you as a friend—as a—as a brother."

He smiled reproachfully. "And you said you would try to say something new!" Then the little upflash of pleasantry died out, and he spoke as one who leaves hope behind. "No, Isabel; I meant it literally. It must be 'Good-bye,' so far as I am concerned. I couldn't go on as we've been going on all these years; I should go mad, some day when the right man turns up, and do that which would make you hate me. No, I shouldn't"—the denial came quickly in response to the distress that crept into her eyes—"no, I shouldn't do that, for your sake; but I should be sore and miserable, and that would hurt you, too. You wouldn't want that, would you?"

She shook her head, and he stood irresolute for a moment. Then he said: "Won't you kiss me, Isabel? You haven't, you know, since we used to play boy and girl games in the old, old days."

She withdrew her hand quickly. "You mustn't ask that. It would—it would——"

How was he to know that she was trying to tell him that it would undo all that had gone before; that it would break down the frail barrier she had been at such pains to uprear? How was he to guess that he stood at last before the open door of the woman's heart of her; that he had but to take her in his arms to possess her?

Not by anything that she said or did, truly; and yet at that moment her love for him sprang full-armed into being, filling her with joy unspeakable, and promising thenceforth to dominate ambition and all else. But her lover knew it not, and he turned away to grope in thick darkness for the door because the vertigo of failure was blinding him. On the threshold he stopped, and when sight returned looked back at her as she stood under the light of the high easel lamp.

He made sure that the picture and its setting would be a lasting memory, and the sight of it brought back a swelling wave of recollection that went nigh to submerging him. There was the piano, where he had so often stood beside her, turning the leaves of her music while she played for him. In the corner, where the cross light from the windows could be shaded and controlled from her chair, stood her easel—the workbench before which she had spent so many patient hours. On the wall opposite, hanging just where she could see it while she worked, was the little Vedder—his one valuable gift; and beside the fire, which was now burning brightly, stood the easy-chair which had come to be called his, so often had he claimed it.

Some such background he had always imagined for his own home—the home wherein he could escape from the growing responsibilities of his work; the home which Isabel was to make for him. But she had said it could never be, and she was sending him away without hope, and with nothing but the remembrance of her pity to fill the place she had made for herself in his life. She might have kissed him once, he thought, and the thought set itself in words before he could check it.

"It couldn't have made much difference to you, Isabel; a kiss is only a little thing. And yet I had an idea that if you gave me one the remembrance of it would tide me over some of the hard places. That was all."

Her eyes met his when he began to say it, but she neither saw nor heard him when he went away. When she looked up and found him gone she ran to the door to call him back, but she was not quick enough. The night had swallowed him, and when she made sure of it she went back to the studio to bury her face in the lounge pillows and to cry bitterly—for what, she knew not, save that her world seemed suddenly to have fallen out of its orbit.

Thus the maid. And the man? As Brant had left the same house a few nights earlier with the devil beckoning him, so went Antrim, stumbling over the curb at the crossing and splashing through the pools made by the overflowing irrigation ditches without once realizing the discomfort. It was mirth for the gods, doubtless. His trouble was only a microscopic bit of side play in the great human comedy. But it was tragic enough to the young man, and many a spoiled life answers to promptings no more insistent than those which gather, buzzardlike, to pick the bones of a starved passion.

In the ruck of it Antrim tramped wearily back to the city, unmindful of all the familiarities until some one spoke to him at the corner of Sixteenth and Larimer Streets. It was Grotter, the division engineer, and he linked arms with the chief clerk and caught step.

"Chilly night, isn't it, Harry?" he said, shouldering his companion diagonally across the street toward a stained-glass transparency marking the entrance to a saloon. "I should think you'd freeze in that light overcoat. Let's go in here and have a nip to go to bed on—what do you say?"

Now, no anchoret of the Libyan Desert was ever less a tippler than was Antrim. But the thought of his great disappointment came and grappled with him, and the devil, to whom some very worthy people are yet willing to accord a personality, tempted him with a specious promise of comfort. So he did no more than hang upon the doorstep while Grotter overpersuaded him.

This was at midnight, and therein lay one of life's little ironies. At the very moment when Isabel, kneeling at her bedside, was trying with innocent cheeks aflame to frame the first halting petition for her acknowledged lover, Antrim was entering the house of temptation with the engineer. And presently he joined Grotter in a cup of some insidious mixture in which beaten eggs and liquid fire seemed to be the chief ingredients, sipping it slowly while he listened to the engineer's stories of his perils by fire, flood, and unruly grade labourers in the mountains.

That was the beginning. In the end the devil's promise was kept after a fashion, inasmuch as Antrim stumbled up the steps of Mrs. Seeley's boarding house some two hours later in a frame of mind which, whatever may have been its lacks or its havings, was at least bullet-proof on the side of sorrow.

CHAPTER XIII
"THROUGH A GLASS DARKLY"

IN her own way—which was the quietest and least obtrusive of ways—Dorothy was quite as intolerant of mysteries as was her father, and after the evening when Brant had gone forth to seek and to save that which was lost, small mysteries seemed to lie in wait for her at every turn.

They began the following day with Brant's brief visit and abrupt departure. She had heard his voice in the hall, and, a little later, the rustle of skirts as some one—her mother, she thought it was at the time—had gone in to meet him. Of what took place in the drawing-room she knew nothing, but a few minutes afterward, when she was going down to join them, he had stumbled out into the hall, snatched his coat and hat from the rack, and left the house without once looking behind him. So much Dorothy saw from the stair, and she also saw that he was excited and preoccupied, and that his face was the face of one upon whom trouble sharp and serious has come suddenly.

When she heard the gate clang behind him she went to the drawing-room and found it empty; whereupon that which had been merely singular became unaccountable. Was it possible that he had taken offense because he had been kept waiting? Dorothy thought she knew him better than that. He was a grown man, and not a foolish boy with a brand new dignity to battle for.

Failing to account for the unaccountable, Dorothy waited. He would doubtless come again, and with his coming the apparent mystery would vanish. But when the days passed and he came no more, she grew curious and asked guarded questions of her mother—and received ambiguous answers, since Mrs. Langford, with maternal self-sufficiency, had deemed it unnecessary to take either of her daughters into her confidence in Brant's affair.

So Dorothy wondered, and laid innocent little snares to entrap her father, who had also grown singularly reticent. And when these traps sprung harmless, she tried Antrim, with no better results. No, Brant was still in town, and the chief clerk was not aware of any impending change in his plans. Thus Henry Antrim, vaguely; but Dorothy's attempt fell upon an inauspicious moment, since it was made on the evening of Antrim's off day, and her questions were put while he was waiting for Isabel to make ready for the jaunt *à l'opéra*.

After this failure Dorothy tried Will, and it was a measure of her concern that she should appeal to him. She had no news of him; had nothing save that which an affectionate sister usually gets in an attempt to fathom the unplumbed depths of a younger brother's churlishness. Knowing Will's weakness, she ventured carefully, but she was quite unprepared for his sudden outburst of petulant brutality.

"You wonder where Mr. Brant is, do you?" he sneered, mimicking her. "Well, you've no business to wonder; that's all there is about that."

"Why, Will——"

"You needn't try to wheedle me. I don't know where he is, and, what's more, I don't care, as long as he keeps away from here."

"But, Will, you must have some reason——"

"Reason enough," he interrupted rudely; "and that's all you'll get out of me in a thousand years." And he lighted a cigarette and put distance between himself and the chance of further questioning.

Knowing nothing of Harding or his story, Dorothy set her brother's anger down to the account of a natural feeling of resentment toward a comparative stranger who had interfered in Will's private affair. None the less, the incident added another shrouding to the mystery involving the draughtsman, and Dorothy's curiosity and concern went one step farther on the road toward anxiety.

It was about this time that she began to notice a rather remarkable change in Isabel. From being the most outspoken member of the family, the younger sister had developed a degree of reticence which was second only to Will's churlishness, though Dorothy fancied it was sorrowful rather than sullen. From day to day she spent less time at her easel, and twice Dorothy had come upon her when her eyes were red with weeping. To inquiry, jesting or solicitous, she was stonily impervious, and when the thing became unbearable Dorothy went to her mother again, meaning to be at the heart of things if persistence could find the way. She chose her time cunningly, attacking after her mother had gone to bed, so there would be no chance of retreat.

"How should I know, dear?" was the mother's reply to her first question about Isabel. "I haven't noticed anything wrong with her."

"But there *is* something wrong," Dorothy insisted. "She hasn't been like herself for days. She mopes, and she doesn't paint; and twice I have caught her crying, though she denied it spitefully."

Mrs. Langford's answer to that was conventionally sympathetic.

"It is another of the unthinkable pictures, I suppose. I do wish the child wouldn't torment herself so over her work. It is all well enough as an accomplishment, but she needn't make a martyr of herself. Harry is quite right about that."

Having a very considerable reverence for art, Dorothy was not so sure of this, but she left the point uncontested and asked a question suggested by the mention of Harry Antrim.

"You don't suppose she has quarrelled with Harry, do you?"

"It is quite possible. It's a way they have had ever since they were children together."

"Still, it might be serious this time."

"No fear of that," said the mother easily. "Isabel thinks a great deal more of him than she has ever admitted, even to herself, perhaps. And as for Harry, I would as soon think of the world coming to an end as of his giving her up."

Dorothy was silenced, but not convinced.

"That was one thing I wanted to speak about, mamma," she said, gathering herself for the plunge; "but there is another. I want to know what has come over us all lately. We seem to be groping about in the dark, trying to hide things from each other. What is the mystery? and why can't I share it?"

"Mystery? Nonsense, child! there is no mystery."

But Dorothy was insistent. "Yes, there is. First, Mr. Brant does us a kindness and drops us, all in the same day. Then, when I wonder at it, you put me off, and father goes deaf, and Will gets angry. And when I ask Harry a civil question about his friend, he snaps me up only a little less savagely than brother. Now Isabel has turned blue and won't talk, and—and, altogether we seem to be turning into a family of freaks. What is at the bottom of it all? Why doesn't Mr. Brant come here any more?"

The mother's smile would have been full of meaning for the daughter if the darkness had not hidden it.

"Mr. Brant probably has his own reasons for not coming, and they are doubtless very good ones."

"What makes you say that? Do you know what they are?" Dorothy demanded, being fully determined not to be baffled.

It was a point-blank question, but Mrs. Langford evaded it with considerable skill:

"I? What a question! Mr. Brant is not likely to take me into his confidence."

For the moment Dorothy had an uncomfortable feeling that she had been making mountains out of molehills, and in that moment she retreated. But when she was alone the perplexities assumed their normal proportions again; nay, they grew even larger when she was reluctantly driven to the conclusion that the late attack on the maternal stronghold had failed because her mother was the better fencer.

After all, it was Isabel who gave her the clew to a startling solution of the mysteries, and the manner of its giving was this: The sisters occupied adjoining rooms connected by a curtained archway, and when Dorothy went from her mother's room to her own she found the curtains dropped—a thing without precedent, and emphasizing very sharply the barrier that Isabel sought to rear between herself and the other members of the family.

Dorothy was hurt, but she was too truly a Langford to take the risk of making unwelcome advances. So she went to bed with eyelashes wet, and with a sore spot in her heart in which the ache was quite out of proportion to the wounding incident of the dropped curtains. Just as she was falling asleep the curtains parted and Isabel stole softly into the room, to go down upon her knees at the bedside. Dorothy made no sign at first, but when her sister buried her face in the bedclothes and began to sob, compassion quickly found words—and a little deed.

"What is it, Bella, dear?" she asked, with an arm around her sister's neck.

"Everything," said Isabel to the counterpane.

"But what, dear? Can't you trust me?"

Isabel shook her head to the first pleading and nodded to the second. Dorothy understood, and pressed the point gently.

"Is it a picture?—won't the new one find itself?"

"It's—it's something a great deal worse than unthinkable pictures," said Isabel dismally.

"Then it must be very bad indeed. Tell me about it, Bella, dear."

"I can't; there isn't anything to tell. He is gone—I sent him away, and he will never come back!" sobbed Isabel, with womanly inconsistency.

Dorothy permitted herself a little sigh of relief. It was only a lovers' quarrel between her sister and Harry, the last of many, and perhaps a little more serious than some of the others, but still only that. The wound would heal of itself, as such hurtings do, yet she made haste to pour the wine and oil of sympathy into it.

"Don't cry, dear. He will come back—he can't help coming back," she prophesied confidently.

Isabel shook her head as one who knows and may not be comforted. "No, he won't—not the man that I sent away. Harry, the good-natured, obstinate boy that we used to tease and make fun of, might; but this grown man that I never knew till the other day is quite different. He will never put it off with a laugh and come back as if nothing had happened—I know he won't."

Thus Isabel, thinking only of the seeming change wrought in her lover by the quick shifting of her own point of view, and Dorothy, with the chill of a nameless fear benumbing her, could only repeat her prophecy:

"He will come back; never fear, Bella."

"I wish I could believe it, but I can't. O Dothy, if you could have seen his face when he went away! I shall never forget how he looked, not if I should live to be a hundred."

Dorothy had a fleeting vision of a man hurrying out through the hall with a look of desperate trouble in his eyes, and in a flash the apparent ambiguity in Isabel's confession vanished. It was her sister, and not her mother, who had gone to meet Mr. Brant. It was he, and not Harry, whom Isabel had sent away, and for whose loss she was grieving.

Dorothy shut her eyes hard, and for a moment the pain of it was sharp enough to make her shrink from the innocent cause of it. Then a great wave of thankfulness swept over her when she remembered that her secret was yet her own. And close upon the heels of gratitude came a growing wonder that she could have been so blind. She might have known from the first that it was Isabel. It was plain enough now. His gentle deference to her sister's moods, his helpful criticism of her work, his evident determination to give Antrim the preference which was his by right, leaving Isabel free to choose between them. All these things pointed to but one conclusion, and Dorothy was thankful again; this time for the darkness which hid the hot blushes. For she remembered how ready she had been to read quite a different meaning into all of his sayings and doings.

And the little sister of fickleness? Dorothy was loyal after her kind, and she quickly found excuses for Isabel. Was it not what always happens when a man of the world and a stranger is pitted against a playmate lover?

So the pyramid of misapprehension was builded course by course until it lacked only the capstone, and this was added in the answer to Dorothy's question:

"When did all this happen, Bella, dear?"

"The last time he was here; years ago, it seems to me—but perhaps it is only months or weeks."

This was the capstone, and there was now no room for doubt. It was nearly two weeks since Brant had stopped coming, and there had been no intermission in Harry's visits. Indeed, it was only a few days since he had taken Isabel to the opera. Dorothy choked down a little sigh, put herself and her own dream of happiness aside, and became from that moment her sister's loyal and loving ally.

"Don't be discouraged, dear," she said caressingly. "You must learn to wait and be patient. I know him—better, perhaps, than you do—and I say he will come back. He will never take 'No' for an answer while you and he live."

Isabel got up and felt under her sister's pillow for a handkerchief.

"You are good and comforting, Dothy," she whispered, "and I think I am happy in spite of my misery." She bent to leave a kiss on the cheek of goodness and comfort. "I am going to bed now; good night. Why, how hot your face is!"

"How cold your lips are, you mean," said Dorothy playfully. "Go to bed, dear, and don't worry any more. You will make yourself sick."

But when her sister was gone she lay very still, with closed eyes and trembling lips, and so fought her small battle to the bitter end, winning finally the victory called self-abnegation, together with its spoils, the mask of cheerfulness and the goodly robe of serenity.

CHAPTER XIV
THE ANCHOR COMES HOME

BRANT awoke on the morning following his excommunication with one idea dominant, and that pointed to flight. Whatever he might be able to do with his life elsewhere, it was evident that the Denver experiment was a pitiful failure. This he said, cursing the fatuous assurance which had kept him from flying to the antipodes at the outset. The city of the plain was merely a clearing house for the mining camps, and sooner or later his story would have found him out, lacking help from Harding or any other personal enemy.

"Anybody but a crazy fool would have known that without having to wait for an object lesson; but, of course, I had to have it hammered into me with blows," was the way he put it to himself on the walk downtown. "Well, I have had the lesson, and I'll profit by it and move on—like little Joey. If they would give me the chance I'd rather be a sheep dog than a wolf; but it seems that the world at large hasn't much use for the wolf who turns collie—damn the world at large! If I hadn't given my word to Hobart I'd be tempted to go back and join the fighting minority. As it is, I'll run for it."

So he said, and so he meant to do; but a small thing prevented. Colonel Bowran was away, and he could not well desert in his chief's absence. But this need no more than delay the flight. The chief engineer's absences were usually short, and a day or two more or less would neither make nor mar the future.

So ran the prefigurings, but the event was altogether different from the forecasting, as prefigured events are prone to be. For three days Brant made shift to sink his trouble in a sea of hard work, but on the fourth he had a note from the front, saying that the chief engineer's absence would be extended yet other days. At the same time, lacking the data contained in the field notes carried off by the colonel, he ran out of work. After that the days were empty miseries. In the first idle hour he began to brood over the peculiar hardness of his lot, as a better man might, and with the entrance of the remorseless devil of regret such poor forgetfulness as he had been able to wring out of hard work spread its wings and fled away.

At the end of twenty-four hours he was fairly desperate, and on the second day of enforced idleness he wrote a long letter to Hobart:

"The devil has another job for me," he began, "and if it wasn't for my promise to you I should take it. Things have turned out precisely as I knew they would, and you are to blame; first, for dragging me out of the pit when I wasn't worth saving, and next, for telling me that I might come to Denver when I should have gone to the ends of the earth. By which you will understand that my sins have found me out. I don't know that you care to hear the story, but I do know that I shall presently go mad if I don't tell it to somebody. If it bores you, just remember what I say—that you are to blame.

"Before I begin I may as well tell you that it is about a woman, so you can swear yourself peaceful before you come at the details. I met her on the train the day I came down from the Colorow district—the day of my return to civilization. Nothing came of that first meeting, save that I got a glimpse of the gulf that separates a good woman from a bad man; but later, after I had begun to look ahead a little to the things that might be, we met again—this time in her own home, and I with an introductory godfather.

"That was two months ago. Up to last Wednesday everything went as merry as a marriage bell. The father liked me, the mother tolerated me, and the young woman—but let that pass. I was welcome enough, and sufficient unto the day was the good thereof. As a matter of course, I was living in a fool's paradise, walking daily over a mine that any chance spark might explode. I knew all that, and yet I was happy till last Wednesday. That was when the mine was fired.

"It came about in the most natural way, but the story is too long to write out, and I don't mean to weary you needlessly. It is enough to say that the mother found me out. You can guess what happened. I went to the house, knowing nothing of what was in store for me. There was a little scene in which I played the heavy villain to the mother's part of outraged virtue—and the end of it is that I am once more a pariah.

"I didn't see the young woman; that wasn't permitted, of course. But I suppose she knows all about it, and the thought makes me want to run amuck. In the whole dreary business there is only this single grain of comfort: I know who gave me away. And when I meet that man, God do so to me and more if I don't send him where he belongs, and that without benefit of clergy. And you won't say me nay when I tell you that his name is Harding.

"I suppose you will want to know what I am going to do next. I don't know, and that is God's truth. The day after the thing happened I meant to vanish; but the chief was away and I couldn't very well shut up the office and walk out. Since then the mill has been grinding until I don't know what I want to do. Sometimes I am tempted to throw the whole thing overboard and go back to the hog wallow. It is about all I am fit for; and nobody cares—unless you do.

"For pity's sake write me a letter and brace me up if you can; I never needed it worse. The chief is still away; I can't do another stroke of work till he comes back with the field books, and there isn't a soul here that I can talk to. Consequently I'm going mad by inches. I suppose you have taken it for granted that I love the young woman, though I believe I haven't said so in so many words. I do, and that is what racks me. If I go away, I give her up for good and all. If I stay I can't get her. If I go to the devil again—but we won't discuss that phase of it now. Write, and hold me to my word, if you love me."

This letter was mailed on the train Wednesday evening, and in the ordinary course of events it should have brought an answer by the Saturday. This Brant knew, and he set himself to wear out the interval with what constancy there was in him, doing nothing more irrational than the devoting of two of the evenings to aimless trampings in the Highlands, presumably in the unacknowledged hope that he might chance to see Dorothy at a distance. He did not see her, did not venture near enough to Altamont Terrace to stand any chance of seeing her, and when the Saturday passed without bringing a letter from Hobart, hope deferred gave birth to heaviness.

"He is disgusted, I suppose, and I can't blame him," was his summing up of it when the postman had made his final round. "God in heaven, I wish the colonel would come back and give me my quittance! If I have to sit here and grill through many more days I shall be ripe for any devil's sickle of them all!"

By which it will appear that despairing impulse was already straining at the bit. None the less, when six o'clock came he went home, ate his supper, read till midnight, and then went to bed, though not to sleep. On the morrow, which was the Sunday, he set on foot a little emprise the planning of which had eased him through the wakeful hours of the night. It was this: Dorothy had a class in a mission school, and this he knew, and the place, but not the hour. For the latter ignorance he was thankful, since it gave him an excuse for haunting the neighbourhood of the mission chapel during the better part of the day. Late in the afternoon he was rewarded by catching a glimpse of her as she went in, and, heartened by this, he did sentry duty on the opposite side of the street until the school was dismissed.

She came out among the last with a group of children around her, and Brant's heart went warm at the sight. "God bless her!" he said under his breath; and then he crossed the street to put his fate to the touch. If she knew—if her mother had told her—her greeting would show it forth, and he would know then that the worst had befallen.

They met at the corner, and Dorothy looked up as she was bidding her children good-bye. He made sure she saw him, though there was no sign of recognition in her eyes. Then she bent over one of the little ones as if to avoid him, and he went on quickly with rage and shame in his heart, and the devil's sickle gathering in the harvest which had been ripening through the days of bitterness.

That night he went to his room as usual after supper, but not to stay. At eight o'clock he flung down the book he had been trying to read, slipped the weapon which had once been James Harding's into the pocket of his overcoat, and left the house. Half an hour later he was standing at the bar in the Draconian kennel, and Tom Deverney was welcoming him with gruff heartiness.

"Well, say! I thought you'd got lost in the shuffle, sure. Where have you been—over the range again?"

"No, I haven't been out of town."

"You took blame' good care not to show up here, then," retorted Deverney. "First you know you'll have to be packing a card case; that's about what you'll have to do."

"I have been busy," said Brant. Then the smell of the liquor got into his nostrils and he cut himself adrift with a word. "Shall we have a drink together, and call it square, Tom?"

Deverney spun a glass across the polished mahogany and reached for a conical bottle in the cooler. "I don't know as I ought to drink with you— you wouldn't drink with me the last time you showed up. What shall it be— a little of the same?"

"Always," said Brant. "I don't mix." He helped himself sparingly and touched glasses with the bartender.

"Here's how."

"Looking at you."

Brant paid, and the bartender dipped the glasses. "Going to try your luck a while this evening?" he asked.

The backslider glanced at the tables and shook his head. "No, I guess not. I'm a little off to-night, and I'd be pretty sure to go in the hole."

Deverney laughed. "That's what they all say when they are broke. I'll stake you."

"No—thanks; I didn't mean that. I have money enough."

He strolled down the long room toward the faro table, turning the matter over in his mind. He had left Mrs. Seeley's with madness in his heart, and with a fell determination to go and do something desperate—something that would make Dorothy's heart ache if she could know of it. But now that he was on the brink of the pool of ill-doing the stench of it sickened him. Calling the plunge revenge, it seemed very mean and despicable.

Halfway down the room he faced about, and but for the drink he had taken would have gone home. But the liquor tipped the scale. It was adulterated poison, as it was bound to be in such a place, and Brant—at his worst the most temperate of men on the side of appetite—had neither touched nor tasted since turning the new leaf. So the decent prompting passed, and he wheeled and went back to watch the game.

After that the descent was easy. A dollar ventured became two, the two four, and the four eight; Presently one of the sitters rose, and Brant dropped into the vacant chair, lighted a fresh cigar, and ordered another drink. It was what he used to do in the old days when his conscience stirred uneasily, and now, as then, the intoxicant had the desired effect. It slew the man in him without unstringing the steady nerve of the gamester.

Since he cared not whether he lost or won, luck was with him from the first and throughout. Play as he might, he could not lose; and when he rose at midnight, Draco, who acted as his own banker, had to stop the game and go to his safe for more money before he could declare the dividend.

"There are your ducats," he said, tossing a thick roll of bills across the table. "It's an open game, and I haven't anything to say; all the same, I'm willing to see you pull out. This outfit isn't any blooming gold mine."

Brant unrolled the money, twisted it into a spill, and handed it back.

"Keep it, if you like; I haven't any use for it." Draco laughed. "Yes, I will!—and have you charging back here with a gun when you're sob—when you've had time to think about it? Not much! I haven't got any time to open up a shooting gallery and play bow-and-arrow with you, George."

Brant stuffed the money into his pocket and went his way. As he was going out, Deverney beckoned him.

"Say, I heard two fellows talking about the way you were winning," he said, leaning across the bar and lowering his voice. "I didn't know either one of them, but they're a hard-looking lot—the kind that waits for you at the mouth of a dark alley. Are you fixed?"

Brant nodded. "You say you don't know them?"

"Only by sight. They've both been here before; though not together till to-night."

"Talk as if they knew me?"

"Yes. They do know you by name. One of them said something about 'spotting' you to-night."

Now, when one has scattered the seed of enmity impartially in all soils a goodly crop of ill-wishers may be looked for in any harvest field however well inclosed. Since he had never turned aside to avoid a quarrel in any one of the ill-starred years, Brant had enemies a-plenty; but holding his own life lightly he had never let the fact trouble him. None the less, he was curious enough to ask Deverney if he could describe the two men. The bartender could and did.

"One of them is tall and rather thin, about the size and shape of the Professor, only he has a beard like a billy goat, and a shock of red hair that looks as if it hadn't been cut for a month of Sundays. The other is—well, I should say he looks like a chunky man gone thin, if you can savez that; smooth face, with a sort of bilious look, and the wickedest eye you ever saw in a man's head."

Brant shook his head slowly. "I don't recall either of them," he said. Then the Berserker in him came to the surface, and he took the pistol from his pocket and twirled the chambers to see that they were all filled. "If they know me, they know what to expect, and I'll try and see that they are not disappointed. Much obliged for the hint. Good night, Tom."

He went out with his head up and his hands in his pockets, bearing himself as if he would as soon end the bad day with a battle to the death as otherwise. At the corner above he saw the two men standing in a doorway on the opposite side of the street, recognised them at once from Deverney's description, and, giving place to a sudden impulse of recklessness, went straight across to them. They paid no attention to him, not even when he stopped and looked them over with a cool glance of appraisal that was little less than a challenge. But when he went on they followed leisurely and at a safe distance. Brant knew they were dogging him, but he neither loitered nor hastened. If they chose to overtake and waylay him he would know what to do. If they did not, the morning newspapers would lack a stirring item, and two footpads would have a longer lease of life.

In the challenging glance he had passed the taller man by as a stranger, but the face of the other haunted him. There was something exasperatingly familiar about it, and yet no single feature by which it could be identified. Analyzed in detail, the puzzle arranged itself above and below a line drawn across the upper lip of the half-familiar face. The broad flat nose, high cheek bones, and sunken eyes were like those of some one he had seen before. But the hard mouth with the lines of cruelty at the corners, and the projecting lower jaw, seemed not to belong to the other features.

"It's a freak, and nothing more or less," he told himself, when he had reasoned out so much of the puzzle. "The fellow has the top of somebody else's head—somebody I have known. I wonder how he got it?"

There was an easy answer to the query, and if Brant had guessed it he would have been careful to choose the well-lighted streets on the way up town. If he had chanced to remember that a thick curling beard, unkempt and grizzled, would mask the cruel mouth and ugly jaw, he would have recognised the face though it chanced that he had seen it but once, and then in a moment of fierce excitement. And if he had reflected further that a beard may be donned as well as doffed, and that the wig-maker's art still flourishes, he would have realized that out of a very considerable collection of enemies made in the day of wrath none were more vindictive or desperate than the two who kept him in sight as he made his way back to Mrs. Seeley's.

They closed upon him, or made as if they would, when he reached the gate, and he fingered his pistol and waited. The few hours which overlaid his late meeting with Dorothy had gone far toward undoing the good work of the preceding months of right living. While he waited, the man-quelling fiend came and sat in the seat of reason, and it was Plucky George of the mining camps rather than Colonel Bowran's draughtsman who stood at Mrs. Seeley's gate and fingered the lock of the ready weapon.

As if they had some premonition of what was lying in wait for them, the two men veered suddenly and crossed the street. Had Brant known who they were and why they had followed him, it is conceivable that their shadows would never have darkened the opposite sidewalk. As it was, he opened the gate and went in with a sneer at their lack of courage in the last resort.

"Two to one, and follow a man a mile at midnight without coming to the scratch," he scoffed. "I have a good mind to go over and call their bluff alone. It would serve them right to turn the tables on them, and I'd do it if I thought they had anything worth the trouble of holding them up."

CHAPTER XV
WHEN HATE AND FEAR STRIKE HANDS

WHEN he was suffered to escape after his attempt upon Brant's life in the private room at Elitch's, James Harding tarried in Denver only so long as the leaving time of the first westward bound train constrained him. Nevertheless, he went as one driven, and with black rage in his heart, adding yet another tally to the score of his account against the man who had banished him.

But, like Noah's dove, he was destined to find no rest for the sole of his foot. Having very painstakingly worn out his welcome in the larger mining camps, he was minded to go to Silverette, hoping to pick a living out of the frequenters of Gaynard's. Unluckily, he was known also in Silverette; and unluckily again, word of his coming preceded him from Carbonado, the railway station nearest to the isolated camp at the foot of Jack Mountain. Harding walked up from Carbonado, was met at a sharp turn in the wagon road by a committee from the camp above, and was persuaded by arguments in which levelled rifles played a silent but convincing part to retrace his steps.

Returning to Carbonado, his shrift was but a hand's breadth longer. On the second day, when he was but barely beginning to draw breath of respite, he was recognised as the slayer of one William Johnson, was seized, dragged into the street, and after an exceedingly trying half hour was escorted out of camp and across the range by a guard of honour with drawn weapons.

Under such discouragements he promptly determined to face the ills he knew, drank deeply at the well of desperation, and, making a forced march to the nearest railway station, boarded the first train for Denver. It was a hazardous thing to do. Brant was a man of his word, and the banished one had known him to go to extremities upon slighter provocation. But, on the other hand, Denver was a considerable city, and their ways might easily lie apart in it. Moreover, if the worst should come, it was but man to man, with plenty of old scores to speed the bullet of self-defence.

So reasoning, Harding stepped from the train at the Denver Union Station in the gray dawn of an October morning, Argus-eyed, and with his hand deep buried in the pocket of his ulster. The time was auspicious, and he reached a near-by lodging house without mishap. Through one long day he remained in hiding, but after dark, when the prowling instinct got the better of prudence, he ventured out. In a kennel some degrees lower in the scale descending than Draco's he met a man of his own kidney whom he had once known in the camps, and who was but now fresh from the Aspen district and from an outpost therein known as Taggett's Gulch.

This man drank with Harding, and when his tongue was a little loosened by the liquor grew reminiscent. Did the Professor recall the killing of a man in the Gulch a year or so back—a man named Benton, or Brinton? Harding had good cause to remember it, and he went gray with fear and listened with a thuggish demon of suffocation waylaying his breath. Assuredly, everybody remembered. What of it? Nothing much, save that the brother of the murdered man was in Colorado with the avowed intention of finding and hanging the murderer, if money and an inflexible purpose might contribute to that end.

That was the gist of the matter, and when Harding had pumped his informant dry, he shook the man off and went out to tramp the streets until he had fairly taken the measure of the revived danger. Summed up, it came to this: sooner or later the avenger of blood would hear of Brant, and after that the end would come swiftly and the carpenters might safely begin to build the gallows for the slayer of Henry Brinton. Harding had a vivid and disquieting picture of the swift sequence of events. The brother would find Brant, and the latter would speedily clear up the mystery and give the avenger the proofs. Then the detective machinery would be set in motion, and thereafter the murderer would find no lurking place secret enough to hide him.

Clearly something must be done, and that quickly. Concealment was the first necessity; James Harding must disappear at once and effectually. That preliminary safely got over, two sharp corners remained to be turned at whatever cost. The incriminating evidence now in Brant's hands must be secured and destroyed, and Brant himself must be silenced before the avenger of blood should find and question him.

The disguise was a simple matter. At one time in his somewhat checkered career Harding had been a supernumerary in a Leadville variety theatre. Hence, the smooth-shaven, well-dressed man who paid his bill at the Blake Street lodging house at ten o'clock that night bore small likeness to the bearded and rather rustic-looking person who engaged a room a few minutes later at a German *Gasthaus* in West Denver. The metamorphosis wrought out in artistic detail, Harding put it at once to the severest test. Going out again, he sought and found the man from Taggett's Gulch, and was unrecognised. Introducing himself as a farmer from Iowa, he persuaded the man to pilot him through the mazes of the Denver underworld, and when he had met and talked with a dozen others who knew the Professor rather better than he knew himself, he went back to the

West Side *Gasthaus* with a comforting abatement of the symptoms of strangulation.

Having thus purchased temporary safety, the castaway began presently to look about him for the means to the more important end. Night after night he haunted the purlieus, hoping that a lucky chance might reveal Brant's whereabouts. But inasmuch as Brant was yet walking straitly, nothing came of this, and in his new character Harding could not consistently ask questions. Twice he met William Langford face to face, and, knowing that the boy could probably give him Brant's street and number, he was about to risk an interview with his *protégé* in his proper person when the god of evil-doers gave him a tool exactly fitted to his hand.

It was on the Sunday evening of Brant's relapse. Harding had been making his usual round, and at Draco's he met a man whose face he recognised despite its gauntness and the change wrought by the razor. A drink or two broke the ice of unfamiliarity, and then Harding led the way to a card room in the rear on the pretext of seeking a quiet place where they might drink more to their better acquaintance. In the place of withdrawal Harding kept up the fiction of bucolic simplicity only while the waiter was bringing a bottle and glasses. Then he said: "I reckon you'd be willing to swear you had never seen me before, wouldn't you, Gasset?"

The big man gone thin was in the act of pouring himself another drink, but he put the bottle down and gave evidence of a guilty conscience by starting from his chair, ready for flight or fight as the occasion might require.

"Who the blazes are you, anyway?" he demanded, measuring the distance to the door in a swift glance aside.

Harding pulled off the wig and beard and leered across at him. "Does that help you out any?"

Gasset sprang to his feet with a terror-oath choking him and retreated backward to the door, hand on weapon.

"Don't you do it, Jim!" he gasped. "Don't, I say. I never meant to hurt her—any of 'em will swear to that!"

Harding struck a match and relighted his cigar. He did it with leisurely thoroughness, turning the match this way and that and ignoring his quarry much as a cat ignores a mouse which can by no means escape. Gasset stood as one fascinated, watching every movement of the slim fingers and feeling blindly behind him for the knob of the door. Whereat Harding laughed mockingly and pointed to the bottle on the table.

"You had better come back here and take a little more of the same to stiffen your nerve, Ike. You couldn't hit the broad side of a barn just now."

Gasset found the doorknob finally and breathed freer when it yielded under his hand. "Give me a show for my life, Jim!" he begged, widening the opening behind him by stealthy half inches. "It ain't worth much, but, by God, I want it for a little while yet!"

Harding laughed again. "What is the matter with you? You would have been a dead man long ago if I had wanted to drop you. Come back here and finish your drink."

Having more than once set his life over against his thirst, Gasset did it once again, filling his glass with hands that shook, and swallowing the drunkard's portion at a gulp. The liquor steadied him a little and he sat down.

"Then you ain't out gunning for me?" he ventured.

"No; what made you think I was?"

Gasset scratched his head and tilted the bottle again. "I don't know, if you don't. But it appears like to me, if anybody had killed a sister of mine I'd want to get square. And I reckon I wouldn't split any hairs about his being drunk or sober at the time, nor yet about whether he went for to do it meaningly or just did it by happen-so."

Harding ignored the implied reproach and went on to the more important matter:

"Damn that! It is enough for me to know that you were trying to kill George Brant," he said coolly. "Do you still feel that way?"

Gasset rose unsteadily and the dull eyes of him glowed in their sockets. "Look at me now, Jim, and then recollect, if you can, what-all I used to be. You know what that was; not any man in the camp could put me on my back unless I was drunk. And now look at me—a poor, miser'ble, broke-up wrack, just out o' the horspital! *He* done it—filled me plum full of lead when I was too crazy drunk to see single; that's what he done!"

"Then I suppose you wouldn't be sorry if you had the chance to even up with him," said Harding, hastily building up a plan which would enable him to make use of this opportune ally.

"Now you are talking! Say, Jim, I'm hanging on to what little scrap of life he has left me for just nothing else. Understand?"

"Good; that is business," quoth Harding. "I am with you to stay. Find him for me, and I'll help you square the deal."

"Find him?" echoed Gasset. "Why, man alive, he is right out yonder at the faro table! You rubbed up against him coming in here!"

"The devil you say!" Harding hastily resumed the wig and the false beard, with a word explanatory. "He mustn't recognise me, or the game will be up before it begins. Pull up your chair and we'll talk this thing over."

Half an hour later the two conspirators left the card room and made their way singly through the crowd in the game room to meet at the bar. Gasset had lingered a moment at Brant's elbow, and, having seen the winnings, incautiously spoke of them to Harding in Tom Deverney's hearing. Harding shook his head, and dragged his companion out to the sidewalk.

"You will have to look out for Deverney—the barkeeper," he said. "He is Brant's friend. The first thing is to find out where he sleeps. We'll go over to the other corner and wait for him till he comes out."

CHAPTER XVI
THE GOODLY COMPANY OF MISERY

HAVING gone so far astray on the Sunday, it was inevitable that Brant should awake repentant and remorseful on the Monday. He slept late, and when he had breakfasted like a monk and had gone downtown to face another day of enforced idleness in his office, conscience rose up and began to ply its many-thonged whip.

What a thrice-accursed fool he had made of himself, and how completely he had justified Mrs. Langford's opinion of him! How infinitely unworthy the love of any good woman he was, and how painstakingly he had put his future beyond the hope of redemption! If Colonel Bowran would only come back and leave him free to go and bury himself in some unheard-of corner of the world! This was the burden of each fresh outburst of self-recrimination.

So much by way of remorse, but when he thought of Dorothy, something like a measure of dubious gratitude was mingled therewith—a certain thankfulness that the trial of his good resolutions had come before he had been given the possible chance of free speech with her—a chance which might have involved her happiness as well as his own peace of mind.

"Good Lord!" he groaned, flinging himself into a chair and tossing his half-burned cigar out of the window. "I ought to be glad that I found myself out before I had time to pull her into it. If they had let me go on, and she would have listened to me, I should have married her out of hand—married an angel, and I with a whole nest of devils asleep in me waiting only for a chance to come alive! God help me! I'm worse than I thought I was—infinitely worse.—Come in!" This last to some one at the door.

It was only the postman, and Brant took the letters eagerly, hoping to find one from Hobart. He was disappointed, but there was another note from the end-of-track on the Condorra Extension, setting forth that the chief engineer's home-coming would be delayed yet other days.

Brant read the colonel's scrawl, and what was left of his endurance took flight in an explosion of bad language. A minute later he burst into Antrim's office.

"Where is Mr. Craig?" he demanded.

"He has gone to Ogden," said Antrim, wondering what had happened to disturb the serenity of the self-contained draughtsman.

"The devil he has! When will he be back?"

"I don't know—the last of the week, maybe."

"Damn!"

Antrim laughed. "What ails you this morning? You look as if you'd had a bad night. Come inside and sit down—if you're not too busy."

Brant let himself in at the wicket in the counter-railing and drew up a chair.

"I am not busy enough—that is one of the miseries. And I want you to help me out, Harry. You have full swing here when the old man is away, haven't you?"

"Why—yes, after a fashion. What has broke loose?"

Brant looked askance at the stenographer, and the chief clerk rightly interpreted the glance.

"O John," he said, "I wish you would take these letters down and put them on No. 3. Hand them to the baggageman yourself, and then you'll be sure they have gone." And when the door closed behind the young man he turned back to Brant. "Was that what you wanted?"

"Yes, but I don't know as it was necessary. There is nothing particularly private about what I want to say. You see, it is this way: Colonel Bowran is out on the Extension, and Grotter is with him. I am alone here in the office, and I've got to leave town suddenly. What I want you to do is to put somebody in there to keep house till the colonel returns."

The chief clerk smiled. "It must be something pretty serious to rattle you that way," was his comment. "You are a good enough railroad man to know that my department has nothing to do with yours, except to ask questions of it. And that reminds me: here is a letter from the general manager asking if we have a late map of the Denver yards. The president is coming west in a day or two, and there is a plan on foot for extensions, I believe."

"Well?" said Brant.

"It isn't well—it's ill. We haven't any such map, and I don't see but what you will have to stay and make one."

Now, to a man in Brant's peculiar frame of mind employment was only one degree less welcome than immediate release. Wherefore he caught at the suggestion so readily that Antrim was puzzled.

"I thought you had to go away, whether or no," he said curiously.

"Oh, I suppose I can put it off if I have to," Brant rejoined, trying to hedge.

"Which is another way of telling me to mind my own business," retorted Antrim good-naturedly. "That's all right; only, if you have struck a bone, you can comfort yourself with the idea that you have plenty of good company. No one of us has a monopoly of all the trouble in the world."

"No, I suppose not." Brant said so much, and then got far enough away from his own trouble to notice that the chief clerk was looking haggard and seedy.

"You look as if you had been taking a turn at the windlass yourself, Harry. Have you?"

"Yes, something of that sort," replied Antrim, but he turned quickly to the papers on his desk.

"Nothing that I can help you figure out, is it?"

"No," said the chief clerk, so savagely that Brant smiled.

"Which the same is none of *my* business, and so we are quits," he rejoined.

Antrim was much too good-hearted to let the matter rest there, and he made halting amends.

"I would give you a chance, Brant, quicker than I would anybody else I know; but it is no use. Every fellow has to take his own medicine."

Brant nodded, and after a little Antrim went on as one who changes the subject.

"Been over to the Highlands lately?"

"No."

"I thought you hadn't. Dorothy was asking about you the last time I saw her."

"When was that?" The question was so eager that Antrim, remembering his unjust suspicion of Isabel, had a pang of honest shame.

"Last Wednesday. She wanted to know if you had left town."

Brant was plunged at once into a problem in which there were many more unknown quantities than integral facts. When he came to the surface it was to catch at a straw. Perhaps, after all, Dorothy was yet in happy ignorance of all the distressing things her mother could tell her; in which case she had merely failed to see him when he had lifted his hat to her the day before. And, if that were true, his late excursion into the realm of things evil was nothing better than the sequence of a hideous mistake. The logic of the thing appalled him, and he made haste to go back to first principles, planting himself desperately upon the assertion that she must have seen him. Having done that, he was immediately swept adrift again by an overwhelming desire to know the truth of the matter beyond peradventure of doubt. A suggestion offered, and he pounced upon it. He would make an unconscious messenger of Antrim.

"When are you going over there again, Harry?" he asked, making the question as incurious as might be.

"I don't know," replied the chief clerk, burying his face in his desk.

"Well, when you do, if Miss Langford asks you any more questions about me, you may say that I haven't been away, but that I am going before long."

Antrim looked up with a puzzled frown.

"I don't begin to know what you are driving at. Why don't you go and tell her yourself; you know the way."

It was Brant's turn to prevaricate, and he did it so clumsily that Antrim stopped him in sheer pity.

"That will do," he interrupted. "You are only getting tangled up in a lot of polite lies, and that doesn't help matters. Besides, if it is a question of carrying messages to Hollywood, I can't help you; I am out of the running myself—no, don't ask any questions, please. I can't talk about the thing, even to so good a friend as you are."

At this conjuncture the stenographer came back, and Brant took up the general manager's letter. "I'll take this and make the map," he said. "Does he want a tracing, or a blue print?"

"A tracing, I guess; they will want to make marks on it," replied Antrim.

And Brant went back to his office and fell upon the task with such singleness of purpose that the day was gone before he realized it.

As he was leaving the office at six o'clock, a messenger boy met him at the door with a note. It was from the editor of the Plainsman, and it was both brief and noncommittal.

"If you have nothing better to do, come down to the office this evening," it ran. "I have a promising little mystery in hand in which you may be interested."

Brant went back to his desk and wrote a reply. He had meant to go on with his work during the evening, but the editor's invitation came as a happy alternative. The making of a single map would not afford surcease from the devil of idleness for very long, and anything which promised to postpone the evil day of emptiness was to be accounted a blessing. Wherefore he accepted gladly, and, when the answer was written and despatched, went to supper with the comforting thought that the next few hours were safely provided for.

CHAPTER XVII
"AS APPLES OF GOLD IN PICTURES OF SILVER"

IT was yet early in the evening when Brant climbed the stairs of the Plainsman building to keep his appointment with Forsyth. The presses were roaring in the basement, but on the top floor the reporters' rooms were untenanted, and the telegraph editor, writing furiously under the sheen of the droplight in his noisy den, was the only member of the staff on duty. When Brant's form darkened his doorway, the man of specials snapped his key and looked up.

"Forsyth's gone down to supper," he said. "Told me to tell you to make yourself at home till he came back."

Brant nodded, and went on through the deserted offices to the night editor's room. The windows were open, but the chill of the October night was in the air, and a bit of fire smouldered in the grate. Brant stirred it into a blaze and was drawing up a chair when Forsyth entered.

"Good man!" he exclaimed cheerily. "Sit down and light a fresh cigar while I unfold you a tale. Did my note stir up your curiosity? or do you disown any such womanish weakness?"

Brant laughed. "I disown nothing in the way of weaknesses, and we'll admit the curiosity, with this qualification: it isn't a womanish weakness—on the contrary, it is altogether masculine. What is the mystery?"

Forsyth took a paper from a pile of exchanges and ran a blue pencil around an advertisement in the "Personal" column. "That is the text," he said. "Read that, and then I'll go on and preach my sermon."

Brant read: "If Mr. George Brant, formerly of Taggett's Gulch, Pitkin County, will communicate with J. B., care of the Herald, Leadville, he will hear of something to his advantage."

"I suppose that is pointed at my namesake," he commented, handing the paper back with an effort at nonchalance. "I hope he will come in for a good thing."

"So do I," rejoined the editor, smiling inscrutably. "But wait till you hear the story. Last night, one of our reporters—Jarvis, you know him—was hobnobbing with a lot of variety people in one of the private rooms in Heddrigg's restaurant. He swears he was sober, but you can draw your own conclusions as to that when I tell you that the company withdrew and left him alone without his knowing it."

"Sleepy, perhaps," suggested Brant.

"That is what he says. When he woke up he was alone, but the box beyond him was occupied by two men who were talking in whispers. Now Jarvis is a good fellow, but he is a reporter first, and everything else afterward, so of course he listened. The men were arguing about an 'ad' in the Leadville Herald, and Jarvis gathered that it boded ill for one of them, though he couldn't tell which one. In the course of the talk your name was mentioned—oh, yes, it was you, because they spoke of your boarding place out in Welton Street," Forsyth insisted, in rebuttal of Brant's incredulous negative, "and Jarvis heard enough to make him think they meant to do you a mischief."

"One moment," Brant interrupted. "What time of night was this?"

"I don't know exactly, but it was between twelve and two."

"All right. Go on."

"That is all. Only, as I say, Jarvis thinks they mean mischief, though he caught only a few words pointing to the necessity for haste in what they had to do. They seemed to be much afraid that you would see the 'ad.'"

Brant leaned forward to flick the ash from his cigar. "I presume Jarvis saw them when they went out. What did they look like?"

"That is just where the otherwise irreproachable Jarvis fell down," said the editor. "He posted himself conveniently behind the curtains of his box when they stirred, but unfortunately there is a back door to Heddrigg's place, and they used it."

"Leaving the Herald behind them?" queried Brant.

"Not much! But Jarvis went through the file and found the 'ad' after he came back here."

Brant smoked reflectively for a few minutes and then rose to go.

"I am much obliged to you, Forsyth. It was good of you to give me the pointer."

The editor made an effort to detain him. "Don't be in a hurry; the night is young."

"Yes, but I think I would better be going."

Forsyth tilted his chair and made a monocle of one side of his *pince nez* through which to quiz his visitor.

"Brant, you are most provokingly cold-blooded, don't you know it? Here I have been at the trouble to put you in the way of opening up a veritable mine of first-class sensation, and you are going away without so much as giving me a squint down the shaft thereof. Do you call that giving a man a fair shake?"

Brant sat down again. "What do you want me to say?" he asked.

"Say? Why, everything. Do you know these men? or is it a case of mistaken identity? Are they after your scalp? or do you yearn for theirs? Can't you open up the blinds and let in a little daylight?"

Brant shook his head. "Not for publication. You don't know what you ask, Forsyth."

"Publication be hanged! Who said anything about printing it, I'd like to know! Don't you suppose a newspaper man has bowels as well as other people? I didn't get you up here to work you for the Plainsman."

"Then that is different," Brant conceded. "I'll tell you what I can, which isn't much. I have seen these men; they followed me home last night at midnight. But if I ever knew them, I have forgotten who they are. As to the advertisement, I can only guess its purport. If the guess is right, there is only one man in Colorado who need be disturbed about it, and he is not in Denver."

The editor turned to his desk and ran through a pile of telegrams, pausing at one dated from Leadville.

"Does that help your guess?" he inquired, handing the message to Brant.

"Advertiser's name is John Brinton," was what the typewritten line said; and Brant nodded.

"Yes, and no; I can't understand. Forsyth, I am going out to hunt those fellows down."

Forsyth looked at his watch. "Will you take a partner? My rush won't be on for a couple of hours yet."

"I shall be glad to have you along, if you don't mind going into the dog kennels. I can't promise you a pleasure trip."

"I'd like to go," said the editor. "I suppose you share the opinion of the public, that all newspaper men are seasoned rounders; but it is a fiction in my own case—and in that of many others too, I think."

They went down together, and in the street Forsyth asked if it would not be well to take an officer along. Whereat Brant laughed.

"You forget my errand, don't you? We might as well look for these fellows with a file of soldiers at our backs as with a 'Bobby' for an escort. We shall get around all right by ourselves, and if we should happen to run afoul of trouble, you just stand from under while I cover the retreat."

"Are you armed?" asked Forsyth.

"Assuredly."

"Well, I am not, and I presume it is just as well. I can't see four feet in front of me with or without glasses."

"Can't you? Then let me take your arm," said Brant, with ready sympathy; and together they turned down Sixteenth Street to plunge presently into the depths of the underworld.

For reasons best known to himself, Brant made the search for the unknown conspirators a very thorough one. If, as he more than half suspected, one of the men should turn out to be Harding in disguise, the solution of the mystery would be reached at once. And in that case he knew his enemy well enough to be sure that nothing short of vigorous measures would serve to beat him off.

As a last resort he could always give the murderer of Henry Brinton up to justice; but he shrank from the thought of this as a brave man would scorn to ask aid in a personal quarrel. Doubtless the wretch deserved hanging, but the more Brant thought about it the more he was disinclined to play the part of the hangman. The alternative was to find Harding and to warn him once again that his safety lay not in reprisals, but in putting distance and oblivion between himself and his accuser.

It was to set the alternative in train that Brant tramped his companion from dive to den, dragging the murkiest depths of the pool, and leaving no place unvisited where he thought there was a chance of unearthing the plotters.

The search proved fruitless, as it was bound to, since Harding and Gasset were at that time closeted in the former's room in the West Denver *Gasthaus*; but Brant did not give over until Forsyth intimated that it was time for him to go back to his desk. Even then Brant begged for five minutes in which to ransack yet one more kennel, and the night editor yielded and went with him.

It was the place in which Harding had met the man from Taggett's Gulch on the day of his return to Denver—an evil-smelling lair half underground, with a bar fronting the entrance and a drug-like heaviness in the air pointing to what was beyond the bar-screened portal. It was Forsyth's earliest sniff of an opium hell. He gasped for breath at the threshold, and had he been alone would have fled precipitately. As it was, he went in with

Brant and stood at the bar while his companion searched the rooms beyond.

In a very short time Forsyth began to wish himself well out of it. First, the bartender scowled at him and asked what he would take, and when he refused to take anything, having a just fear that any liquor sold in such a place would be only less deadly than prussic acid, there was a stir in a little knot of ruffians clustered at the other end of the bar.

"What's that?" demanded one of them, sidling up with threatenings. "What are ye here for, if ye don't buy? Here, barkeep', hand out the red liquor; this here gig-lamps is goin' to set 'em up fer the crowd."

As he had confessed to Brant, Forsyth was short-sighted almost to blindness; also, he was unarmed. But he was no coward, and he pushed the bottle back resolutely and shook his head.

"The gentleman is mistaken," he said; "I haven't asked any one to drink at my expense, and don't mean to."

Then there was trouble, as a child might have foreseen. In the midst of it, Forsyth found himself looking into the barrel of a huge revolver, the weapon thrust so close that not even his short-sightedness availed to obscure it. At the same moment there was a stir in the murky region beyond the bar, a fierce oath followed by the sharp crack of a pistol, and the ruffian's weapon clattered harmless to the floor. Then Forsyth drew breath of relief, for Brant had thrust him gently aside and was standing before him.

"That is my bluff, gentlemen," said the newcomer quietly. "Would any of you like to call it?"

"Holy Smut, it's Plucky George!" gasped one in the rear; and in a twinkling the place was cleared—nay, more, the scowling bartender himself disappeared as if by magic.

Brant linked his arm in the editor's and led him forth into the clean night air. Neither spoke until they were nearing the Plainsman building, and then it was Forsyth who broke the silence.

"You heard what that fellow said, Brant? Are you really the Silverette man?"

"Yes. Don't be alarmed; I'll quit you when I have seen you safe back to your office."

Forsyth stopped, swung around, and put his hands on the stalwart one's shoulders.

"You are a blessed idiot—no less; and I am minded to beat you," he protested. "Why, confound it all, man, haven't you just saved my life?"

"That is nothing. And, besides, you wouldn't have been there if I had not taken you."

"No more would I; but what of that? Say, Brant, don't play the fool. I have known this thing, or suspected it, from the first, and I'll leave it to you to say if it has made any difference with me. I am quite willing to take you for what you are, and I don't care a little curse what you have been. That is no affair of mine, or of anybody's else."

"Do you think so? The world doesn't agree with you."

"The world is an impudent busybody," quoth the editor, catching step again. "Come up to my pigeon-hole and tell me all about it. I'll stave the rush off while you do it."

"No, I sha'n't let you do that, Forsyth; but I shall come up later on, if you will let me. I'll own up frankly; I am in trouble, well up to my neck, and, barring yourself, there isn't a soul in Denver that I can talk to."

"All right; you come up and unload on me. I'll look for you about the time the forms go down."

It was the word fitly spoken, and Brant turned away with a warm spot in his heart. High ideals and puissant resolves are all very well in their way, but a single grain of human sympathy strikes deeper root and bears better fruit. For the time Brant felt at peace with all men, and instead of going back to the purlieus to renew the search for Harding, as he had intended, he went in quite the opposite direction, being minded to go to his office and work on the map while he waited on Forsyth's leisure. So ran the intention; but at the corner he came upon Jarvis, and was straightway turned aside to do a better thing.

CHAPTER XVIII
"LET THE RIGHTEOUS SMITE ME FRIENDLY"

"HELLO, Brant!" said the reporter. "Been to see Forsyth?"

"Yes."

"Then you are posted, of course. What do you think about it?"

"I hardly know what to think of it yet," replied Brant, unwilling to go into details with Jarvis. "You are sure those fellows were talking about me, and not about somebody else?"

"I'm sure they were talking about a man named Brant who boards at Mrs. Seeley's. That makes the peg fit the hole, doesn't it?"

"It seems to. I guess we shall have to call it a mystery, and hope to learn more about it later on. Going upstairs?"

"Not just yet; let's go and liquidate."

"I don't drink," Brant objected.

"The dickens you don't! Since when?"

"Never mind the date—since I quit."

"I'll bet money that was no longer ago than yesterday. Come and take a cigar, then."

"I don't mind doing that, if you are thirsty enough to drink alone."

"I am thirsty enough to envy the fellow who went and got himself drowned in a butt of Malmsey," rejoined the reporter, linking arms with Brant and pointing like a trained retriever for the nearest pothouse.

"That thirst will be the death of you, my boy, if you are not careful," ventured the older sinner, catching step.

"Don't you lose any sleep about that. I know blessed well when to take a drink and when to let it alone."

"Yes, I have met you before," said Brant ironically. "You are one of a fair-sized crowd. The first 'when' is whenever you happen to think of it; the second is when the thing itself is temporarily out of reach."

Jarvis whistled derisively, and his retort was out of the heart of flippancy:

"You missed your calling, old man; your layout is the Prohibition platform. Why don't you join the Salvation Army?"

"For good and sufficient reasons; but that has nothing to do with your bad habits."

"Oh, come off! You're a one-horse lay preacher, that's what you are! Your theory is all right, but the wheels won't go round in practice. Man can't be a reporter and not drink."

"Without knowing more than I have to about the askings of your job, I'll venture to dispute that," Brant asserted. "According to my notion, a man can't be the best of anything so long as he hobnobs with any devil of appetite."

"Oh, let up—you make me limp! I'll bet a gold mine against a skinny little Indian pony that you've got wickedness enough in your system to cover my one little weakness like a bedspread and tuck in all around the edges. Come now, own up."

But for obvious reasons Brant could not own up; and since the random thrust found the joint in his harness, he must needs go dumb. But a little later, when they were standing together at the bar, he was again moved to protest at the spectacle of Jarvis putting absinthe into his whisky.

"The red liquor is bad enough by itself, my boy," he remarked, clipping the end of his cigar, "but the other is enough worse. It will make an idiot of you before your time."

"That's right; share a man's hospitality and jump on his personal preferences all in the same breath. If you've got to reform somebody, why don't you tackle that railroad friend of yours over there in the corner? He is sliding down the stair on the balustrade thereof. Go over and preach to him, while I see if I can't rustle up an eleventh-hour suicide for Forsyth."

Brant wheeled at the word and saw that which suddenly buried his own trouble deep under the *débris* of a shattered ideal. At a small table in the corner of the room two men sat playing cards. One of them was so good a type of his clan that Brant was able to summarize him tersely in the word "rook." The other was Harry Antrim—Antrim, the self-contained, the immaculate, the very pride and pattern of the well-behaved. The chief clerk was evidently much the worse for liquor; his face was flushed, and his hands trembled when he dealt the cards; but he was sober enough to recognise Brant when the latter came up and accosted him.

"It's about time you were going home, Harry," he said. "Get your overcoat, and I'll walk up with you."

The obscene bird across the table took Brant's measure in a swift glance, and, scenting trouble, sought to make his peace with the newcomer.

"We were just having a little game for pastime, you understand—low man pays for the dr—for the cigars," he explained.

Brant ignored the peaceful overture and the maker of it, and asked Antrim what he had done with his coat.

"It's all right about the coat," replied the foolish one, making a pitiful effort to keep the consonants in their proper places. "Man don't need any overcoat in summer time. Le's go home."

Brant saw that the man across the table wore an overcoat, and that he was sitting upon another.

"I'll trouble you to let me have my friend's coat," he said mildly, but the cold gray eyes narrowed and shot a look with the words that made the request a demand.

"Oh, certainly, if he is a friend of yours"—the rook had never laid eyes on Brant before. "But it wasn't no brace game; I win it fair enough."

Brant helped Antrim to his feet and into his coat, after which he walked him home with no word of inquiry or reproach. Truly, the foolish one was far enough beyond the reach of admonition, but he was also sane enough to appreciate the value of the silence which is golden, and he made an effort to say as much when Brant led him into his room and lighted the gas.

"Much obliged, George, for what you haven't said." He steadied himself with his hands on the table and tried to catch Brant's eye: "'Nother fellow would've preached, and a sermon isn't jush what I need."

"I know that. Good night," said Brant, and therewith he left the prisoner of fools to the company of an accuser which is not to be silenced save by many applications of the searing iron.

The night editor of the Plainsman was in the midst of the last batch of copy when Brant redeemed his promise to return, and Forsyth motioned to a chair.

"Sit down; I'll be with you in a minute," he said, and when the desk was cleared he wheeled the pivot chair to face his visitor and drew up another for a foot rest.

"Thanks be; that is the last of it for one more day. It's a 'demnition grind,' but I suppose that is true of every occupation under the sun. Haven't you found it so?"

"Honestly, no. I think I am in love with my profession. If I didn't have other things to trouble me, I believe I could go on making maps to the end of the chapter."

"You think that now because the drudgery is preferable to the other things, maybe. Tell me about the other things."

"I shall, and I'll cut it short. You know what the public knows about George Brant of Silverette and elsewhere, so we needn't go into that, though perhaps you will let me say that I was no worse than other men of my tribe. I mean by that that I never dealt a brace game, and I never picked a quarrel of my own motion."

"These things say themselves. Go on."

"Well, one day I came to the end of things. You may imagine that the life would nauseate any man who has ever known anything better, and that is what it did to me. So I turned short, pasted down the old leaf, and began all over again."

"So far so good. And then?"

"Then I began to hunger and thirst after respectability, and a wife, and a home, and all the commonplace blessings of the well-behaved. And because I can't have them I am minded to do a lot of foolish things."

The editor removed his glasses and fell to polishing them absently. "Perhaps you are not willing to pay the price," he suggested.

"Yes, I am—if I know my own mind."

"Then you have found the—what shall we call her?—the affinity?"

"I have; found her and lost her again."

"Very few things are lost in this world—beyond the hope of finding them again, I mean. What happened?"

"That which was sure to happen, sooner or later. Her mother found me out and sent me adrift with a Scotch blessing."

"H'm! that was a bit hard. Does the young woman know?"

"That is what I can't find out, though I am afraid she does. I met her face to face yesterday, and she passed me without a word."

"Which proves nothing more than that she may be nearsighted. I shouldn't lose any sleep over that."

"But I did; I went mad, and spent half the night in a gambling den."

"You did? That is the worst thing I know about you thus far. It was unworthy of you."

"Don't I know it? Haven't I been eating the bread of bitterness all day?"

"I suppose you have; but you will have to eat a good bit of it before you get through. You say you are willing to pay the price, but I have my doubts about that."

Now Brant could be steel cold in the fiercest fray, but he was not beyond flinching under a friendly lash. Forsyth's doubt whipped him out of his chair, and he made two or three quick turns up and down the narrow walkway behind the desk before the pot of passion boiled over.

"God in heaven, Forsyth, you don't know what you are talking about!" he burst out. "I'd sell my soul and the reversion of it to win that girl's love—and respect."

"Exactly; but you are not required to sell it. You are expected to pay it out of debt."

"I am willing to do that. But what can I do more than I have done?"

"A great deal, I should say. Let me use the knife a little, and then I'll try to sew the wound up. You went your own way—which you admit was not the way of decency—till you got tired of it. Then you faced about and said to yourself that all these things should be as if they never had been. That was right and proper, but it was only the first step in a longish journey. Since that time you have taken several other steps, and now you have reached a point where society begins to concern itself, demanding from you a reasonable guarantee of good faith."

"Hang society! I suppose that is what the mother meant when she said I hadn't repented."

"She was quite right. You haven't repented, in the sense that you are sorry for what you have done. You were merely tired of one thing and so took up another, forgetting that in this game of life he who plays must also pay."

"I am paying now, at any rate."

"No, you are not; you are only suffering the consequences of not having paid."

Brant made more turns in the narrow walkway, and scowled and frowned and otherwise gave signs that the friendly knife had cut deep. It is not every man who can probe his own wound, but this man did it, as his silence-breaking word declared:

"Tell me what I am to do, Forsyth, and I'll do it if it shortens my life."

"The thing that you have to do makes for longevity. It is merely to settle down in humdrum good behaviour and wait."

"For how long?"

The editor shrugged. "*Quien sabe?* Till the price is paid. Society will let you know when it believes you are to be trusted."

Brant sat down again and jammed his hands deep into his pockets. "Wait, you say. That is the one thing I can't do. Set me any task, however desperate, that I can do and have done with it, and I am your man. But the waiting game will first drive me mad and then kill me."

"No, it won't. Other men have had it to do."

"But I shall lose my chance of happiness in any event."

"Not necessarily. Certainly not if the young woman loves you."

"You mean that she would wait, too? Possibly she might, if she knew; but she doesn't, you know."

Forsyth shrugged again. "I presume I am a traitor to my kind for suggesting it, but you are not under bonds not to tell her, are you?"

"No; I might have been, if the mother had seen fit to put it that way. But she didn't. She declared open war, and she needn't complain if I borrow her weapons."

"No. And there is little doubt about your being able to hold your own in any stand-up fight. By the way, speaking of fights, did you shoot that fellow who was trying to bully me?"

"No; I shot his pistol out of his hand."

"Purposely?"

"Of course."

"It is a sheer marvel to me, the accuracy and the fact itself. I don't understand how you managed to hit it; and I didn't suppose a bullet would knock a pistol out of a man's hand."

"It is easy enough if you shoot straight and carry heavy metal. This thing"—he took Harding's revolver out of his pocket—"this thing throws a forty-five, and it would punch boiler plate at that distance."

"Let me see it," said Forsyth, and he took the weapon and examined it as one examines the tools of an unfamiliar trade. "It's a young cannon, isn't it? What is this name on the handle?"

"'J. Harding' is what it is meant for. He owned it until one night when I held him up and took it away from him."

"Another battle royal, I suppose," said the editor, shaking his great head in deprecation of battles royal and brawlings general. "You will have to drop all that, my boy, if you are going to join the great army of the well-behaved. And that reminds me, what kind of a coil are you in with these fellows that Jarvis overheard?"

Brant thought twice before he spoke once. Here was a matter about which the least said would be the soonest mended. If he should tell the facts in the case, Forsyth would insist that he was no better than an accessory after the fact if he should persist in his refusal to give Harding up to justice, and this he could not bring himself to do. Therefore he answered lightly:

"It is an old quarrel, and one which I don't mean to take up. One of the fellows owes me a grudge, but he is in no condition to go to war with me—or with any one."

"And yet you wanted to find him?"

"Yes; I was going to invite him to drop it and go away, but it's hardly worth while," said Brant, getting up to take his leave before he should be drawn into the giving of details.

"Well, keep out of it—keep out of everything that isn't as plain as print and of a nature to be cried from the housetops, and you will come out all right. Don't get downhearted, or, if you do, just come up here and I'll abuse you some more. Good night."

Brant went down the stairs and out into the street, and so on up to Mrs. Seeley's, with his square jaw set and two ideas dominating all others in his thoughts. One was that without Dorothy's love to sustain him he would be unequal to the task of maintaining the long probationary struggle outlined by Forsyth; and the other was an intense longing, born of the militant soul of him, to be given some desperate penance—to be tried by the fire of some crucial test which, should it leave him but a single day to glory in the victory, would prove him once for all a man and a gentleman, worthy to have lived and loved.

This he yearned for, and, yearning, put it aside, little knowing that he had within the hour reached and passed the parting of the ways, or that his feet were already in the path leading straight to the goal of his soul's desire.

CHAPTER XIX
THE LEADING OF THE BLIND

ON the morrow's morning Brant went to his work with a choir of new resolves making melody in his heart. He would get speech with Dorothy by fair means or other and make a frank avowal of his love, telling her what she should know of his past, and pleading only for the time wherein to make good his promises of amendment. Then he would settle down to his work, walking straitly and shunning even the appearance of evil through the weeks or months or years of his probation. And in the end he would win her and wear her in the face of all the world, and none should say him nay.

Thus he planned as he bent over the drawing-board, etching in the scheme of the future while he traced the intricate lines of the map. From summarizing he presently came down to the successive steps in the outworking of the problem, and then he remembered that he still held the money won in the night of madness at Draco's. Then and there he determined to return it, whether the chief gambler would or no, and on the heels of this resolve came a nobler. He would draw out of his bank balance every dollar that had not come to him hallowed by honest toil, and, since it was manifestly impossible to make individual restitution, he would give the money to some worthy charity.

Being a man of action, he did not suffer the good resolution to cool by delay. Within the hour he had made a deposit in his bank, purchased New York exchange for the amount won at Draco's, and cashed his check for six hundred and eight dollars and fifteen cents, the exact sum with which he had left Silverette on the night of the tragedy. Then he begged a sheet of paper and an envelope from the cashier and scribbled a note to Draco:

"Here is the money which you refused to take back the other night," he wrote. "It is not yours, but it is still less mine, and I don't want it. I have put it into New York exchange, so you will know it is out of my hands. Keep it, or throw it away, as you please."

That done, he began to wonder what he should do with the six hundred odd dollars. There were worthy charities a-plenty, but he shrank equally from giving without explanations and from telling any part of his story to a stranger, however charitable or devout. Since it had to be done, he finally chose Dorothy's clergyman as his beneficiary, and, having so decided, sought out the address and boarded a street car for the house of the minister. A servant answered the bell, and, in reply to Brant's inquiry, sent him across the street to the church.

"You'll find the study at the back," she said. "If Mr. Crosswell ain't there, you can go in and wait. He'll not be long gone."

Brant did as he was directed, and when his tap at the half-open door was unanswered, he went in. A young woman was sitting in a corner reading, and when he saw that it was Dorothy he stood abashed like any schoolboy. Only for a moment, however, for Dorothy rose quickly and came forward with hands outstretched.

"Why, Mr. Brant, you fairly startled me! I heard you at the door and thought it was Mr. Crosswell. How do you do? and where have you been all these weeks?"

Brant went dizzy with mingled joy and self-reproach. Then it was a hideous mistake, after all, and Mrs. Langford had kept her own counsel. It was almost beyond belief, and he stammered helplessly in his acknowledgments:

"I—I haven't been anywhere—that is, I've been here—no, not just here, either——"

Dorothy's laugh rang sweet and joyous, and it outran her words in restoring his self-possession.

"It's the atmosphere of the place, you know," she said archly. "People come here to confess their sins, and polite excuses are not allowed. Have you come to confession, Mr. Brant?"

Her jesting question went near enough to the truth to make him wince.

"Ye—yes; something of that sort. I came to have a little talk with Mr.— Mr.——"

"Crosswell?" she suggested. "So did I. Won't you sit down and wait for him? He will be in before very long, I think."

Brant did as he was bidden, and thus having the opportunity for free speech which he would have been willing to buy at a price, went dumb and could do no more than tie idle knots in his watch chain. Dorothy read the questions in his eyes, but she mistook their pointing, and wondered how she could help matters along without betraying Isabel. Much to her relief, he opened the way by breaking ground in the direction of things serious.

"The last time we met you were in trouble," he began. "I hope the cause has been removed."

"It has," she assented; "and—and I have wanted so much to thank you. It was very, very good of you to help us."

"Please don't mention it; any one would have done as much under the circumstances," he protested, adding, "and that without the hope of reward."

She knew what he meant, or thought she did, and steeled herself to lead him on.

"I think we all expect rewards of some kind for our good deeds, and we usually get them, don't we?"

"Rather oftener than we deserve, I think. But I missed mine."

Dorothy had prayed for this opportunity, and for strength to improve it, but she had to turn away from him before she could go on.

"Sometimes we think we have lost things when we have only overlooked them," she ventured; then, brushing aside the figure of speech, she went straight to the heart of the matter. "Mr. Brant, why don't you come to see us any more?"

From the personal point of view it was the cruelest of questions, but she was determined to secure her own safety and Isabel's happiness by forcing his confidence, and she knew no better way to do this. Nevertheless, she was wholly unprepared for his reply.

"For the best of reasons, Miss Langford: I have been forbidden the house."

It seemed incredible that he should put such a harsh construction upon Isabel's refusal, and Dorothy was bewildered. "But I don't understand," she began. "Surely——"

"One moment, please. Do you believe in repentance?"

"In its efficacy, you mean? Why, certainly; otherwise we should all be beyond hope."

"Then let me suppose a case—call it a parable, if you will. There was once a man who was thoroughly bad; quite given over to the service of the Evil One. One day this man saw the error of his way and resolved to live thenceforth a clean life. Then he met and loved a woman"—he paused and got up to pace slowly back and forth behind her chair—"loved her with a love that recked nothing of the great gulf separating him from her; forgetting the gulf, indeed, until the spectre of his evil past was called up to remind him of his unworthiness. Do you follow me?"

Her "Yes" was the faintest of whispers, but he heard it and went on.

"Judge, then, between that man and an exacting world. Is there any hope for such a one? Would patient perseverance in well-doing some time earn him the right to contend for such a prize as the love of a good woman?

Might he venture to look forward to a time when the great gulf would be fairly bridged—when a pure woman, knowing the worst of him, would not turn from him in loathing?"

Dorothy rose and faced him with the light of self-sacrifice shining in her eyes.

"Who am I that I should judge any one?" she asked softly.

"You are yourself, Dorothy; and you know the man—and the woman."

It was a moment of supreme trial. How could she give him the word of encouragement from Isabel without betraying Isabel's secret? And how could she ever forgive herself if she should waste the opportunity and send him away empty-handed. In her embarrassment she again took counsel of frankness.

"It is only the faint-hearted who despair," she said steadily. "Difficulties are made to be overcome, and for one who presses forward steadfastly there is always hope." She stopped with the feeling that all these phrasings were but generalities, and he broke in eagerly:

"That is enough. You have heard the parable; this is the interpretation. I am the man, Dorothy, and you——"

"Are the woman," he was going to say, but she held up a warning finger, and he heard a step at the door. It was the clergyman returning, and before Brant could add the word to which all the other words had been but the preface his chance was gone. The next moment Dorothy was introducing him to an elderly little man with a kindly face and a hand-clasp that spoke of warm friendships and a broad personality.

"I am glad to meet you, Mr. Brant—always glad to know any friend of Miss Dorothy's. Sit down—sit down, both of you, and let us be comfortable."

Brant obeyed, but Dorothy hesitated.

"I wanted to see you a moment about the Crowleys," she said. "They are in trouble again, and this time it is beyond me. Mr. Brant wishes to see you about another matter, and if you can give me a minute——"

"Certainly, certainly; Mr. Brant will excuse us," and they went apart to discuss the case of the unfortunate Crowleys, while Brant took up a book and pretended to read. Presently Dorothy took her leave, giving her hand to Brant at parting and inviting him to call soon at Hollywood.

He told no lie in saying that he should be glad to, and he tried to say with his eyes that other thing which had been denied lip utterance. Dorothy flushed faintly under his gaze and her hand trembled a little in his;

whereupon he made bold to revert to the object of their common solicitude in another offer of assistance.

"About William: be sure to command me if I can ever help you again. I hope the occasion won't arise, but if it does, you must manage to let me know at once."

"Indeed I shall," she rejoined gratefully. "But you must come to see us. Good-bye."

When she was gone the clergyman drew up his chair opposite Brant's. "A most devoted young woman," he said with kindly emphasis. "I don't know how we should get along in the parish without her. Have you known the Langfords long?"

"Not very long; no."

"Charming family—that is—er—all but the boy. He is a little wild, I'm afraid."

"Yes," assented Brant. He was finding his introduction by Dorothy a very considerable hindrance to his errand.

"The judge knows it, and tries to do what he can," Mr. Crosswell went on, following out his own line of thought. "But Mrs. Langford puts the lad on a pedestal and so spoils him. But pardon me, you came on an errand of your own, didn't you?"

"Yes." Brant braced himself and took the simplest way out of the entanglement. "You probably have many ways in which you can use money for charitable purposes, haven't you, Mr. Crosswell?"

"Yes, indeed. You are always safe to assume that in the case of a working clergyman," was the reply.

"I supposed so. I have some money here"—taking the roll of bills from his pocket—"which is, in a certain sense, what you might call conscience money. Would you object to adding it to your charity fund?"

"Not at all, if it be truly conscience money. But you must give me some assurance that it is—that there is no possibility of restitution to the proper parties."

"There is none whatever. It is money which was won across the gaming table—not recently," he added, in deference to the look of pained surprise in the kindly eyes, "but some months ago. I don't know what else to do with it, and it will be truly an act of charity to me if you will take it."

"Under those circumstances I shall be quite willing to disburse it for you, Mr. Brant. It is very commendable in you to take such an honourable view of the matter—a thing as commendable as it is rare, I assure you."

But Brant could not let that stand. "It is a simple matter of justice, and I am afraid the motive is purely selfish. To be very frank about it, the stuff burns my fingers."

"A most hopeful sign, my dear sir," said the little clergyman, warming to Brant as most good people did, without any reason that could be set in words. "It is not often that we are given to see such practical proofs of repentance."

Being an honest man in the better sense of the word, Brant made haste to remove the false impression:

"Don't misunderstand me. I am not at all sure that I am repentant in your meaning of the word; in fact, I am quite sure I am not. I drank the cup of evil living to the dregs, and the dregs nauseated me—that is all."

"But that is a very good beginning—very good, indeed," asserted the clergyman benignly. "Go on as you have begun, and we shall see better things; I am quite sure of that."

Brant remembered his desperate plunge of less than forty-eight hours before, and smiled.

"It is very evident that you haven't sounded all the depths of wickedness in the human heart, Mr. Crosswell, and perhaps it is just as well for us sinners that you haven't. We are a sorrier lot than you have any idea of, I fancy."

"We are all 'vile earth' when it comes to that, Mr. Brant; but I shall continue to consider your case as a most hopeful one." Then, as Brant found his hat, "Must you go? Come and see me often. I want to know more of you."

Brant bowed himself out and went his way musing. As he approached the side gate giving upon the street, a carriage drew up to the curb and a lady descended therefrom. He had opened the gate for her and lifted his hat before he saw that it was Mrs. Langford; but in any case he could have done no less. Notwithstanding, her chilling stare cut him to the quick, and he went back to his office with the comfortable feeling of elation engendered by the meeting with Dorothy and the act of restitution somewhat dashed by the chance encounter.

Meanwhile Mrs. Langford had entered the study and made known her errand, which was to call for Dorothy.

"She said she wouldn't wait," explained the clergyman. "Mr. Brant was here, waiting to see me about a matter which was—ah—er—a matter which I presume Miss Dorothy knew to be private, and so she kindly made room for him."

"Mr. Brant!" Mrs. Langford's frown was quite portentous. "Do you mean to say they were here together, Mr. Crosswell?"

"Why, yes; that is, I—er—I found them both here when I came in." Then, as the lines of displeasure deepened in the lady's brow, he tried to set himself right by adding: "A most excellent young man, Mrs. Langford; I am glad to know that he is a friend of the family."

"He is not," she rejoined with aggressive emphasis. "He was never more than a calling acquaintance, and he is not even that at present. I have forbidden him the house."

"Forbidden him the house?" echoed the good man in unfeigned astonishment. "May I—may I ask your reason?"

"You may; and I will tell you, if you will tell me what he was doing here."

"He came on a very worthy errand, I assure you, Mrs. Langford; he came to devote a certain sum of money to charitable objects—money acquired in a manner which is all too common in this our day and generation, but which he felt that he could not conscientiously keep."

"Humph! Some of the proceeds of his gambling, I suppose. It was a mere trick, Mr. Crosswell, and I hope you won't let him impose upon you. I know his whole history, and it is thoroughly bad and disgustingly disreputable."

"But, my dear madam, are we not commanded——"

"I know what you would say," she broke in, with her hand on the door. "But you know my views, Mr. Crosswell. If a woman had done the tenth part of the evil things this man has, you would be the first to recommend sackcloth and ashes and a sisterhood, if not a solitary cell."

The indignant lady swept down the walk and stepped into her carriage. "Conscience money, indeed!" she said to herself. "It is much more likely that he made the whole thing an excuse to get a chance to talk to Dorothy. Well, I'll put a stop to that!"

But when Mrs. Langford's carriage turned and rolled away, the good little man stood in the doorway of his study and shook his head sadly to the tune of a musing commentary on his latest visitor.

"Strange, passing strange, that she can be so uncharitable, when her own son stands so sorely in need of the broadest charity! I do hope there is no dreadful day of retribution in store for her, but it is certainly tempting Providence to be so pitiless."

CHAPTER XX
THE DEMONIAC

THE rounds in the descending ladder of dissipation are many or few according to the temperament of the man who makes use of them: the man, I say, for women rarely descend—they fall. As in a galloping consumption it is not infrequently the strongest who succumb first, so in a moral lapse it is often the self-contained who set the pace.

Antrim's sudden plunge into the stream of excess was fairly illustrative of this. Beginning with the mild debauch in the company of Grotter, the division engineer, he went from bad to worse with such breathtaking celerity that the end of a single week found him shattered and nerveless, and already dependent upon stimulants for the inspiration needful to keep him up to his work.

It was in such a plight that he began the day following his adventure with the "rook." To be sure, there were, early in the morning, some feeble and shame-prompted motions toward amendment, but these were soon swept away by the onrush of appetite, newborn but mighty; and since he went fasting to his work, he began the earlier to borrow efficiency from the bottle.

As it is prone to do in time of need, the stimulant played him false at first, though he gauged the doses with careful accuracy and repeated them frequently. All through the forenoon he found himself struggling with a vague sense of uncertainty, a mental obscuration which made perplexing puzzles out of the well-known details of the office work. The mail was heavy that day, and in the absence of the superintendent the chief clerk's tasks were multiplied. There was an unusual influx of callers, each with a grievance real or fancied, and a dribbling stream of telegrams trickled insistently through the clicking relay on his desk. To make a bad matter worse, his telegraph operator was sick, and such wire business as came to the office he had to handle himself.

It was some time during this hazy interval that a message, repeated from some station on the Eastern Division, came from the despatcher's office at Lone Pine Junction. It was from the general manager, who, with the president and his party in the private car Aberystwyth, was on the line moving westward. Some member of the party was sick, and in consequence the car was running as a special train, with orders giving it right of way over all other trains. Similar orders were required for the Western Division, and Antrim turned to the stenographer:

"Take a message to the general manager, care car Aberystwyth, running as special train on Eastern Division," he directed; and when Bertram's pencil stopped, he dictated:

"Your message to-day. Car Aberystwyth will be run as special train on Western Division, Lone Pine Junction to Denver, with right of way over all trains."

"Get that off as quick as you can, and when you come back I'll give you the letter to the despatcher," he said, and a few minutes later Bertram took the message to the telegraph office.

When he came back Antrim had something else for him to do, and in the rush of the forenoon's work the stenographer forgot all about the letter to the train despatcher—the letter without which the despatcher would know nothing about the arrangement made for the special. But if Bertram forgot, so did the chief clerk, though the omission hung over Antrim like a vague threat, which he tried vainly to define. At noon the threat had become a part of the general obscurity through which he seemed to be groping his way, and by that time he was so far behind with the business of the day that he went without dinner to save the noon hour, substituting yet other potations for the midday meal.

Such reckless disregardings of the simple necessities speedily brought their own penalties. By half past one o'clock he was little better than an automaton, doing whatever came to hand mechanically and by force of long habit. By three he had fairly entered the drunkard's paradise—that exalted frame of mind in which the most abstruse problems seem to solve themselves of their own motion. After that, all things were easy of accomplishment, and the chief clerk shut and locked his office at six o'clock with the comforting conviction that he was quite himself again; that, notwithstanding the perplexities of the morning, he had acquitted himself with his old-time vigour and perspicacity.

Then he went to supper, and when he found that he had overshot the mark and could eat nothing, he began dimly to realize that he was in a bad way and forced himself to drink a double allowance of strong coffee. The slight stimulant began presently to counteract the effect of the greater, and with the first gleams of returning sobriety the threat of the forenoon renewed itself with added insistence.

When that happened he went to his room and sat down on the edge of the bed to reason it out. For an hour or more he wrestled with the thing, coming no nearer the truth than this: that out of the struggle came a great and growing conviction that he had left something of critical moment undone. That was enough. Things left undone in a railway superintendent's office may easily mean anything in the category of disaster, and Antrim groped for his hat and coat and went out, meaning to borrow yet again of the usurer, and then to go back to his office to search for the slipped cog.

Fortunately for the latter resolve, the brisk walk in the cool night air sobered him sufficiently to send him straight to the office without the preliminary. Letting himself in and leaving the door ajar, he turned the key of the incandescent lamp over his desk and sat down to go painfully over the business of the day. It was slow work. His fingers were clumsy, and there was a curious haze before his eyes which seemed to befog the mental as well as the physical vision. Under such conditions it was not wonderful that he overlooked the message relating to the movements of the president's special train; and when he had gone through the day's correspondence without discovering anything amiss, he was dismayed afresh to find that the threat of impending disaster was increased rather than diminished, and his pulse quickened with a rising fever of apprehension.

"Oh, good Lord," he groaned, "what has come over me that I can't remember? I know I've missed something—something that will drive me crazy if I can't find out what it is. Let me think: there was the Rowland excursion to arrange—that's done; and the holding of Number Seven for the Western mail—I did that, too." He went on through the day's routine, checking off the items one by one. "No, it's something else, and it's gone from me—gone as though it never were. And whatever it is, it will ruin me, world without end. God of mercy, why can't I remember?"

He leaned back in the swing chair and tortured his brain once again—cudgelled it until the sweat stood in great drops on his forehead, but all to no purpose. Once he started up with the thought that he would try to find Bertram, but he knew not where to look for the stenographer, and, besides, the nameless terror seemed now to be so close at hand as to forbid all expedients asking for time. This menacing phase of the unexplainable thing made him sick with fear, and the sickness made him sit down and sweat again and fight desperately for consciousness.

In the midst of this, while he sat staring blankly at the opposite wall, the end came. Having dwelt overmuch upon the day's routine, the events of it now began to chase each other in a round of endless repetition. In this rhythmic round things tangible were presently involved, first the walls of the room, then the furniture. He caught at the arms of his chair to save himself from slipping into the vortex of the spinning whirlpool: something clicked, in his brain or out of it, the twirling maelstrom vanished in a puff of darkness that could be felt, and silence as profound as that in which the deaf live seemed to kill the sense of hearing.

How long he sat horror-sick in the stifling darkness he knew not; it might have been minutes or hours. Then a familiar sound broke the stillness, and he listened with the keen joy of one who hears the babble of running water in a thirsty desert. It was the clicking of the telegraph instrument on his desk, and the tiny tapping was his first assurance that he had not been stricken both deaf and blind in the same instant. At first the clicking spatter of dots and dashes was meaningless; then it slipped into coherence, and Antrim listened with his heart pounding like a trip hammer. The sounder was repeating the wire business of the day.

Like a flash out of the unseen it came to the prisoner of despair that the thing forgotten had to do with some telegram mislaid or overlooked, and here was his opportunity. Sooner or later the tapping sounder would give him the lost clew, and he would lie in wait and listen and pounce upon it.

One by one the messages received hours before were ticked off into the silence, and so single-eyed was the listener that it did not occur to him to marvel at the miracle. Word for word they came, and he could even recognise the varying "writing" of the different operators on the line. At length there was a pause, and then the sounder began again, tapping out the Denver office call with the signature of Lone Pine Junction. Antrim pounced upon the key and answered. Without a break the message followed the closing of the key:

"To CRAIG, Superintendent, Denver:

"Owing to sudden illness of a member of the president's party, we are running private car Aberystwyth as special train with right of way against all other trains. Make same arrangement for Western Division. Must reach Denver at earliest possible moment. On present schedule, will arrive Lone Pine Junction between nine and ten this P. M.

"R. F. ANGUS, G. M."

Antrim heard it through, opened his key and sent the reply:

"To R. F. ANGUS, General Manager, care car Aberystwyth, running as special train on Eastern Division:

"Your message to-day. Car Aberystwyth will be run as special train on Western Division, Lone Pine Junction to Denver, with right of way over all trains.

"CRAIG, Superintendent."

Then he felt in the darkness for the pad of letter-heads, dipped the pen, and began the forgotten letter of instructions to the train despatcher:

"DISBROW, Despatcher, Denver:

"President Carothers, with his party in private car Aberystwyth, is moving westward on Eastern Division. A member of the party is sick, and car is running special to Denver with regardless orders. This special will reach——"

The chief clerk stopped with suspended pen and tried to recall the name of Lone Pine Junction. Though he had but now repeated it, it was gone, and, balanced as he was upon the sharp edge of collapse, the effort to remember the name turned the scale. The pen slipped from his fingers, his head sank upon his arm, and the swirling whirlpool laid hold of him, thrusting him down to oblivion in the black throat of its vortex.

CHAPTER XXI
"A ROD FOR THE FOOL'S BACK"

COMPARING it with the fortnight of yesterdays, Brant reckoned the day of his meeting with Dorothy as one worthy of anniversaries. In good truth, his confession had stopped something short of its climax, and of the coveted personal absolution; but it was comforting to remember that he had spoken plainly, and that she had bidden him go forward hopefully. Notwithstanding the untimely interruption, there could be no reasonable doubt of the major fact: that she fully understood his parable and its application—understood and was glad, and would have let him go on but for the interruption.

So much for the good; and as for the ill, the rebuff at the church gate went for little. Being so well assured of the daughter's—he was about to say "love," but he changed it to "sympathy"—being so well assured of the daughter's sympathy, he could afford to wait for reinstatement in the good graces of the mother. Women, even such women as the Mrs. Langfords, are not implacable, he reasoned; and when he should have shown how sincere he was, her resentment—her natural resentment, he was willing to call it—would be allayed, and she would see the injustice of her sentence of ostracism. Wherein he showed forth an unknowledge of womankind common to very young men, and to some older ones whose walk in life has led them much apart from women worth the knowing.

In the exuberance of his self-congratulation Brant lost sight of the one redeeming thread in the thought-woven fabric of the day, which thread was a brotherly concern for Antrim, and a half-formed resolve to turn bearwarden to the foolish one. By evening the half-formed resolve took permanent shape; and since a physician must first know something of the disease and the cause of it, he began by trying to breach Antrim's reticence at the supper table. For reasons good and sufficient, the effort was bootless; and Brant, driven from ear to eye evidence, and having, moreover, considerable skill in diagnosing the symptoms of bottle sickness, saw with concern that Antrim was tottering on the verge of the abyss.

From that to keeping a solicitous eye on him was but a step; and when Antrim went upstairs, Brant, whose room was just across the corridor from the chief clerk's, went too, mounting guard with a light, a book, and with his door ajar. For a long time there was no stir in the opposite room; but just as he was beginning to hope that Antrim had gone to bed, the door opened and the chief clerk hurried out.

Brant's first impulse was to follow and bring him back without ceremony. Then he reflected that it is an ill thing to meddle, even with the best of motives, and so cast about for a plausible excuse. Luckily, he found one ready to his hand. The papers containing the evidence against Harding were in the drawer of his writing table, and in view of the late stirrings in that pool it would be well to put them under lock and key. There was a safe in Antrim's office, and the errand would give him a chance to probe Antrim's wound, and so haply he might find the bullet or the arrowhead, or whatever it might be that was rankling therein.

So he put the papers in his pocket and went out; and taking it for granted that Antrim would make straight for the nearest barroom, lost a half hour or more in a fruitless search among the drinking places. When he had widened the search circle to the farthest limits of the *quasi*-respectable district, outside of which Antrim would not be likely to venture, he stumbled upon Jarvis and stopped to inquire of him.

"Say, Jarvis, have you seen anything of Harry Antrim this evening?"

The reporter nodded. "Um-hm; saw him heading for his office half an hour ago, plugging along with his head down and his hands in his pockets. What's struck him lately?"

"I don't know," replied the bearwarden truthfully enough; "much obliged." But when he would have gone on, Jarvis turned and went with him.

"Going to hunt him up? I'll mog along with you. The old man says the president of the C. E. & W. is coming in on a special, and I'd like to get the facts for an item."

"Can't you telephone?" asked Brant, remembering the nature of his errand.

"I suppose I could, but I don't mind the walk. Say, it's queer about Harry, isn't it? Never saw a man let go all holds at once like he has."

"He will get over it; it's nothing worse than a fit of the blues," said Brant, taxing his ingenuity meanwhile for an expedient which would rid him of the reporter.

"Blues nothing! Fit of the 'jimmies,' if he doesn't pull up pretty short. He isn't built right to carry bug juice in bulk, and that is just about what he is trying to do."

"What was it you said to me about preaching last night?" asked Brant, as they climbed the stair to the railway offices.

"Never mind about that; you were preaching at me, and I didn't need it. Now, with a fellow like Harry it's different——"

They were at the door of the train despatcher's room, and Brant paused. "Better ask Disbrow about the special," he said, with a glance at the darkened transom of the superintendent's office. "Harry doesn't seem to be here."

The reporter acted upon the suggestion; and when he was alone in the corridor Brant went quickly to the door of the darkened office. It was ajar, and when he pushed it open the light from the hall fell full upon the figure of the chief clerk lying inert and helpless across the open desk.

Brant took in the situation at a glance, closed the door softly, and walked back toward the despatcher's room. Jarvis was a good fellow, but he already knew too much about Antrim's affair, and he must be got rid of at all hazards. He met the reporter as the latter was coming out of Disbrow's door.

"Get what you wanted?" he inquired.

"No. You railroad fellows are all of a piece when it comes to giving up anything that the public would care to read about. Disbrow says he doesn't know anything about a special train—didn't know the president was coming. Between you and me and the gatepost, I think he doesn't know much of anything."

"Then you'll have to forego the item."

"Forego nothing! I'll hang around this old shack till morning, now, but what I'll find out about that train."

Brant laughed. "I like your persistence, even if it is a little out of proportion to the object. Come into my office here and sit down and smoke a cigar while I try my hand at it. I owe you a good turn, anyway."

Brant unlocked the door of the chief engineer's rooms, and, telling the reporter to make himself comfortable while he waited, left him. But since it was no time for half measures he took the precaution to set the catch of the nightlatch as he closed the door, locking Jarvis in.

Hurrying back to the superintendent's office, he turned on the light and tried to rouse Antrim, shaking him roughly and sparing neither blows nor abuse. Nothing coming of this, he was beginning to despair of any measure of success which should antedate the end of the reporter's patience, when his eye lighted upon the unfinished letter to the train despatcher. Written as it had been, in the dark, it was a barely legible scrawl, but he made shift to decipher it, pieced it out with Jarvis's information and Disbrow's ignorance, and knowing much more about building railways than about operating them, jumped at once to the conclusion that the special train was rushing onward to certain destruction. Wherefore he forgot the imprisoned reporter, overlooked the very obvious expedient of notifying the despatcher by word of mouth, and fell upon Antrim with renewed buffetings to which the assumed exigencies lent stinging vigour.

No sudorific could hold out long against such an heroic antidote, and with the first signs of returning consciousness Brant dragged his patient to the wash basin in the corner of the room and held his head under the cold faucet. Antrim came up gasping and struggled feebly with his tormentor, but Brant thrust him down again and held him until he found speech and sanity wherewith to protest.

"For Heaven's sake, let up—you'll drown me!" gasped the victim, and Brant desisted.

"Got your grip again so it will stay?" he inquired grimly.

Antrim staggered back against the wall and groped for the towel which Brant handed him.

"I should hope so. What's the matter? What have you been doing to me?"

"Matter enough. Drop that towel and come over here." Brant was dragging him back to the desk. "Read that letter, quick, and tell me what to do, before somebody gets killed!" he commanded.

Antrim sank into the chair. "Great Scott! I feel as if I had been brayed in a mortar!" he groaned. Then he took up the letter and read it.

"Well?" said Brant impatiently. "Pull your wits together and tell me what I am to do—or is it too late to do anything?"

The chief clerk blinked at the clock and was evidently unable to see its dial. "Will you tell me what time it is?" he said. "I can't seem to see very well."

"It is ten minutes past nine."

"'Between nine and ten,' he said," muttered Antrim, quoting the misplaced message. Then to Brant: "Maybe there is time enough. Can you run a typewriter, Brant?"

"Yes—after a fashion."

"Then let me give you a letter. I couldn't write it with a pen to save my life."

Brant jerked the cover from the machine and thrust in a sheet of paper. "Go ahead."

Antrim handed him the unfinished letter.

"Just copy that, if you will, and I'll tell you what to add."

"But, man alive! have we got to sit here and fool with red tape when every minute may be worth a dozen lives?"

"It isn't so bad as all that," said Antrim soberly enough. "The train can't get past Lone Pine without orders for this division. But I'm a ruined man if Disbrow doesn't get that letter before Lone Pine calls him up. Don't you see?"

"No, I don't."

"Then I'll explain. The general manager is on that train, and he wired me this morning for regardless orders over this division. I answered that they would be given—and they haven't been. If there is a balk at Lone Pine, every operator on the line will know that some one has fallen down, and you can trust the general manager to find out who that some one is. And when he finds out, I'm done."

"I see," said Brant, and forthwith he turned and fell upon the typewriter. When he had written to the break in the unfinished letter, Antrim dictated:

"Will reach Lone Pine Junction between nine and ten this P. M., and you will arrange to give it right of way to Denver over all other trains."

Brant finished with a flourish and jerked the sheet out of the rolls. "Can you make out to sign it?" he asked.

"I guess so," responded the chief clerk, and he dipped his pen and made the supposition good, though with no little difficulty. "Now, if you will copy it in that book and tell me how I'm to get it to Disbrow at this late hour without giving myself away, we'll see what comes of it."

Brant took an impression of the letter, laying his plans meanwhile.

"Can't trust Disbrow, I suppose?" he asked.

"Yes; but he will hold it over me."

"Then we won't give him a chance. Let me have an envelope."

When the letter was inclosed and addressed, Brant told the chief clerk to sit still and wait for him. He was back in a few minutes, and Antrim had not to ask if his errand had been successful.

"How did you manage it?" he queried.

"Never you mind about that. I got two letters to-day in the train mail that didn't belong in our office."

"Oh. What did Disbrow say?"

"Nothing much. Swore a little on general principles, and said it was lucky I found it before the old man had time to raise Cain. It took me longer because I had to go and bake it over a gas jet; it was wet, you know."

Antrim swallowed a lump in his throat and pulled himself together to meet the demands of the occasion.

"Brant, you have played the Good Samaritan to-night, if you never did before. You have pulled me out of the deepest hole I ever got into."

"No, I haven't; but I am going to. Now tell me how the thing happened."

Antrim told the story of the day's miseries, concluding with the curious experience in the darkness.

"It's all plain enough but the miracle, and that is beyond me," he confessed. "Did I know what I was about? or was I beginning to 'see things'?"

"A little of both, I guess," said Brant, and as he spoke the key of the incandescent lamp snapped and left them in the darkness. Brant laughed and got up to turn it on again.

"That is doubtless the snap you heard, and it accounts for the blindness. As for the rest, your brain was simply making another hunt for the missing clew. Does that satisfy you?"

"It will have to, I guess."

"Well, then, it is my turn. I want to know why you have been making a bally idiot of yourself for the last week or so."

Antrim hung his head. "Because I haven't any better sense, I suppose."

"That doesn't go. Give me the facts."

"There is only one to give: Isabel won't marry me."

"Oh, she won't? And so you are going to make a howling wilderness of yourself because a young woman doesn't happen to know her own mind. Is that it?"

"But she does know her own mind," Antrim protested.

"Oh, nonsense! You are no boy, and you ought to know better. If you love her—and I take that for granted—all you have to do is just to hang on and wait; and that is what you are going to do, if I can make you."

Antrim smiled wearily. "The way I feel at this present moment, anybody could make me do anything. I am as weak as a cat, and as sore as if I had been through a prize fight.—What on earth is that?"

"That" was a furious pounding on a near-by door, and Brant sprang up, oversetting his chair in his haste.

"It's Jarvis—that's what it is!" he exclaimed. "Blest if I didn't forget all about him! Sit in the dark a minute, will you?" and he turned off the light and went to liberate the captive.

"Nice fellow, you are!" began Jarvis wrathfully when the door was opened. "Lock a man up while you go off and go to sleep——"

Brant broke in with an apology which ran smoothly and without a break until he had walked the reporter down the stair and out into the street. Then he gave Jarvis the required information about the president's special, and hastened back to Antrim to explain the interruption.

"You see, I had to do something with him," he concluded. "He is a good fellow, but he talks too much, and the less said about this business of yours the better."

"I should say so," agreed Antrim ruefully, adding, "but it's no use; the whole town must know about it by this time. I haven't been at it very long, but I haven't been hiding my light under a bushel."

"Oh, I don't know about the publicity. A man doesn't fill the public eye quite as much as he is apt to think. Besides, you have made your last appearance in the idiotic rôle. Beginning right now, you are going to break it short off and be yourself again. When did you eat last?"

"Supper, last night."

"Humph! I thought as much. No wonder you had wheels in your head! Let me help you into your overcoat, and we'll go up to Elitch's."

"I don't believe I could eat anything, if it was to save my life," objected Antrim, rising laboriously.

"Yes, you can—you have got to; and then you are going to let me take you home and put you to bed; and if we hear of any more foolishness, you will come in for a manhauling that you won't get over for a week."

Antrim reached backward for the sleeves of the overcoat and groaned piteously.

"Great Moses! I feel as if I'd had that already. What the mischief do you suppose makes me so stiff and sore?"

Brant's laugh lacked sympathy. "It is one of the after-effects, I fancy; look out you don't bring it on again." And he tucked Antrim's arm under his own and led him uptown, carrying out his programme to the letter, and playing his new rôle of bearwarden until he had seen his charge safe in bed.

When he reached his own room he found the packet of papers still in his pocket and tossed it carelessly across to the table. Then he thought better of it, and put the envelope back in his pocket.

"It is climbing into the plane of responsibilities, and my conscience isn't clean enough yet to handle it," he mused. "Just now I feel as if I should like to burn the stuff and give the beggar a chance for his life; and yet I suppose there are plenty of purists who would say that I am an accessory in the murder of Henry Brinton for not giving his murderer up to justice. I wonder what *she* would say about it? If I knew, that is what I should do." He stretched his arms and yawned sleepily. "Heigho! it's a queer old round world, from any point of view; but since the morning and the evening of this blessed day, I'm rather glad to be in it."

With which altruistic reflection he went to bed to dream that he was about to be hanged for the murder of one Henry Brinton.

CHAPTER XXII
HOW THE SMOKING FLAX WAS QUENCHED

A WISER than any here has said that as a man lieth down, so riseth he up; and inasmuch as a good deed had rounded out the Tuesday which was to be held worthy of anniversaries, it was Brant the brother-keeper who thrust his head into Antrim's room on the Wednesday morning what time the convalescent was dressing.

"Peace to your ashes, Henry, my son! How do you pan out by this time?"

"Better, thank you; only I'm black and blue in spots and too sore to talk about. Say, do you know, I think I must have been in a fight last night! But I don't remember the first thing about it."

Brant grinned. "I had been aching to get a chance at you, and it came in my way last night—trying to make you come alive to your responsibilities, you know. Never gave anybody such a jolly good beating in all my life. Shall I come in and shake you into your raiment?"

"Oh, no, thank you; I'll be down directly. Wait for me, if you are not in too much of a hurry. I'll eat with you."

Brant waited, and after breakfast they walked down town together. It was a tonic autumn morning, with a crisp clean wind blowing fresh from the snow-capped peaks, and a marvellous clarity in the atmosphere that seemed to bring the nearer foothills within easy speaking distance. On such a morning it was good to be alive, and Brant said something to that effect—an assertion to which Antrim gave conditional assent.

"Yes, if a fellow's head could be as clear and bright as the morning and the atmosphere."

"A fellow shouldn't roil his brains with muddy fire water, then."

"No; but I didn't mean just that. That is only a consequence."

"A very unnecessary consequence in your case. You know you haven't a peg of an excuse to hang your villainy on, Harry."

"I suppose I haven't, when you get down to the marrow of the thing. A man never has a water-tight excuse for making several kinds of a donkey of himself. But I'd like to be allowed to say that it was the worst facer I have ever had. You see, I had been banking on a certain kind of happiness ever since Isabel and I used to go to school together; and then to have to give it up—well, it just knocked me out, that's all."

"But you are not going to stay knocked out, and you are not going to give it up—unless you are a donkey sober as well as a donkey drunk."

"Oh, no; I've had my little fling, and I paid the piper's bill last night. That settles the bottle imp. But as to the other, you don't know Isabel."

"Of course; no one but your own sapient self could know her. How long is it since you have seen her?"

"A week."

"No longer than that? Suffering humanity! You didn't lose any time on the way down, did you? Are you far enough out to transplant a few little cuttings of advice?"

Antrim nodded, and then qualified the nod. "I guess so; anyway, you have earned the right to tell me what I ought to do."

"*Bueno*; and this is what you are to do: Go over to Hollywood this evening, just as if nothing had happened. Keep your wits about you, and see if Isabel isn't quite as glad to see you as you are to see her."

But Antrim's mood was not optimistic. "I know; that is the way it looks to you. But, you see, I have known her all her life, and———"

"And therefore you think you know it all. But you don't. I have seen a good bit of the Langfords in the last few weeks, and if you haven't a mortgage on the future of the younger daughter, no one else has."

Now it is one of the peculiarities of jealousy that it will come alive again and again long after there is reason to believe that it has been effectually killed. Antrim stole a swift side glance at his mentor, and there was a fine-lined frown between his level brows.

"I wish I were as sure of that as you seem to be."

Brant looked up quickly. "Now, what fresh idiocy is this? You know well enough that however little she may seem to care for you, she doesn't care anything for any one else."

"Do I?"

"If you don't, you are a greater donkey than I thought you were."

"Well, let that pass. But if another man hasn't the inside track, art has."

"Oh, art be hanged! Once in a thousand years or so you may find a girl who is an artist first and a woman afterward, but you haven't run up against the exception. If you will bear with me, I'll dare say that Isabel is the merest *dilettante*; she can't paint a little bit."

"She can't, eh? That is all you know about it!" Antrim retorted hotly. "What the dickens do you know about art, anyway?"

Brant chuckled joyously. "Nothing, my son—less than nothing. I did but skewer you to see if you were really jealous of Miss Isabel's poor little passion. Go in and win, Harry, my boy; and may your house be decorated in many colours, as it is pretty sure to be."

In such heartening manner began a day fraught with many happenings. Brant completed the map in good time for the purposes of the general manager, and it was scarcely off the drawing-board when Colonel Bowran returned, summoned by wire to meet the other officials of the railway company. And since the colonel brought the Grotter notebook with plentiful data for more map work, the chance of enforced idleness, which Brant dreaded more than anything else, was pushed forward into an indefinite future.

Moreover, the chief was well pleased with the work done on the yard map, and was gratified to be assured that he had at last found an office man who could go ahead on his own responsibility. So there was hearty approval and commendation for the draughtsman; and what with this, and the blessings which belong rightfully to those of the helping hand, Brant won through the day on the crest of the wave.

But the purely personal point of view, pitched as it may be upon any hilltop of present satisfaction, is necessarily restricted; and beyond the ken of the satisfied one other things were happening which were to bear heavily upon his future.

For one, the train speeding down the cañon on the day run from the region of mining camps was bringing Hobart and his wife to Denver. For another, Antrim's purposed visit to Hollywood was postponed by order of the general manager. The party in the private car Aberystwyth was to go out on a tour of inspection, and, in the absence of his superior, Antrim was required to do the honours of the Western Division. Again, late in the afternoon Mrs. Langford wrote a letter which she put into the post office with her own hands. This was the third happening, and the fourth was still more portentous. At the moment when Mrs. Langford was mailing her letter, two men met behind a locked door in a West Denver lodging house to lay the train of a mine in which the explosives were already stored.

In this conference behind the locked door there was a slight disagreement arising in a very natural reluctance on the part of one of the plotters to play the cat's-paw for the other.

"Coming right down to brass tacks, Jim Harding, I don't see why I want to monkey with your end of the game, anyhow," said the cat's-paw. "All I need is to get even with him for knocking me out, and I can do that the first time I get the drop on him, 'thout mixin' up any in your deal."

"Yes, and you can get yourself choked with a rope for doing it," added Harding. "Now, on the other hand, if my scheme works—and it will work if you will do your part—the sheriff will do the evening-up business for you, and you can sit back and read all about it in the newspapers the next morning."

"Yes, 'if'; but that there 'if' is bigger than Pike's Peak. You seem to think if you can get hold o' them dockyments he's got, you can change a few words in 'em and make out that Plucky George is the man they want—chuck him plumb into your shoes. Maybe you can; but there's a heap o' holes in a skimmer. Seems like you've lived long enough to know that."

"That is all right; I know what I am doing," was the confident assertion. "As it stands now, it is between me and Brant. It was an all-around free fight, and he was mixed up in it, too. Once let me get hold of those papers, and he will have his hands full to prove that *he* didn't kill Hank Brinton."

"I don't savez it that way; but that part of it is your funeral—not mine. What is it you want me to do? Measure it off."

"You know; I want you to get the papers."

"Why don't you do it yourself?"

"It's out of my line. I don't happen to have been over the road for house-breaking—as you have—and I am not up in that branch of the business."

Gasset scowled and gritted out an oath at this, but finally asked, "Well—when?"

"The quicker, the sooner; the first night we can be sure he isn't in his room."

"Reckon he keeps the papers in his room?"

"Surely. Where else would they be?"

"I don't know. But it appears like if it was me, I'd lock 'em up somewheres where they'd be safe."

"He might, if he thought anybody was trying to lift them. But he doesn't suspect anything of the kind. He doesn't even know I'm in Denver."

"All right; it's a go. I'll swipe the papers for you if I can find 'em, and after that you fork over, and we're quits. I tell you right now, though, I'd a heap rather play it alone."

"Do what you please after you get the papers. When you hand them over to me, it's a cool hundred in your clothes. After that, if you would rather take the chance of dancing on nothing instead of letting him do it, why, go ahead. You may kill him and welcome, so far as I am concerned."

"Oh, yes; you're all right. You've got everything to gain, and nothing much to lose, as near as I can make out. But let her go. Better try it to-night?"

"One time is as good as another, if he will stay out late enough to give you a chance."

"Enough said. Let's go and have a drink on it."

"Not too many drinks, Ike, if you want to earn your money. Keep your head clear till this job is done, and then you can fill your skin to the queen's taste, if you feel like it."

They went out together, and Harding locked the door. In a neighbouring barroom, while they were drinking to the success of the plot, the cat's-paw asked one other question:

"How are we going to find out if the coast's clear? Had you thought o' that?"

"Yes; we'll shadow him from the time he leaves his office and see where he goes," was the reply. "And it is about time to begin that right now. Come on."

Thus the varying lines of events converged upon the unsuspecting one, who a little later cleaned his pens and put away his drawing instruments in deference to the failing daylight. It had been a comfortable day, and, contrary to his habit, which was abstemious even on the tobacco side, he lighted a cigar to smoke on the way up to supper. While he was putting on his coat a footstep echoed in the empty corridor. It was the postman making his final round. The letter slide in the door clicked, and a square envelope fell to the floor. Brant picked it up, read his own name in the superscription, and went to the window to save the trouble of lighting the gas.

The daylight was nearly gone, but there was enough of it to enable him to pick out his correspondent's message from the tangle of fashionable angles and heavy downstrokes. Also there was light enough to show forth the change from disinterest to astoundment, and from astoundment to dull rage and desperation that crept into his face as he read.

"In view of his clandestine meeting with Miss Langford yesterday," said the writer, "Mr. Brant will not be unprepared for such interference as Miss Langford's natural guardian is constrained to make. Up to the present time the writer of this has refrained from discussing, even in the family circle, a subject which is as repugnant to her as it must prove humiliating to Mr. Brant; but if Mr. Brant does not find it convenient to relieve her of further disquietude in the matter by leaving Denver at once, it will become her unpleasant duty to take her daughters into her confidence—a duty which she sincerely hopes Mr. Brant will not make obligatory."

There was no signature, and none was needed. Brant read the letter through twice, and then tore it slowly into tiny fragments, opening the window to brush the bits of paper out into the twilight, and watching them as they disappeared like circling snowflakes. Suddenly his clenched hands went up and he swore a mighty oath, and in that oath was a recantation of all the good resolves which had been writing themselves down throughout the day of comfort.

The outburst of cursings seemed to steady him, as the earthquake subsides when the volcano finds vent. He closed the window carefully and fastened it, and then went to spread the dust-cloth over his work on the drawing-board, folding it smoothly down at the corners, as one might drape the pall over the corpse of a thing dead. Some thought of the simile must have suggested itself, since he broke out in bitter speech:

"That is precisely what I am doing; it is a pall, and it covers the corpse of my little nursling of decency. God help me! Two hours ago—two minutes ago, I thought I had a chance for my life; and now it is all done and over with, and I am banished like an unclean thing. I'll go. She knew I'd go when she thonged that whip for me. I'll go to my own place."

Thereupon one may conceive that all the good in him would rise up and plead strenuously for a little respite, for a few hours of sober second thought in which the soul-destroying possibilities of such a relapse might be weighed and measured; but to such a plea such a man must needs harden his heart and drive out the better prompting with muttered curses, as thus: "No, by God! I have listened to that song for the last time! From now on there is nothing to do but to forget, if I can. And I shall forget, I will forget, if I have to smother myself in the reek of the bottomless pit to do it!"

As he passed the colonel's desk on his way to the door his hand sought the train mail box mechanically and from force of habit. There were two letters in the box, letters written by the chief engineer before going out with the party in the private car, and Brant slipped them into his pocket, excusing himself to himself for letting the bit of routine obtrude itself into the presence chamber of desperate resolves. "I'll take them down and put them on the train. It is my last day of honest work, and I'll round it out fairly."

The masthead electric lamps over the platform at the Union Depot lighted the customary train-time pandemonium when he passed through the archway and made one in the jostling crowd under the arc lamps. It was before the day of gates and gate keepers, and the unquiet throng filled the open space opposite the archway. From the open space as a fountain head little rivulets of humanity filtered away to trickle up and down between the trains headed in either direction.

A symphony of sound, pitched in the key of preparation, rose upon the still air of the outer night. The hum of human voices; the rumblings of the baggage trucks piled mountain-high with outgoing luggage; the monotonous "Look out!" of the baggagemen as they steered the rumbling mountains slowly through the throng; the measured beat of the air-brake pumps on the waiting engines, drowned at irregular intervals by a cacophonous blast from some overloaded safety valve—these contributed to a din which was rather harmonious than discordant.

But if the savage scowl of him told the truth, Brant was in no mood to find harmony in anything—to find it or to contribute to it. Having mailed the two letters in the baggage car, he pushed his way aggressively through the narrow space between the trains, intent only upon getting free of the crowd. At the steps of the Pullman he jostled one man so rudely that the victim turned in pardonable heat. It was Hobart; and when he recognised the offender resentment gave place to gladness.

"Why, George! By all that's good, this is lucky! I had given up all hope of seeing you on this trip."

Brant shook hands as if it were a thing which could not be avoided, and his greeting was anything but cordial. "How are you?" he said; and then, reverting to the hope, "I guess it wasn't very hard to give up; I haven't been hard to find."

"Perhaps not, but I managed to miss you all around; drove first to your boarding house, and have just come down from your office. I have been in town only an hour and a half, all told, and a good bit of that was used up in taking Kate over to Judge Langford's. But never mind about that; luck is with us for a minute or two. How are you getting along? and why don't you write once in a while?"

Brant ignored the friendly questions, and went back of them to the statement of fact.

"Do you know the Langfords?" he asked.

"Why, yes; didn't I tell you? I meant to send you a note of introduction to them. The judge is one of the stockholders in our mine—the vice-president, in fact."

"And you say Mrs. Hobart is at Hollywood?"

"Yes; I brought her down on a visit. Too much altitude for her on Jack Mountain. But tell me about yourself. How has the world been using you?"

"As well as I deserve, I suppose," answered Brant shortly—so shortly that Hobart knew not what to make of it. Then the conductor's cry of "All aboard!" warned him that he had but a moment more, and he took a card from his case and scribbled a line on the back of it.

"Take this and call upon them—only you won't need it if you will make yourself known to Kate. Sixteen, Altamont Terrace, is the number; but if you know Hollywood, you know the place. They are good people to know, and Kate will put you on an old friend's footing from the start." Hobart tossed his handbag up to the porter and turned back for a last word. "Now don't put it off; go soon—this evening, if you have time." And seeing that Brant stood as one indeterminate, he bent to whisper: "Kate knows nothing but good of you, if that makes any difference."

Now in the face of all this kindly interest none but a churl could withhold the decent meed of gratitude. Brant did not withhold it, but if the light had been better Hobart must have seen that the thanks were little more than perfunctory—or, at least, less than hearty. Then the wheels began to turn, and there was time only for a hasty leave-taking; this also without heartiness on the part of the one who was not going. He stood scowling after the receding train until the two red eyes of the tail lights disappeared around a curve; then he turned and walked slowly uptown, with his hands deep in his overcoat pockets and his eyes on the sidewalk. There was little comfort to be got out of the late incident on the station platform. To be sure, it proved that Hobart was still stanch, and that he had not received the letter which was a cry for help. But Mrs. Hobart's presence at Hollywood could only complicate matters.

What was in Brant's mind as he tramped up the street was not readable in the face of him, but just before he turned out of the shop-lined thoroughfare he strode into a drug store and called for a pint of brandy. He had the bottle in his pocket when he reached his room, and when he had locked the door he stripped off his coat, found a glass, and poured himself a drink vast enough to drown a very amphibian trouble. At the moment of pouring the gas burned blue and sank to a pin point, as poor gas will, and the sheen from the arc light in the street set the liquor afire in the glass. The illusion was strong enough to draw him to the window, where he stood holding the glass to the light and watching the play of the electric beam in the brown liquid. In the act the gas burned brightly again, and two men who had been watching the house from the opposite sidewalk darted into the blue-black shadows of the curbstone cottonwoods.

Brant put the liquor down untasted, and waited long and patiently for the two figures to reappear beyond the cottonwoods. When it became apparent that the blue-black shadows were still concealing them, he turned out the gas and went back to the window to look again. This time his patience was rewarded by a glimpse of the two men; and when he had made sure of their identity, he drew up a chair and sat at the window to await further developments, with the big revolver laid across his knees.

And it was thus, sitting in his shirt sleeves, with his hand on the big revolver, that the morning sun shining broadly in at the casement found and aroused him; aroused him with a start for which there was no apparent call, since the room and its belongings were undisturbed, even to the uncorked brandy bottle on the dressing case, and the untasted half glassful on the window seat.

It was characteristic of the man that when he came out of his bath a half hour later, breathing the fragrance of cleanliness, he should pour the untasted drink back into the bottle, corking it therein against a time not of greater need, but of less responsibility. For he remembered that Colonel Bowran was again out of town, and until his chief returned he could by no means have his quittance from the claims of duty—or of decency.

CHAPTER XXIII
HOW DOROTHY BLEW THE EMBERS ALIVE

THE railway inspection party of which the chief engineer was a member did not return to Denver until late in the afternoon, and by consequence Brant wore out the day like a caged wild beast, tramping miles on end up and down the long apartment which served as a workroom in the chief engineer's suite. Not once during the lagging hours did he uncover the drawing-board; but on the other hand, if he did not work, neither did he put himself in the way of temptation, spirituous or other. It was as if he had promised himself that he would quit clean-handed and clear-headed; that, until the colonel should release him, he would remain, as nearly as might be, the man whom the colonel had befriended.

The day was drawing to its close when the burly little man who was partial to college graduates bustled in and struggled out of his greatcoat. Brant assaulted promptly, saying what had to be said in terms of the simplest. He had made up his mind to leave Denver at once, and he would be glad if the colonel would give him his quittance and let him go.

The struggle with the greatcoat paused in the midst, and the burly one, who knew a capable man when he found him, protested vigorously:

"What's that? Leave me just when I am beginning to know what a comfort it is to have you about? What's gone wrong with you? Is it too much work, or not enough pay?"

"It is neither; it is nothing that you have done, or failed to do, my dear colonel. On the contrary, your kindness will be one of the things that I shall always be glad to remember. But I have never been able to stay long in any one place, and the time has come for me to move on."

"But surely, my dear boy, you haven't taken time to think about it! Why, it was only yesterday that you seemed perfectly contented."

"I know; but I have been thinking about it for a week or more. I am afraid I can't reconsider."

"Well, well, I'm sorry; only that doesn't half express it. I hope you haven't to go right away. You can stay on a few days till I can look around a bit, can't you?"

"I am sorry to have to say that I can't do even that," Brant began, and just here the entrance of the postman interrupted the colloquy. There were letters—several for the colonel and one for the draughtsman. Brant opened and read his, while the chief engineer hastily glanced through the others. Brant's was a dainty note, and it appeared to move him strangely. His cheek flushed under the bronze, and his eyes kindled as he read; and when the talk was presently renewed he promptly stultified himself.

"You were asking if I could stay on until you had found some one else," he said. "On second thought, I don't know but I can, if it will be an accommodation to you."

The colonel was too well pleased with the sudden change of front to show his surprise, though he could not help putting two and two together and wondering who was the writer of the dainty note which had evidently countermanded Brant's marching orders.

"Of course it will be an accommodation," he hastened to say. "I shall have to go back to the Extension to-night to figure on Hurlcrow's estimates for next month, but I'll come in as soon as I can, and then, if you are of the same mind, I'll look around for some one to relieve you. But I hope you will find it possible to reconsider. I like you, and your work is as thorough and accurate as I knew it would be when you told me you were coached by my old friend Thirlwill."

Brant did not commit himself, and the colonel tossed the lately opened letters into his desk and drew down the roll-top. "I shall be with the general manager and the president in the Aberystwyth till train time, and to-morrow you can reach me at the front," he went on. "Take things a bit easy while I am gone, and see if you can't make up your mind to stay with us."

Being just then devoured with an impatience in comparison with which the restlessness of the long day was but a sedative, Brant did not seek to prolong the interview; and when he was once more alone he read and reread his letter until he could repeat it word for word. It was from Dorothy; and she had kept her promise to call upon him in the time of need. She wrote:

"DEAR MR. BRANT: You were kind enough to offer to help us again if the occasion should arise. It *has* arisen. Will left home yesterday afternoon, and we have not seen him since. Mamma is wild with anxiety, and my father is so greatly discouraged that he will do nothing. Won't you please try to find my brother again?

"P.S. Mrs. Hobart, whose husband is a friend of yours, is with us, and she will be glad to see you when you find it convenient to come."

When he had quite committed the note to memory Brant set about answering it. Whatever else he was or might become—and under the sentence of ostracism this question seemed settled beyond peradventure of doubt—he was none the less Dorothy's loyal liegeman, and while he could serve her, the future, good, bad, or indifferent, might wait for its due. Therefore, after a half dozen false starts, he wrote:

"MY DEAR MISS LANGFORD:

"Your note, which makes me both sorry and glad, has just found me. Be assured that, while I grieve with you in your present trouble, I am only too happy to place myself at your service. Be of good cheer. I trust we shall speedily find your brother, and that nothing serious has befallen him. If he should not come home to-night, send me a line in the morning; and believe me, now as always,

"Your sincere friend,
"GEORGE BRANT."

He read it over when it was written, and made as if he would tear it up. Certainly it was anything but loverlike in its measured coolness and conventional formality. He laid it aside and tried again:

"MY LOVED ONE:

"May I write as I should if Mr. Crosswell had not come in upon us the day before yesterday? If I may—if your own heart says I may—I shall not need to tell you how glad your note makes me; what a joy it is to have you turn to me in any time of need. Be very sure, my dear one, that I shall run to do your bidding. There will be difficulties in the way this time—difficulties which did not exist before. An old enemy of mine has prejudiced your brother against me. But if the obstacles were ten times as many I should overcome them for your dear sake.

"Your note found me when I was in the depths of despair, and while it has comforted me by giving me something to do for you, the future is still very dark, and I know not what it holds for me. But this I do know: that if your love may shine for me as a light in great darkness, I shall have strength to keep from turning back; nay, courage and strength to go forward, if only you will stand at the end of the snare-beset way and beckon me.

"Let me have a line from you again in the morning if William has not returned.

"Faithfully and lovingly——"

He paused at the signature, and read and reread the two replies. And, after all, it was the formal note that a district messenger was presently bearing awheel to the transplanted Southern mansion in the Highlands, and the love letter lay torn into tiny fragments in Colonel Bowran's wastebasket.

The answer to Dorothy's note despatched, Brant began to cast about for ways and means to the end she besought. As he had intimated in the letter which was not sent, there were difficulties. Harding had doubtless sown the seed of prejudice and ill will, harrowing it well in; in which case young Langford, when found, would have nothing to do with the man against whom he had been warned. Brant gave the difficulty a thoughtful half hour, at the end of which he sought Antrim. The chief clerk was just closing his office to go to supper, and he was glad enough to have company.

"What are you going to do with yourself to-night, Harry?" Brant asked, when they were free of the downtown six-o'clock sidewalk throngs.

"I am just in from the inspection trip, and I meant to go back to the office and work a while. Why?"

"I want you to do something for me, if you will."

"After what you did for me last night, you have only to ask," was the grateful rejoinder. "State your case."

Brant stated it at some length, omitting none of the details save those which might have defined his own motive in playing the knight-errant.

"I think I know where to look for the boy," he said in conclusion; "but I am more than afraid that any argument that I could bring to bear on him would be so much wasted eloquence. I want you to go along, and when we find him it will be your part of the job to persuade him to go home."

"He hasn't much use for me, as I have told you," Antrim objected. "But I'll go along and do what I can. It's a great pity the judge doesn't set him to work at something."

"What is his bent? or has he any?" asked Brant.

"I don't know that he has any now. At school he was the best mathematician in his class; and there was a time when he wanted to learn your trade. Mrs. Langford was quite willing until it came to field work, and then she put her foot down. Her Willie was not to go careering around all over the world with a lot of rough engineers, she said."

"Oh, no; of course not," assented Brant, not without scorn. "She was quite right; we are a hard lot."

The emphasis was so bitter that Antrim glanced up in surprise. "Has she been giving you a lecture on the subject?" he asked quizzically.

"Who—Mrs. Langford? Certainly not," denied Brant, hedging promptly. "She has never mentioned my present occupation to me."

"She will, some day; especially if—" But Antrim was not sure of his ground in the matter of Brant's leanings, and he broke off abruptly to go back to the former question. "I suppose you will want to start out right after supper?"

"Yes," said Brant, and they went into the house and entered Mrs. Seeley's dining room together.

After the meal, which was hurried in deference to the urgencies, Brant went up to his room to prepare for the quest. While there he appeared to be drawn into a struggle which, in view of all the wicked things he had sworn to do, was scarcely less than trivial. It manifested itself in sundry takings up and layings down of the big revolver, ending when he finally put the weapon, together with the unbroached bottle of brandy, into the drawer of his dressing case.

"No, I'll be hanged if I do!" he muttered. "I'll not go armed like a desperado on any errand of hers. If I find the boy with Harding, there will probably be a row; but while I am about her business I'd rather suffer violence than do it." Whereupon he ran down to Antrim, and together they set out on the quest for William Langford.

Contrary to his expressed assumption, the first half of the undertaking proved more difficult than Brant had expected. Beginning with resorts of the Draco type, they went from bad to worse, working their way downward through the substrata of vice until Antrim held his breath and hoped for William's younger sister's sake that the search would be unsuccessful in that direction. And so, indeed, it proved to be, though Brant was indefatigable, dragging his companion from dive to den as he had once dragged Forsyth, until the chief clerk was half intoxicated with the mingled fumes of tobacco and opium and alcohol—half intoxicated and wholly disgusted.

"Good Lord! and this is what I was coming to!" he gasped, as they emerged from a particularly noisome kennel. "Let's give it up, old man, and go home. I'm sick and nauseated."

"Not yet," Brant objected. "We are sure to find him, sooner or later; and it is early yet."

Antrim looked at his watch. "Eleven o'clock. I call that late. But go on; I'll stay with you."

Eleven it was, and the policeman, whose beat included the quiet neighbourhood of which Mrs. Anna Seeley's select boarding house for young men was the centre, had finished his round and had dropped into the nearest uptown saloon for a bite of bread and cheese and such other refreshment as the bartender was wont to set unasked before the guardians of the city's peace.

"You have a picnic on the uptown beat, don't you, Sam?" said the licensed dispenser of stimulants, drawing a second glass of beer for the officer.

"Pretty near that. Might jog around up here all night and never see nothing out of the way," responded the civic soldier, helping himself to another sandwich. This he said, and yet, not ten minutes before, he had met a man carrying a ladder in a quiet street within an hour of midnight, and had not thought the matter curious enough to warrant looking into.

But if the officer had been unmoved, the man with the ladder had not. On the contrary, he was greatly disturbed, and was deterred from casting down his burden and taking to his heels only by the fear that a bullet from the civic soldier's pistol might outrun him. When the danger was overpast, he rested the ladder against the fence and took a long pull from a flat pocket bottle.

"Whooh!" he growled, stopping to take breath, and glancing up at the darkened windows of the Seeley house. "I'll just about get my blooming leg pulled for twenty years before I get through with this deal! Run right smack against that cop, when I'd been dodging him for a half hour and better!"

The flat bottle gurgled again, and then the ladder was lifted and dropped quietly over the fence, to be reared presently behind a tangle of evergreen vines at the end of the veranda. A minute later the man appeared at the top and made his way cautiously over the tin roof, which bulged and crackled under his weight until the sweat of fear made him damp and uncomfortable. He paused before Brant's window, and, inserting a thin-edged bit of steel beneath the sash, tried it gently.

"Fastened, of course," he muttered, and a knife blade was slipped deftly between the upper and lower sash. There was a muffled click, and then the window opened noiselessly. Once safely inside, the burglar's first care was to close the window and to draw the curtains. Then he lighted a dark lantern and flashed its beam around the room.

"So far, so good," was his comment. "Camp cached, and nobody at home. Now for them dockyments."

He took another pull at the flat bottle as a preliminary, and then proceeded to ransack the apartment with the skilful rapidity of one to whom the craft was not new. The belongings of a man's room are soon overhauled. Brant's impedimenta were of the lightest, and in a short time the burglar came to the end of his quest without finding anything more to the purpose than a large revolver and a bottle of brandy. Laying the weapon aside, he unstoppered the bottle and sampled its contents.

"Brandy—ten-year-old cognac, as I'm a sinner!" He held the bottle up and flashed the beam of the lantern on it. Then he gave a toast. "Here's to you, Mister Snap-shot Brant; and may you live happy and die suddint—when I git the drop on you!"

The liquor paid the penalty of the toast at a frightful cost, and the burglar smacked his lips and wiped them on the sleeve of his coat.

"Blast him! he knows what good liquor is," he remarked. "I'll say that much for him, anyway. Now, then, I'll have a squint among his clothes."

He dived into the closet and came out with an armful of clothing, and when the pockets yielded nothing he broke out in a monologue of thick-tongued malediction, and again had recourse to the brandy bottle. After a deeper potation than any of the preceding he did that which was afterward to prove his undoing. He drew up Brant's easy-chair and sat down to curse his ill luck.

The process was a long one, and it was eked out by many more tiltings of the bottle. When it was wrought out to its conclusion the bottle was empty, but the man was not. Some glimmerings of sanity remained, but they pointed only to his bafflement, and not to the necessity for escape. When he staggered to his feet it was to determine what spoil, lacking the papers, would best repay his hazard.

So he fell to rummaging again, and after much dubitation decided to carry off the easy-chair as the thing most greatly to be desired. Failing to get the chair through the opened window, he compromised upon a suit of clothes; and after trying vainly to roll them into a portable bundle, he cut that Gordian knot by struggling out of his own garments, kicking them into the depths of the closet, and arraying himself in the suit of black.

That done—it took so long that the china clock on the mantel was tinkling out the midnight hour—he put the big revolver in his pocket and sat down on the edge of the bed to gather himself for the passage perilous over the crackling tin roof of the veranda and down the ladder. But in the midst of the gathering the foolishness of those who tarry long at the wine came upon him, and the bed transformed itself into his bunk in the West Denver *Gasthaus*. That being the case, there was no occasion for further efforts, perilous or other. He tried to remember how he had got out of the house of peril; how it was that he came to be sitting on the edge of his bunk in safety; but in the thick of it sleep laid its heavy hand on him, and when the china clock on the mantel chimed the quarter past twelve the man who had tarried too long was snoring brazenly with his head on Brant's pillow.

CHAPTER XXIV
"WHOSO DIGGETH A PIT SHALL FALL THEREIN"

IT was between two and three o'clock in the morning before Brant would consent, at Antrim's solicitation, to give over, or at least to postpone, the search for William Langford. The midnight wanderings in the realm of Abaddon were a wholesome corrective for the chief clerk, whose late aberration lay heavy on his self-respect; but, as he himself phrased it to Brant, he knew when he had enough. One of the results of this glimpse into the deeper depths of the pit he had so narrowly escaped was a fresh stirring of the pool of gratitude, and at the home-going he sought to put his debt to Brant into fitting terms of speech. But Brant cut him off with curt brutality:

"Let up on that. You don't owe me anything."

"Yes, I do," insisted the grateful one.

"I say you don't. But if you choose to think so, you can even things up by doing your part when we find this addle-brained boy."

"Oh, I'd do that anyway, and without charging it to your account. He is Isabel's brother."

"Yes—and Dorothy's." The last two words said themselves, and it is conceivable that Brant would have bitten his tongue before letting that unruly member betray his secret. But Antrim's quick apprehension and ready sympathy were answerable.

"I thought maybe she was the power behind the throne," said the chief clerk, linking his arm in that of his companion. "You know my story, George; won't you tell me yours?"

"There is nothing to tell," said Brant shortly; and then, after an interval in which one might cuff ill humour into subjection: "That is to say, not anything out of the ordinary. I think a great deal of Miss Langford—I suppose you guessed that much long ago; but there is nothing between us—of the sort you have in mind, I mean. And there never will be. When I shall have found her brother I shall go away and probably never see her again."

"Go away?" echoed Antrim. "I thought you had given up that idea. Why are you going away?"

They had reached the house, and Brant turned on the doorstep to put his hands on Antrim's shoulders.

"Don't ask me, Harry," he said gently. "Passing your own words back to you, it is a thing I can't talk about, even to you. You will know all about it some day, perhaps, and then you will understand—if you don't go over to the enemy, horse, foot, and artillery, with the rest of them."

Antrim laughed. "I'm not much on making rash promises, and talk is pretty cheap; but when that day comes you will have a friend who will stay with you if you haven't another on the face of the earth."

"Don't commit yourself blindfold," warned Brant, fitting his key to the nightlatch. "The chances are that you will be ashamed to admit that you have ever known me."

They climbed the stair quietly, so as not to disturb the house, and Antrim entered his room and closed the door. While he was lighting the gas there was a tap on the panel and Brant came in.

"Will you give me a shakedown on your lounge till morning?" he asked. "Mrs. Seeley evidently thought I was going to make a night of it, and she has put some one into my room."

Antrim made haste to be hospitable, but he looked mystified.

"Surely. But I don't understand that a little bit. It isn't at all like Mrs. Seeley."

"No; it is rather odd."

"I should say so. Are you sure there is somebody there?"

"On the evidence of two separate senses. I struck a match and saw a man in my bed; and besides that—listen." The subdued murmur of the intruder's snoring was quite audible, and Brant went on: "Moreover, to add to the oddness of it, the man has been drinking. The room reeks like a pothouse."

"Well, that is queer," mused Antrim; and then: "Maybe it is one of the boys gone wrong and couldn't find his room. But in that case I can't imagine who it could be."

"Nor I," rejoined Brant, stretching himself wearily on the lounge. "Never mind; we'll find out all about it in the morning."

So he said, and fell asleep; but the morning event discredited the confident assertion. When they went down together to a late breakfast and mentioned the matter to Mrs. Seeley, the good lady was quite as astonished as her lodgers had been. Moreover, she was touched in a tender part, and her inn-keeping pride resented the imputation put upon it by Brant's suggestion.

"Put any one in your room? Why, Mr. Brant! to think you would suspect me of doing such a thing! Why, never in all my born days did I——"

A chattering shriek from the upper regions cut the protest in half, and the three occupants of the dining room rushed into the hall in good time to meet the housemaid flying down, the stair, wild-eyed and incoherent.

"A man—a man in Misther Brant's room!" was all she could say, and, at the word, Brant and the chief clerk darted up to the second floor three steps at a bound. Arrived on the scene of the mystery, they found an empty room smelling strongly of brandy, an open window, and a little heap of Brant's clothing in the middle of the floor. Antrim made a dash for the window, and was out upon the tin roof of the veranda in a twinkling. When he climbed back into the room there was the light of discovery in his eye.

"There is a ladder standing against the end of the porch. That is how he got away."

"Yes; and it is how he came," said Brant. "He was a—" He stopped abruptly and clapped his hand upon his pocket. There was only one thing among his belongings that any one would risk life or liberty to obtain, and that thing was safe. He drew out the packet of papers and gave it to the chief clerk.

"He was a burglar," he said, finishing his sentence, "and he made the mistake of taking a drop too much."

Antrim was turning the packet over and reading the superscription: "To be opened at my death. George Brant." "What is this?" he asked curiously.

"It is what the burglar was after. Take it and lock it up in your safe, and I'll tell you about it later. Now we'll go down and get the fellow's description from Mary."

That was easier said than done. The housemaid was too thoroughly frightened to be successfully cross-examined. The intruder was tall, he was short. In one breath he wore a beard and was a very buccaneer in general appearance; in the next, he was smooth-shaven. Picked out and pieced together, her facts were but two: she had seen a strange man dressed in black, and he had rushed first at her and then toward the window.

Mrs. Seeley and Antrim badgered the servant for further data and sank deeper into the mire of wonderment at each fresh rendering of her adventure; but Brant stood aside as one who rides upon his own train of thought. The burglar's object defined, there was only the question of identity to be answered. Harding was a coward, and he was much too shrewd to defeat his own end and risk his neck for the sake of a bottle of brandy. Wherefore, Harding must have employed an emissary. But who could he find who was at once brave enough to take the risk and foolhardy enough to get drunk in the midst of it? No seasoned house-breaker, certainly; it was more like the hare-brained prank of a reckless boy; such a boy, for instance, as William Langford.

Brant bided his time, and when Mrs. Seeley went above-stairs to view the scene of the invasion he lagged behind with Mary McCarthy.

"You say he had on black clothes, Mary. Are you sure of that?"

"'Deed I am that, sorr."

"Did you have time to notice the kind of a coat he wore?—how it was cut, I mean."

"I did that. It was as like to the wan ye're wearing as two peas in a pod. On'y but I knowed ye'd gone down to breakfast, I might have been misdeluded intirely till I saw the oogly face av him."

Inasmuch as both garments had been cut by the same tailor from the same measurements, there was every reason for the similarity; but Brant did not know this, and he tallied his score and went on:

"At first you said he had black hair, and just now you told Mrs. Seeley it was brown. Take time to think about it, and tell me which it was."

"'Deed, sorr, it was both—lastewise, it was that darrk it might be ayther wan."

"Was it long, or short?"

"Nayther the wan nor the t'other; joosht betwixt and betune, like."

"Exactly." Brant nodded assent. The answers came so readily, pointing step by step to the inevitable conclusion, that they drew out a leading question:

"One more point now, Mary, and we have him. Pull yourself together and try to remember his face. He was a young fellow, wasn't he?—smooth-faced and rather thin, with heavy eyebrows, a straight nose, and a mouth turned down a little at the corners?"

"That's it—that's joosht him to the parin' av a finger nail! 'Deed and ye might be readin' aff from his photygraph, Misther Brant!"

Brant asked no more questions. Slipping a dollar into the housemaid's hand, he laid a finger on his lip. "Mum's the word, Mary, and it will be a favour to me if you will let the thing die out as soon as it will. I know who it was, and it was only a bit of boy's play, meant to frighten me instead of you. You will help me keep it quiet, won't you?"

"'Deed and I will, then. It's a fine gentleman ye are, intirely, Misther Brant; and it's never an intilligent wurrud will they get out o' me at all at all forninst the b'y. But joosht to think av the impidence of the young spalpeen!"

Brant thanked her and ran up to his room, where Mrs. Seeley and Antrim were debating what should be done. Mrs. Seeley appealed to the draughtsman.

"What do you think about it, Mr. Brant? I was just asking Mr. Antrim to notify the police on his way downtown, but he thinks we ought first to know what has been taken. Will you look through your things and see if anything is gone?"

Now, in view of the inevitable conclusion, an investigation by the police was not to be thought of. So Brant made his examination perfunctory, missing nothing but the revolver and the bottle of brandy—and not missing the suit of clothes.

"There is nothing gone—nothing of any consequence," he said. "If I were you, I shouldn't call in the police. If we had lost anything valuable, it would be different; but as it is, we should gain nothing but a lot of newspaper notoriety, and that would hurt the house. Don't you think so?"

Mrs. Seeley demurred at first. She did not quite like the idea of having her house broken into, and then to be denied the poor consolation of stirring up the lazy, good-for-nothing police. But when Antrim added his word, she yielded. On the way downtown Antrim asked Brant a single question and no more:

"Tell me one thing, George. Did you give Mrs. Seeley your real reason for wanting to keep the thing quiet?"

"No," said Brant.

And as he volunteered no further information, the chief clerk dropped the subject and took up another.

"I suppose you will keep on hunting for Will Langford?"

"I shall; if he hasn't already turned up at home. I asked Dorothy to send me a line this morning, and if he is still missing I shall keep on till I find him."

"All right; I'm with you. Let me know what she says, and I'll do what I can to help. I shall be too busy to do much through the day, but after supper I'll be yours to command again."

Dorothy's note came just before noon. She had been delayed by the difficulty of finding a trustworthy messenger, she wrote. Her brother had not returned, and the situation at home was most trying. Her mother was sick with anxiety, and her father would hear to nothing less harsh than the turning of the matter over to the police. Mrs. Hobart had not been told; and, altogether, the household was in a most grievous state. Wouldn't Mr. Brant send her a line of encouragement?

Brant would, and did; sat down at once to indite it, ringing first for a messenger, so that no time should be lost.

"I was not able to find William last night," he wrote, "but I have every reason to believe that he is alive and well; indeed, I may say that I have had speech with a person who saw him as recently as nine o'clock this morning. From this person, and from some circumstances connected with her sight of him, I have obtained a clew to his whereabouts—no, not quite that, either; but I know what he is doing and what company he is keeping. Owing to the peculiar nature of the affair, this clew can not be followed up until to-night; but again I say, be of good cheer, and by all means dissuade your father from calling in the police. This would merely complicate matters, and it would doubtless prove disastrous to any hopeful future for your brother."

After this note was signed, sealed, and despatched, Brant drowned the remainder of the day in hard work over the drawing-board. It was the best antidote for impatience, and, since his task chanced to be more or less mechanical, he was able to lay his plans for the evening as he wrought. Following out the theory verified by Mary McCarthy's answers, the mystery of William Langford's disappearance was easily accounted for. Harding had doubtless broken his parole and returned to Denver. He had managed in some way to get hold of young Langford, and, with the help of the bottle imp, to turn the boy into a house-breaker.

Just how the cautious fugitive from justice could bring himself to trust the lad with the information necessary to an intelligent search for the papers was unexplainable. But that it had been done was beyond question.

One small fact, and one only, refused to fit into the chain of circumstantial evidence. It was this—and to one unfamiliar with the progressive stages of the liquor disease it might have appeared trivial: Brant had found the empty brandy bottle on the floor of his room, and it seemed incredible that a mere boy in the beginnings of the case-hardening process could drink so deeply in a single night and still be able to run away in the morning. But stubborn as this fact was, Brant would not allow it to upset his theory. It was William Langford who had broken into his room; and it was James Harding who had planned and instigated the raid. Therefore, when Harding should be found, the search for the boy would be successful.

With these premisings Brant renewed the quest in the evening methodically. He took Antrim into his confidence, but only so far as to hint that Will would be found in the company of a man whose description was thus and thus; and the chief clerk's part in the search was to make the round of the hotels and lodging houses.

Reserving the more dangerous share for himself, Brant went first to Draco's; and when Deverney assured him that nothing had been seen of Harding since the night of his banishment, he set the peg of conclusion one hole farther along. In his dealings with young Langford, Harding would be likely to keep up the fiction of respectability; hence there would be no frequenting of the more public resorts.

Acting upon this suggestion, Brant began a round of the more exclusive "clubhouses," making guarded inquiries of doorkeepers, and using his reputation with the craft unsparingly as a pass-key to unlock doors which would have been so many dead walls to a detective or a policeman. Since this was a slow process, it was well upon midnight when he ran his quarry to earth. It was in a club called the "Osirian," a very palace of the goddess of Chance. The doorkeeper was known to Brant, and under question he was able to answer in the affirmative. Two men tallying accurately with Brant's description had come in early in the evening. They were still upstairs in one of the private rooms, the man thought; which room the attendant in the upper corridor could doubtless point out.

Brant went up, and at the stairhead found himself in a large apartment richly furnished, with a high wainscot of polished mahogany and walls and ceilings of bronze pacrusta wrought into curious designs centring in clusters of softly shaded incandescent lamps. The central space, which served as a vestibule for a series of ceilingless private rooms built out from the walls, was fitted as a club parlour, and Brant made his way noiselessly over the thick carpet to the room whose number he had obtained from the attendant at the stairhead. The door was closed, but since the walls of the private room were merely an extension of the high wainscoting, there was no obstruction to sound. Beyond the door there was a clicking as of ivory counters, and the swish of cards across a table. Brant laid his hand on the doorknob, and at that moment the noises ceased and a boyish oath dropped into the gap of silence.

"I won't pay it—that's all there is about it!"—this in the voice of the boyish oath. "By gad, I'm tough enough, Mr. Harding, and I don't like him any better than you do; but I'm not a sneak thief yet!"

"I don't see but you will have to pay it, Willie; it is a debt of honour, you see," the gambler insisted. "You put up your promise for a stake in the game, and you have lost, fair and square. It won't be much trouble—knowing him as well as you do."

"But you don't understand; or rather you won't understand. I can't do a thing like that, tough as I am, and nobody but a cursed cad like you would try to make me. And, by gad, I believe you cheated me, anyway! Let me see those cards."

"Oh, I cheated you, did I? And you are going to kick out, are you? You're a nice, innocent kid, you are! Now, see here: you have gone too far, a good deal too far, to back down; and, by God, you know too much! You are going to do just what you promised to do before we played this game, or I'll give you dead away for what you did last night.—No, you don't!—just keep your hands on the table right where they are! I've got the drop on you."

Silence for a leaden-winged half minute, and then Harding spoke again. "Are you going to do it, or not?"

The boy's voice was hoarse with passion. "I sha'n't say anything as long as you hold that gun on me! Put it down, if you want me to talk to you."

Brant's big jaw was set like a mastiff's. The knob turned silently under his hand and the door swung noiselessly inward. The card room, with its red-brown walls of polished mahogany, was lighted by a single incandescent globe bracketted from the wainscoting at the right of the doorway. A square table stood in the midst. On the farther side of it sat the gambler, glaring up at the intruder, with mingled terror and ferocity yellowing his lean face and burning in his evil eyes, and with his right hand creeping by hairs' breadths toward the revolver lying upon the table. The boy was on the nearer side of the table; he was half out of his chair, poising catlike for a spring, and at the instant of Brant's entrance he pounced upon the weapon.

Like a stone from a catapult Brant was upon them, smashing the globe of the bracket light in passing, and while one might draw a quick breath three pairs of hands clutched fiercely in the darkness for the weapon on the table. In the midst of the struggle—if that which has no duration in time can be said to have a middle part—came the crash of a pistol shot. There was a moment of ringing silence and darkness, broken by the clatter of a heavy weapon on the floor and a sudden burst of light from a suspended chandelier. Then, as if the light-burst had been a trumpet call to summon them, the attendants and *habitués* of the place rallied quickly, filling the small room to overflowing.

The first comers found Harding sitting bolt upright in his chair, with a clean-cut hole in his temple from which the blood was trickling in a thin stream. The boy was shrinking opposite, with his face averted and his hands held out before him as if to ward off a blow. Brant was leaning against the wainscoting near the broken lamp bracket, his arms folded and his gaze fixed upon the upturned face of the dead man.

That was all, save that on the floor at Brant's feet lay the big revolver with an empty shell in one chamber.

CHAPTER XXV
"SILENCE IS AN ANSWER TO A WISE MAN"

WHEN the rumour of the tragedy ran through the clubhouse the small card room on the second floor filled quickly with a curious throng. Some made haste to ease the limp body of the slain to the floor, and others examined the pistol and tried to dig the bullet out of the wainscot. A brother craftsman knelt to unlace the victim's shoes, but he desisted at a word from one who had thrust his hand into the dead man's bosom.

"No use doing that now; he's dead," said the objector; and at the announcement William Langford sank back into his chair and covered his face with his hands. Whereat the witnesses exchanged significant glances.

"He's only a boy," said one under his breath, and there was a touch of commiseration and rough pity in the comment that ran quickly from one to another of those who heard.

Jarvis, busy with pencil and notebook, was among the earliest comers, writing at top speed and asking questions which no one could answer. But the lack of answers was no bar to a very succinct and complete story of the tragedy which grew under the flying pencil.

As his chief had said of him, Jarvis was a reporter first and everything else afterward, and the diploma of that degree is given to the man who can make the most of the visible facts. This is why every good reporter is more than half a detective; and Jarvis saw and noted some things which escaped the more morbid and less investigative curiosity of the others.

Brant stood aside, seeing and hearing, it is to be presumed, but only with the outward eye and ear, if his face were any index. To those who saw him when the light first leaped into the big chandelier overhead, his face was the face of one dazed; but later the shrewd eyes narrowed and the rapture of those who can isolate themselves and think to the mark in any crisis wrote itself in the square-set jaw and compressed lips and far-seeing gaze. What turmoil of soul these crucial minutes measured none knew and none could know, least of all those whom the balder facts of the horror held spellbound; and so it came about that Brant was ignored until he pushed his way through the throng to bend over the boy. What he said was whispered, and it went no farther than to the ear for which it was intended.

"Brace yourself quickly, and don't let them rattle you," he commanded. "The police will be here in a minute, and you must deny it and stick to it through thick and thin. Do you understand?"

The boy looked up, and blankness was in his face. "Tell them I didn't kill him?" he began vaguely; and Brant had no more than time to nod before two officers pushed through the throng and laid hands on the cowering figure in the chair. The boy started to his feet in a sudden panic of awakening, protesting his innocence with such passionate vehemence that Brant's warning seemed to have been quite unnecessary, and those who looked on wondered at the boy's hardihood.

"My God, I didn't do it—as God sees me, I didn't!" he cried. "Perhaps I might, if he'd given me a chance, but he didn't; he held a gun on me at first, and then when he laid it on the table I couldn't——"

The sergeant of police shook him silent and gave him his warning. "Least said's the soonest minded for you, me b'y. Ivery wurrud ye say'll be used against ye. Come on wid us."

"But I say I didn't!" quavered the boy. "Ask Mr. Brant, there; he was here, and he knows."

All eyes were turned upon Brant. In the excitement of the moment no one had thought of him as having been a witness to the tragedy. It was known that Harding and young Langford had occupied the card room together, and the earliest comers had supposed, if they thought anything about it, that Brant had merely outrun them in the rush to the scene. Jarvis alone seemed to comprehend the situation, and his pencil flew swiftly in the moment of strained silence following Langford's appeal. Brant faced the battery of eyes without flinching and stepped forward.

"The boy is right," he said quietly. "I do know—and I am ready to go with you."

It was characteristic of time and place that a low buzz of applause greeted the announcement. "That's Plucky George, every day in the week!" said one who knew him; and at the mention of the name the buzz went around again. But Sergeant McCafferty was not to be so easily turned aside.

"Do I understand that ye surrinder yourself as the murtherer of this man?" he demanded, with a jerk of his thumb toward the limp figure on the floor.

In the hush that followed Jarvis's pencil paused, and the reporter thought it a measure of Brant's fortitude that he could smile.

"I am not required to criminate myself before witnesses," was the reply. "I neither deny nor affirm; but I am ready to go with you and to answer to the charge at the proper time and place."

He held out his wrists for the handcuffs, but the sergeant ignored the gesture and contented himself with searching his prisoner for weapons.

"You come along wid us quietlike, and there won't be no use for the darbies," he said. "Officer Connell, ye'll bring the b'y."

But Brant protested quickly. "What for?" he demanded.

"As a matther of discreetion. I know fwhat I'm doing," retorted the sergeant. "Come on wid you."

"Not a step till you turn the boy loose," said Brant firmly; "at least, not peaceably. I appeal to the crowd. You have just as good reasons for arresting every person in this room as you have for taking this young man. You may say he is a witness; but in that case I ask who gave you the authority to arrest witnesses?"

It was a bold stroke and the argument was altogether specious, but Brant knew he could count upon the moral influence of the onlookers, and in this he was not disappointed. A murmur of encouragement answered the appeal, and when the sergeant hesitated Jarvis put in his word.

"You know me, McCafferty," he said. "I'll vouch for the young man. He is the son of Judge Langford, and you can find him when you want him."

The mention of the judge's name turned the scale, and William Langford was released. Brant looked his thanks, and the reporter nodded. Then the officers moved off with their prisoner, and in the slight confusion Jarvis got speech with Brant.

"Is there anything I can do for you, old man?" he whispered.

"Yes; get the boy into a carriage and send him home."

"Is that all?"

"Yes."

"I'll do it. Keep a stiff upper lip, and you'll come out all right."

The reporter fell back when they reached the street, and a few minutes later Brant was ushered into the presence of the lieutenant on duty at the police station. The officer took his name and entered it in the record; and since the prisoner would answer no other questions, he presently found himself safe behind bolts and bars in the city jail, charged with the murder of James Harding.

There was a cot in the corner of the cell, and when the turnkey left him Brant flung himself down upon it in sheer weariness. He had been up the better part of two nights, and whatever tangle of thought there was asking to be set in order, sleep was more insistent. But the trials of the night were not yet at an end. While he was but dozing, the door bolts clanked and the door swung open to admit Forsyth. Brant would have risen, but the editor prevented him and came to sit on the edge of the cot.

"Don't disturb yourself," he made haste to say. "I haven't come to fight with you. Jarvis has told me all about it, and I just came over to let you know that you have a friend or two left, if you are the biggest fool on record."

"That was good of you," Brant rejoined, and he would have been less than human if the editor's kindness had not touched him. "I was sure you would come, but I wasn't expecting you to-night."

"You might have known I'd be with you as soon as I could get away from the desk. I presume you will get your preliminary in the morning?"

"I suppose so; though I don't know anything about it."

"It's safe to count on it, anyway," Forsyth continued, "and there are two matters to be arranged in the meantime—counsel and bail. Give me a list of your friends, and I'll go out and hustle for you."

Brant laughed. "I haven't reputable friends enough to furnish bail in a case of assault and battery. There are plenty of the other kind, but I don't mean to call on them—or to let any one else."

"Oh, pshaw! what difference can it make now? You can't hope to preserve your incognito through all the publicity of a murder trial."

"I wasn't thinking of that; and it makes all the difference in the world to me," said Brant doggedly. "I want none of their help, and I sha'n't accept it—that's all."

"Well and good," replied the editor cheerily. "In that event I shall have to see what I can do on my own account."

"My dear Forsyth, you will do nothing of the kind. The case will come up at the next term of court, and I shall stay right where I am until the sheriff's deputy comes for me."

Forsyth did not press the point. The day of reckless shooting affrays had passed its Colorado meridian—in the cities, at least—and a healthy public sentiment was beginning to demand a more stringent interpretation of the law. Moreover, the Plainsman had kept well to the front in the law-and-order movement, and its editor had protested often and vehemently against the laxity of judges and juries in murder cases. For this cause he went not unwillingly from the question of bail to that of counsel.

"Have you made up your mind whom you will have to defend you?" he asked.

"No one," said Brant.

"Nonsense! And why not, pray?"

"I shall plead my own cause."

"Be your own lawyer and have a fool for a client, I suppose. But that won't do at all. I know you have been living in an atmosphere where, as we say, 'everything goes,' but you mustn't bank on mining camp methods in Denver at this late day. The prosecution here won't leave you a leg to stand on; it can't, under the present pressure of public sentiment."

"Nevertheless, I shall plead my own cause," Brant insisted stubbornly.

"You are not going to be allowed to hang yourself after that fashion. I shall retain the best lawyer I can find, and send him to you early in the morning."

"If you do I shall send him away again."

The editor got up to tramp back and forth in the narrow limits of the cell. "What the devil is the matter with you, anyway?" he demanded. "Can't you see that you are sending yourself straight to the gallows? I tell you, Brant, you don't realize the change that has been wrought here even in the last few months. The jury that acquitted Steve Basket last spring did what no jury will ever do again in Denver. And if Jarvis tells a straight story, you haven't a ghost of a show without the best legal help you can get."

"What you say is all true enough, and I realize it as clearly as you do," was the calm reply. "But you are talking quite beside the mark. I am here, charged with the murder of James Harding, and I am ready and willing to take what shall befall. I don't need a lawyer to help me do that, do I?"

Having no doubt of Brant's guilt, Forsyth made haste to interrupt what he feared might lead to an incriminating confession. "Don't tell me anything about it," he broke in quickly. "We are known to be intimate, and it is quite as likely as not I shall be called as a witness against you."

Brant smiled. "Don't worry about that. If you should happen to be summoned you must tell the whole truth. I sha'n't gainsay it by so much as a single word."

"You are a queer fellow," was the editor's comment after a pause. "Most men in your hard case would be catching at straws. Are you quite sure you don't want counsel?"

"Quite sure."

"Then is there anything else I can do for you?"

The jailer was returning.

"No, I think not—yes, there is, too. You can keep young Langford's name out of the papers, if you will."

Forsyth shook his head. "It is too late to do that now, even if it would have been possible earlier—which it wouldn't have been, under the circumstances. Is there nothing else?"

"Nothing that I think of."

"All right. Keep up your nerve, and try to argue yourself into a reasonable frame of mind—about employing counsel, I mean. I'll see you again in the morning."

CHAPTER XXVI
IN THE VALLEY OF THE SHADOW

MISTRESS KATE HOBART, California-born and bred, was of the cheerful salt of the earth, a frank and outspoken young woman whose vivacity was unfettered, and to whom mystery and melancholy were alike insupportable. Having twice entertained the Langfords on Jack Mountain during the summer, she thought she knew the family well enough to enjoy a visit in the Denver household, and so had accepted Mrs. Langford's invitation willingly. But after two such depressive days as had never before been ticked off in any calendar of hers, days which made her homesick for Jack Mountain, she went down to breakfast on the Saturday morning determined to make some excuse—any excuse—for flight.

But at the breakfast table she was moved to reconsider. In some manner quite as inexplicable as its gathering, the storm cloud had lifted in a night; and for the first time since her darkening of the Hollywood door she was made to feel that an atmosphere of gloomy mystery was not the normal respiratory medium of the household.

As yet, no one save his mother had seen the returned prodigal, but they all knew he was safe at home. And since he had seen fit to account for his absence by a most ingenious paraphrase of the truth, there was no hint of the terrible story wrapped up in the damp newspaper beside the judge's plate to mar the good cheer of the meal. Isabel alone appeared to lag in the ascent of the mount of cheerfulness; whereat her father rallied her, as fathers will:

"What is it this morning, Bella? Is it the unattainable Paris art school, or just an everyday picture that doesn't paint itself? You look as if you had lost a friend, or gained an enemy."

Isabel choked at the unintentional pointing of the thrust, and Dorothy came to her rescue:

"Don't be a tease, papa," she begged. "Isabel is going to surprise us all some day, and then you will lose your courtesy title and be known as the father of Miss Langford, the artist."

"'A prophet is not without honour,'" quoted Mistress Kate. "I think Isabel does very good work; don't you, Mrs. Langford?"

"I refuse to call it work," the mother asserted, pouring a second cup of coffee for the guest. "It is a very proper accomplishment for a young woman, and as such I have always encouraged it."

"Oh, *don't!*" said Isabel, and when the judge looked up and saw the real distress in her eyes he changed the subject, or thought to.

"I wonder what has become of Harry lately," he remarked, and thereupon Isabel quaked afresh and nerved herself for the worst that could possibly be said.

No one seemed to know, and it was Dorothy who ventured the suggestion that possibly the superintendent's prolonged absence and Antrim's added responsibility were accountable.

"And who may 'Harry' be?" inquired Kate.

"Young Mr. Henry Antrim, the son of an old friend of ours in Tennessee," Mrs. Langford explained. "He is almost a member of the family, I may say," she added, with a glance in Isabel's direction which was not thrown away upon the guest.

The younger daughter dropped her napkin, stooped to recover it, and so had an obvious excuse for the painful flush called up by the suggestive reply. Her self-control was beginning to sag threateningly, and she gave a little sigh of relief when her father began to smooth out the morning paper.

"I saw in the paper yesterday that Harry was out with the president's car," he said, straightening the damp sheet and unfolding it. "Let us see if——"

They all looked up at the abrupt pause. The judge was sitting very straight in his chair, his thin lips compressed in two colourless lines, and a gray shadow of grief and anger spreading slowly from cheek to brow. The paper trembled a little in his hands, but he read steadily through the leaded nonpareil under the staring headlines. Mrs. Langford was the first to find speech.

"Robert!" she cried. "What is it?"

The judge pushed back his chair and rose stiffly, as one upon whom the palsy of old age had come suddenly.

"Send William to me in the library," he said, and his voice had in it something of the judicial sternness which had so often struck hope out of a culprit's heart in the courtroom days. He turned away, and then he remembered the guest, and came back to apologize with grave dignity. "You must excuse me—excuse us all, Mrs. Hobart. We are in great trouble; you can see for yourself." And he gave her the newspaper.

He left the room, and Mrs. Langford followed at once. Kate looked askance at the paper, but she took it up at Dorothy's nod. A glance at the staring headlines appalled her, but she saw that it was no time for nice distinctions in the conventional field, if she were to be of the helpers.

"Shall I read it aloud?" she asked.

"If you please," Dorothy assented, slipping her arm around Isabel's waist.

So Mistress Kate read, and stopped to gasp and read again:

"'SACRIFICED TO OSIRIS!

"'WILLIAM LANGFORD AND JAMES HARDING
PLAY CARDS, AND GEORGE BRANT
KILLS THE WINNER!

"'Last night, at the solemn hour of midnight, another murder was added to the long list of crimes that have made bloody abattoirs of the temples of chance here and elsewhere. The "Osirian" clubhouse was the scene of the grim tragedy. The details of the killing are somewhat obscure, but it seems that William Langford, the young son of one of our most respected citizens, and James Harding, better known as the "Professor," met in one of the private rooms of the Osirian for a quiet game of draw. About midnight a pistol shot rang out, and those who rushed to the scene found Harding weltering in his blood. He had been shot in the face as he sat in his chair, the bullet—a 45-calibre Colt—entering beside the left eye and passing out at the back to bury itself in the wall.

"'The affair is shrouded in mystery, which will probably not be cleared up until the facts are brought out at the trial. It was at first supposed that young Langford had fired the fatal shot, but when the officers were about to arrest him, Brant, whose presence in the card room is unexplained, stepped out and surrendered himself. The motive for the crime is not far to seek. It is said, by those who know both, that Brant and the "Professor" have long been deadly enemies; and as the former had been seeking the latter at the various resorts in the city, it is supposed that the killing was the culmination of an old feud.

"'Harding's record is most unsavoury, and he has more than once been a fugitive from justice. The reports about his slayer are conflicting, some asserting that he is no other than "Plucky George" Brant, the notorious snap-shot faro dealer of the mining camps, while others say he is a civil engineer in the employ of the C. E. & W. Ry.'"

Dorothy went white at the third line of the heading and drew closer to her sister; and Kate was scarcely less moved when she put the paper down at the end.

"Isn't it just simply dreadful!" she said; and the trite phrase showed how far beyond adequate speech the dreadful thing was.

Dorothy's lips moved, but they were too dry to form even the single word of assent, and it was Isabel who answered:

"Indeed it is; it's too awful to realize. But we all ought to be so thankful that Will was cleared so quickly and so easily."

Dorothy drew herself up and stared at her sister as if she doubted that she had heard aright. Was it so easy, then, to choose between one's lover and one's brother?

"But, sister, is it any less terrible for that?" she cried out reproachfully.

"Oh, no; I suppose not. It is too awful to think about, anyway. But it is just what one would expect of Mr. Brant—the giving himself up, I mean. I wonder if what the paper says about him is true—about his double identity."

"How can you think of that now!" Dorothy burst out passionately. "Of course it isn't true; and even if it were—" She stopped short and caught her breath in a quick gasp, suddenly remembering Brant's parable.

"I am afraid it is true," said Kate sorrowfully. "He is an old friend of Ned's, and Ned would never tell me how he came to meet him in Silverette, or what Mr. Brant was doing there."

Dorothy's heart was too full for any kind of utterance. The open disgrace brought upon the family by her brother; the terrible tragedy for which she felt that her letters to Brant were partly responsible; the dreadful fate that awaited the slayer of James Harding, and Isabel's apparent indifference thereto—these were all past speech. And when there came a dim suspicion of a more horrible thing—a bare suggestion that Brant had shielded the real murderer by giving himself up in his stead—she burst into tears and ran from the breakfast room.

In the meantime William Langford was having an exceedingly painful quarter of an hour in the library. Much to her dissatisfaction, Mrs. Langford had not been permitted to accompany her son in the capacity of special pleader, and for once in his life the young man was compelled to face his father's wrath unsupported, while his mother awaited the outcome with what fortitude she could summon in the deserted drawing-room.

"Tell me the whole story, and tell me the truth," was the judge's stern command when his son appeared before him.

William did neither. From long practice in presenting his own case at home in the most favourable light the young man was blankly unable to tell a straightforward story in plain words, though for this once his will to do it was good. But what he did tell put his father in possession of a fairly consistent series of facts. On the day before the tragedy the boy had met Harding and had become his guest at a hotel. There had been liquor and cards, he admitted—so much of the former that he had been afraid to come home. That was all.

"And how did you come to be in this place last night?"

"Harding took me there. He said it was a gentlemen's club."

"Didn't you know it was a gambling house?"

The boy hung his head. "I—I guessed it was—after we got in."

"Well, go on."

"We went upstairs and began to play cards. Harding won everything I had, and then—" He stopped, but the lash of his father's command struck him smartly.

"Tell it all. What then?"

"Then he got me to put my promise to get some papers away from Mr. Brant up against all the money on the table. I thought he was just joking, y'know, and I did it—and he won."

The judge groaned in the bitterness of his spirit. "It wasn't enough for you to be a knave; you must be a fool as well. Go on."

"Then he said I must pay; that if I didn't, he'd give me away for what I did the night before."

"And what was that?"

Again the boy hung his head and went dumb. "I don't know. I can't remember."

"Which is another way of saying that you were too drunk to know what you were about. God help us!" said the judge, and he got up to walk to the window. When he could trust himself to speak he began again:

"About these papers that Harding wanted you to get from Brant: what were they?"

"I don't know—some affidavits or something that Brant was holding over him."

"How were you to get them?"

"Any way I could. I was—to—steal them—I suppose."

"And you—you deliberately put your honour, my honour, the good name you have made a hissing and a reproach, on the table as a stake in a game of cards!"

"I—I thought it was only a joke—before God, I did! And when I found out it wasn't, I kicked, and we quarrelled."

The dreadful suspicion that had just sent Dorothy sobbing to her room seized upon the judge and gripped him till his knees trembled. "You—you quarrelled?" he echoed. "Go on—go on, my son; let me know the worst."

It is a hardened son indeed who can look unmoved upon the vicarious anguish of a father. William Langford was not unmoved, but the churlish habit had grown to be second nature, and all the gates of generous expression were closed and barred. He went on as if it were another's story, and not his own, that he was telling.

"He cursed me, and said I'd have to do it. I swore I wouldn't, and when I started to get up he held his gun on me. That scared me, but it made me madder, too, and I told him I wouldn't talk any more till he put that gun down. He did put it down—laid it on the table—and I jumped for it. I don't know just what I meant to do if I got hold of it. Part of the time I wanted to kill him, and part of the time I was scared stiff for fear he'd kill me."

The culprit stopped to take breath. The effort of such continuous truth-telling was exhausting.

"Go on," said the father.

"I don't know as I can—so that you'll understand. When I jumped for the pistol everything seemed to happen at once. The room was only a little box of a place, lighted by an electric globe sticking out from the wall at the end nearest the door. There was a big chandelier hanging from the ceiling right over the table, but that wasn't lighted. Just as I jumped up the light went out with a smash, and there were three of us grabbing for the pistol on the table, instead of two. I got hold of it, somebody snatched it and pushed me back, and the shot was fired, all in the same breath. Then some one on the outside snapped the key of the big chandelier, and I saw that Harding was shot right where he sat."

The judge crossed the room unsteadily and laid his hand on his son's head. "William, you say 'the shot was fired'; tell me, as you hope to be forgiven, did you fire that shot?"

The boy hesitated, doubting for the moment his ability to answer the question truthfully. The memories of the past eight-and-forty hours were like those of a fantastic dream in which a single incident more or less was hard to affirm or deny.

"I—I don't think I did," he stammered. "Most of the time I'm sure I didn't; I was sure of it when the officers started to take me, and told 'em so. But there is a queer thing about it that I can't understand. I told you that I grabbed the pistol in the dark, and that somebody snatched it from me just as the shot was fired. That's true, and I'd swear to it if I stood on the gallows. But when the thing was done, I found that pistol in my hand just as if I'd never let go of it, and I threw it on the floor as if it had been hot and burned me."

"But surely you can remember whether you fired it or not!"

"It seems as if I'd ought to, but I can't. I was stunned and scared up and crazy mad all in one breath, and the whole thing happened before you could swallow twice. I'm glad I don't have to remember."

"Don't have to remember? What do you mean?"

"Why, Brant settled it when he gave himself up, didn't he? And yet, if he hadn't done that, I'd have been ready to swear that he didn't fire the pistol, either."

The judge shook his head despairingly. "This uncertainty of yours is simply maddening, William. If you know you didn't fire the shot yourself, why do you think Brant didn't fire it?"

"Because the noise didn't seem near enough, and I didn't see any flash. The room was dark, y'know, and rattled as I was I'd ought to have seen it if it had been fired as close to me as that."

The judge shook his head again, and began to pace the floor in a fresh access of grief and humiliation. But the exigencies of the case presently asserted themselves.

"I believe you have told me the truth, or that you have tried to tell it. But you must pull yourself together and get the facts in the shape of a consistent story. You will be put upon the witness stand, and Brant's life may depend upon your testimony."

The clang of the front-door bell broke in upon them, and the painful interview was at an end. The caller was an officer, come to summon

William Langford as a witness in the preliminary examination, which was set for ten o'clock. The judge groaned inwardly at this fresh proof of the relentless march of publicity and disgrace, but he got his hat and coat and went with his son.

There were no new developments in the courtroom. William Langford told his story more coherently than the judge had believed it could be told; and, in accordance with his expressed determination, Brant refused counsel and maintained a stubborn silence. Hence the magistrate, having no alternative, ordered a plea of "Not guilty" to be entered for him, remanded him to jail, and fixed his bail at the sum of ten thousand dollars.

Forsyth and Antrim were both present at the preliminary examination, and after it was over the latter introduced Judge Langford and the editor. True to his promise to befriend Brant in the time of need, the judge immediately offered to procure bondsmen, but Forsyth shook his head.

"It is no use," he explained. "He won't accept bail, and I can't even get him to consent to employ counsel."

"But, my dear sir, that is sheer folly! Indeed, in this case it is worse than folly—it is suicide." So said the judge, and so he fully believed.

"I know it; that is just what I tell him. But he is as stubborn as a mule."

The lawyer in the judge awoke at this, and he became interested at once on the part of the mulish one. "What reason does he give, pray?"

Forsyth hesitated, not knowing precisely how far he might confide in the questioner. So he felt his way:

"He doesn't give any reason; he simply refuses to talk. But I have my own theory. We are all friends of his, I take it, and I may speak plainly?"

"Certainly; go on."

"Well, he is a singular fellow in some respects, and you can't apply the law of averages. I believe he did the thing deliberately, and for some reason which does not appear on the surface. And, having done it, he means to let the law take its course without opposition—to take the consequences."

"H'm," said the judge reflectively; then he remembered how easy it would have been for Brant to have shifted suspicion to Will, and his heart warmed toward the culprit. "We mustn't allow that, Mr. Forsyth. Of course, the court will assign him counsel at the trial whether he wants it or not, but we mustn't let it come to that. Do you see him again, and endeavour to make him listen to reason."

Forsyth promised to do what he might toward that desirable end, and the judge and his son left the courtroom together. The editor followed with Antrim, and when the Langfords were out of earshot the chief clerk put in his word:

"You may say what you please, Forsyth, but I am not going to believe that Brant did it till he admits it himself."

"But, my dear boy, hasn't he as good as admitted it already?"

"No. In what little he has said he has dodged that point very cunningly."

"Of course he has; that is the proper thing to do. He is not obliged to criminate himself."

"It is proper enough, as you say, but, don't you see, it doesn't fit into your theory. If he killed the man and is determined to take the consequences, why on top of earth shouldn't he plead 'Guilty' and be done with it?"

That was a logical question, and Forsyth was unable to answer it. When he had said as much the inevitable alternative suggested itself, and he spoke of it:

"If you exonerate Brant, you put the boy in a bad box."

Antrim had thought about that. "I can't help it," he said promptly. "The tree will have to lie where it falls. If you go back to motives, you will have to admit that, according to his own story, the thing looks bad for Will. He was the one who was quarrelling with Harding."

"Yes, but—pshaw! I can't believe it, Antrim. Why, he is only a boy!"

"That is true. But it is also true that he is a young tough, hot-headed and quick-tempered. I have known him all his life, and neither the thing itself nor the denial of it is much beyond him."

They had reached the corner where Antrim should turn aside to go to his office, and the editor stopped and regarded his companion curiously.

"You are a friend of the Langfords, aren't you?" he asked.

"If they have a better one, I don't know it. But right is right. I should say the same if Will Langford were my own brother," Antrim asserted stoutly. "I know you won't agree with me, and I don't expect any one else will, but I say George Brant isn't guilty, and, unless he admits it himself in so many words, I am going to stick to it till the last dog is dead."

Forsyth went his way unconvinced, but it was inevitable that Antrim's suggestion should colour the editor's talk with Brant that afternoon. And the colouring had its effect, too, though not in the way Forsyth would have wished. While the prisoner said little, and no thing of that little that could be construed into an admission of guilt, the editor left the jail with his own assumption confirmed and fortified beyond a question of doubt. Furthermore, he had failed utterly in the renewed attempt to make Brant listen to reason in the matter of employing counsel.

CHAPTER XXVII
SHOWING HOW FAITH MAY OUT-BUFFET
A FACT

WHEN a great misfortune threatens, the heavens are darkened and the smaller ills are obscured; but when the eclipse passes, the lesser evils magnify themselves, assuming abnormal proportions in a field wherein they are no longer secondary. What time Judge Langford was oppressed by the fear that his son had added a murder to the sum of his iniquities, the disgrace consequent upon the dragging of the family name into the public prints seemed trifling. But when it became apparent that William was not to be hanged, the lesser misfortune demanded a hearing, and the judge shut himself up in his library to mourn over the wreck of the good name he had builded.

To him in his sorrowful seclusion came Dorothy, grief-stricken and incoherent, staggering under a burden of remorseful anguish too heavy to be borne alone. The judge loved his elder daughter with an affection which was both tenderer and less prideful than that shared by the younger; and he postponed his private grief in the effort to measure and assuage hers.

"What is it, Dorothy, daughter—anything worse than the worst?" he inquired.

"Oh, yes, papa; and it is all my fault!" she sobbed, leaning against the high mantel and covering her face with her hands.

"Your fault? But I don't understand. What is it that is your fault?"

"A good part of what has happened, and all that is going to happen. Mr. Brant was in that place last night because I had asked him to go. He was looking for Will, to bring him home."

"But you say you had asked him. How could that be?"

Dorothy dried her eyes and told the whole story bravely, beginning with the chance meeting in Mr. Crosswell's study, and ending by handing her father the two notes received from Brant. The judge read the notes thoughtfully and the lines of anxiety deepened in his face.

"You did it for the best, and no one could have foreseen such terrible consequences. It was a most natural thing for you to do, and I am far from reproaching you. But you are right; this complicates the affair most grievously. It makes us in a certain sense responsible, and that without helping to clear up the mystery. If the young man's purpose was to rescue William—and that seems to be very evident—why under heaven should he spoil a good deed by committing a murder in the very midst of it?"

"Oh, I don't know, I don't know! But if I hadn't sent him he wouldn't have been there!"

"No, probably not; but you mustn't try to carry more than your proper share of the burden. Whatever his motive for killing the man, it must surely go back of Harding's connection with William."

"If I could only be sure of that!" sighed Dorothy; and then she added hopelessly: "Not that it would make any difference. It is done, and it can never, never be undone."

"Yes, it would make some difference," said the father reflectively; "not in fact, but in the ethics of the fact. Nevertheless, it would not greatly lessen our responsibility. We must make this young man's cause our own now, at any cost." Here spoke the loyal Southern gentleman.

"And he can be cleared—you can save him?" she faltered, brightening up a little.

But her father shook his head doubtfully at that.

"It would be more than any one could promise at present; he is acting very singularly"—and Dorothy's hopes were slain when the judge told the story of the preliminary examination. When she had heard him through, the horrible suspicion came again and refused to be driven away, but she could not bring herself to speak of it to her father. Will a murderer? Oh, no; anything but that!

Not until his daughter had gone away and he had sat down to go thoughtfully over the details again did the judge realize what his championship of Brant would require of him. Then it became evident, with a keen pang of fresh misfortune, that he was bound hand and foot; that any effort made to clear Brant must inevitably result in entangling his own son. As the matter rested, William was free and unsuspected, and George Brant would hang—if the jury so willed. But if by any effort of any one Brant should be proved innocent— The alternative was as plain as the handwriting on the wall of Belshazzar's banquet hall, and to the full as appalling.

The luncheon hour came and went unheeded, and the autumn afternoon waned toward a cloudy evening, and still the judge plodded wearily back and forth in the narrow space between his writing table and the bookcases, striving with his paternal love as many a father has striven since the day when Abraham the Just was commanded to make trial of his faith. It was the father against the man, and what wonder if, after all the hours of stern conflict, the father won?

"I can not do it," he said at length, setting his face flintwise against all arguments. "A man's first duty is to his own flesh and blood. If William were guilty it would be different; though even then I doubt if I could play the Roman. No, Brant must take his chance; I can't help him."

So saying, the judge went up to dress for dinner; but his decision did not prevent him from telephoning to Antrim as he came down again, asking the chief clerk to come to the house that evening.

Antrim promised readily enough, the more willingly since he suspected the reason for the summons and hoped to be able to do something in Brant's behalf. Accordingly, he boarded a car immediately after supper and was presently set down in the Highlands. Isabel met him at the door and would gladly have been plastic; but Antrim was, in his way, a man of one idea at a time, and at that moment he was too full of concern for his friend to think overmuch of his own affair. Whereat Isabel was piqued, and the angel of reconciliation spread its wings and flew away.

"Is your father at home?" Antrim asked, after what Isabel thought was the coldest of greetings.

"Yes, my father is at home, and he is in the library," she replied, with the accent precise. And when Antrim disappeared she went back to the drawing-room and played many unmusical staccato exercises on the piano.

"Good evening, Harry," said the judge, greeting his visitor cordially. "Come in and sit down; you have been neglecting us lately."

Antrim admitted it in one word, not wishing to go a-swimming in that pool.

"I asked you to come over because I wanted to have a talk with you about Brant," the judge went on. "You know him better than any of us, and I thought you might have some suggestions to offer. He mustn't be allowed to hang himself without benefit of clergy."

"That is exactly what he is going to do," replied Antrim, who had been to see the prisoner in the city jail during the afternoon. "He won't talk about bail; and I can't get him to listen to a word about having a lawyer."

"What does he say?" queried the judge.

"As nearly nothing as a man can and keep on talking."

"Do you know anything about the affair yourself, Harry?—any more than the newspapers tell, I mean."

"How much do you know?" asked Antrim cautiously, not wishing to betray Dorothy.

The judge smiled. "I know all that Dorothy can tell me," he rejoined.

"All right; then that lets me out, though I haven't much to add. We were out together nearly all Thursday night, looking for Will, and we arranged to go out again last night. Brant seemed to have found out something during the day, for in the evening he gave me a description of this man Harding, and told me I'd be likely to find him and Will together. When we separated I was to go to the hotels and lodging houses, and he was to make the round among the dives."

The judge remembered his talk with Brant after the Draco raid and William's first home-bringing, and was once more able to put two and two together. "It is very evident that there are some earlier chapters to the story," he said, "and if Brant won't tell us about them we must find some one who will. It may be there are extenuating circumstances in the background which will help out at the trial."

He rose and pressed the bell-push; and Antrim made haste to define his own position before an interruption should slay the opportunity.

"You are going on the supposition that Brant is guilty," he said quickly. "I don't believe he is."

"You don't?" The judge's tone evinced more deprecation than he could honestly lay claim to. "But, my dear boy, have you considered the alternative?"

"No." Antrim admitted it frankly. "I haven't looked at it in that light at all. But I know Brant, and I think I know him pretty well. I don't believe he is any more capable of killing a man in cold blood than I am."

"I know; but that is only inference. You forget the evidence—" The judge was going on to summarize the evidence, but the coming of the servant interrupted him. "Yes, I rang," he said to the housemaid. "Ask Mrs. Hobart if she will be good enough to come to the library."

Kate complied at once, and the judge introduced Antrim. "Have this chair, Mrs. Hobart," he said. "We were discussing the mur—the tragedy of last night. Mr. Antrim is a friend of Brant's, and I understood you to say that your husband knows him well. Can you tell us anything of his history?"

Kate shook her head slowly, and, being inclined at times to be wary out of all proportion to her sex and age, replied guardedly: "Nothing more than that he and Ned were college classmates."

"Have you written to your husband yet?"

"No; I thought he would get the papers before he would my letter."

"So he will; but I think it will be well to ask him to come down. You might write to-night, and Mr. Antrim will mail your letter."

"I'll do better than that—I'll wire," said Kate. "May I write at your table?"

She wrote the message and gave it to Antrim, and after a little more talk the chief clerk took his leave. He found his way to the front door alone, and Isabel watched his departure from the stairhead; after which concession to her pique she went to her room and did penance after the fashion of quick-tempered lovers the world over.

Antrim took a car and left it at the corner nearest the telegraph office. Ten steps from the crossing he ran upon Jarvis, and the reporter began forthwith to ransack him for details in Brant's affair. Antrim set his teeth upon a resolve to tell nothing, and ended by telling all he knew, salving his conscience by reasserting his belief in Brant's innocence.

"Right there is where I am stuck myself, but I am going to settle that point before I'm an hour older," quoth the reporter, adding, "You may come along and help, if you want to."

"Settle it?" echoed Antrim. "How can anybody do that?"

"You stay right with me and I'll show you."

They went on together, first to the Western Union office, that Antrim might do his errand, and then to the Osirian. On the way to the clubhouse Jarvis stopped short and smote his thigh.

"By Jupiter, Harry, but your part of the story turns on an oxy-hydrogen side light that beats the moon! I'll bet a gold mine to an Indian cayuse that I've got the whole play down pat. Here is the layout: He is soft on the girl; he goes on a still hunt for the girl's brother; he catches his Toughness killing him a man for breakfast, and coolly steps into Mr. Brother's shoes—all for the sake of the girl. That is George Brant to a hair, if I'm any judge of my kind. Come on till I prove it to you like twice two."

Antrim went aghast at the bare possibility, but he held his peace and followed Jarvis blindly. The reporter's calling procured them ready admission to the exclusive palace of Chance, and they found the room on the second floor untenanted, as it was sure to be. Jarvis posted his companion near the door and in line with the end of the table where Brant must have stood. Then he placed the chairs on either side of the table, about where they were when Harding and Langford had sat in them. The stage set, he began his demonstration:

"Now, we know that Harding was hit on the side of his face nearest to you, but that proves nothing more than that he might have turned away just at the moment of the firing. But if you will hold the end of this tape, I'll show you that Brant couldn't have fired that shot from your end of the table, unless it turned a corner in Harding's head."

He unwound the tape, gave one end of it to Antrim, and drew it taut as nearly as might be through the space where the murdered man's head must have been. That done, he turned and stared blankly at his assistant.

"What is it?" Antrim demanded.

"B'gosh, I've proved too much!" said the reporter. "Can't you see? The bullet that made this hole in the wall was fired from about where you stand. By Jove! that lets young Langford out, but say, it puts Brant in head over ears!"

Antrim dropped his end of the tape and thrust his hands into his pockets. "Just the same, I don't believe it," he said doggedly. "And, what's more, I never will until Brant admits it himself."

"Bully for you!" cried Jarvis heartily. "You are the kind of a friend to have at a pinch! Well, there is nothing more to be found out here. Let's go down and have a drink, and then you'll tell me more about that burglary business. I was so full of this other thing that I didn't quite catch on."

"No drinks," said Antrim briefly when they were once more in the street and Jarvis was pointing for a barroom. "Come up to Mrs. Seeley's with me, if you like, and I'll tell you and show you all there is to be heard and seen."

Jarvis acquiesced, grumbling, and the chief clerk was as good as his word. But if the reporter made any fresh discoveries in Brant's room he kept his own counsel. By this time Antrim was catching at straws. The meeting with Jarvis and the experiment with the tape measure in the card room damped his courage, and left his belief in Brant's innocence more nearly shaken than it had been at any time during the eventful day. None the less, he remained steadfast, as his last word to Jarvis testified.

"You are interested in getting to the bottom of this thing on general principles, aren't you?" he asked, as he let the reporter out at the street door.

"Sure thing."

"I supposed so. Well, you just go ahead on the supposition that Brant didn't do it, and you will be more likely to succeed. Good night."

"You are a crank," said the reporter, laughing, as he ran down the steps.

And yet such is the impact of one man's assertion hurled repeatedly against a wall of self-evident fact that Jarvis actually found himself ignoring the evidence and building theories based on the major "if." He toppled them over as fast as they rose, but they straightway grew again, and it took another conference with his chief, the night editor, to fully fortify his reason against the assaults of Antrim's insistent faith.

CHAPTER XXVIII
HOW THE JUDGE GAVE OF HIS BEST

HAVING done what he might for his friend on the Saturday, Antrim thought he should not err in devoting the Sunday afternoon to his own affair, and to this end he turned his face to the Highlands as soon as he could break away from the Sunday duties which entangle the railway servant. He was a little later than usual; and Isabel, after waiting half an hour, avenged her pique by going out with Mrs. Hobart. Dorothy, meeting Antrim at the gate as she was starting for the mission school, was unable to tell him whither they had gone. Wouldn't he go in and wait?

Piqued in his turn, Antrim decided he would not go in and wait. He had meant to do no more at present than to try to resume the old relation with Isabel, and he thought she might have suffered this, the more willingly since it was her own expressed wish. But if she were not yet complaisant——

Before he had argued the case to its irritant conclusion he found himself walking townward with Dorothy. They missed a car by a minute or two, and Antrim halted at the corner to wait for the next.

"I have time enough, and we can walk on until a car overtakes us, if you care to," said Dorothy, who had a reason of her own for desiring an uninterrupted interview with her companion.

"I'd like to walk," replied Antrim, whose mood welcomed a diversion of any sort.

They went on together, and mutual constraint immediately thrust a barrier of silence between them. Antrim thought he knew enough of Brant's secret to make him hesitate to speak first of the thing which he imagined was uppermost in Dorothy's mind; and Dorothy was made dumb by a great sympathy for Antrim in his disappointment. None the less, she was the first to break the silence.

"Have you—have you been to see Mr. Brant since the—" She could not give it a name, and Antrim promptly forestalled the necessity.

"Yes; I was with him for half an hour yesterday afternoon."

Dorothy meant to go straight on to the end she had in view, but her courage failed, and she had to bridge the gap with a commonplace. "Isn't it dreadful!" she said.

"That depends upon how you look at it," rejoined Antrim, forgetting for the moment to whom he was talking. "I don't believe Brant is guilty."

"O Harry!" Dorothy stopped, and the quick tears blinded her.

Whereupon Antrim realized, with a pang of remorse for his thoughtlessness, what such an assertion must mean to William Langford's sister, and he made haste to comfort her.

"You mustn't take it for granted that I am accusing Will. I am not; I just leave him out of the question altogether, and stick to Brant for what I know of him. He wouldn't do such a thing any more than I would."

Dorothy could not so easily avoid the apparently inevitable conclusion, but her enthusiasm rose unbidden at the tribute to the worth of the man whom she loved.

"I want to think so too, Harry—oh, *so* much! But papa says he doesn't deny it."

"No, he doesn't; and he doesn't affirm it, either. And till he does, I am not going to believe it," said Antrim stoutly.

At this conjuncture it occurred to Dorothy that Antrim was behaving very nobly toward his successful rival, and she found space to lay a little offering on the altar of manly friendship.

"It is very generous of you, Harry, to feel that way after what has happened. I have been afraid you might feel just the least bit vindictive."

"Vindictive? You don't know what I owe him, Dorothy. It is a bigger debt than I ever owed any one before, and I'd pay it if it took the last thing I have in the world."

"It has taken the thing you valued most, hasn't it?" said Dorothy, with heartfelt sympathy in voice and eyes. "Poor Isabel! It is a dreadful blow for her! And she is taking it so strangely."

Antrim was properly mystified, but he got no farther than to say: "Isabel? I am afraid I don't quite understand."

"Surely she has told you," said Dorothy, who could not imagine anything like duplicity on the part of her outspoken sister.

Now Isabel had told him but one thing of any considerable importance to a lover, and Antrim's thought naturally reverted to that thing.

"Oh, yes," he rejoined, trying to speak lightly. "She gave me my quittance for good and all a while back, but——" He was going on to add that it is a long lane that has no turning, when Dorothy interrupted:

"I knew she would tell you first! And now this dreadful thing has come between them. Harry, I believe it will kill her if she has to give him up now. She is acting so strangely that I fairly tremble for her reason."

Antrim throttled a wild impulse to give place to madness and forced himself to say, as calmly as might be, "Then she has told you that—that she loves Brant?"

Dorothy decided on the spur of the moment that it was no time for half confidences.

"Yes; and that isn't the worst of it. She sent him away because—because she didn't know her own heart, I suppose. I told her he would come back; and now he never can. Isn't it too pitiful!"

Antrim thought it was—in more senses than one. More than that, it was blankly incredible, or rather it would be apart from Dorothy's positive assertion. Could he have been so purblind as not to have seen what was going on before his very eyes? Reason said No; but a misconception, once endowed with the breath of life, is sure to find plenty to fatten upon, and the atoms of corroborative evidence began to assemble quickly with Dorothy's declaration for a nucleus.

This was why Brant had been so sure that he knew Isabel's preference; and he had been mistaken, after all. This was why he had stopped going to Hollywood, and why he had been so quick to deny even the hint of a love affair with Dorothy. And Isabel: had she not steadfastly refused to say in so many words that she did not love any one else?

Antrim called himself hard names under his breath, and in the first flush of the new misery would have been glad to be able to charge his friend with insincerity. He saw the injustice of that in time to fight it down, and then rancour gave place to honest admiration. How unselfishly Brant had effaced himself, and how quick he had been to succour and to offer comfort and countenance to his rival! That, too, seemed incredible, even to Brant's best friend; but since incredible things were the order of the day, it was decently in keeping with all the other happenings of a time which was hopelessly out of joint.

So Antrim assured himself, with what resignation he could command; but for all that, this latest buffet of the boxer Misfortune was as a bolt from the blue, and he staggered under it, though not toward the abyss, since he had lately had his lesson and had profited by it.

While he was trying to face the necessity of discussing this newest phase of the many-sided problem with becoming stoicism a car overtook them and privacy was at an end. By the time the car had reached the crossing nearest the mission school he had fought and won his battle—the fiercest, and, as it chanced, the most unnecessary, that had ever been thrust upon him—and was ready with an assurance of good faith which was quite as sincere as it was costly.

"We mustn't be discouraged, and we must just go on hoping against hope," he said, when he took Dorothy's hand at parting. "It is a most intricate tangle, and I can't begin to unravel it yet; but you may count on one thing: what one man may do to help Brant will be done. You have told me some things that I didn't know before, but I shall work all the harder for knowing them. And if—if you think it will do any good, you may tell Isabel that."

After which generous confession of faith he left her and went to his office, being minded to dull the keen edge of the new trouble on the grindstone of hard work. The dulling process was but fairly in train when the door opened to admit Forsyth.

"Do you allow a man to trespass on Sunday?" he asked, feeling for the latch of the gate in the counter-railing.

"Surely, when the man is as good a friend as you are. Come in and sit down."

"It is about Brant, or I shouldn't trouble you," explained the editor, drawing up a chair. "I have been to see him again, and he is more obstinate than ever—if that be possible. He said you were there yesterday, and I came to see if you had been able to do anything with him."

"I wasn't."

"I was afraid you wouldn't be. Have you anything new to offer?"

"No."

"Well, I have. It is pretty plain to you that Brant will hang, lacking strong counsel, isn't it?"

"Plainer than I wish it were."

"Very good. Now there is just one lawyer in Christendom, so far as I know, whose services he can't well refuse."

"Who is it?"

"Judge Langford," said the editor, crossing his legs and nursing one knee.

"But, good Lord, Forsyth, you are losing your grip! Have you forgotten that the judge is William Langford's father?"

"I have forgotten nothing. From your point of view it would be out of the question, I grant you; but so far as heard from, you are the only person who doesn't believe Brant did it. Now I am convinced that he did, and the judge is quite as sure that he did; so the difficulties on that side vanish. I don't see what is to prevent the judge from taking the case, if he chooses to."

"I do. If he should clear Brant it would reopen the entire question as to Will. You know that as well as I do."

"He can't clear him; nobody can do more than get him a light sentence. But if he could clear him, the boy is well out of it. You were with Jarvis last night, and you helped him make the discovery that the shot was fired in line with the door; that it could not well have been fired from young Langford's position."

"Yes, but——"

"But what? Will you say that the judge is an invalid? or that his family connection with the affair should exempt him?"

"Ye-yes; either or both. That is about what I was going to say."

"Waiving the first objection,—the judge is a good deal better than a sick man,—the second is precisely the reason why he should be willing to offer his services—why he must offer them."

"How so?"

"Because the thing happened while Brant was in the service of the family. You know what I mean."

"I do; but I'd like to know how you found it out."

Forsyth laughed. "You have forgotten that you told Jarvis the whole story last night. But no matter about that: don't you see the judge's necessity now?"

"Yes, I don't know but I do. But supposing the judge doesn't see it?"

"He must be made to see it; and that brings me up to date. You know him well; can't you undertake to enlist him?"

"Frankly, I can't; and you have given the reason: I know him too well. He has been a second father to me since my own died."

"All right; I didn't know," said the editor, rising to go. "Somebody has it to do, and I thought perhaps you might be able to do it best."

"Who else have you in mind?"

"Nobody. I am going to tackle him myself."

"You?"

"Yes. Why not? I know the facts, and not being a personal friend, I sha'n't scruple to use them. I am going over there now. Will you come along?"

"Not unless you make a point of it. I should only hamper you."

"I don't make a point of it. Let me see; the house is Number Sixteen, isn't it?"

"Yes, Altamont Terrace. Don't be too savage with him, Forsyth. He has had lots of grief lately."

"He will have more if he shirks in this affair. But I sha'n't be any harsher with him than I have to be."

Half an hour later Forsyth rang the Hollywood door bell, and sent his card to the judge, who presently received his visitor in the library.

"I am right glad to see you, Mr. Forsyth," he said, rising and shaking hands cordially with the editor. "No, don't apologize for coming; you are very welcome. Be seated."

Forsyth took the proffered chair and plunged at once into the midst of his errand.

"It is about Brant, as you will infer. Yesterday you asked me to try again to make him listen to reason in the matter of employing counsel. I have tried thrice, and failed."

"Does he still refuse to give his reasons?"

"He does."

"And is he fully aware of the probable consequences?"

"As fully aware as we are."

"H'm! that is bad. Have you anything to suggest, Mr. Forsyth?"

"Yes. There is one person whose services he can not well decline."

"There is? And who is this person?"

"Yourself."

The judge rose quickly and went to the window, turning his back upon his visitor. It was full five minutes before he spoke again, and the editor waited patiently.

"I can scarcely believe you know what you ask, Mr. Forsyth," said the judge at length, coming slowly back to his chair. "If the circumstances were different, if my own son were not unfortunately involved, I should be the first to volunteer."

"My dear sir, that is precisely the reason why you should volunteer," said Forsyth firmly. "Bear with me a moment while I show you how the matter presents itself to an unbiassed outsider. Your son absents himself, and, knowing his habits, you and the other members of the family are justly anxious. In response to a request from one of your daughters——"

"Pardon me, but how did you learn that? From him?"

"No, indeed. I learned it, indirectly, from Miss Dorothy herself. As I was saying, in response to this request my friend undertakes the not unhazardous task of finding and rescuing your son. He does the first, and in trying to do the second he commits a crime which, account for it as you may, would not have been committed at that time and place if Brant had been less willing to help you and yours. Do I make my point of view quite clear?"

"Quite."

"Very well. Under such circumstances the least you can do for my friend is to defend him. No one else can do it as well. Your mere presence in court as his counsel may well save his life. Ask yourself the question seriously, Judge Langford, and if your own sense of justice will allow you to refuse, I have nothing more to say."

The judge leaned back in his chair and stared absently at the handful of fire in the grate. Forsyth's appeal reopened the question which he thought he had settled once for all the day before, and the arguments for and against began once more to marshal themselves for a fiercer conflict. Before the battle began he made one more effort to postpone it.

"You ignore the fact that I might end by directing suspicion against my own son, Mr. Forsyth."

"I do. I ignore everything but the question of simple justice and a just man's obligations."

The fight was on, and the judge left his chair to pace the floor with his hands behind him and his head bowed. Forsyth had told him no new thing. His duty had been clear enough from the moment of Dorothy's confession. But the frankness of the editor's appeal; the grave ruthlessness with which he held the responsibility up as something to be decided apart from personal considerations—a thing affecting justice, and honour, and uprightness—this touched him very nearly. But opposed to this his fatherhood rose up in mighty protest pleading as only paternal love can plead for the supremacy over all abstractions of whatsoever kind or degree. The struggle was long and bitter; and seeing the story of it writing itself in deeply graven lines upon the judge's face as he paced slowly back and forth,

Forsyth had to harden his heart more than once while he awaited the outcome. "It is the father against the man, but the man will win," he said to himself; and as he prophesied, so it came to pass.

"You have won your cause, Mr. Forsyth." The judge stopped before the editor's chair and spoke abruptly. "Go you to the young man and tender him my services, and let me know as soon as may be if he will accept them."

Forsyth sprang to his feet and wrung the elder man's hand gratefully.

"God bless you, Judge Langford; it is a noble thing for you to do! Don't think for a moment that I undervalue the cost. And now let me tell you something which will make your task easier. One of my young men made some experiments last night in the card room at the Osirian. The result proved conclusively that the shot was fired from some point in line with the door; that it could not well have been fired from the chair in which your son was sitting."

"Thank God for that!" exclaimed the judge fervently; but he added quickly: "I am glad you withheld that—glad you gave me the opportunity to give of my best. You will see Brant at once?"

Forsyth hesitated. "As my friend's friend, I am entirely at his service and yours. But don't you think it will be as well if you go to him unannounced?"

The judge thought about it for a moment.

"In view of his most singular obstinacy, perhaps it will. It is worth trying, at all events. I will go to-morrow morning."

"Thank you again," said the editor, finding his hat. "I presume I need not say that we have little time to lose. The Grand Jury meets to-morrow, and Brant will doubtless be indicted during the week."

"So I have been informed. No matter; we shall be diligent. If the young man will only confide in me we may be able to discover something which will serve to—to palliate his crime and to mitigate the severity of the inevitable sentence."

So spoke the judge, as though the question of his client's guilt was a question fully answered. But when he went to the door with his visitor he ventured a query which seemed to admit the thin edge of the wedge of uncertainty.

"There is no shadow of doubt in your mind, is there, Mr. Forsyth?—as to his guilt, I mean."

"None whatever," rejoined the editor sorrowfully. And he went his way saddened by the thought that he could answer no otherwise.

CHAPTER XXIX
IN WHICH A WILFUL MAN HAS HIS WAY

SINCE obstinacy, like a hound that is beaten, is constrained to course the truer for the blows of the whipper-in, two days of confinement and the anxious expostulations of Forsyth and Antrim appeared to have no mellowing effect upon the man who stood charged with the murder of James Harding. So far from it, time and the friendly efforts of the allies seemed but to crystallize reticent impulse into a fixed purpose strong to defeat any helpful emprise on the part of his friends.

Failing to beat down the guard of reticence in any face-to-face encounter, Forsyth had not been above bribing the turnkey to spy upon his prisoner; but if the man's report was to be believed, the bribe was money wasted. Brant spent the time in reading, was calm and cheerful, and cared not to know what the newspapers were saying about him. A model prisoner in every respect, and a man whom he (the turnkey) would be sorry to see hanged.

So ran the purchased report, and to all outward appearances the morning of the third day of his confinement found the prisoner in the same equable frame of mind. But if he fancied he had fortified the gate of silence until it was proof against the batterings of friendship, he had left unguarded a postern opening upon the innermost citadel of whatsoever resolution he was defending. By this postern he was presently to be assaulted, as was apparent when the jailer unlocked the cell door to admit Judge Langford. None the less, he welcomed his visitor heartily, and with becoming warmth.

"Good morning, Judge Langford. This is kind of you. I hardly expected to see you here," he said, doing the honours of his cramped quarters as best he might.

The judge stood his cane in a corner and sat down on the edge of the cot.

"That doesn't speak well for your good opinion of me," he rejoined genially. "At our last meeting—in your office, if you remember—I gave you to understand that you had placed me under obligations which I should gladly repay. Since then you have added somewhat to the score, and I am here to do what I may to square the account."

Brant bowed. If he suspected what was coming he made no sign, choosing rather to let the judge find his own way to what was toward.

"After the examination, Saturday, I met your friend Forsyth—and, by the way, he is a good friend of yours, too. He tells me that you refuse to employ counsel, and that without giving any reason. Now we can not allow that, you know, and to make it impossible for you to persist, I have this morning taken out a license to practice in the Colorado courts for the express purpose of defending you."

"Of what?" exclaimed the prisoner. It was a hopeful sign that the judge had beaten down the guard of self-possession that Brant sprang up and began to tramp, three steps and a turn.

"Of defending you, I said. And I am here now to beg you to speak freely to me as client to advocate."

"But, my dear sir! it is impossible—utterly impossible! You don't know what you have undertaken."

"I think I do; and I am ready and willing to do my best for you. But to that end you must be candid with me."

"I say you do not know," Brant insisted, going back of the admonition and speaking to the assertion. "Let me ask you one question, Judge Langford: Have you remembered that, as my counsel, you would be obliged to cross-examine your own son?"

"I have."

"Good God! And you would do it? Why—" The prisoner checked himself suddenly, as one on the verge of a precipice, faced about, and went on more calmly: "But you must know that I wouldn't allow it. It is the height of generosity and unselfishness on your part to offer it, but I can not accept—indeed, I can not."

"You must accept; it is my privilege to insist."

"And mine to refuse, ungracious as it may seem. I can not give you my reasons, and you must not ask them. But I'll say to you what I have not said to anybody else. If I should suffer you to do this thing which you propose you would never forgive me as long as you live!"

The judge met him firmly on his own ground. "That is only adding mystery to mystery. Be frank with me, Mr. Brant, at whatever cost to yourself, or to any one."

There was no reply to this, and the judge pressed his advantage vigorously. "Let us put away all equivocation and seek only to understand each other," he went on. "You have committed this crime"—the prisoner looked up quickly, and seemed to draw breath of relief—"you have committed this crime, and for some reason, real or fancied, you are determined to make no effort to save yourself. From a purely self-centred point of view this may seem right and proper; but you must remember that no man lives or dies to himself. You owe something to your friends; you owe something to me, since it was at least a part of your errand last Friday night to find my son and to send him home."

"Then you know—" Brant began, but the judge went on quickly:

"I know that much, and no more. It is for you to tell me the rest."

"I can't do it, Judge Langford, and you must forgive me if I still insist that you do not know what you are asking of me. I appreciate your kindness more than I can tell, but I can not suffer it. I have sins enough to answer for, God knows, without adding another for which there would be no forgiveness in this world or the next."

The judge shook his head slowly. "Your point of view grows more and more inexplicable, Mr. Brant. In what possible way could your confidence in me wrong any one?"

Brant leaned against the wall with folded arms, the gray eyes narrowing and the firm jaw settling itself in rigid lines.

"Perhaps the word was ill chosen. But if I should do as you ask, there would be sorrow and grief and misery where I would fain see happiness. And for myself there would be regrets deep and lifelong. You will say this is more mystery, but I can not help it. I know quite well what I am doing, and I have counted the cost to the last farthing. My life has been a sorry failure, Judge Langford—so poor a thing that I can afford to give it freely if the law shall demand it."

The judge pursed his lips and made another step in the outworking of the problem of deduction.

"Am I to understand by this that free speech on your part would involve others besides yourself?" he asked.

"It would involve others—yes, many others."

"Without making your defense less hopeless than it appears to be at present?"

"Without bringing me anything that I could endure with half the fortitude that I shall take to the gallows. No; your sympathy and loving-kindness are very comforting to me, but you must pardon me if I say that they are quite undeserved. Whatever the jury sees fit to give me will doubtless have been earned, and well earned."

The judge saw that the time for winning his client's confidence was not yet ripe, and he rose and buttoned his coat.

"You are still giving me riddles, Mr. Brant, and while you elect to do that, no one can help you intelligently. I am not going to press you further this morning, but I shall come again—and yet again. Meanwhile, I am ready and anxious to act for you the moment you will permit it. I can't say more, can I?"

He held out his hand, and Brant's grasp of it was not without emotion.

"No one could be kinder than you, Judge Langford; and some time, in this world or another, you shall know that I am not ungrateful."

When the judge was fairly out of the cell and the sound of his footsteps had died away in the corridor, Brant threw himself upon the cot and groaned aloud. But his speech was of gratitude.

"Thank God, that trial is over! If they could devise many more such torments as that, I'd hang myself to the grating and have done with it!"

That evening, at nine o'clock, a fact leaked out which Forsyth hastened to telephone to the house in the Highlands: the Grand Jury had found a true bill against George Brant for the wilful murder of James Harding.

CHAPTER   XXX
HOW LOVE AND FRIENDSHIP THREW A MAIN

FOR two weeks after the judge's first interview with his unwilling client the possibility of successfully defending Brant receded steadily, and no new discoveries came to countermine the wall of evidence which was slowly and surely closing in upon him.

In this interval Colonel Bowran had returned, and, contrary to Brant's expectation or desire, had at once championed his draughtsman's cause. There had been more than one stormy interview—they were tempestuous on the colonel's part, at least—in which the chief engineer's wrath was directed at Brant's obduracy. And when expostulation and friendly abuse had failed, the colonel sought out Judge Langford and Forsyth, joining forces cordially with the prisoner's friends, but bringing nothing helpful in the way of additional information.

On the other hand, the prosecution lacked nothing but the culprit's confession of having a complete case. Brant's record was exploited, and the details of his previous quarrel with Harding, or so much of them as were known to Draco's bartender, were dragged out of Deverney as sound teeth are extracted from the jaw of an unwilling patient.

So much of the State's side of the case was known to Brant's friends—by what means Forsyth's young men could best have explained—and there was consternation among them in just proportion. If the tide could not be stemmed before the rapidly approaching day of the trial, the judge knew he should go into court without any case. And, making due allowance for the change that had recently been wrought in public sentiment, he had every reason to fear the worst for his client.

"I tell you, Forsyth, the man will hang in spite of everything we can do."

So much the judge was impelled to say in one of the many conferences with the editor, and Forsyth had nothing to offer in rebuttal.

"I'm afraid he will," said the editor. And then: "We are all in the same boat, and on the same side of the boat—all but Harry Antrim. He still asserts his belief in Brant's innocence. In his way he is as obdurate as Brant himself. But it is entirely sentiment on his part. I wish his faith had a better foundation."

So Antrim had wished many times; and after having racked his brain for a fortnight for something tangible wherewith to buttress his belief, he was finally indebted to the chapter of accidents for a clew which seemed to point most hopefully.

It was in the afternoon of that day in which Judge Langford had summed up Brant's case in the talk with the editor. Antrim had been rummaging in his safe for a missing paper, and had chanced to come upon the sealed envelope given him by Brant for safe-keeping on the morning after the burglary at Mrs. Seeley's.

His first impulse was to send it posthaste to the judge; his next was to break the seal and read the sworn evidence of Harding's guilt in the year-agone crime committed in Taggett's Gulch. Five minutes later he was writing a note to Dorothy, begging her to come quickly to the office.

Dorothy answered the note in person, and Antrim took her into the superintendent's room and closed the door. What he had to say brooked neither listeners nor interruptions.

"I'm awfully glad you came right away," he began. "I was afraid something might hinder you, and what I want to talk about won't wait."

Dorothy sat down in the superintendent's big chair and unpinned her veil. "I was just getting ready to come down for Isabel when Tommie came. He said it was a 'rush message,' so I caught the next car."

"That was lucky." Antrim was tramping up and down before her, full to bursting with his news. Suddenly he stopped and confronted her. "Dorothy, would you still be glad to believe that Brant isn't guilty?"

She sat up very straight at this and the sensitive chin quivered a little. "That is a hard question, Harry. If it wasn't Mr. Brant——"

"I know what you are thinking about," he broke in. "But just leave Will out of it entirely; try to forget that he was there."

"If I could do that, the question—your question—would answer itself."

"That is all I want to know. Now I have believed all along that Brant didn't do it; and a little while ago I found some papers which go to show that he could have no possible motive for doing it. It isn't necessary to go over the whole thing, but you will understand what I mean when I tell you that these papers are Brant's, and any time he wanted to get rid of Harding all he had to do was to turn them over to the district attorney of Pitkin County. That would have been the end of Mr. Murderer Harding as soon as they could catch and hang him."

"You say you found these papers—where?"

"In my safe. Brant gave them to me to keep for him."

"Do you know why he did that?"

"No."

"I do." She tugged at the fingers of her glove and a light came into her eyes that told Antrim more than she would have admitted by word of mouth under torture. "It was because he was afraid to keep them; afraid he might be tempted to let the law do what everybody is saying he did with his own hand. Harry, he is innocent!"

"Of course he is; that is what I've been saying all along. Now there are two of us who believe it, and something has got to be done quick."

"What had you thought of?"

"I can't think—I'm too foolishly rattled to think; and that is why I sent for you. You can plan all around the rest of us. What do you say?"

Dorothy sat back in the great chair and thought it all out in the turning of a leaf.

"Mr. Brant must be made to listen to reason," she said decisively. "He must let papa defend him; he must let papa use these papers; and he must tell us all the things we don't know."

Antrim's gesture was of despair. "Pity's sake! that is just what we have all been trying to get him to do for two whole weeks!"

"I can't help it; that is what must be done."

"And done it shall be, if you will only go a step farther and tell me how we are to bring it about."

"Can't you persuade him?"

"Persuade nothing! Why, Dorothy, you haven't an idea what a mule the man is! Your father, and Forsyth, and Colonel Bowran, and I have fairly worn ourselves out trying to make him open his head. There isn't a thing any of us could think of that hasn't been tried; not a— Yes, by Jove, there is one thing, too!"

An inspiration much too large to be readily clothed in words came to Antrim, dazzling him with its invincible simplicity. Dorothy divined it with quick intuition, and her heart sank within her at the bare suggestion.

"What is it?" she asked faintly.

"Why, it is the simplest thing in the world! Brant won't talk to any of us, but if you will go to him——"

"O Harry—I can't, I can't!" she wailed.

But he would not be turned aside. "Yes, you can, Dorothy, and you must. It is life and death with him now. Only this morning Forsyth told me it was all up with him. Think of a man being hanged for a thing that he didn't do; think how awful it would be if you had to remember that you might have done something to prevent it, and didn't! Think of—think of Isabel, Dorothy, and be a brave little sister of mercy, as you have always been to every one in trouble."

"Oh, don't, *don't!*" she pleaded pitifully. "Don't say any more, Harry. You haven't any idea of what you are asking me to do, but I—I'll go. Can we do it now—right away—before I have to go home and face them all again?"

Antrim made a quick dash for his hat and coat, and they were halfway to the jail before she spoke again.

"Isn't it a very dreadful thing for me to do?" she asked shamefacedly. "Do—do ladies ever go to see the prisoners?—alone, I mean."

"I don't know; and you must not care, Dorothy—not for this once. I'll go as far as the corridor with you and wait till you come out. You must just keep saying to yourself that it is life and death; and—and Isabel's happiness," he added softly.

She caught the inspiration of his unselfishness, and answered it in kind.

"You are very good and noble, Harry. I'll remember; and I'll try to do my part—as you are doing yours. Is this the place? Oh, what a terrible Castle of Despair!"

CHAPTER XXXI
A FEAST OF MINGLED CUPS

BRANT was lying down when he heard the heavy step of the turnkey in the corridor; heard the heavy step and a lighter one, and the rustle of a woman's dress. He made sure it was another of the cut-flower faddists who had lately been making his prison life a hot bath of vicarious shame, and sprang up with a muttered malediction comprehensive enough to include the entire procession of the sentimentalists. A moment later the key grated in the lock, the bolts clanked, and the door swung back. He stood transfixed for an instant, hardly daring to believe his eyes. Then the clamour and crash of the closing door brought him to his senses and he turned away and hid his face.

Dorothy stood still, abashed at her own boldness and waiting timidly for some sign of recognition. When it was overlong in coming she plucked up courage and went to him.

"Haven't you a word of welcome for me, Mr. Brant?" she asked softly.

"Don't ask me. What can I say? Why did you come?"

"Because you made me," she said simply. "You wouldn't listen to any of the others, you know; and—and—but you will listen to me. You must."

He turned to face her, and even in the dim half-light of the cell she could see that he was nerving himself for a struggle.

"Please sit down," he said, pointing to the single chair. "I think I know what you have come to say, but it isn't any use—indeed, it is not."

She ignored the pointing and the invitation, and leaned against the wall within arm's reach of him.

"Please don't say that—not to me. None of the others had my right. It was I who sent you."

He flinched at that and gave ground a little. "You have a good right, Miss Langford, though it isn't builded upon your little cry for help. What would you have me do?"

"Whatever papa wants you to do," she rejoined quickly, deeming it best not to go too deeply into particulars.

"I am sorry to have to refuse you anything; but this that you ask is altogether impossible."

"Why is it impossible?"

"Because—God in heaven!—none of you know what you are asking!"

"Then tell me, so I may know."

"I can't do that, either."

"Won't you tell me if I guess it?"

The pleading eyes unsteadied him, and he receded yet another step. "Perhaps," he said, hesitating.

"Are you afraid that if you defend yourself my brother will be in danger?"

Is there something in the washing of tears that gives insight to sympathetic eyes? She saw deep into him at that moment; saw that to deny her accusation would be to lie; saw also that he could not look into her eyes and find words to frame the falsehood. So she was prepared for the evasion.

"And if that were true, what then?"

"You would be making a terrible and utterly useless mistake. Don't you know—haven't they told you? It has been proved that my brother could not have done it."

He did not ask how it had been proved. It was enough that she believed it, and it was the final drop of bitterness in the cup of expiation that he had thought to drain bravely to the dregs. To her, as to all others, save only Antrim, he was a murderer. It was more than he could bear unmoved, and he turned from her lest she should see the anguish in his face and be moved by it to say the thing which was not true. When he did not reply she spoke again:

"That was the reason, wasn't it?"

"It was—it *is*." The words said themselves because there was no strength left in him wherewith to hold them back.

She gave him no time to draw again the sheathed sword of denial. "I was sure of it. But you won't hesitate any longer now, will you?—not after what I have told you."

"Hesitate—to tell them I am guilty? No, I shall not hesitate; I'll confess to you—here—now, if you wish." He faced her suddenly, but again the tear-brightened eyes and their pleading unmanned him. "No, I can't say it to you," he went on, softening and becoming as the clay on the potter's wheel in spite of himself. "In the eye of the law—in the eyes of the whole world—I am a murderer, taken in the very act. But I can not go to my death with the thought that the only woman I have ever loved believes me guilty of such a cowardly crime. I did not kill James Harding."

Dorothy forgot her errand, forgot the papers, forgot everything in the horror of a great doubt and the ecstasy of an unchartered joy still greater than the doubt which suddenly threatened to suffocate her. Nevertheless, a misunderstanding, rooted and grounded as hers was, dies hard.

"You mean that I should—that you want me to—to tell my sister," she faltered; and she could no longer look him in the face.

"Your sister!" Brant fought a good fight for self-control and won it. "No, Dorothy; it is not Isabel's belief that troubles me; it is yours. How could you have misunderstood?"

Dorothy felt her lips growing cold, and the solid floor of the cell swayed under her feet until she clung to the wall for support.

"How could I? But she told me—" She broke off in pitiable confusion, and Brant gave her the helping hand of a question:

"What was it she told you? I have given you the right to say anything you please to me now."

She saw instantly that she must go on or leave Isabel under an imputation too dreadful to be contemplated. "She told me that—that she sent you away."

"Sent me away? But she didn't send me away; that couldn't be, you know. It is all a mistake, Dorothy—an awful mistake. It was not I whom she sent away; it was Harry."

"Harry!" said Dorothy faintly. "Oh, dear, what have I done? Tell me one thing, please. Whom did you meet the last evening you came to see us?"

It was Brant's turn to be confused and tongue-tied, and he answered her with his eyes on the floor.

"I met—your mother. I went over that evening to tell you that—I—loved you, my darling; to tell you what I had been, and what I hoped to be, and to ask you to wait until I could make my promises good. Your mother met me, and— But no matter about that. It was she who sent me away—for good reasons, you will say now. None the less, bad as I am, and good as you are, I love you—you and no other, my dear one; how truly and passionately you may know some day."

"Some day!" She knew at that sublime moment, and the keen joy of the knowledge made her lose sight of everything save the heart-quelling fact.

"Thank God, I know it now!—know that you are here in prison because you thought it was the only way to save my brother. Oh, how could I——"

"Be so faithless," she would have said; but he caught her in his arms and his kisses put the remorseful exclamation to death.

"Say but two words, my darling," he whispered. "Tell me that you love me, and that you believe me innocent of this last horrible thing, and I shall die happier than most men live."

But, after all, he had to take the first of the two words for granted. His saying that he should die happy brought her back to the peril of the moment.

"Oh, please don't say that! I know you are innocent; but so is brother!"

He shook his head gravely and drew her closer. "I wish I could believe that, but I can't, Dorothy, dear," he said sorrowfully. "I should not have been weak enough to betray him, even to you; but now you must keep my secret and help me to save him. Try to think of it as I have. You remember what the Man of Nazareth said: 'They that take the sword shall perish with the sword.' I have lived a life of violence, and it is only just that I should pay the penalty."

But her sense of right and wrong was keener and truer than his. "No, you must not say that. Two wrongs never make a right. Can't you see that your blood will be upon the head of the judge and the jury, and every one who has anything to do with punishing you for a crime you did not commit? Oh, you mustn't, you must not!"

"I have thought of all that, dear," he said, "and at times it has shaken me. But there is no other way. It is my life or your brother's. He is young; the lesson will be a terrible one, and he may live to profit by it."

His words carried such deep conviction of William's guilt that she gasped and gave a little cry of anguish.

"Oh, are you sure? Did you see him do it?"

"No, dear; it was done in the moment of darkness. But when they turned the lights on from without he had the pistol in his hand, and I saw him throw it upon the floor. Will you tell me why they say he couldn't have done it?"

"I don't know well enough to make it clear; but Harry and one of Mr. Forsyth's young men made some measurements, and they both say that the shot couldn't have been fired from where Will was sitting; that it must have been fired from the direction of the door."

"From the door?" A great desire to live and love and be loved came quickly to Brant, and he made haste to put it away before it should possess him. "I wish I had known that sooner, but it is too late now. I wasn't near the door; I was trying to get between them when the shot was fired."

"It must not be too late!" cried Dorothy eagerly. "Oh, why didn't they tell you? Why——"

She broke off abruptly and struggled out of his arms at the sound of a footstep in the corridor. It was the turnkey coming to release her, and there was time for no more than a breathless question.

"May I tell—" she began; and he bent over her till his lips touched her forehead.

"I am yours in life or in death," he said gently. "Do with me what seems best to you, my darling."

A moment later she had rejoined Antrim in the corridor, but neither spoke until they were out of the building. It was in the half-light between day and dusk when they reached the street, and the chief clerk curbed his impatience until they were hurrying to catch the North Denver car. Then it slipped the leash.

"What luck?" he demanded, as they threaded the crowded sidewalk in Larimer Street. "Did you find out anything? Would he talk to you?"

Dorothy blushed hotly and drew down her veil.

"Ye-yes, he talked very freely, and I found out a great many things. Wait till we get out of the crowd and I will tell you."

They missed the car, as a matter of course, and had to wait on the street corner. Whereupon Antrim drew his companion into a sheltered doorway and refused to be kept longer in ignorance and suspense.

"For pity's sake, tell me, Dorothy, what did he say? I'm on tenter-hooks, and it seemed as if you would never come out."

"He didn't do it, Harry. He is innocent," she began triumphantly, and Antrim could see her eyes shining behind the veil.

"I have known that all along," he interrupted impatiently. "What then? What about the papers?"

"Oh, dear, I forgot all about them! I can't talk about it, Harry; not here in the street. But there is one thing I must tell you"—the hot blush came again and its attendant emotion threatened to stop her, but she went on bravely—"it is about—Mr. Brant and—and Isabel. I was just dreadfully, horridly, stupidly mistaken. Isabel meant—that is, it's not Mr. Brant; it is somebody else. There is nothing at all between them, and there never has been. I——"

Antrim waited to hear no more. There was an idle carriage standing at the curb, and before she knew what he meant to do he had put her into it, slammed the door, and swung himself up to a seat beside the driver.

"To Judge Langford's house, over in the Highlands. I'll show you the way if you don't know it," he said briefly; and then, "The quicker you make it the more money you'll earn."

In an incredibly short time he was helping Dorothy out at the Hollywood gate. "Fix it some way so that I can have ten minutes alone with Isabel," he begged as they hurried up the walk, "and then I'll be ready to hear all about Brant. You will do that much for me, won't you, Dorothy?"

Fortunately, it needed not to be arranged. Isabel met them in the hall, and Dorothy had but to dart quickly into the library and so leave them alone together. Two weeks of utter neglect had humbled Isabel rather more than she would admit even to herself, but they had also made her affectionately vindictive. Hence she gave him no more than a cool little "Good evening, Harry. Won't you come in?"

"I am in; and I'll stay to dinner if you will ask me," he retorted promptly, penning her into the corner between the door and the stairfoot. "But first I want to say something that I am going to repeat every time we meet, regardless of time, place, or present company. I love you, Isabel, I have always loved you, and I am always going to."

"Indeed!" said Isabel with sweet sarcasm.

"Yes, in deed, and in thought, and in word. More than that, I know now that you love me—oh, don't take the trouble to deny it; it's wrong to tell fibs. You told Dorothy you did, and she gave it away without meaning to. So you see it is no use, and you may as well give me that kiss I asked for the last time you told me the biggest fib of all the——"

"Not now—or ever!" she retorted, slipping under his arm and darting down the hall to the drawing-room door. He caught at her as she eluded him, and then ran after her. She paused with her hand on the doorknob.

"Keep your distance, or I vanish!" she threatened. "Stand right there where you are and tell me why you went off in a dudgeon that night; and why you froze me out two weeks ago; and why you haven't been back since; and why——"

But the catechism was never finished. With a most lamentable want of vigilance she took her hand from the doorknob, and Antrim— But sufficient unto the day of youth are the small triumphs thereof.

Twenty minutes later Kate Hobart, coming down to dinner, stumbled over two young persons sitting on the lowest step of the stair. She recognised them even in the darkness, and being but a Sabbath-day's journey beyond her own love affair, understood at once why the hall was not yet lighted.

Antrim sprang quickly to his feet and made the explanation which does not explain; and Kate benevolently helped him out by asking if there were anything new in Brant's affair.

"No—yes, there is, too, by Jove! And we have been sitting here talking— that is, ah—er———"

"Spooning, Harry, dear," cut in Isabel with refreshing frankness; "tell the truth and shame———"

But he went on without a break—"while Dorothy is waiting to tell us about Brant. Let's go in and hear her story."

Isabel tapped at the library door, and they all saw within when the judge opened to her. Dorothy was sitting on the lounge, her hat and gloves still on, her face pale and tear-stained. The judge waved them back.

"In a moment," he said; and then he crossed the room to bend over the still little figure on the lounge and to whisper a word of encouragement.

"It is hard to win and lose in the same moment, but you must be brave, my child—for your own sake and mine. I shall keep your secret; your mother mustn't suspect—now or ever."

She nodded, and the tears came afresh.

"Go you up to your room," he added, seeing that there was no present balm for the hurt. "I'll make your excuses at the table."

Then he joined the trio in the hall. "Dorothy brought astounding news," he explained, leading the way to the dining room, "but it comes too late. From what she tells me there seems to be a reasonable doubt of the young man's guilt; but there is nothing that can be used in evidence, and his conviction is none the less certain."

There was manifestly nothing to be said, and a sympathetic silence followed the announcement. While they were taking their places at table the telephone rang, and the judge excused himself to answer it.

"Don't wait on me," he said. "Harry, lad, take my place and carve, will you?" and he went out and carefully closed the door behind him. And inasmuch as the hall was not yet lighted, he failed to see a shadowy little figure on the stair. It was Dorothy, and she paused and leaned over the balustrade when her father answered the call.

CHAPTER XXXII
SUCH FRIENDS ARE EXULTATION'S AGONY

"ARRAH, now, Misther Jarvis, 'tis no use your flatthering me the like of that. Fwhat I know, I know; and that I'll keep to myself. Besides, wasn't it Misther Brant himself, poor dear! that says, says he, 'Mum's the wurrud, Mary, me jool; sure 'tis but a b'y's thrick, and I'll not be having it talked about at all at all.'"

"Yes; but that was before it all came out in the newspapers," Jarvis cut in glibly. "He doesn't mind your talking about it now; in fact, he told me to ask you."

For something better than a week the reporter had been assiduously cultivating Mrs. Seeley's housemaid, and one of the results of the intimacy was a second visit to Brant's room, made in the landlady's absence and connived at and arranged by Mary McCarthy. Jarvis hoped little from a second inspection of the room, and not much from anything the housemaid could tell. Yet he lied brazenly to make her talk, and the lie accomplished that whereunto it was sent.

"Ah, then, did he tell you that, poor man?" said the unsuspecting Mary.

"He did, for a fact; couldn't come himself, you know, poor fellow!" rejoined the reporter, clinching the falsehood promptly. "Now show me just what you did and tell me what you saw."

Thus absolved and adjured, Mary McCarthy went circumstantially over the account of her discovery of the burglar, Jarvis absorbing the story as it was told, and leaving the journalistic compartment of his brain to sift the salient facts from the mass of embellishment and exaggeration.

"Black clothes, you say?" he interrupted, when the housemaid came to the describing of the intruder.

"Black as Father Callahan's cassock."

"Then he didn't look like a tramp or a tough?"

"On'y for the oogly face av him I might have mistook him for Misther Brant himself."

Jarvis strolled to the window and stood with his hands deep in his pockets, looking out upon the tin roof of the porch.

"Dang the thing!" he muttered. "It gets blinder with every move. Now, who the mischief is this gentleman burglar whom Brant wants to screen, and what was he here for? By Jove! I wonder if it was young Langford? He always wears gamblers' mourning. But what the dickens was he trying to steal?"

He turned away from the window and made another slow circuit of the room in the vague hope that he might stumble upon some overlooked clew to the puzzle. There was none, and he was about to give it up when he came to the closet at the foot of the bed.

"Does this door open into the next room?" he asked.

"No, sure; 'tis on'y the closet where Misther Brant does be keeping his clothes."

Jarvis turned the knob and glanced at the garments hanging in an orderly row at the back of the shallow recess. "These are all Brant's, I suppose," he said carelessly.

"'Deed and they are, then. Whose else would they be?"

"Are these all he has?"

Mary McCarthy picked a fancied suspicion out of the meaningless question and promptly resented it.

"D'ye think annybody would be shtealing them?" she demanded. "Av coorse they are all there, barring fwhat Misther Antrim and the b'y tuk to him at the jail."

"Boy? What boy was this?"

"'Deed, then, I don't know; some little scaramouch from the sthreets, I'm thinking. But he did be bringing a letther from Misther Brant; 'tis there on the table."

Jarvis sauntered across the room and took a dirty scrap of paper from beneath a paperweight on the small writing table. It was a misspelled pencil scrawl, signed with Brant's name, but he did not have to look twice to decide that it was the clumsiest of forgeries, written evidently by some one who had never so much as seen Brant's handwriting.

"Mary, dear," he said feelingly, "you are a pearl of price, and the mate to you has never been found."

"Be off wid you wid your flatthering tongue!"

"It's not flattery—never a word of it. Did Mrs. Seeley see this letter?"

"Sure, she did that same. 'Twas to her that the b'y did be giving it."

"And she gave the boy the suit of clothes it calls for?"

"Av coorse she did. And 'tis myself as was wondering fwhat Misther Brant would be wanting wid them ould rags."

"From all our friends—so they be women—good Lord deliver us!" said Jarvis under his breath; then aloud: "That was quite right, of course. Did you happen to see the clothes yourself, Mary?"

"I did that; an ould dirty suit of pepper-and-salt it was, the likes of fwhat Misther Brant never did be wearing in the whole swate life av him."

"Exactly."

Jarvis slipped the note into his pocket and got away as quickly as he could. It was but the slenderest thread of a clew, but it spanned one of the many gaps he had been vainly trying for a fortnight to bridge.

At the very beginning of his investigation the reporter had stumbled upon Harding's disguise—the wig and the false beard—in the West Denver *Gasthaus*; and a painstaking inquiry into the habits of the red-haired and fiery-bearded lodger had developed the fact that he was seen often in company with another man whose description Jarvis had gathered from many sources, but whom he was as yet unable to identify.

So far as could be ascertained, the unidentified one had disappeared on the night of the tragedy. He had been seen alone at Draco's in the earlier hours of that night, and he had not been seen by any of Jarvis's informants since that time. Apart from the overheard conference in Heddrigg's restaurant—a conference in which Jarvis had long since recognised Harding in his character of red-beard and the unknown man as the two participants—there was nothing to remotely connect the unidentified man with Brant's affair; nothing, unless the forged letter to Mrs. Seeley might be taken as a connecting link. But just here the reporter's incomplete knowledge of the facts hampered him. He knew nothing of the papers at which the burglary pointed, and could only guess from the overheard conversation in Heddrigg's restaurant that the burglar was an emissary of Harding's. At the finding of the forged letter he had jumped to the conclusion that the house-breaker and Harding's unknown companion were one and the same person; but cooler after-thought brought doubt, and a leaning toward the William Langford hypothesis.

"I am afraid it was the young fellow, after all," he said at the summing up. "That guess fits the other guesses a little more as if it belonged. Nobody but a fool of a boy would do such a thing and get stone blind in the middle of it; and there is nobody else in the whole shooting match that Brant would go out of his way to shield. As for the clothes and the letter, they don't count very hard. Even as big a fool as the boy would have sense enough not to wear his everyday clothes while he burgled a house."

So Jarvis concluded; and he did not change his mind when, later in the day, in another talk with Deverney, he learned that Harding's unknown companion had always appeared in dingy "pepper-and-salt." That was a mere coincidence, he argued; and the pattern was certainly common enough to warrant the supposition.

It was in the evening of this same day that the reporter asked his chief to procure him an order to visit the prisoner, or, rather, asked if such an order could be procured.

"I don't know," said the night editor. "It's after hours. But we can try. What have you stumbled upon—anything new?"

"Nothing much. Write me the request for an order, and I'll tell you about it when I come back. I have an idea."

The request was written and Jarvis forthfared to the jail. His idea was but the piecing together of some irrelevant facts. He had learned from his chief that Brant had at one time taken a pistol from Harding, and from the editor's description the weapon was a *facsimile* of the one found on the floor of the card room after the murder. Out of this the reporter built a new theory, and an interview with Brant was needed to confirm or disprove it.

———————————

CHAPTER XXXIII
TE MORITURI SALUTAMUS

IF it was late in the day when Jarvis left the Plainsman building armed with his chief's request for an order to visit the prisoner in the jail, it was still later when the formalities were finally appeased and he gained access to the inner fastnesses of the city's house of detention and to Brant's cell.

Having but now parted from Dorothy, Brant was in the seventh heaven of love's aftermath when the cell door opened to admit the reporter; and since love breaks ground for far-reaching kindliness, the news-gatherer's welcome was all that could be desired.

"I wonder if any unlucky dog of them all ever had better friends or more of them than I have, Jarvis? The way you all stand by me would warm the cockles of a worse heart than mine ever was." Thus the prisoner of good hope, love-tempered; and Jarvis laughed.

"You don't deserve to have any friends. May I sit on your bed? Thanks. A fellow that loses the combination on his tongue the way you have ought to be hanged on general principles. But you've got to talk to me, or thrash me, one of the two."

"I'll do both, if you insist," said Brant with cheerful levity. "Which will you have first?"

"The answers to two or three questions first, and then, if there is any fight left in you, we'll see about the thrashing."

"Go ahead. What is it you want to know?" said the aforetime bondsman of reticence.

"A lot of things that you can't tell me, and some few that you can. Did you at one time have a gun—a Colt's forty-five—that had once belonged to Harding?"

Brant lost levity and freedom of speech in the dropping of an eyelid, but he could not in common fairness refuse to answer.

"I did."

"Did you have this admirable weapon about you on the night of the shooting?"

"No."

"Where was it at that time?"

"I don't know."

"I think I do know," said the cross-examiner placidly. "You had lost it, hadn't you?"

"Yes."

"I thought so. Now I am going to hazard a guess—dang the thing! it's all guesses, so far—and I shall know if I've hit it whether you admit it or not. You left that gun in your room the night of the burglary, and you haven't seen it since."

Brant did not attempt to deny it. "That is also true," he admitted.

"So far, so good. Now, do you know who it was who broke into your room, and slept in your bed, and stole your artillery?"

"I think I do, but I don't care to discuss that point with you."

"You needn't, if you don't want to. But it will be discussed in open court next week."

Brant's start was not lost upon the young man, who had apparently missed his vocation in electing to be a journalist rather than a detective.

"Why should it come up at the trial?" Brant demanded.

"Because it is going to have a very considerable bearing on the case," said Jarvis coolly. "The man who took the pistol from your room gave it back to Harding."

"How do you know he did?"

Jarvis leered. "He did, or he didn't; one of the two. I believe he didn't."

"More theories," said Brant, not without sarcasm. "What difference does it make?"

"It makes all the difference in the world when you come to tie it to the fact that Harding was killed with that same weapon."

This time Brant's start was visible to the naked eye of the least critical observer, but his rejoinder was well measured and calm:

"What is your theory? Set it in words."

Jarvis settled himself on the cot, nursing one knee in his clasped hands and chewing an extinct cigar. "It's as simple as twice two. You heard young Langford's testimony at the preliminary examination?"

"Naturally, being within a few feet of him when he gave it."

"Very good. You were in that card room at the Osirian and saw what he saw. Did he tell the truth?"

Brant was silent.

"You know he didn't tell the truth; or, at least, he didn't tell all of it," Jarvis went on. "He said that Harding drew a pistol on him, but he did not say that he had already drawn his own. Also, he left the inference wide open that the big pistol on the table, the pistol from which the shot was fired, was Harding's—that Harding had laid it there. That wasn't so."

Brant sprang to his feet in a frenzy of impatience. "For God's sake, have done with this beating about the bush and tell me what you know or what you suspect!"

Jarvis complied in set phrase. "This: Young Langford was the man who broke into your room. He was the man who took the pistol, who carried it all the next day, who drew it upon Harding, who—" He broke off abruptly, leaving the categorical accusation unfinished. "You know what happened just as well as I do. It was that young cub who did the shooting, and you are here because—well, I know the why and wherefore of that, too, but we needn't go into it. You've been all sorts of a Don Quixote, and I believe you'd keep it up to the finish, if you had your way. But it won't go, George."

Brant said nothing. He was leaning against the wall, just where Dorothy had stood a little while before, and there was a far-away look in his eyes—the look that comes into the eyes of a soldier when duty calls and death beckons. But Jarvis was not skilled in reading face signs, and he went on, secure in the worldly wisdom of his own point of view.

"I'm not saying it wasn't a fine thing. If you had lived two or three centuries ago they would have drawn and quartered you first and made a demigod of you afterward. But it won't go now. When people find out, half of them will laugh at you, and the other half will say you ought to be sent to a lunatic asylum. If you could have carried it through——"

Brant came out of his reverie and sat down on the cot beside the exponent of worldly wisdom.

"You say, if I could have carried it through," he broke in. "But now?"

"Now there is nothing to do but to switch over and pull in harness with common sense. It will all come out at the trial—it's bound to. The judge is making believe that he is going to be your counsel, whether or no; but you know you are not going to allow it, and the upshot of that will be that the court will appoint somebody else to defend you, and it is ten to one that it will be some keen young fellow with nothing to lose and everything to gain.

There are a dozen young lawyers keeping up with the case, and any one of them will snap at the chance. And you know as well as I do what will happen if any lawyer in the wide world, save and excepting his own father, gets a chance to cross-examine Will Langford."

Brant nodded, as one who may not controvert a self-evident fact. But what he said brought the reporter's card house of hypotheses tumbling in ruins.

"You have made your case, Jarvis, and summed it up, but there is one small flaw in it. You are taking it for granted that young Langford killed Harding, and that I did not. What if I say that your basic premises are wrong?"

Jarvis laughed, but it was not the laugh of assurance. "You can't bluff me out, George; I know what I know."

"You don't know anything. You are merely guessing from beginning to end."

Jarvis took time to think about it, and assurance slipped still farther into the abyss of incertitude.

"If it is only a guess, you can make it a certainty," he said at length.

Brant smiled. "You would hardly expect me to tie the rope around my own neck, even in a confidential talk with you. But I will tell you a little, and you may infer the rest—you are pretty good at inferences. My quarrel with Harding was of the deadly sort, and it had been going on for years. A few weeks ago I ran him out of town, telling him plainly that if he came back I should kill him. After he had gone I learned that he had done a thing for which there was no such word as forgiveness, and I swore then, and wrote it down in a letter, that his chance for life lay in keeping out of my way. Can you put two and two together?"

Jarvis nodded slowly. "You've buried me and my little theory six feet deep, with a stone atop, and—and I'm honestly sorry. I couldn't believe you'd do a thing like that in cold blood, George."

"Do you call it cold blood? There were three of us in that eight-by-ten shambles that night, and somebody had to die."

The turnkey was unlocking the door, and Jarvis rose.

"I guess there isn't anything more to say," he said. "Can I do anything for you?"

"Yes; you may take a line to Forsyth for me, if you will." And then to the jailer: "One minute, Carson, until I write a note."

The note was written, and Jarvis took his leave, wringing Brant's hand at parting quite as heartily as he would if the card house of guesses had not been wrecked.

"You've simply made another friend, old man," he whispered. "It was mostly curiosity with me before, but now I'll stand by you while the lamp holds out to burn."

Brant returned the hand grip, but his smile had in it more than gratitude. "I'll let you know when you can do anything," he promised; and then the iron door came between.

The reporter found his chief waiting impatiently for his return, and Forsyth was soon acquainted not only with Jarvis's guesses, but with the main points in the late interview.

"That's all," said Jarvis in conclusion, "except that he gave me this note for you."

Forsyth read the note and swore gratefully.

"You are to be congratulated, Jarvis; you have done what none of the rest of us have been able to do. He consents to accept Judge Langford as his counsel." And the editor went quickly to the telephone to call up the house in the Highlands.

This was the skirling of the bell which had interrupted the master of Hollywood as he was sitting down to his dinner, and which had made Dorothy linger on the stair to hear what should come of it.

"What is it, papa?" she asked, when her father replaced the earpiece in its hook.

"It is a message from Mr. Forsyth. Brant has notified him that he will accept me as his counsel, and has promised not to obstruct us any more. You may take that for a grain of comfort."

But Dorothy still lingered. "Is the time set for the trial, papa?"

"Yes; Tuesday of next week. But don't grieve till you must. We shall be ready, and we shall do all there is to be done."

"One week from to-day—one little week!" She said it over and over to herself in the darkness after her father had gone back to the dining room, and the grain of comfort was swallowed up in foreboding.

The week of waiting was outworn at length, slowly for the State's attorneys, since their case was already made, but all too swiftly for Brant's friends. At the end of it Judge Langford went into court with as little of weight to say for his client as any advocate of a man who was already tried and found guilty by public opinion could have. Of that little he made the best possible use, and his eloquent plea to the jury had in it all the fire and fervour and pathos of a strong man who had once been the ablest special pleader in a section where eloquence is in some sort a birthright.

But the judge fought a losing battle from the beginning; he knew it, and all the others knew it. Though the prisoner had receded from his original determination, and had pleaded "Not guilty," the plea was taken to be wholly a matter of form. His guilt was tacitly admitted by all, and the judge's appeal was for clemency rather than for acquittal. "*If* this man had done this thing," was the preface to each fresh outburst of eloquent beseeching.

None the less the effort proved unavailing. Forsyth had prophesied truly. Public sentiment was aroused, and there was need enough for a stern example on the side of strict justice. Brant's friends saw all this written out large in the faces of the jury, and were prepared for the verdict. As a mere matter of decent formality the twelve men left the jury box at the close of the judge's charge to them; but they were back again before the hum of comment in the crowded courtroom was fairly a-buzz. And in the silence which fell upon all the foreman announced the verdict. The prisoner at the bar had been found guilty as charged.

There was a little hush, the electrified stillness which precedes a death sentence in any court, and then Judge Langford rose to give notice that an appeal would be taken. The court heard him through patiently, and sentence was suspended accordingly. Then the prisoner was remanded to jail, and the trial was over.

Judge Langford had no hope of securing a new trial, and he admitted as much when Forsyth got speech with him. "It was the only thing there was left for us to do," he said, "and we shall gain nothing by it save a little delay. But having undertaken to plough this young man's furrow, I shall plough it faithfully to the end."

Once more, as on a former occasion, the judge's forecasting was rooted in the event. The motion for a retrial was argued, heard, and denied; the prisoner was sentenced, and the day of execution was set for the Friday before Thanksgiving. And at the pronouncing of the sentence that Friday was no more than a fortnight in the future.

CHAPTER XXXIV
THE WING-BEAT OF AZRAEL

AND Dorothy? Truly, these were terrible days and weeks for one who loved, and had lost and found, only to lose again. But, believing in her lover's innocence as no one else save Henry Antrim did believe in it, she was yet powerless to break a single thread of the net which enmeshed him. She could do naught but grieve despairingly, and that in secret, since none but her father and Antrim guessed the depth of her hurt.

To her in her misery came an angel of light masquerading as one Parker Jarvis. She knew the reporter by sight, and better by repute, since Antrim had spoken much of him and of his friendly movings in Brant's affair. She also knew that he was of those who would have held Brant excused though guilty; but at this point her knowledge of him paused until, one black Thursday evening in late November, but a single sweep of the clock hands from the fatal Friday morning, when she had stolen out of the house to be alone with her misery, he stood uncovered before her holding the gate for her to pass out.

"Do you know who I am, Miss Langford?" he asked; and when she signed assent he turned and walked beside her.

"I don't mean to intrude, and I could have only one excuse for waylaying you," he went on. "If there is any blame, Harry Antrim must answer for it. He doesn't mean to tell all the things he knows, but sometimes he tells a good bit more than he sets out to, and he has told me enough to make me understand why to-morrow will hurt you worse than it will any of us."

There was manifestly no answer to be made to this, and she let him go on without hindrance. For to-morrow would end it all, and anything less than death seemed too trivial to be opposed.

"I wanted to ask you to help me at a pinch where I am unable to help myself," he continued. "But before I come to the helping part, I'd like to tell you just where I stand to-night. May I do that?"

Her "Yes" was no more than a whisper, but he heard it and took his cue promptly, beginning in the midst.

"At first I thought Brant did it, as a matter of course. Everything pointed that way, and the mere fact of his giving himself up seemed as good as a confession. But afterward when I began to dig a little deeper into it I wasn't so sure; in fact, I came to believe that your brother had done it, and that

Brant was trying to screen him—to—well, to stand in the way until your brother had a chance to run for it. You mustn't mind my saying these things, because they have to be said before I can come around to the present state of affairs."

Again she gave him liberty. "It does not matter; nothing matters any more."

"Thanks. Well, about that time I had a talk with Brant, and I'm ashamed to say he made me fly the track again—made me believe he did do it, after all; and I went on believing it till one day about a week ago, when Harry Antrim told me what you told him Brant had told you. That is pretty badly tangled up, but I guess you know what I am driving at."

"Mr. Brant told me he was innocent—is that what you mean?" she asked.

"That's it precisely, and I just put it up that he would come pretty near telling you the truth; that you are the one person in the world he wouldn't lie to. So I had to climb over the fence again, and—well, to cut a long story short, I haven't had ten hours' sleep in the last sixty-odd; and—and to-morrow is the day."

She caught despairingly at the straw, as any poor drowning one might. "O Mr. Jarvis, what have you done? what can be done?"

"I don't know that I have done anything. I've been desperately tangled up in two theories, and one of them is no good unless I can get rid of the other. Miss Langford, you will know how hard pressed I am when you hear what I came over here to ask you, but you must let to-morrow be my excuse for anything and everything. You have seen your brother and have been with him more or less every day since this thing happened: is he the one who ought to be counting the hours as George Brant is probably counting them this evening?"

The early dusk of the winter day was beginning to prick out the arc lights in the downtown circuits, and she stopped to turn back; and so facing him she gave him his answer:

"No, Mr. Jarvis, my brother did not do it. I have thought of that—I have been driven to think of it, dreadful as it is; and I have watched him—God forgive me!—I have watched him as an enemy might. *He did not do it!*"

Jarvis threw up his head and drew a deep breath of the crisp night air, as a swimmer who feels the bottom under his feet while yet the shore of ultimate safety is afar off.

"That helps out a whole lot," he said; and his involuntary sigh was a measure of the relief which her assurance gave him. "May I walk back with you? I'm not half through."

She suffered him, and he went quickly forward in the path she had cleared for him.

"We are now a long way ahead of any point that has been reached hitherto," he began. "Brant didn't do it, and your brother didn't do it. But a man was killed, and if he did not commit suicide, somebody must have killed him. Happily, we don't have to wrangle with the suicide theory, so we may safely fall back on the alternative. Do you follow me?"

Her "Yes" was not a whisper this time; it was an eager little gasp of expectancy.

"Good. Now, while I have been holding the William Langford possibility in suspension, as it were, I have been filling in the time by hunting desperately for this shadowy 'somebody.' That is why I haven't had much sleep since Monday night."

"O Mr. Jarvis! Have you found any clew at all?"

"If I say Yes, you must understand that it isn't any bigger than a spider's web—just one strand of a spider's web, at that. For a week or so before the shooting Harding was seen here and there and everywhere in company with a man whom everybody can describe after a fashion and nobody can identify. They seemed to be friends, but that doesn't count for much among people of that kind. Still, there is only one little thing to connect this unknown man with the murder, so far."

"And that is?"

"That is the fact that he was seen just before the shooting, and he has not been seen since."

"But surely he can be found?" So much she said, and then she covered her face with her hands and a dry sob shook her. In a few short hours the clearest proof of Brant's innocence would come too late.

Jarvis understood, and he held his peace until she grew calmer. Then he said: "I've told you my errand, or at least the biggest part of it. But there is one other little thing in which you can help. The time has come for the forlorn hope to make its last dash. Antrim tells me that Mr. Hobart, Brant's oldest friend, has just got word, and he is coming hotfoot to Denver on this evening's train. I want to have a final rally of Brant's friends at Forsyth's office to-night to see if we can't cook up some sort of an excuse to beg the Governor for a reprieve. It's the only hope now."

"But I—how can I help?" she asked eagerly.

"You can persuade your father to come down after dinner. Harry will call for him with a carriage."

She did not reply at once, and when she spoke it was as one who feels the way. "Will you understand me if I say that my father thinks he has done his whole duty? You must remember that he believes firmly in Mr. Brant's guilt—he has believed in it from the very first."

"I know; but it must be your share in this last pull to make him believe as we do."

"Oh, how can I?" she cried.

"I think I can put you in the way of doing it, but you must forgive me if I dig still deeper into a matter which is your own private affair, Miss Langford. You have had one interview with Brant since he was locked up, and any man with blood in his veins could guess what happened in that half hour you were together. I'm not going to ask you to repeat that talk for my benefit, but I do ask this: Didn't Brant give you to understand that he believed your brother to be the guilty one?"

She was choking with mingled grief and humiliation and embarrassment, but she made shift to answer him:

"He did."

"Then, of course, you knew at once why he was there; that he had stepped in voluntarily to save your brother—not for Will's sake, perhaps, but for yours?"

"I knew it then—I know it now."

"And you knew that, rather than let the shame and disgrace and horror come upon you and yours, he would keep it up to the bitter end—that end which is coming to him to-morrow morning?"

"Yes; I knew that, too."

Jarvis paused, and then he clinched the nail he had driven:

"Have you ever tried to make your father understand all this?"

"Oh, you are hard—bitter hard!" she broke out passionately. "I did try at first, but my father said it wasn't in human nature. And how could I hope to make him believe it when he was so thoroughly convinced of Mr. Brant's guilt?"

"None the less, you have it to do. You must convince him, and persuade him to come down to the office with Harry to-night. Luckily, I can help you a little. It so happened that I went to see Brant the same day you saw him. I was with him in less than half an hour after you left him. In that talk I came within one word of making him admit to me that he wasn't guilty, and also of making him confess that he believed Will did the shooting. Shall I tell you how I know this?"

"If you must—if you will."

"I had told him that it wasn't any use to try to keep up the fiction; that the truth would all come out at the trial; that the court would appoint a lawyer to defend him, and that any counsel he might have, save and excepting only your father, would break your brother's testimony down in five minutes. Do you know what he did when I told him this?"

"No."

"He sat down and scribbled a note for me to take to Forsyth. In that note he told Forsyth that he had reconsidered; that he would accept your father as his counsel. He believed it was the only way to save your brother from a cross-examination which would undo what he was staking his life to do. That is all."

They had reached the Hollywood gate, and he opened it for her, and when she stood beyond it, lifted his hat.

"I hope I haven't said too much, or asked too much, Miss Langford."

She came close to the gate, and he could see her eyes shining in the twilight.

"No, you haven't said too much, and you haven't asked too much. I shall go down on my knees to my father, Mr. Jarvis, and—and as God helps me, he shall go to you believing as we do. And for yourself—" But he was gone before she could thank him.

CHAPTER XXXV
THE WISDOM OF MANY AND THE WIT OF ONE

IT was quite dark when the reporter left the Langford gate and set out at a rapid walk toward the nearest street-car corner. As he was turning out of Altamont Terrace a four-wheeler with two men on the box swung into the curving street of the suburb from the boulevard. Jarvis gave a shrill whistle, and the carriage drew up at the curb.

"Is that you, Jarvis?" said Antrim, from his seat beside the driver.

"Yes. You're 'way too early; they haven't been to dinner yet."

"Did you see her?"

"Sure."

"Can she do it?"

"She knows she's got to do it."

"Good enough; I'll go on up to the house and help her."

Jarvis reached up, felt in Antrim's vest pocket, found a cigar, and coolly purloined it. "Begging your pardon, you will do nothing of the kind, *savez vous*? That little battle is one she will have to fight for herself. You go away and kill time for an hour and then come back."

Antrim held his watch down so that the flare of Jarvis's match lighted the face of it.

"Six-thirty—seven-thirty. The train Hobart is coming on is late, and I'll time things so we can go by the station and pick him up. That gives me a clear hour to spare. Get in, and we'll take you back to town."

The reporter took his place in the empty four-wheeler and rode cityward in solitary state, rode as far as the Union Depot, and then got out to walk uptown. Recalling the incidents of that eventful night, he could never quite account for the impulse which led him to drift aside from the straight course to the Plainsman building, to turn the corner at Blake Street, and finally to stroll aimlessly into Draco's. At that early hour the place was all but deserted, and Tom Deverney was glad enough to have some one to talk to. As a matter of course, he reverted to the impending fate of the one known to both.

"Poor old George!" he said in rough sympathy. "To-morrow morning winds him up, doesn't it? By cripes, if the old town was what it used to be, they'd have to call out the soldiers before they could hang him!"

But Jarvis would not speak of Brant.

"Tell me once more, Tom, about that fellow who was running with the Professor—about how he looked, I mean."

"Still a-twanging on that old string?" laughed the bartender. "I have told you till I can't remember how he looked myself."

"Never mind; dig it over once more," begged Jarvis "It's the last time I'll ever bother you about him." And thus besought, Deverney racked his memory and described the unknown man for the twentieth time.

"Old clothes—always the same old clothes," Jarvis groaned in despair. "Didn't he ever change them, I wonder?"

"Not that anybody ever saw or heard of. I—" The bartender stopped short and knitted his brows till they met above his eyes. "Say, I told you he was in here to get a drink the night of the killing, didn't I?"

"Yes."

"Well, he'd changed 'em that night, for once—gone into mourning. I recollect, because I joshed him about the misfit; asked him which one of his uncles had died and left him the blacks."

"What!"

"It's a fact. Didn't I tell you that before?"

"No." Jarvis grew suddenly cool and wary. "That is, I don't remember it if you did. Now, cudgel your brain once more, Tom, and try to guess me at about what hour that was."

"It just so happens that I can tell you to a dot. A minute or two after 'his Blacks' was in here a fellow came up from the faro game and wanted twenty-five cases on his watch. I let him have 'em, and when I went to put the ticker in the safe I noticed the time. It was half past eleven."

Jarvis bought a bad cigar, but he did not light it. On the contrary, he was absently crushing the little roll of alleged tobacco in his hand as he went out and up the street. And a little later, when he was crossing Larimer Street on his way to the rendezvous, he was still scattering the powdered cabbage leaves in a thin trail of brown dust behind him as he strode along.

"It is a sheer miracle—nothing less!" he muttered. "Tom Deverney has told me that story more than a dozen times before, and he left out the whole heart of it every time until to-night. That knocks out one of the mysteries with a good clean body blow. It wasn't young Langford who ransacked Brant's room; it was 'his Blacks,' as Deverney calls him. And if he was drunk when he did it, he was sober enough when he sent the boy for the cast-off pepper-and-salts that might have betrayed him. Lord of love! if I only knew what he was after!"

Like a flash of inspiration the answer tripped upon the heels of the question. Antrim had told the reporter about the packet of papers given him by Brant for safe-keeping, but not until this instant had Jarvis been able to put two and two together.

"That's it—that is the whole thing in a nutshell!" he ejaculated. "This fellow and Harding were partners and Harding put him up to steal those papers. Lord, Lord, what a flock of purblind bats we've been!"

But the night of miracles was yet young. When the reporter had crossed the street, narrowly escaping the wire scoop net of a passing cable car in his abstraction, he stumbled upon one of the employees of the Osirian Club, the doorkeeper who had been on duty in the upper corridor on the night of the tragedy. Jarvis stopped to buttonhole the man from sheer force of reportorial habit.

"Hello, Binkie! Going on watch?" he queried.

The man nodded.

"One demnition grind, isn't it? Anything new?"

"No. Business has been mighty quiet with us since that scrap in Number Seven."

"Go shy, do they? That will wear off in time. By the way, Binkie, there wasn't anybody else in the big room that night when George Brant went in, was there?"

"Not a soul." The man shifted uneasily from one foot to the other, and then added, as one who seeks to divide a harassing burden: "That's what I told the police, and it's what I say now. But for all that, there was a blamed queer thing happened that I haven't told anybody, and I've sweat about it till I'm galded raw."

"What was it?" Jarvis forced himself to ask the question carelessly, but anxiety and eagerness were fairly suffocating him.

"Why, it was this: George came up and asked me about those two fellows, and which room they were in, and I told him. Then I saw him go swinging up the middle of the big room with that get-out-of-my-road gait of his as plain as I see you now. Well, about two minutes afterward I got up to go and close a window in the far end of the hall, and when I got back to my chair at the door there he was yet, still going up the room the same as I'd seen him before. Blame me, if I didn't think I'd got 'em again, for a minute!"

"You are sure it was Brant?" said Jarvis, hungering and thirsting for the negative answer which he did not dare to so much as suggest.

"Sure enough," said the doorkeeper briefly. "At first I wasn't so cocksure; it seemed like he'd gone thinner just in that minute or two, so that his clothes didn't fit him so well; and he wasn't swinging along any more—he was going cautiouslike, as if he were listening for something that he couldn't hear. But of course it was George. It couldn't have been anybody else, or I'd have seen him come up the stairs. See?"

If the man craved buttressing in his own belief it was not denied him.

"Of course, it couldn't have been any one else," Jarvis agreed. "Most likely George came back to ask you something, didn't find you at the door, and went on again. Well, I must get a move. Good night."

Thus Jarvis, with every word of the nonchalant reply carefully weighted down with disinterest. But when he had left the latter-day Egyptian on the corner, repressed excitement found speech commensurate with the importance of the new miracle.

"Holy Smoke! and yet they say there isn't any such thing as a miracle nowadays! Why, good Lord! here there have been two of them within an hour—within fifteen minutes—and they go together like the foot and the shoe! Yes, it was Brant—like fits! It was his double in the stolen suit of black clothes—that's what Binkie saw! And he has been keeping it dark because he was afraid of losing his job if he admitted that some one might have made a sneak on him."

This time Jarvis went straight to the editorial rooms of the Plainsman, and, finding them untenanted, sat down to wait with what patience he could muster for the others to come in. The interval was not ill spent. Before the reporter's reverie was interrupted he had cleared up more of the mysteries—so many of them, indeed, that only one of any magnitude remained to baffle him. But that one was impregnable. If the unknown one were the murderer—and with this Jarvis had closed as with a fact assured— why had the man shot his late confederate?

In the meantime Antrim had killed his hour, and had driven once more to Altamont Terrace. He found the judge ready to accompany him, and from the elder man's grave preoccupation he argued that something of moment had occurred in the interval of slain time.

As prefigured, they drove by way of the Union Depot and stopped to pick up Hobart. The train was not yet in, and Antrim had time to run up to the telegraph office. When he came down he was scowling and cursing his luck.

Whereupon the judge came out of his preoccupation enough to ask what had happened.

"Oh, it's that despatcher at Voltamo again; he is always getting sick at the wrong time. I've got to drop everything and 'sub' for him, and I suppose I shall have to go up on Seventeen. That lets me out of the conference, but I don't know that I could do any good if I stayed. It isn't going to make any difference. It's all up with poor Brant."

The judge shook his head. "I must confess I don't see any light; but since Dorothy has told me——" He broke off abruptly. "Do you know what she believes, Harry?"

Antrim nodded.

"I—I more than half believe it myself, now," the judge admitted, and his voice had in it a tremulous quaver which was not of age. "It is the height of incredibility; it is more like a chapter out of some old romance of the dead-and-gone age of chivalry, but—but——"

"I have believed it all along," said Antrim.

"I know; I know you have. As you say, I don't see how we are to accomplish anything by talking it over again to-night, but this I have determined: when we have sifted it down to the last grain of evidence, I shall go to the Governor and get him reprieved, if one man may, with God's help, move another to do a little deed of mercy."

"God bless you!" said Antrim fervently; and then: "After it's all over I wish you would drive by and give the facts to the train despatcher upstairs—Disbrow, you know. He'll wire them to me on Seventeen and I sha'n't sleep much till I hear."

The judge promised, and a moment later caught sight of Hobart in the stream of outcoming passengers from the delayed train. There was no time sacrificed to the formalities, and when the assayer had shaken hands with an old friend and a new one, the judge passed quickly to the matter in hand.

"You are barely in time, Ned; we had despaired of reaching you. Leave your valise at the check stand and come uptown with me. I can explain what we hope to do as we go."

As he promised, so he performed; and by the time they reached the editor's room at the top of the Plainsman building, Hobart knew all that the judge could tell him. Forsyth welcomed the newcomer heartily, and then Jarvis was introduced.

"Here is a young man whom I have been misjudging from the first," said the night editor, by way of preface to what the reporter had to tell. "While we have been content to accept one theory, following it blindly to its present desperate conclusion, he has built up and torn down half a dozen, with the result that he is ready to-night to open a most astounding budget of discoveries.—Jarvis, do you begin at the beginning and go over the ground carefully, remembering that Mr. Hobart knows none of the details."

Jarvis drew up his chair, lighted a fresh cigar, and told his story succinctly and with commendable clarity. Hobart heard it through without comment, but at the close of the narrative he fetched a sigh of relief.

"These mysterious details, with their open doors of possibility, help me out wonderfully," he said. "As you all know, I had my first news of the tragedy last night, and it was meagre enough. But, from information in my hands—in fact, from a letter which Brant wrote me a short time before the shooting—I had every reason to believe that he had simply avenged himself on his enemy. Indeed, he swore he would do it if the man ever crossed his path again."

"His enemy?" echoed the judge.

"Yes. Listen, and I will tell you his story, so far as I know it."

He fulfilled the promise literally and truthfully, beginning with their intimacy and close friendship in college, and ending with a description of the impressive parting in the moonlight on Jack Mountain, when Brant had promised to turn his back upon his evil past and to set his face toward better things.

"What has happened since that night you all know better than I do," he concluded. "But I may add this from my knowledge of the man: As boy and youth he had his faults, and the chiefest of these were impulsiveness and a reckless uncounting of the cost when he had set his heart upon doing a thing. But he was always as loving and tender as a woman, and as chivalrous as any Bayard of them all. Every one in college knew what Harding's sister was, and Brant was merely a scapegoat for a half dozen worse men. But because he, too, had sinned, he paid the penalty—would be paying it to this day if the woman were alive. That was one of his redeeming characteristics; and another was his absolute and fearless truthfulness. If he says he did not do this deed for which he is to suffer to-morrow morning, that settles it. He wouldn't lie about it if the lie would save his life a dozen times over."

The judge was profoundly moved. Twice he essayed to speak, but what he had to say would have naught of formal phrasings. And when he began, the words came haltingly, and there was generous emotion at the back of them.

"My good friends, this is no time to let false pride or a strained sense of family honour stand in our way. I have that to add to Mr. Hobart's story which makes the young man's hitherto inexplicable reticence a part of a most chivalrous and heroic purpose—a deed worthy of the noblest knight that ever figured in ancient story. From the moment of darkness in which the deed was committed up to the present time Brant has believed that my son was the murderer of James Harding, and it was in this belief that he determined to sacrifice himself to save the boy. What the ulterior motive was you may perhaps divine for yourselves when I tell you that it was to my daughter, and after she had guessed his purpose, that he admitted the fact."

A silence more eloquent than the loudest praise fell upon the little group gathered around the editor's table. Hobart was the first to break it.

"It was very like him," he said softly; "like the George Brant I used to know and love in the old days. But in our admiration we mustn't lose sight of his peril. What are we to do?"

The judge shook his head. "While we have cleared up many of the mysteries, we are still far from having a reasonable excuse for asking the Governor's intervention. If I go to him with the story of these later discoveries he may justly say that these things have no bearing upon our case and refuse to grant a reprieve. I presume it is sufficiently clear to all of us now that this unknown man who broke into Brant's room and stole his clothes is the man who killed James Harding. But we can neither prove this nor establish the motive. If we could identify this man, and so be enabled to find him, we might be able to show why he shot a person with whom, by all accounts, he was on friendly terms."

While the judge was speaking, Jarvis was sketching a crude outline of a human face on the blotter under his hand. He did it mechanically, and without realizing that he was trying to draw the features of the man of many descriptions. When he did realize it, he passed the blotter across to Hobart with a query.

"Does that remind you of anybody you have ever seen?"

Hobart shook his head.

"I didn't suppose it would," said the reporter, taking the blotter and beginning to obliterate the picture by adding a bushy beard and a bristling mustache to the face.

The judge and Forsyth were anxiously discussing the advisability of calling in the senior member of a great law firm to act as a go-between in the appeal to the Governor, the editor urging it and the lawyer objecting on the score of time.

"It is my impression that he isn't in town," the judge was saying. "And, in any event, what is done must be done quickly. It is a matter of hours for Brant now."

Hobart took no part in the discussion. He was leaning over the reporter's shoulder watching the strokes of the idle pencil. Suddenly he put out his hand and stopped it:

"Hold on a minute; that begins to look something like a man I've seen somewhere. Let me think."

The exclamation drew the attention of the others, and they examined the sketch while the assayer was trying to recall the suggestion.

"Let me look at it again," he said, and he knitted his brows over it for a breathless minute while they waited in silence.

"I can't place it," he added, at length. "I thought at first it looked a little like the man Isaac Gasset."

"Who is he?" asked the reporter.

"Didn't I mention him by name? He is the ruffian who shot Harding's sister in the affray at Gaynard's—the fellow that Brant winged and would have killed, if I had let him."

The editor's pivot chair made a quick half circle, and Forsyth smote upon the table with his fist in an ecstasy of exprobration.

"What an infernal lot of idiotic chumps we are!—saving your presence, judge," he burst out. "Why, the thing is as plain as daylight! Gasset is the man who was plotting with Harding against Brant, and he is the man who followed Brant into the Osirian that night and fired the shot which killed Harding. And that shot missed its mark; it was meant for George Brant!"

Hobart's pose was self-repression, but he sprang to his feet with something very like an imprecation. "Why, of course! If I'd had any time at all to pull myself together! Why, gentlemen, I *knew*—knew all about it, but it didn't occur to me. This man Gasset got out of the hospital before I left Silverette, and it was the talk of the camp that he was hunting for Brant with blood in his eye. I meant to write George about it at the time; but since he had cut the whole business I didn't think there was any great danger."

But it was the judge who went to the heart of the matter in two words. "Thank God!" he said earnestly, "at last we have something with which to go to his Excellency, the Governor. And afterward, if we can only lay hands on this man Gasset——"

There was a volley fire of suggestions from Hobart and Jarvis, but the night editor's genius for organization came quickly to the fore:

"We shall have him, if he is anywhere this side of his master's smelting pot, and——"

"And when you find him," Jarvis cut in, "he will probably have in his possession a big 45-calibre Colt's with the name 'J. Harding' scratched on the butt."

"What's that? how do you know?" demanded Forsyth; and the marshalling of forces paused while Jarvis explained.

"I know, because the existence of that same big pistol has been the one thing which has kept me alive. Everybody took it for granted that the murder was committed with the pistol which was found on the floor. I wasn't sure of that, and when I began to doubt, I saw the possibility of another weapon and another man behind it. Gasset was the man who had the original 'J. Harding' weapon at the time of the killing, and if he still has it when we catch him—if we catch him—it will be a strong point in evidence if he happens to have the pistol he stole from Brant's room in his possession."

"It is a good point, and we'll put it in the telegrams," said the editor. "Now, gentlemen, to work. Judge Langford, if you will go with Mr. Hobart to the Governor's house, Jarvis and I will see to the telegraphing, and I'll have my young men ransack the city—they will do it better and quicker than the police. Jarvis, send the boys in here, and then chase over to the jail and get word to Brant—if it costs money." Then to the judge: "You think there is no doubt about your being able to make your case with his Excellency?"

"None whatever now, I think."

"Good. Then we'll all meet here in two hours and compare notes, if you please."

It was an hour after midnight when Despatcher Disbrow was finally able to answer Antrim's impatient inquiries from Voltamo. He gave the chief clerk the story of the later discoveries, closing the long message with a succinct account of what had been accomplished up to date:

"They have ascertained that Gasset left town on night of the murder, and the wires are hot after him with a big reward out. Governor has granted a reprieve, and Brant has been notified. Judge L. says Gasset must be found and made to confess; otherwise Brant's case still hangs on the ragged edge. Call up again in the morning.

"DISBROW."

CHAPTER XXXVI
IN WHICH A FOX DOUBLES ONCE TOO OFTEN

IT is conceivable that Henry Antrim clicked his "O. K." at the close of the wire talk with Despatcher Disbrow with a lighter heart than he had carried for many a day. Truly, everything still hinged upon the capture of Gasset, but the blessed optimism of youth is always ready to make light of contingencies, and the chief clerk threw himself upon the night operator's bunk to snatch a few hours' rest, little thinking that the conclusion of the whole matter still hung in a balance whose beam would tip as his own energy and presence of mind might decide. And while he slept, the net spread so promptly by the whispering wires was already entangling the murderer.

With the criminal's instinctive distrust of small towns to narrow his choice of a refuge, Gasset had put his fate into the keeping of chance by spinning a coin: heads, to lose himself in the untabulated crowds thronging the streets and byways of Leadville; tails, to drop from the train at some lonely station in the mountains, whence he could make his way on foot to one of the more isolated camps. The chance of the spun coin sent him to Leadville; and when, on the second morning of his sojourn in the carbonate camp, he learned from the newspapers that his bad aim had disposed of an inconvenient accomplice without materially marring his plan of vengeance on Brant, he exulted openly, and from that on went his way without concealment, believing that he had safely outrun his evil hour.

For this cause it came about that the Leadville reduplication of the telegram offering a reward for his arrest was scarcely an hour old when a police officer interrupted a quiet game of cards in a den in lower State Street, laid hands upon the winner, a big-boned man in an ill-fitting suit of dusty black, searched him, and took from him a big revolver with the name "J. Harding" scratched on the butt.

Gasset surrendered at discretion, not suspecting the nature of the charge against him, and, having a due regard for the possibilities of escape, made no resistance which should warrant the use of the handcuffs. So all went amicably until the officer, who was less discreet than his prisoner, told Gasset for what he was wanted. At the naming of the thing the ex-house-breaker caught his breath, set his teeth upon a fiercely growled oath, smote his captor skilfully upon the point of the jaw, and made a wild dash for liberty.

The policeman gave chase courageously, ignoring the broken jaw and firing ever and anon at the dodging fugitive. But Gasset made good his escape, threading the intricacies of alleys and streets in the lower town until, by the time the hue and cry was properly raised, he was free of the houses and skirting the slope of the mountain which overlooks California Gulch. Here he might have rested, but the terror of it was too new upon him. So he pushed on and always on over the bleak mountain side, doubling and twisting on his course, and cursing the snow which at day dawn would point a sure trail for his pursuers to follow. And thus running and stumbling and cursing, he came out finally in the stunted pine *chapparal* opposite the railway station at Malta.

From this point three ways were open to him. He might turn his face northward toward the new camps beyond Tennessee Pass, avoiding the railroad and trusting to the hospitality of the mountains for succour of bread and meat on the way. He might push westward over one of the passes to the sparsely settled gulches beyond the main range, but this was a still more precarious bread-and-meat hazard. Or, lastly, he might follow the railroad to the eastward, putting the chance of better speed and fewer privations against the greater risk of discovery and capture.

He knew well enough that either of the foot flights would be safer than the alternative; but it was late in the season, and the early snows promised hardships a-plenty. While he was yet weighing these hardships against the perils of the easier route, an east-bound freight train crawling slowly through the Malta yards turned the scale, and dashing swiftly across the tracks he climbed catlike into an empty box car what time the train was gathering headway for the rush down the valley.

At the moment of decision he had no plan more definite than the putting of as great a distance as possible between himself and the scene of his late encounter with the Leadville officer; but by the time the morning sun was gilding the snow-capped peaks of Princeton and Harvard he had hit upon a strategic series of moves which was not less ingenious than it was daring. Knowing that he could not hope to remain undiscovered in the box car after daybreak, he determined to leave the freight train at the first stop, to wait for and board the early east-bound passenger, to ride thereon openly until his identity and ostensible intention were discovered, and then to take the chance of out-witting everybody by doubling back to the westward from the meeting point of the two day trains.

It was a hazardous game to play, with the noose of the hangman at the end of it as a penalty for unsuccess; but he could think of no better. The chief hazards were two: If his identification should come too soon, he would be obliged to leave the east-bound train before it should reach the meeting point, and there would be the desperate risk of waiting at some small station until the west-bound train should arrive. And if it should be delayed until the moment of doubling, he would lose all upon the single throw. But, on the other hand, if the stratagem succeeded, if he should be lucky enough to send the hunt eastward on a false scent, much precious time would be gained and present safety would be fairly well assured.

In pursuance of this plan he dropped from the freight train while it was slowing into Buena Vista, and was so far successful as to find a hiding place in which he could watch and wait unobserved for the east-bound passenger. When that came, and he had taken a seat in the smoking car, the perils began. The conductor eyed him suspiciously, took his fare to Denver, and a little later came back to sit down for a friendly chat which soon developed by insensible degrees into a cross-examination. Gasset answered as best he might, writhing and swearing under his breath. It was what he had expected and provided for, but it had come too soon. The conductor desisted finally and went about his business, but Gasset drew fresh breath of alarm when he saw the brakeman lounge forward to take his seat on one of the newsboy's boxes. And when the brakeman kept his place doggedly past station after station, ignoring his duties, Gasset argued that he was already under surveillance and began to nerve himself for whatever desperate struggle was in store for him.

The fugitive's surmise was entirely correct. Since early morning the wires had been buzzing with the news of the night; and inasmuch as the railway afforded the most obvious line of escape, every trainman was on the watch for the man whose description had been sown broadcast by the telltale wires. For this cause, and knowing both the fact of the reward and the figure of it, Conductor Harker thought himself in luck. Voltamo was the first station ahead where a constable could be found; and to Voltamo the conductor wired at the first opportunity.

Antrim was at his post in the telegraph office, filling the place of the invalided branch despatcher, when the conductor's message arrived, and he took it upon himself to make sure that the town marshal and two deputies were at the station to meet the train. That done, he waited in a fever of impatience for the event to mature, and when the suspense indoors became unbearable, he gave his place to the day operator and went out to be in at the death.

He had not long to wait. The whistle of the coming train was echoing in the upper cañon, and the little knot of loungers which had gathered about the marshal and his deputies broke apart and fell back to give the officers free play. There was a west-bound freight in the upper yard, waiting, with a man at the switch, to pull out after the passenger train should arrive; and the rear trucks of the latter were no more than fairly over the movable rail before it was set for the siding, and the freight began to worm its way out around the double curve.

The incoming passenger train slid down the grade to the station with brake shoes smoking, and Conductor Harker swung off and caught himself with a quick little run.

"I've got him!—alive and kicking. He's in the forward end of the smoker," he cried; and in a flash the marshal darted into one end of the car while his deputies cut off the retreat at the other.

Something to the surprise of all three, they met in the middle of the car without their quarry. There were not more than a dozen passengers in the seats, and no one of them remotely answered the requirements of the Gasset description. The marshal threw up a window and yelled to the conductor:

"Come in here and show us your man!"

Harker was with them at the word, but there was blank astoundment in his face. "Suffering Moses! you've let him get away!" he gasped. "He was right there in that second seat not more than a minute ago when we pulled down over the switch!"

"Well, you can see for yourself he isn't here now," quoth the marshal. "You hold the train a minute while we look through the other cars."

The detention was not called for. Voltamo is a locomotive division station, and before the engines were changed the marshal and his aids had searched every possible hiding place in the train. Antrim knew that they had done their duty faithfully, but he was exasperated at the conductor's apparent neglect.

"It is all your fault, Harker!" he said hotly. "You ought to have had sense enough to keep your eyes or your hands on him!"

"I ain't saying a word," said Harker. "But what can I do now?"

"Do? Why, take your train and go on. There isn't anything to stop for now that he's gone."

The conductor obeyed, glad enough to be out of it, and Antrim turned to the marshal. "I'm sorry I got you out on a wild-goose chase," he said. "What do you suppose became of him? Or did Harker only imagine he had him?"

"Oh, he was there, right enough. I asked some of the passengers in the smoker and they all saw him. By gravy! look at that, will you?—fell plum from the top o' the car and never turned a hair!"

Antrim looked, and saw much more than did the marshal. The west-bound freight had stalled on the double curve, and during the detention of the passenger train had been backing and filling to get headway. Just as the marshal spoke a drawbar pulled out, and the sudden jerk of the forward section flung a man who was clinging to the roof-hold of a box car far out into the ditch. He was on his feet again in a twinkling, making a quick run for a hand car which stood blocked on a siding.

Antrim yelled as he saw him kick the block from beneath the wheel and scramble upon the deck of the car.

"That's your man! Wing him as he goes by or he'll get away yet! There's a safety switch at the lower end, and the car will jump it and keep the track!"

The man threw himself fiercely upon the driving lever of the hand car, and the light gear truck came spinning down the grade under his vigorous strokes. The marshal and his two aids coolly drew their weapons and waited. The fugitive would have to pass within thirty feet of the platform, and the marksmen could afford to wait until the flying target was at short range. At the critical instant the three pistols cracked as one, and the toiling figure at the lever dropped behind the gear casing as the car shot past with ever-increasing momentum.

"Heavens and earth, I hope you haven't killed him!" panted Antrim, while they were running down the track after the retreating hand car. "He's got to talk some before he dies."

"He'll never do that," said the marshal confidently. "He'll never wag his jaw any more this side of the range. I don't miss—By gravy! do you see that?"

The four pursuers stopped in speechless astoundment. The hand car had reached the safety switch, clearing it at a bound and alighting fairly upon the rails of the main line, and at the same instant the prone figure behind the gear casing straightened up and flung itself once more upon the rocking lever. Two pistols crashed simultaneously, and then the car with its labouring burden dodged out of sight and range around an elbow in the lower cañon.

"G-g-great Scott! M-m-missed him all the t-time!" stammered one of the deputies, whose speech failed him at a crisis; and the big marshal flung his weapon down and ground it into the ballast under his heel in a fine frenzy of impotent wrath.

Antrim was the first to recover presence of mind, or some semblance of it. "Come back with me and we'll catch him yet!" he shouted, leading the race up the yard toward the relieved passenger engine, which the engineer was about to back under the coal chute. A breathless minute later they were clambering aboard, and the engineer recognised the chief clerk.

"Catch that hand car for us, Tom!" gasped Antrim, fighting for breath and coherence. "There's a—there's a man's life depending on it. Turn her loose!"

The engineer nodded and dropped the reversing lever forward with a crash. One of the yard men saw them coming and ran to set the switch, and in a gathering tempest of clamour the engine shot out on the main line and the chase began afresh.

Two miles down the cañon they came in sight of the hand car darting around the curves ahead of them. Gasset had abandoned the lever when the increasing speed of the car made it dangerous to try to keep up with the quick strokes of it, and was crouching on the deck, screening himself as well as he could behind the driving mechanism. Seeing this, the marshal borrowed the stuttering deputy's revolver and watched his chances for another shot. Antrim saw, and shook his head, shouting to make himself heard above the din and clamour of the flying locomotive:

"Don't kill him; we must take him alive, if we can."

The marshal lowered the weapon, and the engineer signed to Antrim to come closer. "We can't make it," he protested, giving the spinning wheels a taste of the air brake. "He's got the hill with him, and that light car will keep the track when we can't. See?"

Antrim nodded. "Keep him in sight, if you can," he shouted back. "If you can hold your own till we come to that let-up in the grade at Berg Siding, maybe we can run him down."

But the end of the chase was nearer, though it need not have been if Gasset could have had the courage of his despair. Before the "let-up" came in sight there was a series of blood-chilling curves around which the hand car lurched with increasing velocity. Gasset's hand sought the brake lever. The fusillade of pistol shots, the swift down-rush between the echoing walls of the cañon, the hopelessness of any escape from the shrieking monster in the rear, all went to the unnerving of him, and he applied the brake before he fully realized what would follow any sudden checking of speed in that tortuous pathway.

What did follow brought the chase to a calamitous end. The flying wheels of the light car answered promptly to the pressure of the brake, and the car plunged sullenly through a cutting, promising to come to a full stop on the curve beyond. The hunted one sprang to his feet and kicked savagely at the brake lever. It was jammed, and he was too late. The pursuing locomotive dashed through the cutting and was fairly upon him before he could jump and save himself.

Antrim saw the doomed one kicking at the jammed lever and heard his scream of terror and the crash of the collision in the same pulse beat. What came after seemed like the awakening from a hideous dream, though the realities asserted themselves once more when they were lifting him from the wreck of the shattered hand car. "There is life in him yet; handle him gently, boys," he said. "If he dies before he can talk an innocent man will hang for it."

They made a rude bed for him with their coats in the empty coal pit on the engine, and so got the crushed body of him back to Voltamo and to a bunk in the freight shed at the station. Antrim could not neglect his duties, but the physician's verdict cheered him a little.

"He is a dead man," so ran the verdict, "and that probably within twenty-four hours. But there is a chance that he will revive a little toward the last."

"A chance that he will be able to tell us what we have to know?" asked Antrim.

"Yes. Have your lawyer here, and the witnesses. When the man begins to find himself, call me, and I'll try to keep him alive till you get what you need—that is, if he will give it to you."

"He has got to give it to us," returned Antrim desperately; and when he had made all the preparations suggested by the physician he telegraphed the facts to Forsyth, and settled down to work his way through the grimmest day of waiting that has ever been marked off in any calendar of suspense.

The end came in the dusk of the evening when the shadows were beginning to fill the deeper clefts in the mighty cañon. Gasset opened his eyes, stirred feebly, and asked for liquor; and Antrim called the lawyer and the witnesses, and sent out in hot haste for the physician.

As it fell out, there was time and to spare; time for a halting confession from the dying murderer, in which he told no more lies than he could help; time, needless time, after that for the slow and reluctant passing of a hopeless soul from a maimed and tortured body. Antrim drew breath of blessed relief when it was all over, but it was a full hour afterward before he could compose himself sufficiently to send a second telegram to Forsyth.

"Gasset died at 7.12 this P. M. He was conscious at the last, and made full confession and deposition in legal form. Same to you by express on

Number Two to-night. Hearty congratulations to Brant. Will be in Denver day after to-morrow.

"ANTRIM."

CHAPTER XXXVII
THE LAW OF THE MEDES AND PERSIANS

"SO you have quite made up your mind to leave Denver, have you?"

It was the day of deliverance, and Hobart, claiming the elder right, had met Brant at the opening of the prison doors, whisking him off straightway to Elitch's and to a private box therein, where they could have a quiet talk over their luncheon and a quiet smoke afterward.

Brant shrugged. "That says itself, doesn't it? I am not wholly shameless. After all the free advertising I have been getting lately, people will stop and point me out in the streets."

Hobart's laugh was a friendly jeer. "That is what you get for trying to play the part of Providence—a not altogether blameless Providence, either, since you were going to let a judge and a jury hang an innocent man. How did you come to get so befogged in the ethical part of you?"

Brant waved the question aside in the gesture which flicked the ash from his cigar.

"'There are more things in heaven and earth, Horatio, than are dreamt of in your philosophy,'" he quoted. "We'll drop that part of it, if you don't mind."

"But I do mind; I am curious to know."

Brant did not hasten to explain, and when he spoke again it was to ask a seemingly irrelevant question.

"Do you know what it means to love a woman, Ned?"

"I'm supposed to, am I not?"

"I don't know. There's many a man married—happily married, too—who doesn't know what it means. Luckily for the common good, the kind of love I have in mind is a thing apart. It is both more and less than a passion; it is a mania in the sense that it blinds the eye to everything save the present happiness of its object. Can you grasp that?"

"Ye-yes, in a measure. But in your case there were so many things to be considered——"

"There was no time to consider them. In such a crisis one must act first and think afterward. At the critical moment I thought of but one thing—the misery of one woman if her brother should not have a chance to run for his life."

Hobart nodded. "I can follow you that far. But afterward, when you found he wasn't going to run for it?"

"That was another matter. I was bitter, at first; I had given him his chance, I thought, and he was contemptible enough to deny me mine. But I had time enough to think then; to see that the object to be attained remained the same; to see what a sorry sham I was and had been. It broke me, Ned; and while I was down I made a clean sweep of it. I hadn't killed James Harding, as it happened, but under other conditions I might have killed him—should have killed him, I said. In which case the judge and jury couldn't err greatly in hanging me."

Hobart heard him through, but at the summing up he scoffed openly. "That is the baldest sophistry, George, and you know it," he asserted.

Brant smiled. "Perhaps it is; but you must remember that I loved the woman. I meant never to speak of this to any one, Ned; none the less, I am glad you have made me speak of it to you."

"Why?"

"Because if you can't understand it, nobody else ever will. Shall we bury it and talk about something else?"

"It is dead and buried from this time on," rejoined Hobart loyally. "But you are wrong when you say that I don't understand. It is precisely because I do understand all you've admitted, and a lot more besides, that I am willing to give you all the rope you want. When a man makes seventeen different kinds of a knight-errant of himself in this cold-blooded age, he earns privileges that we ordinary mortals are bound to respect. This is my last word. Now, then, what are you going to do with yourself?"

"The one thing needful has been done for me. Colonel Bowran did not wait to be told that I should probably want to disappear. He took it for granted, and got me an appointment as engineer in charge of the work on the Chipeta Ditch down in the San Juan."

"Is it a good billet?"

"Good pay and a deep grave; and the latter is all I yearn for just now. The colonel says there has not yet been so much as a stake driven on the preliminary survey. If I take it I can drop out of sight and hearing for a year or two at least."

"You say 'if.' Of course, you will take it."

Brant took time to balance his fruit knife accurately on the edge of his plate before he made answer. "I am not so sure about that," he said finally. "It will depend very much upon the outcome of a little talk I mean to have with a certain lady."

"Miss Langford?"

"No; Miss Langford's mother."

Hobart whistled softly. "Going to carry it up to the supreme court, are you?"

"Yes, and at once. Then I shall know better what I am going to do."

"It is none of my business, George, but I am afraid the time isn't propitious."

"So am I; but it is all the time I have."

"Oh, that doesn't follow. And if you were to go away and stay till the edge has time to wear off—from what you have told me I fancy Dorothy will wait indefinitely."

"She will; and we shall have to wait in any event; but that isn't the point. When I go, if I go, I must carry with me the assurance that bygones will be bygones when I come back."

"Doesn't that smack a little of doing good that good may come?"

"Perhaps. You see that, notwithstanding your good opinion, there is nothing superhuman about me. But it is more than that, Ned. I mean to marry Dorothy some day, God willing, but it sha'n't be until I have had it out with myself, nor even then without her mother's fullest consent and approval. This last I am willing to try to earn, but I want some assurance that it is among the possibilities."

Hobart followed out his own line of thought, and it presently led him back to the original proposition. "You will 'gang yer ain gate,' as you usually do, I suppose; but, as I remarked a minute ago, the time isn't ripe. I have seen something of the family in the last few days—with my eyes open—and I can tell you pretty nearly how you stand. Dorothy would go to the stake for you, the judge would divide his ultimate dollar with you, Isabel worships you from afar, William the Curst swears by you, and Mrs. Langford—well, she doesn't say much before me, as a matter of course, but it is as plain as the nose on your face that she has small use for you in spite of everything."

"That is no more or less than I expected. None the less, I am going to see her—to-night."

"Amen. I like your pluck, even if it is a bit like the zeal not according to knowledge that we read about. I shall be there—under the same ridgepole, at least. Is there anything I can do to help out?"

"Nothing; unless you will be charitable enough to stand by to pick up the pieces after she has demolished me. Shall we adjourn?—if you are through. I have some writing to do, likewise a bit of provisional packing."

CHAPTER XXXVIII
IN WHICH DARTS ARE COUNTED AS STUBBLE

IN the course of a somewhat diversified experience Brant had been constrained to fight his way through a few measurably perilous passages, and in such crises those who liked him least were fain to concede his courage. None the less, when the day of liberation darkened to its evening he went leaden-footed to the interview with Dorothy's mother.

Now Hobart, in the goodness of his heart, had caused it to be whispered about that Brant would probably make his farewell call that evening, and for this reason it was Dorothy, and no hireling, who answered the bell.

Whatever may be said of Brant (and his most loyal apologist is fain to admit that his shortcomings were many and variegated), he was no laggard in love; and when he made sure of the identity of his unexpected welcomer, Dorothy had no cause to doubt the warmth of his passion. Nevertheless, she blushed and struggled a little—as what modest young woman, however affectionate, would not in a well-lighted reception hall which was a thoroughfare for the entire household? And so, mutely protesting, she drew him quickly into the library.

"Only a moment with you, my love," he said tenderly; "just long enough to hear you say it again. Are you quite sure you love me?"

She hid her face on his arm—she was not tall enough to reach his shoulder. "I—I'd be ashamed to tell you how long I have been sure of it," she confessed with sweet *naïveté*.

Whereat he kissed the parting of her hair.

"Thank you for that word, my darling. It would hold a worse man than I ever dared to be true to his purpose. Now there is but one thing more: we must have your mother's consent and approval. Will you go and send her to me?"

But Dorothy hesitated, as well she might.

"If you are sure you must speak to her now," she ventured to say. "But, oh, I am afraid——"

At that he drew her closer, and for some ecstatic moment the hard thing that remained became as naught. "The day of fear and trembling is past, little one, and whatever befalls, whatever your mother may say, we shall still belong to each other. And I will wait and serve for you, my love, as Jacob served for Rachel, if need be. Now kiss me good-bye, dear, and go—before the love of you unmans me."

She lifted tear-brimmed eyes to his and said: "Oh, no; it must not be good-bye."

"Only for a little while, sweetheart. I'll join you with the others when I have done what I must do."

"With the others? But how shall I know what she has said?"

He smiled and once more kissed the parting of her hair. "You'll know without the telling, my beloved. And if you are the first to welcome me, I'll know you know. Now go, and let me have it over with."

She went obediently at that, and when she was gone, Brant began to walk the floor and to call up all his reserves of fortitude and courage, being well assured that he would presently need them.

While he was yet planning the assault, and before the flanking regiments were properly wheeled into line, the door opened behind him and he turned to confront not Mrs. Langford, as he had anticipated, but her son. The "unlicked cub" came in, swaggering a little as was his wont; but when he had closed the door and so shut himself in with his redoubtable preserver, he had an attack of embarrassment which quickly put to flight the offhand greeting he had meant to offer. Whereupon, instead of carrying it off with the easy nonchalance of a man of the world, he stammered like any schoolboy and Brant had to come to the rescue.

"How are you, Will? I am glad to see you," he said, truthfully enough.

The unchastised one felt that some acknowledgment of his immense obligation to Brant ought properly to precede any mere desultory talk, but to save his life he could not twist his tongue to anything like the adequate speech. So he spoke of Brant's plans rather than of the obligation.

"Heard you were off to the San Juan; Harry told us, you know. Jolly good layout, too, isn't it? By gad, don't you know I envy you?—no, that isn't what I meant to say. Fact is, Mr. Brant, you see I've been hanging 'round the door so long waiting for Dorothy to come out that it's got me rattled. What I wanted to ask was if you wouldn't take me along. I reckon I don't know enough about engineering to hurt me any—nothing much but what I learned at school—and folks say I'm too dead tough to breathe, but I'd like to learn, and—well, I don't know, but I reckon I'll never be any account till I get to work, and if anybody can brace me up, it's you, and——"

Brant was generous enough to break in and so supply the period the boy was so helplessly pursuing; and he did it the more readily since he felt the sudden and urgent prompting of a new and imperative duty.

"If you will agree to carry chain and drive stakes to begin with, you may count it a settled thing so far as I am concerned," he said. "But how about your father and mother? Will they let you go?"

"The governor's all right; I've just had a talk with him, and he is so glad to get rid of me that he is scared to death for fear you won't take me. And the mother will be all right, too; she'll do anything I want her to, same as she always does, you know. I'll go and tell her now, before——"

But just then the door opened again, and Mrs. Langford needed not to be sought. She came in with the air of one who does an unavoidable thing reluctantly, but her stateliness abated visibly at sight of her son. The "cub" promptly forestalled anything in the way of preliminary formalities.

"Just this minute talking about you, mother," he burst out, in happy ignorance of constraints or embarrassments, social or other. "Come and shake hands with Mr. Brant and congratulate him on getting out of the horrible scrape I got him into. But that isn't what we were talking about, you know; he starts for the San Juan to-morrow morning—going down to take charge of the Chipeta work—and he has promised to take me with him."

"Subject, of course, to your approval and Judge Langford's," amended Brant, with a bow in Mrs. Langford's direction.

"Oh, of course; but I told you that would be all right. What's the matter with you, mother? Can't you manage to thank Mr. Brant? It's jolly good of him, y'know."

"I—why, William, dear, this is dreadfully sudden! I didn't know you were even thinking of such a thing!" The good lady had formulated quite a number of cool little speeches wherewith to dampen any small spark of ardour which the unwelcome visitor might attempt to blow alive, but here was a contingency for which no forethought could have made provision. So she hesitated, and before the needed access of severity came to forbid it she was doing very nearly as her son had commanded.

"We are glad—very glad, I am sure, Mr. Brant," she faltered, not knowing just how fittingly to congratulate a man upon having got out of jail—out of the very noose of the hangman. "This is really an unexpected pleasure—no, not quite that, either, for I got your note. But about this—this expedition; I am afraid— Hasn't William been taking too much for granted?"

"Not on my part," rejoined Brant civilly. "I assure you I shall be glad enough to have him with me, if he may go with your consent."

"But it is so very sudden," the mother protested, still unable to orient herself. "I had thought—that is, I had been led to believe that you came upon quite a different errand, Mr. Brant."

"Oh, of course; he came to see Dorothy," said William with brotherly brutality. "But that's all right. They'll have time enough to say any quantity of good-byes while you're helping me to pack. Come on upstairs with me, please; I can't begin to find half of my things if you don't help me."

Mrs. Langford gave up in mute despair; and Brant was beginning to fear that his errand would have to go undone; but at that moment the "cub" rescued the vanishing opportunity by rushing off to begin his preparations. Thus the mother and her visitor were left alone together, and Brant seized his courage with both hands:

"Mrs. Langford, one moment, if you please. You know why I came here to-night, and what I meant to ask. My happiness, which you may justly ignore, and that of your daughter, which is of far greater moment, depend upon your answer. Will you give it me now? or must I wait till I have earned a better right to it?"

He spoke hurriedly as the occasion compelled, and she heard him through without interrupting. When he paused she took his arm a little stiffly and led him toward the door.

"You will find the family in the drawing-room, Mr. Brant; and I hope you will excuse me if I go upstairs to help William. And, as I may not come down before you go, I will bid you good-bye now. I hope you will do well, and—and that you will succeed in whatever you undertake."

They had reached the hall, and she turned and held out her hand. Brant took it and bowed low over it.

"Then I am to understand——"

"This: that I am willing to be neutral, and to wait."

"It is all I ask," he said gratefully, quelling a sudden and mighty insurrection of joy that threatened to unseat his self-control.

"It is all I can promise, now. Be lenient with me, Mr. Brant, as I shall try to be with you. You know my views, and you also know whether they are unsupported by reason and justice. I will say frankly that I came down a few moments ago to urge you to spare me; to tell you that I could not reconcile myself to this thing that you and my daughter have set your hearts upon. But while I delayed, you forestalled me with my son. He is my hostage, and I surrender him to you because I can not help myself; but when you return I shall require him at your hands. Deal gently with him, I beg of you—for his sister's sake, if not for mine."

She turned to go upstairs, and he stood aside to let her pass. "God do so to me, and more, if I do not regard him as the son of my own mother," he said solemnly, and the promise touched her.

"I believe you—and trust you," she added, pausing on the step above him. "Now go and join the others in the drawing-room. They will all be glad to welcome you."

And they were; but Dorothy the most of all. For in his eyes she read the promise of the future, and ran to be the first to greet him. And though the others pressed upon him with kindly words and hearty hand-grips, he saw but one—the woman for whose love he lived, and would have died.

THE END

Milton Keynes UK
Ingram Content Group UK Ltd.
UKHW030623061024
449204UK00004B/384